MW00913890

A Man
You Could
LOVE

JOHN CALLAHAN

A Man
You Could
LOVE

JOHN CALLAHAN

Fulcrum Publishing
Golden, Colorado

HEY JUDE © 1968 (Renewed) Sony/ATV Tunes LLC. All rights administered by
Sony/ATV Music Publishing, 8 Music Square West, Nashville, TN 37203. All rights
reserved. Used by permission.

A DAY IN THE LIFE © 1967 Sony/ATV Tunes LLC. All rights administered by
Sony/ATV Music Publishing, 8 Music Square West, Nashville, TN 37203. All rights
reserved. Used by permission.

(WHAT DID I DO TO BE SO) BLACK AND BLUE Music by THOMAS "FATS"
WALLER and HARRY BROOKS Words by ANDY RAZAF © 1929 (Renewed) EMI
MILLS MUSIC, INC. and CHAPPELL & CO., INC. All Rights Reserved. Used by
Permission of ALFRED PUBLISHING CO., INC.

Library of Congress Cataloging-in-Publication Data
Callahan, John F., 1940-
  A man you could love / John Callahan.
     p. cm.
  ISBN 978-1-55591-620-6 (hardcover) -- ISBN 978-1-55591-649-7 (pbk.)
1. Politicians--Fiction. 2. United States--Politics and government--20th century--
Fiction. 3. Male friendship--Fiction. 4. Political fiction. I. Title.
  PS3603.A443M36 2007
  813'.54--dc22
                        2006101594

Printed in Canada by Friesens
0 9 8 7 6 5 4 3 2 1

Editorial: Sam Scinta, Katie Raymond, Faith Marcovecchio
Cover and interior design: Jack Lenzo

Fulcrum Publishing
4690 Table Mountain Drive, Suite 100
Golden, Colorado 80403
800-992-2908 • 303-277-1623
www.fulcrumbooks.com

To Christine

. . . And could politics ever be an expression of love?

—Ralph Ellison, *Invisible Man*

. . . America, having about it still that quality of the idea, was harder to utter—it was the graves at Shiloh and the tired, drawn, nervous faces of its great men, and the country boys dying in the Argonne for a phrase that was empty before their bodies withered. It was a willingness of the heart.

—F. Scott Fitzgerald, *The Crack-Up*

I

CHAPTER 1

Growing up between the claws of eastern Long Island, I was sure I was in cahoots with the world. Never mind that stuff about the unexamined life not being worth living—on Shelter Island, I had no need for an alarm clock or a wake-up call. At daybreak, when the sun came out of the sea, I watched Gardiner's Bay turn the color of fire. Flying along the causeway between Little Ram and Big Ram on my three-speed, it was a rare summer morning I didn't see an osprey swoop back to its nest or spot a great blue heron stalking the shallows in the tracks of the Manhanset chief who, long before any white men arrived, named the island Manhansack-aha-quashawamock, or "Island Sheltered by Islands."

But now, on the Oregon coast during the millennial Indian summer of 2000, I lay in bed beneath Neah-Kah-Nie Mountain watching the sky turn deeper shades of blue. Waiting for my test results, I couldn't shake the feeling that life was winding down. I felt a chill, a sudden dread that my health would put an end to the dream of returning to Shelter Island with the woman I'd left behind in Washington.

As a former man of politics and the vote, I also wondered if my soul's low tide had anything to do with being far from the action of the presidential election of 2000. I had folded my hand almost ten years before, but politics is like any other addiction—the moment you think you have it licked, its insistent rhythms sneak up on the beating of your heart. I followed Al Gore's up-and-down campaign, but, like a recovering alcoholic, I kept my distance, even when a couple of old cronies called the day after the election. They had been taken out of mothballs and rushed to Florida to act as seconds for Gore's duel in the sun with George Bush the younger. Meanwhile, out in Oregon, my red and white blood cells were going haywire, the count dangerously unstable. I'd prepared for bad news and prepared for good news, but I was not prepared for things to be up in the air. Maybe that's why I was impatient with the Team Gore strategy of seeking recounts only in the two or three counties with the largest Democratic majorities.

"Roll the dice," I said into the phone.

"Dice mice, roll troll," responded the media maverick I'd worked with in the days before hip-hop made sassy spoken rhymes fashionable. "You living in the United States or the twilight zone, Bontempo?"

Usually he called me Gabe, or, if he wanted to pull rank, Gabriel, my mixed blessing of a Christian name.

Breaking the silence, a second voice came on the line, this one belonging to the former congressman from New York with whom I'd conspired during my days as an administrative assistant on Capitol Hill.

"Look, man, you know the rules in the Bush league. Leave every vote behind ain't his."

"Take him to court," I said grumpily.

"He got *us* in court."

In the old days, I would have pressed my case like a trial lawyer working for a percentage. Now, I only wanted to clear my mind.

"Count the whole state by hand. Let the good times roll."

"Good times, my ass," the former congressman growled. "Our boy Al's instinct was to recount everything, but the consultants talked him out of it. Now, far as I can tell, ain't no saints marching in this man's Everglades."

From the abrupt pause, I thought the line had gone dead. On my end, the immense, deceptively calm rollers of the Pacific broke toward shore, while in my mind's eye, my two old brothers-in-arms looked at each other across a conference table in a hastily commandeered law office on the Atlantic coast of Florida. Finally, from the thick silence, I realized they had remembered the state of my health.

"Listen," I said in valediction, "keep me posted on the vote count, and I'll keep you posted on my blood count."

The recount was shaping up as a donnybrook, but the results of my blood tests threw me off balance. If the numbers had been borderline or better, I would have taken it as a reprieve and, like old Daedalus, flown off to Florida. In my heyday, I could soar without losing sight of the Earth, and, from what I could tell, Gore needed a savvy old hand to keep him from getting burned by the Florida sun. Or, if the tests had fingered me as a marked man, I might have taken a last fling. But mine was the middle ground. Like the middle of the road, it was not a safe place—more like purgatory, where, the Sisters of Mercy taught me years ago, your good and bad angels join forces to prepare an elixir of fire exquisitely designed to defy your threshold of pain.

Driving to Portland for consultations, I snaked northeast on Route 53, passing humpbacked hills whose Douglas fir kept watch like Indian braves over patches of earth, raw and ragged in the sunlight, where ancestral trees had been felled one by one during clear-cutting massacres by the logging companies. In the distance, the mountains of the Coast Range rested under a deep, dazzling coat of snow, heralding an early winter. From his office overlooking the Willamette River, my oncologist told me that nothing was decided. Years before, I'd helped him prepare testimony before a Senate committee. Now, when he compared my unstable red and white blood cells to undecided voters, I told him I wanted nothing of the kind associated with my fate. Undecideds were not only fickle, you could never tell why the hell they did what they did. So, as the alligator's tail of the recount thrashed back and forth from the Florida panhandle to the Keys, holding the nation hostage, I learned to live with my life's uncertainties.

With November storms ranting and raving along the Oregon coast, the Florida sun seemed a speck of dust light-years away, and my dreams remained free of the recount. No cell phones ran out of juice, no out-of-season tornadoes left me stranded, no nubile Republican posing as a journalist lured me to her room, and no word came from Vice President Gore that I had cost him his victory by conducting wildcat recounts in the wrong counties. No, my anxiety came from the approach of a new decade, a new century, a new millennium, for God's sake, and also from the feeling I'd had during the phone call from Florida that someone was missing.

My friend Michael J. "Mick" Whelan, senator from Oregon, was missing. But as I lay in bed, reluctant to face another day, the fog in my mind burned off and I imagined him standing there. Without speaking, his intense black-Irish face sized up my condition, a look of concern in his eyes before he melted away. Mick Whelan was the brother I had wanted . . .

But even before I met him, politics was the salt in my blood, words the bounce in my shoe. When I was an undergraduate at Dartmouth, I introduced Jack Kennedy at a Young Democrats' meeting during the 1960 New Hampshire primary. I was also writing stories for the literary magazine and, that same weekend, bribed a desk clerk at the Hanover Inn to let me show my date the attic room F. Scott Fitzgerald had stayed in during the 1939 Winter Carnival. Still, most of the time at Dartmouth I was a long way from home.

My father inherited the liquor store on Shelter Island from his father, Giuseppe Bientempo, an immigrant from the corner of the Alps where France, Italy, and Switzerland converge within sight of Mount Blanc. When I was a boy, my grandfather and his cronies sat under the grape arbor telling stories about an Irishman who made furtive trips to the island during Prohibition. They swore that the man, dressed in banker's pinstripes and wearing black horn-rimmed glasses, a trench coat over his arm, looked like a Sinn Fein gunman, or maybe one of the Fenians who had connived with Garibaldi during the Risorgimento. The fact and fiction of the Mafia in America galled my grandfather. Maybe that's why he kept quiet about the Irishman's shady liquor concessions up and down Long Island. Only after the stranger's son became a senator from Massachusetts did I realize that old Giuseppe and his friends had been talking about Ambassador Joseph P. Kennedy. My grandfather never made any comparisons between old Joe's son Jack and me, but from his pats on the head I got the message. Others of Italian descent could go the way of Valentino, Fermi, or Caruso, but if he had his way, his grandson would be an American caesar, duly elected, of course.

So in the early sixties, I left Shelter Island for Washington.

By then, Senator Kennedy was President Kennedy, and things were heating up with civil rights. After graduating from Georgetown Law in the summer of 1963, I was hired by Bobby Kennedy's Justice Department. People forget how scared the Kennedys were of the civil rights movement. Unable to talk Negro leaders out of a massive march on Washington, the attorney general took extraordinary measures to prepare for violence in the nation's capital by thousands of unruly Negroes. One of his deputies assigned me to snoop around the Student Non-Violent Coordinating Committee and report any plans that might be afoot to embarrass the administration. But I quickly discovered that these SNCC characters had heard too many screams, smelled the ashes of too many smoldering black churches, been beaten too many times, hustled off to too many county jails, and broken bread with too many local black citizens liable to disappear in the middle of the night to let some white boy turn them around, even if he was working for the attorney general of the United States.

Excluded from the SNCC tent the night before the March on Washington, I cooled my heels on the Mall, and met Mick Whelan. Like me, Whelan was an errand boy; unlike me, he knew it.

It turned out that while I was a senior at Hanover, we had unknowingly crossed paths when Whelan, a year behind me at Holy Cross, had won the trophy as best affirmative speaker at the annual tournament hosted by Dartmouth's Daniel Webster Society. Irish to the bone, Whelan's face was a slip of the chisel away from the classic black-Irish face: brown curly hair, a touch nappy at the edges, milk-white complexion with an easy blush, flashing blue eyes, nostrils that flared from a wide nose, which some of the hip brothers later kidded him about, and a decisive chin sometimes tempered by the faintest of dimples. His tenor voice stayed with you, too: it was full of lilt, though sometimes when he told stories he had heard at his fugitive Irish grandfather's knee, his voice was haunted by desolation.

I was no slouch at stories either. But because I'd seen my grandfather roll his eyes at my mother's great-aunt's tale of an exiled ancestor's trek over the Pyrenees in the sixteenth century, I sometimes slipped into a defensive key. Wearing a seersucker suit and straw boater at Georgetown parties, I wasn't above answering questions about where I was from with a telltale bravado: "Out on eastern Long Island, across from the Hamptons." I wasn't ashamed of my Italian background or my Shelter Island address, understand; I simply wanted to belong to the big world. In any case, the night before the March on Washington, I was disarmed to hear Mick Whelan say that many a summer afternoon he had looked east at the long blur of land across the sound from Connecticut yet never set foot on Long Island.

"The closest I got was a summer job driving an excursion boat through the Thimbles," he said with a grin.

I laughed, because I knew about those tiny thumbs of land off the Connecticut shore. In the fifties, more than once during hurricane season I'd heard on the radio that the Thimbles had been evacuated, and now I imagined my earnest new friend helping refugees out of rowboats on the suddenly turbulent Connecticut side of Long Island Sound.

Whelan's curiosity prompted me to tell him that my Long Island was not mansions in the Hamptons, or gridlocked traffic crawling out of New York City, or tract homes as far as the eye could see, or concrete county roads that crisscrossed family truck farms, or strip malls at the end of sprawling, desolate townships. To reach my Long Island, you ferried across from New London to Orient Point, or drove out the north fork, past fields of onions, corn, beets, and potatoes. From Greenport, the last real town on the fork, you could see Shelter Island, but you reached it only by ferry. But by the time I finished explaining all this, Mick was scanning the blue-black clouds tumbling in west of the Mall.

"It's funny. During JFK's blockade last October, I wasn't sure anything would be left." Whelan swept his arm toward the Lincoln Memorial, where no one knew how many people would march the next day. "When I heard Russian ships were hours away, I drove up Route 1 to check on a rumor that a sub had surfaced just beyond the breakwater."

Down the sandy path adjacent to the Smithsonian, two volunteers, one black, one white, both dressed smartly in slacks and turtlenecks, emerged from the organizers' tent with stacks of leaflets that announced the next day's points of assembly.

"That's when you knew it was real."

"No," Whelan said, slowing down to pull me into his story. "After I walked through some marshes and heard a rooster crowing at noon, I climbed a hill and noticed that the sky was deep blue and the leaves were on fire. Everything was alive, and the world seemed to be waiting. When I looked east, Long Island was closer than I'd ever seen it." He shook his head. "I'd never gone there, and now it might turn into a cinder."

He accepted a bundle of leaflets from the young black woman with processed hair, interrupting his story to thank her.

"I know," I said, remembering that in my urge to be on Shelter Island if the world was going to end, I'd gone up to the top of the belvedere alongside an unfinished beach house and suddenly felt as carefree as I had as a boy. Now, on the Mall, I looked down at the leaflet's blurry Associated Press photograph of a girl cowering from the German shepherd tugging at her dress and turned back to Mick.

"I could see Connecticut across Long Island Sound," I told him. "I cocked my ears, listening for the whoosh of missiles, before it hit me that I had no idea what a nuclear exchange would sound like."

I fished a cigarette out of my shirt pocket, and Mick gave me a light from his Camel.

"Funny." He took a long drag. "You looked my way, I looked yours, but nothing happened, and here we are trying to turn the country around."

Despite our memories of the Cuban Missile Crisis, Mick Whelan and I were too young to know we were mortal and that our escape from doomsday was an accident. The world was stirring our blood. Moved by black students who had had ketchup poured on their heads at southern lunch counters, and sickened by Bull Connor's police dogs and cattle prods in Birmingham, we were going to change American society. Yet, that night before the march, outside tents on the Mall, within range of thunder and impending drops of rain, we knew we were summer soldiers, stationed well behind the front lines of the struggle for freedom.

The next morning, Mick Whelan stood on top of the ledge above the reflecting pool to get a better view of the marchers striding down the Mall from the Capitol by the tens of thousands. In the sun, the water sparkled white and blue. Several boisterous black boys in Dodgers and Giants baseball caps dodged past Whelan, single file, playing tag with slick moves. Touched on the arm, one slight boy, pink blotches disfiguring his dark-brown skin, stood still, one leg in the air. Like his companions, he knew that although he had faced down fire hoses in Birmingham, a tumble into the reflecting pool meant the end of the game and a stern reproof from any relative or marshal who heard the splash.

Before long, Mick jumped down and knifed through the crowd like a broken field runner, feinting and darting past every opposing player between him and the goal line. Turning abruptly to avoid an old woman with a cane, he bumped into a nut-brown man who kept to his rhythm. Shorter than Mick, the man was dressed in his Sunday best and wore his hair cropped neat and natural in one of the original Afros. I was too far away to hear what was said, but I saw a flush of red deepen the color of my new friend's face.

Presently, a little brown boy wearing a shiny blue suit over a white shirt and red bow tie and holding a homemade sign with the words *Ship of Zion* crayoned in green, black, and red, appeared beside the man with the Afro. The man bent down, buttoned the top button of the boy's suit jacket, and straightened his sign on its rough wooden stick. Then, hand in hand, Odetta's deep, dark voice resounding around them, father and son stepped off down the Mall toward President Lincoln's far-reaching gaze.

"I'm on my way to the freedom land. . . .
I'm on my way, and I won't turn back."

From a distance, I sensed a sea change come over Mick like the turn of the tide on a cloudless summer day on the Sound. Like me, he wore a Black and White Together button the size of a silver dollar pinned to his shirt. Now, his face suddenly as grave as Lincoln's, he picked his way forward through the crowd.

Self-conscious among the flow of dignitaries and the endless black faces of every shade and shape, I drifted off to one side to hear the music. I lost sight of Mick Whelan until after Martin Luther King brought down the house and raised high the nation with his promissory *amen*: "Free at last! Free at last! Thank God Almighty, we're free at last!" Against the grain of the departing crowd, Mick Whelan reached the spot on the steps of the Lincoln Memorial reserved for members of Congress. Beyond dozens of joyous handclapping marchers, I saw him shake hands with the tall graying senator vaguely familiar as the man who had briefly brought down another house back in 1960 with his speech nominating Adlai Stevenson for president.

CHAPTER 2

Three weeks after President Kennedy walked up to Martin Luther King at the White House like it was Saint Patrick's Day and said, "I have a dream" in his flat Boston accent, four black girls were blown up during Sunday school in the Sixteenth Street Baptist Church. If you couldn't smell the coffee after Birmingham, you sure as hell could two months later. One minute Jack Kennedy was waving from an open limousine at high noon in the Dallas sunshine and telling Jackie to take off her sunglasses so people could see her, and the next his brains were all over her lap. After that, if you listened, what you heard blowing in the wind was closer to the wail of the banshee than the call of the trumpet.

At Arlington National Cemetery, I fell in with Mick Whelan—a fellow straggler at the rear of the procession that was bearing John Fitzgerald Kennedy's body uphill to the gravesite. Afterward, we walked back to Washington over the Key Bridge, past Georgetown boutiques with their black bunting and waxy, tinted photographs of the fallen president, until we came to the One Step Down, a hole-in-the-wall jazz joint on Massachusetts Avenue. We downed beer after beer and talked and talked, but neither booze nor words did us much good. At closing time, Whelan stood unsteadily, waved two fingers in the waiter's direction, and, as the horn player swung his harshly tender solo to a close, began to sing: "And before I'll be a slave, I'll be buried in my grave." Several black faces along the bar picked up where Mick left off. "Oh, freedom over me," they sang, their glasses raised in salute. Applauding the saxophone player, Mick said to me in a low, husky voice, "Sweet Jack's gone, but at least you and I have that old Sound Connection."

Like some Kilroy of the sixties, Mick Whelan lived on the cusp of the action. Half brooder, half wild man, Whelan was of that archangel breed unafraid of the demons between him and the light. In 1964, he quit his job as a page at the Democratic National Convention in Atlantic City to sign on as a volunteer for Fannie Lou Hamer and the Mississippi Freedom Democrats. In March of sixty-five, he went to Selma for Bloody Sunday— and stayed on until the march to Montgomery was accomplished. In the same spirit, Whelan joined the first teach-ins against the war in Vietnam, and prodded me to join one feeble little protest after another.

"You leap before you look," I told him. "I'm still looking."

I kept on looking, until, in a recurring nightmare, my grandfather, waving a bottle of Chianti, dispatched me in my three-piece suit to carry a message to a stranded American patrol. *For hours I walked in sunlight beside pale-green rice paddies, the sun burning a hole in my neck. In the jungle, enormous tiger butterflies dive-bombed until the markings on their wings stretched into a livid red-and-yellow silk-screened map of Vietnam. Soon, parrots' staccato cries turned into automatic-weapons fire, and bright flashes lit up the noontime dark like giant fireflies. When I broke into a clearing, a pagoda I recognized from the movies dissolved into a helicopter gunship, its rope ladder dangling out of reach. On all sides, parrots dressed in black pajamas surrounded me. "You, American of free world," they shrieked, "to be saved, you must die!"*

In my waking life, America—my country, damn it!—thrashed in terror like its larger-than-life president Lyndon Johnson. Two years before, in his Texas-hill-country drawl, LBJ told a joint session of Congress and the nation, "And we shall overcome." Now, in private, he was calling Martin Luther King "that nigger preacher."

Battered by black power and white backlash, civil rights became a more and more ambiguous holding action. Between jobs, with time on my hands, I was curious enough about the March on the Pentagon to cross the Potomac arm in arm with Mick Whelan and a ragtag crowd of protestors. But my game was politics, not protest, so I ran with the old crowd from Bobby Kennedy's Justice Department and listened to the young Turks, their pupils dilated by second martinis, make the case for Bobby challenging Johnson for the 1968 presidential nomination. Always cautious, I went home and wrote a confidential memo advising Kennedy to stay neutral, speak out on the issues, and wait for 1972.

In the meantime, I heard from Whelan that Senator Eugene McCarthy had gone to see Kennedy, urged him to run, and, after Bobby's thanks-but-no-thanks response, dropped the other shoe. "Someone's got to do it," McCarthy told Kennedy. "If you won't go, I guess I will." They shook hands—hell, I could see why Clean Gene thought Bobby wouldn't change his mind without some serious give-and-take. But later on, Bobby played it like McCarthy lacked the stuff to be a serious candidate and wasn't tough enough to be president. Deep down, he must have felt remorse over not running, because, while Jack was president, Bobby'd been all out for counterinsurgency and the Green Berets. And he did a slow burn at Gene McCarthy invoking Jack in speeches around the country as if he, and not Bobby, was the worthy successor.

Bobby Kennedy wasn't the only one who couldn't look Vietnam in the eye. Washington insiders made sport of Gene McCarthy's campaign the way Russian aristocrats mocked Napoleon's battles in East Prussia before they realized that the little Frenchman was seriously bent on kicking their asses. The pros forgot about the Mick Whelans of the country, but I remember sitting with him at the One Step, watching the news the night of McCarthy's announcement. Mick's father in Connecticut had passed away suddenly before Thanksgiving. Like so many fathers and sons in the sixties, the two had been so much at odds they were all but estranged. When Gene McCarthy's self-possessed fatherly face flashed on the black-and-white television above the bar, Mick put down his beer. Right away I could see that the senator's measured, earnest words were a healing balm for Whelan's sorrowing heart.

I hung back from the McCarthy insurgency, but Mick didn't stop hounding me. In late January of 1968, I got a card postmarked Laconia, New Hampshire. From the hastily scrawled message, it was plain that he was up in the snow, setting up storefronts, training students to canvass, and writing news releases in one little Christmas-card town after another. He tried to get me to join the campaign. I declined, but this time steered a little money his way. Frankly, I didn't think LBJ could be stopped. But on election night, when the votes were counted, Gene McCarthy and Lyndon Johnson ended up in a virtual tie. The next day, Bobby Kennedy told reporters he was "reassessing his position."

Once RFK declared, I signed on as an advance man and troubleshooter— working for the Kennedys, there was always some of that. His guys didn't send him to Berkeley or Cambridge or Ann Arbor. Like Caesar conquering Gaul, Bobby went to Manhattan, Kansas. Not even Jack Kennedy's Roman procession through Connecticut's Naugatuck Valley the Sunday before the 1960 election equaled the pandemonium, the old hands said. On that first foray to the campuses, I took along a stash of signed photos to barter with the crazies who snagged Bobby's *PT-109* tie clips or JFK cuff links. It was frustrating work, because even if a nutcase grabbed one of his shoes while he stood on the hood, Bobby wouldn't let the cops intervene, and he expected his advance men to keep the carnival going.

Toward the end of that first blitz, I did some work out West in California and Oregon. Oregon was tough. Most of the antiwar activist students were for McCarthy and against Kennedy with the vehemence of a rejected former suitor who had since exchanged vows with another girl and now found his old sweetheart at the front door. These kids had watched the New Hampshire primary on television, and now they acted as though they'd held McCarthy's coat in the snow. But what the hell, every blacksmith's apprentice in Pennsylvania and New Jersey probably told his grandchildren that he'd crossed the Delaware with George Washington on Christmas night in 1776.

After Kennedy's speech at Portland State University, I invited movers and shakers from four or five colleges to meet, figuring that after seeing Bobby in person and hearing my pitch, two or three would switch from McCarthy to Kennedy.

I rented a conference room at the downtown Holiday Inn. When I stopped at the front desk to check arrangements, there was Mick Whelan, wearing a McCarthy button in the lapel of his brown tweed sports jacket.

"Gabe," he said. "For God's sake."

We clasped each other's shoulders and shook hands.

"Wisconsin looks good—it's just Johnson and McCarthy," he said, his expression changing as he noticed my Kennedy button. "You working for Bobby, Gabe?"

His voice was full of the old quick candor and enthusiasm, but his eyes signaled the wariness of someone new to party politics and unsure how much distance to pace off from an old friend in the enemy camp.

I stalled. I wanted to thrash out the choice between Kennedy and McCarthy over a few beers while jazz blew in our ears, instead of in the lobby of a godforsaken Holiday Inn.

"That's right," I told him.

"Like old times. You on the inside, me on the outside."

I looked at my watch. "Listen, Mick, I've got a meeting upstairs."

"The Freemont Room," he said with a quick laugh. "A couple of the students asked me to sit in."

"And they talk about Kennedy spies."

I'd counted on a clean, clear shot at the McCarthy students. In other states, I'd won over a few, to the delight of two interns from Kennedy's Senate office who were along for the ride. Standing awkwardly at the front desk, tense about the coming encounter, I mumbled excuses about things to do while Mick shook hands with the clerk, whose free hand was cupped around an object I figured was from Whelan's stash of McCarthy buttons.

Upstairs in the meeting room, the young people were a mélange of mostly impressive, serious kids, a belligerent, hostile character here, a know-it-all there. The guys had long hair, some wore beards and ponytails, and the young women looked out from mascaraless eyes with alert, compassionate faces, their svelte legs flowing smoothly out of corduroy miniskirts.

"We need staff," I began, lighting a cigarette. *Staff*, I had learned, was the magic word for young people hooked on politics. "We're running in every state, and we'll need smart, tested, dedicated young people in Washington to get the country moving again when Senator Kennedy is president." Looking at Whelan out of the corner of my eye, I revised my spiel. "*If* Senator Kennedy is elected, and that depends on you."

It was the best recovery I could manage from the sense of inevitability I deliberately conveyed in sessions like this. My task was to flatter the best students away from McCarthy, pay them, and give them a title, because we really didn't need them, but McCarthy did. After I left town and the press release announcing defections went out, the kids would come back to Earth.

"I'm glad you said *if*," Mick said, more to the group than to me.

Instead of titters, there were knowing smiles. I had a disciplined bunch on my hands, tougher nuts than those I'd cracked in other states. My glance lingered on Mick until a big-shouldered, open-faced guy sporting an unruly red beard that grew off to the sides like ground cover spoke up.

"Hey, you guys know each other?"

He looked like a mill-town kid on a football scholarship, but in fact his father taught classics at Stanford, and the young man played mixed doubles on the Reed College tennis team.

Mick looked my way as I turned sideways toward the cigarette I'd left burning in the Holiday Inn ashtray.

"We met at the March on Washington," I said. "We were in Atlantic City in 1964, Selma in 1965. And we're together now," I opened my hand, "trying to stop this crazy war."

The scuffing of sneakers and sandals disturbed the silence.

"That's why Gene McCarthy declared last November," the big, bluff, bearded guy said.

"And ran in New Hampshire," a blonde girl said, seizing the baton.

"Robert Kennedy was on the line in the South five, six years ago," I resumed. "We need black votes as well as white votes. Bobby can get them."

"We've had an ego trip with LBJ," the big guy said. "If it's issues that matter, why didn't Kennedy support McCarthy?"

I snuffed out the cigarette. Though I wanted another one, I put the pack down on the table and reached into my gut for the reasons why I was for Bobby Kennedy. "Gene McCarthy opened things up in New Hampshire, but he doesn't have the clout to take Johnson down. Senator Kennedy knows Democratic officeholders and politicians all over the country. He fasted with César Chávez in California, held hungry black kids on his lap in Mississippi."

"That's cool," interrupted a short, olive-skinned guy with black curly hair wearing a Resist! button. "It's cool," he repeated, "but why does he have to be president in '68? Hey, man, my cousin lost his leg in Vietnam."

"Yeah, Kennedy's been supporting Johnson," a black-eyed young woman in bell-bottoms chimed in. "McCarthy's establishment, but he was the only politician to run when we needed him."

"It's going to be a nasty fight," I said. "Switching to Kennedy is loyal to America, and America's always been Bobby Kennedy's cause."

Suddenly, Mick Whelan stood up. "We've been over that," he said, as if it were his meeting. "Senator McCarthy is running in primaries and caucuses. Running anyplace he can. He'll be a president with the mind and heart and the soul to stand up to the establishment. He's not afraid to say he'll fire J. Edgar Hoover and General Hershey."

Whelan was tougher and savvier than before. And he knew his troops, knew I had made no inroads. Wincing, I admired his timing. *Lay off,* he was telling me, his voice cool but not nonchalant. *These young people are McCarthy's and mine, but mostly they belong to each other.* Surveying the conference room, appointed with bland plastic furniture in the green and white colors of Holiday Inns worldwide, my belly quailed. Was Mick baiting a trap? In my mind's eye, I could see the headline "Oregon Students Fooled by Cynicism of RFK Camp."

"Thanks for hearing me out," I told the students. "Senator Kennedy is right when he says Gene McCarthy's lucky to have young people like you working for him."

The two interns from Kennedy's Senate office, their arms full of brochures and a cache of red, white, and blue Kennedy buttons and bumper stickers, were standing by the door, their eyes and mouths wide, waiting for me to play the invisible card they were sure I was hiding in my sleeve.

"Here's my card," I said. "Headquarters opens next week."

"In case we change our minds?" one of the young woman teased, the freckles on her nose bobbing up and down.

The big guy stood up, the last word his. "You're offering money to work for Kennedy. Tell the senator we'll work for free for a politician we believe in, someone who needs us: Eugene McCarthy."

To murmurs of assent, I ushered them out, feeling stares from the Senate interns, who held their unclaimed Kennedy wares in their arms like day-old bread.

In the hall, Whelan lingered.

"You free, Gabe?"

"I'd love to go to the mat with you, Mick, but my flight leaves in an hour."

Down the hall, past the Coke machine and a stainless-steel cart stacked with monogrammed towels and tiny bars of soap, several students turned around to see if Mick and I were still talking.

"No hard feelings?" Whelan asked, walking along next to me.

"We've got to keep this split from getting out of hand like that war between the Irish—I forget what you called it."

"The Troubles," Mick said, and stopped before we caught up to the McCarthy students waiting on one side of the elevator and the Kennedy interns on the other. Listening to his next comment, I heard eggshells crack under my feet. "Doing duty like today doesn't help," he confided in a low voice. "Though I don't think they'll send you back to Oregon."

The elevator dinged; its faded gunmetal doors opened. Before they could creak closed, the big red-bearded guy pushed them back and held them ajar. Interrupting the silence, warning bells began to ring inside the elevator.

"I'll be right down," Whelan told his cadre. "You, too," he said, pointing at my forlorn sidekicks.

After the elevator began to hum its way down, Mick rested his hand on my shoulder. "Sorry we're on different sides, Gabe. I guess it's all that salt water between Connecticut and Long Island."

"The Sound Connection," I said, feeling my chest untighten.

"The Sound Connection," he repeated.

As we shook hands, Mick slid his bony thumb around mine and twisted until we finished with a pretty good imitation of the black handshake then in fashion among white aficionados.

In retrospect, 1968 never flows in a straight line. Like the wheel of fortune, the months whirl around and around, the arrow stopping at random points on each revolution. My path did not cross Mick Whelan's again until after McCarthy beat Kennedy in Oregon. We ran into each other at the bar in the St. Francis in San Francisco the afternoon of the Kennedy-McCarthy debate. Anxious about an event in whose outcome we had an emotional stake but no say, we drank margaritas by a plate-glass window while outside in Union Square competing lines of marchers waved Kennedy and McCarthy placards and chanted their man's name to passersby who lingered as if this were a political remake of the Summer of Love.

"With luck, it's over Tuesday," I told him.

"No," Mick said. "Kennedy said he'd quit if he lost Oregon. If he loses California, he'll stay in."

"And Clean Gene?" I licked salt off the rim of my glass.

"The same. He can't wait for a crack at Bobby in New York."

Mick scanned the scene outside the hotel window. Across the street, a couple of beefy men wearing Confederate Army caps and Wallace for President T-shirts crowded a Kennedy girl and a McCarthy girl against a low concrete wall until the girls' signs pressed tightly against their breasts.

"Look at those creatures," I said.

"They're not the worst," Mick replied, shaking loose a Camel from his pack. "Yesterday I was in San Jose, advancing Gene. Bobby was speaking at the same shopping center, so I hung around. Afterward, he was working the crowd, and some guy slapped his outstretched hand. I'm not talking about a hard hat with a Love It or Leave It button. This dude wore a white shirt and tie."

Mick looked out toward the palm trees in Union Square where a pair of San Francisco's finest, outfitted in Plexiglas helmets and billy clubs, escorted the Wallace supporters away from the girls as if they were conventioneers who had lost their way.

"Bobby looked sort of puzzled. He reached out his hand. Next thing I knew, the guy snarled, 'Fuck you, and fuck your dead brother!' Bobby flinched like he'd been hit," Mick finished as the two men across the street stopped in front of a black girl with a Kennedy placard and rubbed their hands lewdly on the image of George Wallace stretched tight over their bellies.

After we drank another round of margaritas, a covey of Whelan's fellow McCarthy workers approached, all smiles until they saw my Kennedy button. I felt like the guy in the *New Yorker* cartoon who comes late to the cocktail party—as soon as he shows up, the ice melts, the sun disappears behind a single small cloud, the neighbor's dog overturns the hors d'oeuvres table, and the guests fall into despondent silence. I departed with an ironic bow and didn't see Whelan again until after Bobby Kennedy's assassination . . .

Jesus, two months after King, Kennedy. I missed the funeral at Saint Patrick's because I was advancing Bobby's last journey—that awful train ride taking him and the whole Magical Mystery Tour to Washington so that he could be buried next to Jack on the little hillside in Arlington.

I was still numb by early August when, having taken a job in the political section of the National Education Association, my boss sent me out to Oregon to size up Wayne Morse's reelection campaign. Before leaving, I had beer and chowder with Whelan a stone's throw from the Willamette River in downtown Portland. After the waiter took our bowls away, Mick stretched out his foot, crushed a few peanut shells on the sawdust floor of the Oyster Bar, and made a hesitant confession.

"When I heard Bobby was shot, I was putting together the McCarthy advance teams for New York. The reporter wasn't sure it was serious—Gabe, I had visions of Bobby leaving the hospital with his arm in a sling. I thought, *Here comes the great Bobby. He's survived his Dallas; now he's president.*" He put his hands over his face.

"Don't beat yourself up," I said, putting my hand on his arm. "Everybody's demons were loose."

Mick freed his arm and his eyes bore in on mine. "By then, I didn't see Bobby as a man anymore. And I remember Gene McCarthy looking ravaged beyond anything he could say."

The counterman was sweeping up peanut shells in preparation for sprinkling fresh sawdust the next morning. Mick grabbed a couple of peanuts from the bowl on the table. Instead of shucking them, he flipped them toward me like he was tossing dice.

"Did I tell you I'll be teaching constitutional law out here in September?" he asked before hopping back on the boxcar of politics.

"Gabe, I've been trying to bring some of the Kennedy people over to McCarthy. They're against the war as I am, but after I worked with them on the grape boycott, they said they appreciated my help, but they couldn't support Gene McCarthy after the things he said about Bobby." As Mick talked, accusing tears filled his eyes. "Goddamn it, I was going on to New York to help Gene. But if he'd won California and been assassinated, I'd have been in Kennedy headquarters the next morning, McCarthy button in one lapel, Bobby's in the other."

I heard those same tears in Mick Whelan's voice over the phone from Chicago a few weeks later during the Democratic National Convention. He and I were both outsiders—Whelan on the scene as a volunteer for Gene McCarthy's doomed campaign and I stealing a few days in the sun on Maryland's eastern shore. Tanqueray and tonic in hand, I watched on television as the delegates rejected the Vietnam peace plank and nominated Hubert Humphrey while the networks also showed bonus coverage of Mayor Daley's police clubbing protesters and cameramen alike outside in the streets of Chicago. In the wee hours after the convention adjourned, Mick told it like it was from a phone booth in the lobby of the Conrad Hilton on Michigan Avenue. He'd been kibitzing with some McCarthy staff people on the fifteenth floor when squads of Chicago's finest burst in to empty out the rooms and introduce malingerers to the wrong end of a billy club. "No one's safe, Gabe," he said. I commiserated long-distance until the background noise on Whelan's end of the line suddenly yielded to the taut, barely self-controlled tones of Senator McCarthy. According to Mick, McCarthy twice asked the police, "Who's in charge?" Getting no answer, he raged against the wave of blue silence: "Just as I thought, no one's in charge."

After the chaos of 1968, I became deputy assistant to the chief counsel for the House Judiciary Committee, while out in Oregon Mick Whelan settled in at Northwest School of Law. He turned up in Washington every so often and twice finagled invitations for me to speak to his classes about the Constitution and the legislative process. In the meantime, Gene McCarthy's question unnerved the republic as the Nixon administration began to govern by incursion at home and in Southeast Asia. By June of 1972, when masked men broke into the office of the Democratic national chairman, there was little doubt about who was in charge and who was safe. That November, the Nixon-Agnew ticket carried every state in the Union but Massachusetts, leaving only that old Greek magic—nemesis— between the president of the United States and the Bill of Rights.

Chapter 3

Like the tail that glows in the sky long after a shooting star is gone, the sixties' feel of my friendship with Mick Whelan lingered into the seventies.

"Sinn Fein, Bontempo," he yelled when I called him on Saint Patrick's Day in 1974.

"Listen, you old Mick," I told him, "Kate had a baby boy this morning. We named him Patrick Michael."

Across several mountain ranges, I could see Whelan's smile spread as wide as the amber fields of grain. He had been best man at my wedding, and now he insisted on a toast over the phone, so I hauled down the bottle of Jameson's he and I had all but polished off on his last trip to Washington and poured an inch or two into the handiest glass.

"To Patrick Michael. May he banish the snakes from America, starting with the one in the White House!" Mick shouted on his end, clinking the ice cubes in his glass. "Gabe, I must have known Patrick Michael had come into the world—I filed for Congress today."

I shook my head. You never knew what Mick Whelan would do on Saint Patrick's Day. Back in March of 1966, after we drank Irish whiskey, smoked a few joints, and listened to songs of the Easter Rebellion together, Mick grew militant and moody, then slipped alone into the night. The next day, "Up the Republic" appeared in green paint on the side of the Georgetown Law Library in a large, furious hand. Fortunately, President Johnson was coming to campus, and what was a little green paint compared with taunts of "Hey, hey, LBJ, how many kids did you kill today?" But a man who will carry out a prank like that under orange riot lights in his last semester of law school harbors a Fenian gene liable to break out at any time. So, when filing day in the year of our Lord nineteen hundred and seventy-four fell on Saint Patrick's Day, Mick Whelan came out of the shadows and wrote his name on the big board in the great room of the Oregon state capitol in Salem that listed candidates for federal and state office.

"The seat for the new Fifth District," he told me.

"Did you write your name in green?"

"No, my man, in black ink on white paper—like Vanport."

I wished him luck and finished the last of the Irish whiskey.

Vanport was an anomaly, a scar airbrushed out of Oregon's past until the sixties. I stumbled across the story in 1968 while researching Portland's black population for Bobby Kennedy. Henry J. Kaiser, builder of the great western dams in the thirties and Liberty ships during World War II, created Vanport City in 1942 on the floodplain of the Oregon side of the Columbia River. As soon as Kaiser put out the call that black workers were welcome, word traveled via the underground railroad of porters and preachers, musicians, sporting men, and domestics that good jobs were up for grabs in the Pacific Northwest. Better still, Vanport was outside the jurisdiction of Portland, a town that had marched to Jim Crow drummers going back before the Civil War when, I learned from the newspaper of record, many proponents of statehood for the Oregon Territory were allied with the "fire-eating, slaveholding disunionists of the South." I also learned that in the 1859 referendum on the state constitution, Oregon citizens banned slavery by a two-to-one majority, then voted more than eight to one to exclude free blacks from the state. And as late as the twenties, the Ku Klux Klan rode high in Oregon, placing its preferred candidate in the governor's chair. Nevertheless, in one more triumph of hope over experience, black Americans answered "Can Do" Kaiser's call and migrated north by northwest from Oklahoma, Texas, and western Louisiana. In Vanport, they found a freewheeling town outside the color line that was enforced in Portland on the Oregon side of the Columbia and Vancouver on the Washington side.

I don't claim that Vanport was paradise, but White Trade Only signs were absent from storefronts, and public schools were integrated more than a decade before the Supreme Court declared "separate but equal" unconstitutional. The town soon boasted a post office, a library, a movie house, a police station, three fire stations, eleven schools, and a small hospital. Vanport may have been bottomland, but it was a true city for Oregon's new black and white citizens, and by 1944, it was the second-largest town in the state.

After World War II ended, so did the brief blooming of Vanport. Shipyards closed, competition for the jobs that remained was fierce, and white GIs returning home were not happy to find strange-speaking blacks doing work that, before the war, had been reserved for whites. To this day, some Oregonians say that without the flood, racial tensions would have seethed out of control until one incident or another led disgruntled former GIs to clean out the town as if it were a renegade settlement defiling the old Oregon Territory. In any case, without warning, on Memorial Day 1948, waters long held in check boiled over like nature's fifth columnist and roared in a torrent past the dike at Smith Lake. Within an hour, Vanport City was ten feet under. Because of the warning flashed by an amateur shortwave operator, most residents had ten minutes to grab their children and evacuate. Contrary to later rumors of racial hostility, blacks warned whites and whites warned blacks. Most people survived, but Vanport ceased to exist.

Faced with several thousand black folks with no place to go in segregated Portland, whose black population was far too small to absorb them, charitable agencies relocated victims north to Seattle and south to California. It was as if these homeless citizens of the defunct city were war refugees and the war was the lingering Civil War. Like the floodwaters, Vanport soon receded from public memory, until the sixties when African American students and scholars, amateurs and professionals alike, inspired with the turn toward black history and the oral tradition, began to track down survivors. Preachers and porters, maids, bootblacks, and old-timers of every persuasion—especially barbers, puzzled and amused by the youngbloods hanging around their shops, Afros on their heads, tape recorders under their dashikis—told their stories. For years, many had dreamed of returning, and late in the sixties, spurred by urban-renewal money and a coalition of black and white former residents, Vanport rose phoenixlike from the lowlands. After the 1970 census, Oregon, one of three states in contention for the nation's last congressional seat, proposed a district anchored by flourishing Vanport. While the case dragged on in the courts, Mick Whelan drafted an unsigned pro bono brief arguing that a seat centered in a resurrected city with a significant black population had a political and moral claim far more compelling than the gerrymandered districts submitted by Texas and Florida.

Whelan's bona fides were unimpeachable. I know, because in 1970, after I spoke to his constitutional law class at the Northwest School of Law, I sat in a folding chair along the wall of the law library among a delegation of students who wore red and blue bandannas, tie-dye shirts, and buttons sporting the peace sign and the clenched fist of the Black Panthers and heard him lead the fight to establish a branch campus of the law school in reconstructed Vanport.

"Vanport was history forgotten," Whelan told his colleagues. "So were thousands of homeless black people who had built Liberty ships during the war. Most whites in Portland turned their backs. Some thought the 1948 flood was an instrument of divine Providence. One minister quoted the old slave saying 'No more water, the fire next time,' then told his congregation, 'Look like those old-time Nigras had it wrong. The Lord sent so much water, ain't no need for no next time.'"

At Mick's words, a founding member of the faculty exhaled a sigh expressive of all the exasperation ever felt by elders at the presumptions of the young.

"But, Professor Whelan," he interrupted, "what has this to do with the academic issue before us?"

"Damn, Mick Whelan, you preach it," exhorted a black law student in a dashiki and a stovepipe Afro.

"It's a fair question," Mick said, walking away from the podium until he stood directly in front of his senior colleague. "Professor Whitlaw, not long ago, this law school was founded in the spirit of Lewis and Clark and Thomas Jefferson."

Whelan paused—the pause of the stump, not the courtroom.

"During the 1968 presidential primary, the national media called Oregon one great white suburb. They didn't count African Americans in northeast Portland, wheat farmers in eastern Oregon, salmon fishermen on the coast, loggers in the mill towns, factory workers in Portland, Mexican Americans in the fields of the Willamette Valley, or the citizens of Vanport."

The murmurs in the room were hard to read, and Mick looked around, as if to pluck an ending out of the air.

"Founding a branch campus in Vanport would be a sign of our commitment to become a great law school," he said, looking slowly from colleague to colleague, becoming conversational. "And if you need a member of the faculty to carry out your instructions on curriculum and standards, I volunteer to take it on. Pro bono," he added, his smile lighting up the room as he sat down to good-natured laughter and a quick round of applause before the dean's secretary clicked off the tape recorder.

The resolution requesting the Board of Governors to authorize a provisional branch campus on the site of the former Vanport city library narrowly passed. At the urging of black students, the faculty named the Vanport campus after York, the slave William Clark never freed, but whose spirit some folks swore had wandered west to one of the islands north of Vanport in the middle of the Columbia River.

In the unsigned brief he wrote two years later on behalf of Oregon's case for the additional congressional seat, Mick Whelan told the story of the new Vanport—not a black town or a white town, but a town in which, this time, come proverbial hell or historical high water, black folks and white folks were going to stay. Taking his cue from Whelan's argument, Congressman John D. "Blackjack" Phillips, dean of the Oregon delegation and a former state supreme court justice, went to work behind the scenes. Both the judge and the politician in Phillips were impressed by Whelan's shrewd mix of geography, diversity, and politics. The lead attorney for Oregon was state senator Alexander Stephens Corbett, a former Phillips protégé. Thinking ahead, Phillips held a press conference commending Senator Corbett for the brilliance of his legal analysis and his masterful courtroom presence. Blackjack Phillips knew his praise would set Corbett up for appointment to the new seat pending elections in 1974. And things worked out exactly that way. Whelan expected no public credit—and received none. He had been working for a cause, and the cause was Vanport and a reborn Oregon.

Mick Whelan knew that in the abstract, ours is a government of men as well as laws, but, like baseball, politics is a world all its own, and in March of 1974, his campaign for Congress was a lost cause. For one thing, Congressman Corbett was a compliant, regular Democrat, a nonentity with few enemies and excellent committee assignments orchestrated by Blackjack Phillips. For another, Whelan was an unknown who had waited until the last minute and lacked money. Finally, he was a part-time candidate unable to afford unpaid leave from his teaching duties.

Mick knew the score, and so did I. But in the spirit of the Sound Connection, I dropped in on my way back from House Judiciary Committee business on the West Coast. There, I found Vanport the epicenter of a district whose long border with the Columbia River made it shimmer. Shaped like a heron with a beak that curved slightly east of Hood River, a slender neck that stretched past Vanport and the confluence of the Willamette and Columbia, and a breast that rose and fell for fifty miles north by northwest before a long-legged run down the coast, the new district struck me as mammy-made for a candidate like Whelan. Television coverage and advertising from Vanport or next-door Portland could reach every voter, and a personable candidate could do more than a little good touring the tree farms, lumber mills, schools, and main-street luncheonettes in the river towns beyond Vanport and the fisheries and cheese factories along the coast.

In this district, a Democrat needed to appeal to labor and to the family businesses dotting the landscape. And during the mid-seventies, it was easy to be a friend to the clean high-tech companies beginning to favor Oregon over California's more expensive Silicon Valley. Demographically, also, Vanport's burgeoning black population together with an influx of professionals, young and retired, made the district more heterogeneous than the rest of the state.

To double-check my impressions, I stayed overnight on York Island. There, in the middle of the Columbia, a modest hotel had sprouted, along with several two-story condominiums and a small museum in the shape of a nineteenth-century packet boat. Coming over from Vanport on the ferry, I saw a wildlife refuge where herons nested, joined of late by a pair of bald eagles. The island also offered a pleasant view of downtown Vanport, especially the two comely signature malls designed by Northwest architects tired of the chockablock shopping centers springing up like dragon's teeth along the beltways surrounding Portland.

Early the next morning, I drove east from Vanport along the Columbia toward the mountains. Everything people in the Boston-to-Washington Northeast corridor were beginning to rave about stretched out before me. In the distance, halfway between the Columbia and Mount Hood, was Mount

Loowit—the only Cascade peak bearing its original Indian name. On the left, the river, lit by sudden bursts of morning sun, sparkled blue and white. Between the mountains and the river stood stands of Douglas fir. North-west of Mount Hood, a snow-white triangle gleaming in the iridescent light, I could see Loowit half in light, half in shadow, its round face curving proud and pitiless like the old woman in the Klickitat legend to whom the Great Spirit gave youth and beauty in exchange for the use of her fire.

Beyond the sprawl of bedroom communities and industrial parks that had been cannibalizing berry patches and farmland since the sixties were high-tech landscapes that were also virtual spaces, designing chips for the approaching electronic revolution of the eighties. Unlike earlier industrial parks hidden behind cedar fences, these did not scar the landscape. Half an hour from Vanport, I entered a world of water and sky, rocks and trees, sun and snowcapped mountains. Later, from the air, the territory I had explored seemed an idealization of the actual Oregon. My mind drifted back to Bobby Kennedy and his advice to friends who asked him if they should run for office: "If you can win, run. If you can't, don't."

Son of a bitch, I thought. *Mick Whelan, why didn't you do this right? Why didn't you wait for Corbett to bumble and stumble until he became everybody's caveman and go after him in 1976? Or, if the itch was irresistible, why didn't you plan a brilliant campaign far enough in advance to give him a run for his money? Goddamn it, I forgave you for choosing Gene McCarthy over Bobby K. in '68, why couldn't you run as a serious candidate?*

When I returned to Washington and called Mick, he cut me off three sentences into my report.

"Gabe, my man, don't take this so seriously."

Hearing my new son crying in the background, I walked over to his cradle, picked him up, and paced back and forth as far as the phone cord would stretch.

"So, you're looking to 1976?"

"Nineteen-seventy-six might be the end of the world. I just didn't want Corbett to have a free ride."

After more back and forth, I was convinced that Mick was serious about not being serious. For a while, between monitoring Patrick's entrance into the body politic and smoking out Watergate perjuries for the Judiciary Committee, I lost touch with his campaign, until one day on the Hill, when I heard Congressman Corbett brag about putting "that whippersnapper Whelan" in his place. Responding to Mick's criticism of his vote against funding a seismic tracking station halfway up Mount Loowit, Corbett called him "that Earthman from Con-neck-tee-cut." When I checked less than a month before the primary, the Oregon poll put Corbett at sixty-five percent, and had Whelan surging ahead of the undecideds eighteen to seventeen. Still, I was encouraged. Corbett was so confident and so far ahead, I figured his backers wouldn't put much money into television. If Mick caught a bit of a tailwind, he might end up with thirty percent, and maybe I could talk him into doing it right in 1976. But as time passed, our long-distance conversations became more aimless.

"Christ, Gabe," Mick told me one evening, "I'm talking politics in my classes and law on the stump . . . "

He didn't say any more, and I didn't push. I had promised to come out for the last week of the campaign. À la Heisenberg, I thought that by being on the scene in Oregon, I might change the phenomena and fulfill the prophecy I'd made in my cups that Mick would get thirty-five percent.

The Friday before I was leaving, I slipped away early to check Kate's report that Patrick was smiling. When I got home, she met me at the door.

"Gabriel, did you talk to Mick Whelan?"

"No," I said, hurt, because I had been thinking of her and Patrick.

In the living room, the television was on and I saw a freeze-frame of angry gray smoke billowing from what remained of a mountain sharing the screen with live pictures of a gray-white funnel of debris rising higher and higher into an immense blue sky.

"A volcano erupted in Oregon," Kate said.

"That's crazy."

"The whole thing's crazy, but the one with that Indian name blew a couple of hours ago. I saw Mick on television. He got caught in the blast up on some logging road."

I reached for Patrick, who cooed his way into my arms.

"He rescued a black man and his son," she continued. "He's a hero."

With my free hand I dialed and redialed Mick's number, but the lines were jammed. There was nothing to do but watch the special coverage. Like their elders in Dallas after Jack Kennedy was shot, the correspondents ad-libbed, telling over and over how, a little before noon Oregon time, the bulging top of Mount Loowit disappeared in a gravity-defying explosion precipitated by an earthquake grinding away below the crater of the ten-thousand-foot summit. A pilot flying a light plane over Loowit shot Polaroids of boulders spinning into the avalanche of lava (*pumice*, they started calling it on television) that blasted down the mountain, flattening stand after stand of Douglas fir. In live shots, the fallen trees looked like blackened toothpicks. Hundreds of miles away in Idaho, the afternoon sky turned so dark, residents thought they were experiencing a total eclipse, until they ventured outside and felt bits of pumice hailing down on their heads. More than a hundred people were missing in the blast zone; dozens had been killed. But terrible as the eruption was, it was fortunate that old woman Loowit—Keeper of the Fire—had blown her top a few hours before hundreds of Oregonians headed east for a warm May weekend in the mountains.

Scrambling for names and faces, the television stations ran the same clip of Mick Whelan in the lobby of Mercy Hospital.

"How were you able to drive the father and son to safety?"

Whelan hacked loudly in sympathetic vibration with his two comrades-in-disaster. "Mr. Fitch got us through."

Knowing Mick was unharmed, I calculated the amazing turnabout for his campaign. As I patted Patrick's back after his ten o'clock feeding, the phone rang. From Kate's relieved tone, I knew it was Mick. When my turn came, he told me he was okay in body but not in soul.

I tried to imagine what Mick had been through but couldn't come close. After an uncomfortable silence, I plunged ahead anyway, and mentioned the pig in the parlor, as grainy pictures of mudslides on the Clark River ran up and down the television screen.

"I wouldn't want to be Corbett—he made such a big deal of voting down seismic stations."

On the tube, close-up shots of a van up to its door handles in mud yielded to a wide-angle shot of a helicopter, blades whirring above the former tree line, checking for survivors.

"Look, Gabe, maybe I should let this go."

"Don't be crazy. Don't feel guilty about the attention you're getting for saving a couple of lives."

In the silence that followed, it hit me that despite his disclaimers, Mick was looking for a way to make a real campaign of it.

"We'll work it out when I get there," I said, then, cupping the receiver, turned to address Kate. "You don't mind if I leave Sunday instead of Tuesday, do you, sweetie?"

Her hazel eyes blazing, Kate took the phone out of my hands.

"It's news to me," she told Mick, tossing her head, "but I'd rather have him helping you in Oregon than moping around here. Just promise me you'll veto any stunt that could get you both killed—like Gabriel sending you on an aerial tour of the crater."

After Mick's sign-off, I looked at the television set. With the sound turned down, the images took on greater force as the picture dissolved from the prerecorded moonscape of devastation to a live shot. The smoke, steam, and ash no longer spewed from the mountaintop in an angry column of grays and blacks. Now, backlit by the setting sun, the plume billowed slowly into the sky like the tail of a tropical bird, while in our D.C. townhouse I paced back and forth, telling Kate my plans to book an early flight on Sunday and set up a Monday-morning press conference for Mick.

"Gabe," she said finally, her eyes smoldering, "we were going to have this weekend."

"I'm sorry," I said. "I just need to be there."

Sunday morning I landed in Portland well before noon, rented a car, and drove through the flats of Vanport to Ship of Zion AME Church, where Mick was attending a thanksgiving service. In its previous incarnation, Ship of Zion had been the first black church built in Vanport City and the first to be restored when the town was resurrected in the sixties. In homage to the flood of 1948 and biblical Zion, the faithful brought in truckloads of fill, and on the highest point of not very high ground, they, their children, and grandchildren built the Lord's house in the shape of a ship. As I climbed the steps to the entrance, I heard singing backed by a piano, a bass fiddle, and a tambourine.

In the vestibule, an immaculate young man in starched white tails extended his hand. "Welcome to Zion."

He handed me a program written in several childish hands. "Service of Thanksgiving for the Deliverance of Brother Jonas and Brother Martin Fitch" it read above a crude drawing of an exploding mountain and a dark angel in the midst of an ash cloud pointing toward a car in the forest. As the handsome young man with a close-cropped Afro opened the swinging door, the singing reached a crescendo. I marveled at the human warmth. After the blood and fire of the sixties and early seventies, not to mention all the decades before, these black Christians treated me, a strange white man come to their church, as one of God's chosen, and therefore one of their own. Suddenly, their voices surged in unison to a tempo accelerated by syncopated handclapping.

"On Calvary's hill, He died for us," the choir behind the pulpit gave the call, and every voice in the congregation rocked out the response: "And that's love."

Reverend Elbert Harris had cobbled together the program on little notice. To the right of the pulpit were the three crosses left from Easter, and in his sermon the reverend recalled the angel's words to the two Marys who came to anoint the body of Jesus the Sunday morning after his crucifixion: "Why seek ye the living among the dead?" With a deep basso flourish, Harris thanked the Lord for bringing Deacon Jonas Fitch and his son, Martin, back from the dead.

In a sweeping gesture, he turned the gaze of the congregation and the television cameras along the wall toward the Fitch family in the front pew. Four girls, two little ones with pigtails and two in their teens with microscopic braids, surrounded Mrs. Fitch, who wore a lavender suit topped by a wide-brimmed pale yellow hat set off by a corsage of white rosebuds and baby's breath pinned to her jacket. Like sentinels on either side of the women, father and son were dressed in dark suits and wore shoes shined to a transparent black. Next to the Fitches sat Mick Whelan in his three-piece navy-blue suit.

"My staff," Minister Harris said, introducing Deacon Fitch, "without whom I could not make straight the way of the Lord."

The humming of *amens* came from young and old nodding in rhythm to the minister's words.

"Brothers and sisters, 'No more water, the fire next time'—old folks been singing that since slavery days. I don't have to tell you about the water flooded this very spot in the year of our Lord 1948. Brothers and sisters, I don't have to tell you that two days past, a cauldron of fire boiled out the Earth's belly. I don't have to tell you that the Lord spared His own—the good Lord spared Brother Jonas and his son, named after that great preacher taken from us by a white man's gunfire in Memphis, Tennessee."

The congregation answered with a thunderous *amen* and rose, clapping, as Harris moved away from the microphone and Jonas Fitch moved slowly to the podium, dragging his left leg. A bandage covered the burns along his right temple and cheek where falling ash had singed his skin.

"Praise the Lord, brothers and sisters," he said, breaking into a dazzling brown-and-white smile. "Praise the Lord."

His words triggered a further eruption of applause.

"Brother Jonas, you in Abraham's bosom now," a very large dark woman shouted as she moved out into the aisle, swaying in lithe arabesques as mesmerizing as Josephine Baker's.

Looking tired, Deacon Fitch raised his hands to quiet the renewed shouting.

"Brothers and sisters, the good Lord showed me fire and brimstone, and I trembled. 'Take me, Lord, if that's your will,' I prayed. 'Take me, but spare my only son, Martin.'"

"Praise the Lord, who took you out that fiery furnace."

The red lights on the television cameras were on, but no one paid any attention. Even strangers like me were drawn into a circle where the lives and history of the folks at Ship of Zion were no more finished than their stories from the Bible were finished.

"I'm telling you," Jonas said, "the Lord sent a man to lift his servant Jonas out the belly of the fire. That man is named for the archangel Michael and the whale that spouted Jonah out onto dry land. Lord, I didn't recognize the man you sent to deliver us, but my boy, Martin, did."

Nudged by their mother, the Fitch girls stepped into the aisle so that Mick Whelan could pass between them and ascend to the pulpit. I could tell that Deacon Fitch's mysterious reference to the past made it easier for Mick to come forward. As he approached, Fitch held out his arms, and the two men embraced. The tears in their eyes did duty for words, and so did the music, as choir and congregation clapped in a slow dance of hands. Finally, Deacon Fitch pointed to the microphone, then tapped it, an aside to Mick Whelan that he had no choice but to address the congregation.

"Minister Harris," Mick began. "Brothers and sisters—"

A chorus of *amens* filled the silence as Mick looked for a way into the story he wanted to tell.

"Maybe I'm named after the whale," he said, "but instead of spouting like a whale, I wailed like a lost soul while fire fell from the sky. I thought hell was swallowing me. Then a man with a fishing pole beckoned—a fisher of men. I wanted to go on through the gates of hell, but that man opened the rear door of my car and pushed in his son. Then he rode shotgun. All the way down to the highway, he kept his head out the window and wiped hot ash off the windshield with his sleeve and bare hand so he could tell me when to swerve and when to keep straight."

"You know you our brother," the large dark woman who had been swaying in the aisle called to Mick.

"I couldn't place what was familiar about Brother Jonas," Mick continued, "until Martin tapped me on the shoulder and said, 'I know you. You the guy almost knock my daddy down at the March on Washington.'"

"Ain't that the Lord's way?" an old woman answered.

"When I turned my head," Mick said, picking up the thread, "I recognized Jonas—the look on that logging road was the same look he gave me after I bumped into him on the National Mall in 1963."

"Lord, Lord, we know that look," one of the old men who had passed the collection plate said, drawing a belly laugh from the congregation.

"There's another thing," Mick said, looking at the row of reporters and their cameras. "You television and newspaper people got it wrong before, so please get it right this time."

"*Please, please, please, please,*" the young people in the choir rocked the church in imitation of James Brown's famous falsetto, and a few of the elderly members shook their fingers at the cameras.

"Brother Jonas, Brother Martin, you were your brother's keepers. You were in the mountains, but I was in the valley of the shadow of death when you appeared in that noontime darkness."

The handclapping resumed, beating out a slow, stately syncopation, as if the brothers and sisters were miming the Lord's own footsteps as He prepared to set foot on Earth again.

"I didn't rescue Jonas. He rescued me," Mick told the congregation. "He plucked me out from hellfire. I'm here to thank him and Brother Martin. And I'm here to tell you that Reverend Harris's words about the living and the dead are written on my heart."

"Preach it, Brother Michael, preach it."

I listened, wanting Mick to bring in politics without being political. But his words flowed, oblivious to anything as self-interested as a campaign.

"Because I was saved, I *do* seek the dead among the living."

A hum rose among the congregation.

"You in the whirlwind, brother," a baritone voice cried out. "Hold on tight, the Lord ride you through."

"I feel the whirlwind but I am not worthy," Mick answered, a cloudy look dimming his face.

An old man in a wheelchair waved his cane in the air. "Brother, we all unworthy, the Lord make us worthy."

"I feel . . . ," Mick repeated, "I felt . . . " He hesitated in the face of words that belonged to a different tone of voice, a different story. "'*Domine, non sum dignus,*' I used to answer when I was an altar boy in a little church in Connecticut. I rattled off the words and never considered what they meant. But this morning, I knew." His lips whispered a quiet *amen.* "You're the Lord's crew on the Ship of Zion, and this morning you've made me worthy."

The piano, bass, and tambourine started up again, and the old man in charge of the collection plate shouted a response. "You sailing with us, boy. You got ship's papers."

As Mick stepped down from the pulpit, the congregation swayed and waved, singing, "On Calvary's hill, He died for us—and that's love." Now, between the lines of the refrain, the brothers and sisters filled in amens of praise for Jonas and Martin Fitch; praise for their minister, Elbert Harris; praise for the young man in their midst, Michael J. Whelan; praise for one another; and praise for the Lord whose spirit flowed though them like cool, cleansing water rushing down Mount Zion. Afterward, they didn't mob Mick like I'd seen black churchgoers mob Bobby Kennedy. But they looked like they were on the way to being friends.

"I won't speak ill of any man in the Lord's house," Mrs. Fitch told Mick in the vestibule, "but I want you to whip that old Corbett. Don't have to put a bad mouth on him. Just tell the truth."

Whelan clasped a few hands, touched a shoulder here, an elbow there, and made his way outside to Jonas and Martin. I told the hovering television people that Mick would speak briefly with them. I wanted the Fitches included, so, pretending to trip over a cord, I bumped the cameraman into the circle.

"You heard the people," Deacon Fitch announced before a man and a woman in network jackets had a chance to ask a question. "We'll walk through fire for this man."

Whelan bantered with Jonas, and after Mrs. Fitch fished something out of her enormous black handbag, Martin approached with one hand behind his back.

"Hope it fits, Michael," he said, holding up a T-shirt with Ship of Zion etched across the front in red, black, and green.

"So I know you next time you run into me," Jonas laughed.

Mick nodded. I couldn't imagine a better prop. There were hugs all around, then he and I walked down the steps to the lower ground of the street.

That night, I sat in Whelan's little house, not far from where tons of water had flooded Smith Lake twenty-five years before. Sarah, Mick's off-again, on-again companion, was there too. Throughout the evening, Mick was attentive to her with the self-consciousness of a man touched on the shoulder two days before. As he kept watch over the imported pasta boiling in a huge pot with a built-in colander, Mick dipped into the bubbling water with a wooden forklike utensil designed to snare individual strands of pasta. Three or four times, he held the contraption out to Sarah.

"Just cook it, Mick," she finally raised her voice in good-natured exasperation. "You know when it's done."

"Al dente," he said. "Gabe knows the difference."

After dinner, Sarah served black coffee and brandy and we talked about the campaign. Before the eruption, Mick had had a sparse schedule planned for the last week, but now with his pick of speaking engagements, he needed to choose ones that would generate the most-effective free television.

"We need to move the press away from the hero on the mountain, toward the hero as the next congressman," I said.

Sarah nodded vigorously, her presence generating an electric charge in Mick's direction. I looked down at the homemade coffee table—a laminated wooden plank set on cinder blocks painted a discreet forest green. Staring up at me was the headline of Sunday's paper: "Dozens Killed by Loowit Blast." Underneath, in smaller print, was a subhead accompanied by a photo that made the havoc of the volcano real and tragic: "Congressman's Daughter Feared Dead." I felt a catch in my throat as unbidden images of the slender, raven-haired girl grown into a true beauty fast-forwarded through my mind from the grainy newsprint. I remembered Rebecca Phillips arriving on the Hill to work in her father's congressional office the summer of 1967, while her contemporaries back in central Oregon were working drive-in windows at the Dairy Queen, taking riding lessons, or, in a notorious case, escaping God's country for San Francisco and the Summer of Love.

"Jesus, Mick, you didn't tell me about Rebecca."

"They're not sure," he lowered his voice a notch as he took Sarah's hand in his. "That's why I cringe about campaigning. Loowit's not a photo shoot for *National Geographic*."

Despite my shock at the fate of Rebecca Phillips, I couldn't afford a reluctant candidate, so I brushed her image out of my mind.

"But Mick," Sarah leaned close to him, "it's too late to take your name off the ballot. Besides, people are counting on you, like those people at the black church—like me." She crossed and uncrossed her long legs.

"Sarah's right," I told him. "There was a lot of talk about you at the airport this morning."

"Gabe, what were you saying about the next few days?" she asked, like a Saint Bernard come up in the snow with a mug of rum.

"To raise money for television, I've got to show the boys in D.C. that the campaign is exploding like the volcano. And people are coming your way—before I flew out, L. A. Jackson told me he's pulling for you."

Jackson was a black congressman from New York City. I had introduced Mick to him in the Senate gallery after Kent State, on the day Gene McCarthy presented an amendment to require presidential authorization for a National Guard unit to carry live ammunition.

"What'd he say?" Mick asked.

"'Get your ass out there. Any white dude saves two bloods he don't know needs help.' That's what he said."

"Gene got two votes the day I met Jackson," Mick mused, looking out the window at the lights flickering in the distance, "his own and Ted Kennedy's." He sighed, then lifted his foot off the Sunday paper, grazed his mouth with his hand, and stood up. "Let's play it by ear."

I rose to go.

"Mick needs your help," Sarah said, her arm around his waist in the doorway. As Mick disengaged to walk me to my car, Sarah's words took on a tone similar to Kate's the night of the eruption. "Keep him away from Loowit. He can't resist those little roads."

Outside to the east, the moon was rising over the Columbia.

"So peaceful," Mick said. "One minute the world is so serene, you think it's nirvana, and the next, you're in hell."

I put my arm around his shoulder. "It's okay, Mick."

"It's not," he said softly.

I knew he was right, but I had no consoling words. For all that had happened, Mick was my tiger, and I had to keep him focused. "We'll make something out of this shit, like we tried to do in the sixties."

"Maybe," he said.

We shook hands, and I drove off, my mind buzzing with timelines for the campaign and a one-liner or two I wanted to jot down before his press conference the next morning.

CHAPTER 4

To reinforce the catastrophe, I scheduled the press conference at the Vanport Historical Society adjacent to an exhibit on the 1948 flood. Whelan opened with a brief off-the-cuff statement that drew blood with a single flick of the lash. He called it tragic that it took a volcano, a natural phenomenon able to be understood and perhaps foreseen, to focus Congressman Corbett's attention on the environment. Immediately, Harry Hacker, pockmarked veteran reporter for the *Vanport Statesman* whose tongue was as mean as his pen and whose antipathy for whippersnappers equaled his contempt for windbags, rose to his feet.

"Professor Whelan, are you saying that Congressman Corbett is to blame for the Loowit eruption?"

"The congressman may not have had his wits about him," Mick answered as a laugh or two floated toward the front, "but I hold him responsible for his vote against funding seismic stations up and down the Cascade Range."

The lights on the television cameras glowed bright red, but reporters' pencils stopped scratching along their steno pads as Mick began to review the special provisions given to the House of Representatives by the Constitution.

"The framers decreed elections every two years to make the House the people's House. And they charged the representatives with initiating spending legislation," he said, as if he were talking to a civic group about the genius of the American political system. Then he was back on track.

"Mr. Corbett is an interim appointed congressman, not yet an elected representative of the people. The people of the Fifth District need to be informed about the choice they'll make next Tuesday. Therefore, I am challenging Mr. Corbett to debate the issues."

Mick stopped and paused long enough for the reporters to take up their pencils again.

"In case our paths don't cross,"—there were smirks because the reporters knew Corbett's schedulers were under orders to make sure the congressman didn't set foot in the same county on the same day as Mick Whelan—"I offer to meet him at a time and place of his choosing."

After a fractional pause, Whelan left the lectern. Satisfied with the rising buzz in the room, I thanked the press and told them that Mick would be available daily for the rest of the campaign. On our way out, a couple of cameramen asked him to pose beneath a black-and-white poster-size Associated Press photo of the Vanport flood. In the grainy print, a man rowed a battered boat toward his terror-struck son, who sat on top of an old Chevy watching the floodwaters swirl across the windshield. Afterward, the press guys smoking outside parted to let Mick pass, as if he were already a fellow professional.

Before heading out of town, I looped around on the beltway. Dead ahead, a thin trail of vapor wound its way upward from Mount Loowit like the smoke from Mick's cigarette burning in the ashtray. What for centuries had been a forest of brilliant prismatic green was now a graveyard of ragged sticks. For an instant, the remains of the mountainside loomed so close that I swerved instinctively, almost missing the exit to the road west to the lumber mill where Mick was speaking during the lunch hour. Jolted, he reached over and steadied the steering wheel.

"Sorry, Gabe," he said, breaking a silence as thick as the mudflow of debris that had buried Clark River and Lake Sacagawea in the aftermath of the blast.

On the right, the Columbia River flowed irresistibly toward the sea beyond Vanport. In the rearview mirror, the crumpled peak gradually yielded to the flow of cars and trees.

As I saw it, Mick's chance to win the election depended on how well he fused his sudden identity as an unlikely hero who had saved the lives of a black fisherman and his son with the biography of a savvy young politician.

Slouched in the bucket seat next to me, his words began to surge— slowly at first, then in a torrent, like the lava flow I'd seen in television footage of the eruption.

"Friday morning, I was going to speak at a coffee up near Loowit. It was a gorgeous day, so I took a detour on an old logging road—I've spotted loons up there."

After sneaking a look at the burned-out case of a mountain faintly visible in the side-view mirror, his face contorted.

"Damn it, that's not true." His words and expression turned fierce. "I was going to Lake Sacagawea," he said in a low, charged voice, with the look of someone who'd gone too far to turn back haunting his eyes. "I couldn't say it last night, but I was on my way to the Phillips cabin to see Rebecca."

His eyes watering, Mick stopped.

"After law school, she stayed on to work at the legal-aid clinic. I'd see her around from time to time. Easy and casual. Then, right after I declared for Congress, there was more. For a while, I avoided her, and she avoided me. But neither of us wanted to . . . "

Mick shifted his knees away from the gearshift and stretched his legs as far forward as they would go.

"During the McCarthy campaign, Sarah was the best. When I made my rounds of the storefronts, she'd be cadging chairs and tables from the furniture dealer down the street who was against the war but didn't want his customers to know it, or consoling a young mother who'd been called 'a goddamn hippie traitor' going door to door in east Portland to run-down houses with chain-link fences and no sidewalks, or sticking up for black folks who wouldn't change the name of their McCarthy for President storefront, to compete with the Kennedy Community Center up the street, or persuading union wives to bring their husbands to a coffee to hear Senator McCarthy tell them why the Vietnam War was bad for working people, or refusing to come down to the main headquarters on election night because she wanted to hear the returns with the volunteers in north Portland."

He took a cigarette from the pack I held out and put his, then mine, close to the glowing coils of the cigarette lighter.

"Sarah and I were new to Oregon and to each other. But underneath the politics, we didn't have . . . you know, that ease. Over the next few years, we walked up to the line several times—splitting up, I mean—then we'd miss each other. It was a relief bumping around together, lonely when it seemed like we were through."

A long drag brought the glow back to the tip of his cigarette.

"When I filed for Congress, she thought I should wait until I could win. But she's been a good sport."

Mick shifted sideways so that now he was looking directly at me.

"Maybe I was just committed enough to appreciate Rebecca more."

Mick sighed, then leaned forward and replaced his still-glowing cigarette in the ashtray.

"You introduced me to her back in sixty-seven." He clasped his hands together around the back of his head, a faraway smile softening his face. "Her amazing brown eyes with those violet highlights," he said, a blue twinkle invading his.

As he talked, I saw a mirage of the girl who had returned more and more grown up and beautiful each summer after 1967. In the years when many of the sweet young things in Washington weren't so sweet, she showed up at a few antiwar demonstrations, but unlike most congressional brats, she didn't exaggerate her feelings to spite her old man. She didn't sneak around either. She and Blackjack obviously had an understanding that she could work for him and drift around the edges of the protest movement as long as his enemies didn't use her. And it worked. In a *Look* article about the generation gap on Capitol Hill, she came off respectful of her father but not afraid to say she opposed the war in Vietnam. And I was struck by the way she told the writer that she was proud of her older brother, Jack. He was neither a hawk nor a dove, she said, just a young man who signed up and shipped out to Vietnam because he didn't feel right about taking a deferment or using his father's pull to get out of what ordinary guys his age faced.

God, she was beautiful. I remember sitting in the Hawk and Dove more than once during the summer before her junior year in college when she came in with a guy who worked for her old man. Permanent Press, I called him, because he went around so cocksure and buttoned down. When Rebecca walked in, my gang would lower our voices, swivel around, and look at her as if our heads were attached to the same body.

"Anyway, Gabe," Mick broke into my reverie, "early last Friday, she called to tell me she needed to talk. I took a shortcut to the little cabin on Lake Sacagawea that belonged to her mother's family."

We swung away from the river into farm country interrupted every now and then by a copse of alders.

"I was on an old logging road that became a dirt trail and ended at the lake across from the cabin. Passing huge fir on either side, all of a sudden I heard a boom. I looked through a break in the trees to spot the jet fighter, but all I saw was blue sky. I bumped along faster, thinking about Rebecca, until I saw a plume of smoke curling up from the top of Loowit. Hell, Gabe, it was so quiet, I remembered the Indian legend about the old woman in her teepee and imagined the smoke was from her morning fire."

An expression between a smirk and a smile struggled though the crease of pain on Mick's face.

"I heard a low rumble. Before I could get my bearings, there was a roar, and a huge black-and-white cloud rushed out of the mountain—it *was* the mountain. Then everything was haywire—debris shot into the sky and kept going. Boulders flew where the peak used to be, and there were violet flashes of lightning."

Mick picked up his cigarette from the ashtray while I watched a single strand of smoke thread its way up the windshield.

"In my mind, the mountain was collapsing on Rebecca. But the road was clear, and, to the South of Loowit, Mount Hood shimmered in the sun. For a minute, the sun streamed through the trees, and I heard mountain larks. Then, around the next bend, the northern sky was pitch black where the ash cloud was spewing mud and rock down the glacier. Before I heard the cry, I knew Rebecca's name had come from my mouth. I sped up. *Keep your head. Drive. Follow the road.* By now, time and space were gone. Images of Rebecca were all I had to cool the heat from the ash and lava pouring down toward the timberline."

While Mick talked, I drove automatically, snatched from the bright May morning into a nightmare. His rising and falling words put me in the scene, and I half heard, half imagined what he must have felt, his insides turning over as he careened up that washboard road, flinching whenever the ungodly purple lightning knifed through his concentration.

"I saw Rebecca like she was the last time I'd been with her. I wasn't sure I'd make it, and she wasn't there to meet me, so I paddled across the lake to the cabin. She heard water lapping as I tied the kayak to a branch in the middle of the fallen fir tree that old Jack and young Jack had converted into a dock. Coming out to the deck, she smoothed her black hair. She looked as good offhand in a crewneck sweater and jeans as she did in an after-six dress with her hair done up.

"'Hi,'" she said. "'I wasn't sure—'

"Ever since the first sparks flew between us, right after I announced for Congress, I always saw her eyes first.

"She put an index finger to my nose.

"As we embraced, I caught the scent of pine in her hair.

"'Keep me company while I add enough greens for two,' she said, scuffing her tennis shoe on the deck. 'It's okay if you don't get here as long as I haven't already made lunch. Then I miss you too much.'

"She led me inside. Despite her words, she'd set two places at a square cedar table. Once we sat down, she put her hand on my arm.

"'I wish I could help more, Mick. I've been around campaigns since I was a little girl. My father was good at glad-handing people, showing them he knew the ropes. I'd smile like I was proud of him. You know—a guy with a daughter that pretty can't be all bad. It was worse for my brother, Jack. He started out with his father's name: John Davis Phillips Jr. Because Daddy was Jack, you'd think his son could have been John, but no way. He was little Jack from before he could talk. Daddy never said it, but part of him lived through his expectations for Jack. Daddy thought that if Jack listened to him, he could get elected senator, and eventually maybe even vice president on the national ticket. When Vietnam came along, Jack thought it was a point of honor to go.'

"She looked at me, her eyes saying so much, it was hard to look back.

"'But for you, Mick Whelan, politics isn't some macho trip. I've seen you get your kicks when some clown stumps you and you think of something new. Your face lights up—like when that radical black guy with the beard and red bandanna mocked you. Remember? "Whelan," he said, "What would you do to stop the FBI from harassing the Panthers? Nothing! You're worse than Corbett," he sneered before you could answer. "At least he knows he's a fake." You asked him if he was through. "You sure?" you said when he said yes. You looked cool, but you weren't. I knew you were waiting for something.'

"I moved closer and counted her toes with mine under the table. Then I put my arms behind my head and closed my eyes.

"'Then, Mick Whelan, you told bandanna man if the FBI violated the constitutional rights of the Panthers or anyone else while you were in Congress, you'd introduce a bill to cut off appropriations. You knew it wouldn't *pass, but you'd keep pushing until you got the president's attention. You said you couldn't stop FBI harassment by yourself, but you'd try under the authority Congress had under the Constitution. I was so proud of you.'"*

Gaining on us while Mick conjured Rebecca, an eighteen-wheeler blew a crude blast on its horn. When Mick turned around, he winced as distant Loowit came into view, dirty bright in the sun.

"Rebecca was like that," he said.

Now that he was talking directly to me again, his voice rose above the melancholy murmur I had been hearing.

"She was so straight up, I didn't have any choice but to be at my best."

In front of me, the road narrowed. A sudden wind leaned the alder trees toward each other. Their leaves quaked, and Mick's voice dropped back into the language of reverie.

"We went up to the little bedroom over the kitchen and made love—you know, when you hurry not to be in a hurry, then you forget everything, and afterward is as good as before."

Driving alongside the Columbia in the sun, imagining chinook salmon swimming upstream by the thousands to spawn and die, I glanced at Mick and realized that he had no idea I'd heard anything he'd said.

"Maybe the best was when we told each other it couldn't be this good again, knowing it would be."

Whelan sighed, his legs scrunched cross-legged on the seat.

"The sense of time and no time came back on that goddamn logging road. I floored the gas pedal, and as I bounced up and down that roller coaster, the cloud got thicker and louder. Rebecca was trapped somewhere between the volcano and me. I was closing in, and she was on the outskirts of hell. *Maybe she'd gone inside to get her sketch pad; maybe she figured she had a couple of hours, then I'd be there and we'd look at the mountain together and leave. When did she know the thing was headed right for her? What did she do? Why didn't I leave Vanport earlier? . . .* The more my mind raced, the faster I bumped up that dirt road. Now the fir were swaying, their tops dark. Bits of ash flew into my path. I swerved around a bend, and a figure in the road was waving something. *Ah, Rebecca,* I thought. *Thank God you didn't wait at the lake. Thank God you knew if you rowed across and started down the trail, you'd meet me.* I hit the brakes and heard a strange voice.

"'Hey, man, you crazy? Where you think you going?'

"He was a black man, and next to him, a young guy was kneeling on the ground, coughing.

"'To the goddamn lake!' I shouted.

"The guy took off his slouch hat and slapped it against his knee, knocking off little chunks of cinder. Then he pointed his fishing pole toward the dark cloud to the north.

"'Ain't no lake, man. Look, we got one chance—you, me, and my boy here. Turn that sorry-ass car around and drive like there's no tomorrow. And there won't be unless you move. Hear?'

"I didn't see Rebecca anymore. I was stupefied. I would have obeyed him if he'd told me to turn right at the stoplight after the next Shell station."

"'Fitch,' he said, after he pushed his son onto the floor in the back and directed me to back up and turn hard until the car pointed west. Then he climbed in beside me. 'Jonas Fitch.'

"He put his left hand in mine, because his right was blistered red where a fiery twig from a flaming tree had caught him on the palm.

"'Mick Whelan,' I said.

"'Drive like this the Indy 500, Mick Whelan. Stay close to the shoulder. That way, when the road curves, you got room to swerve without slowing down.'

"Far ahead, I could see the blue sky that had been there when I hit the road for Mount Loowit and Rebecca. But overhead in front of me, there was no sky, only an ash cloud heaving this way and that.

"'Left, boy, left. Now right. Steady, bro,' Jonas chanted, as if he were the lead voice on a chain gang. 'Steady, bro, got to make it.'

"I obeyed him, keeping my eyes on the road and my hands at the top of the steering wheel. To the right, where the cloud steamed on ahead of us, trees were down, and those still standing were black and orange, their bark glowing in the dark. Passing tree after tree on my left, I noticed that the patches of green were turning black. But I could see the end of the cloud—maybe the road would stay straight instead of bending into the path of the volcano."

Mesmerized by Mick's story, I had entered a passing zone, and now a long, earsplitting shriek from an air horn followed by a nudge against the rear bumper made me lift forward in the driver's seat. In the rearview mirror, the cab of the enormous eighteen-wheeler loomed high over the rear of my tin-can Toyota. I swerved into the right lane while on my left a beefy truck driver in a logger's cap raised his fist in a curse as he strained to pass before the extra lane ended. Next to me, Mick took his hands off the dashboard, which he'd used to brace himself, and resumed his story.

"In a clearing at the edge of the road, a doe paused. Head high, she sniffed the wind. Then she looked down, and I saw why she'd stopped. At her flank was a fawn, white spots all over it, its tail dusted gray and black from the ash. Hearing the car, the doe looked at me, and the flecks of violet in her chestnut eyes reminded me of Rebecca.

"'Christ,' I yelled, slamming my hand on the steering wheel.

"'Easy, boy. The good Lord help us more if you say His name in prayer,' Jonas Fitch chided. 'Hug that shoulder. Give this heap some gas, boy. You ain't got time to look after no damn doe.'

"Seeing my distress, he turned gentle.

"'Son, that doe got this far. Let the Lord help her the rest of the way.'

"By now, the doe was the farthest thing from my mind. Following the twists of the road, I peered into the forest, and the crackling trees brought Rebecca's story about her brother's ordeal in Vietnam rushing back. Jack Phillips went to Vietnam as a second lieutenant—just like any other college graduate. Old Jack was easy about it—too easy, Rebecca told me one afternoon when the weather had turned fiercely hot and we were sitting outside on beach towels. So she wasn't surprised when young Jack wrote from Saigon, furious that he'd been assigned to show reporters from the States around, because before long they'd realize he was Blackjack's son and find out that back home, the congressman was bragging that his only son was in Nam while Senator So-and-So's boy was marching in protests and Secretary Whosit's son was burning his draft card. But little Jack bided his time and got tight enough with the staff sergeant to grab his personnel file one afternoon while the sergeant was in a topless bar in some Saigon back alley. Jack changed his orders, put them in the stack of transfers, and within a week shipped out to the Mekong Delta to spell a second lieutenant on R and R in Manila. No one knew anything about it until after the platoon got caught in a firefight that wiped out half the men, wounded Jack in the head, and left him subject to bouts of vertigo and blackouts. Afterward, the Army gave him a medal and hushed up the forged papers.

"Congressman Phillips was furious at the Pentagon, but little Jack had his father by the short ones. If there was political publicity about him being a hero, little Jack would blow the game by admitting that he had tampered with his orders in protest against the military's (and his father's) favoritism. He was pretty far gone, but once he was back in the States, he confided in his sister. The official story was that Lieutenant Phillips had performed with valor, commanding his unit under fire and inflicting heavy losses on the enemy until the medevac helicopters arrived. But that hot afternoon at the lake, Rebecca gave me the story that Jack told her after swearing her to secrecy. She told it so slowly and with so much feeling that I saw the tiger butterflies, heard the birds, and felt the vines tripping Jack and his men as they patrolled the jungle looking for a missing Vietcong battalion.

"'Jack wasn't ashamed because he did something he shouldn't have done or didn't do what he should have done,' she told me. 'He hadn't known the first thing about combat, but orders were orders. As soon as he landed at the firebase, he reported to a colonel who sent him to a captain who was short a platoon leader. Jack couldn't tell the truth without getting court-martialed or knowing that Daddy's pull was the only thing keeping him out of the stockade.'

"Gabe," Mick said, and lines creased his face as Jack Phillips's story intersected with the story about Rebecca, too painful to tell together in a straight line. "When I looked out at the forest below Mount Loowit, half torn up by the volcano's artillery, half green and untouched, I saw Jack Phillips in camouflage fatigues leading a dozen scared young soldiers through a landscape about to be assaulted by screams, smoke, and automatic-weapons fire—another green precinct in hell."

As Mick and I drove farther from Vanport, a battalion of puffy gray-and-white clouds tracked the northwest course of the Columbia. Only if I looked carefully did I see tiny wisps of vapor drift loose and bob across the sky like the jellyfish in Long Island Sound. Downriver, the clouds were shifting in the sky, their reflections shattered every once in a while by sunlight sparkling on the flowing water while Mick talked on.

"There I was, Gabe, driving like a maniac down a dirt road, Jonas Fitch burning my ears, Rebecca breaking my heart. I was following Jonas but hearing Rebecca. 'Mick,' she told me, 'Jack was in front of his men when he heard a noise in the jungle—maybe a twig, maybe a snake, maybe an enemy soldier. "Take cover," he ordered before all hell broke loose. Two of his men got hit right away; the rest flattened out on the ground and returned fire. After a while, the shooting stopped. It was heart-stoppingly quiet except for a Vietcong who was screaming in the bamboo six feet away. Finally, one of Jack's men killed him. Jack heard the rounds, then saw a grenade hit the ground and stop halfway between him and Carlos DeJesus, a nineteen-year-old grunt from Fresno. Before Jack could react, DeJesus jumped toward the grenade but tripped and fell on it. Jack hollered, but the only sound he heard was the explosion. DeJesus's canteen whistled past his face, and Jack felt pieces of flesh and bone, cloth and shrapnel stinging him. Somehow he got his men to the helicopters, wounded and all. He's haunted, Mick. He blames himself, not for not saving DeJesus—he knew that was impossible—but for forging the papers. He says that his defying his father cost DeJesus his life—one of his Latino buddies said DeJesus stayed close because he knew Jack had no experience,' Rebecca finished, tears streaking down her face like tracers.

"Gabe," Mick leaned toward me, "I was living that scene as I drove out of the blast zone, and it saved me. I was a crazy man anticipating Jonas's calls of 'left, right, and steady, bro' while branches snapped and Douglas fir crashed across the road behind us. I realized that his and his son's lives were in my hands. Finally, blue sky broke out in front of us—we were going west and, thank God, the cloud had caught a strong east wind.

"'Man, we almost out of it,' Jonas hollered.

"'That was some driving, bro,' Martin, no longer crouched on the floor, choked out from the backseat.

"Gabe, I was in shock. For the last mile, I didn't know before from after. I blocked out Rebecca, the lake, everything.

"'Look like you got us the hell out of hell,' Jonas said when he saw how wasted I was.

"I put my head on the steering wheel and started bawling. I slowed down, and straight ahead under a pine tree still green with only a dusting of ash in its highest branches, I saw that damn fawn. I saw *that* fawn, Bontempo— I didn't know whether it was the same fawn, but I knew it was the fawn. There was no doe to be seen. I braked the car to a stop. Didn't say boo to Jonas or Martin. Put on the emergency brake and opened my door.

"'Where you goin', boy?' Jonas yelled. 'We not out the woods yet—not any which way.'

"I looked from the fawn to Jonas, and he sighed a why-in-the-world-did-I-expect-anything-different-from-this-crazy-ass-white-boy sigh. Then he grasped my arm.

"'Son, if you were carrying a bottle of milk, I'd say go ahead. But all you gonna do is scare that poor creature the rest of the way out of its wits.'

"I paused with the door half open.

"'Besides,' he added, 'any minute now, the wind might shift that evil cloud back in our direction. I'm telling you, that old gray bitch not through blowing her top. Best thing you can do for every living thing here, including that fawn, is get out the woods and on the highway to Vanport.'

"I nodded and closed the door. As I drove on, Jonas fiddled with the radio dial until his blackened fingers reeled in a Vanport station carrying reports alternately calm and hysterical. I turned my head. There was blue on three sides, and the monster cloud was still heading east, taking up less and less of the sky.

"'Oh, God,' I said out loud.

"Rebecca was back there somewhere. I knew that and had to face it. After driving out of the volcano, I felt nothing inside.

"'God,' I kept mumbling.

"Jonas wasn't nosy. He'd gone back to his own thoughts, and we were quiet until Martin started to wheeze and cough.

"'His asthma's starting to kick up bad,' Jonas told me. 'Better drive straight to Vanport Mercy.'

"Looking at Jonas now that the sun was out, I saw blotches of gray and pink on his face that covered blisters as big as half-dollars. I'd forgotten that he'd craned his neck out the window for ten miles, braving a hail of ash in order to wipe splotches of pumice off the windshield. "'You need a little mercy yourself, Jonas,' I said.

"He didn't argue, just nodded as if he had done his part and he'd let me take care of business from here. I was at the end of my rope, inside and out, so I became an automaton, counting off the distance to Vanport by the tiny signs posted on the shoulder of the highway every tenth of a mile. Over and over, I heard Rebecca's sweet voice on the telephone saying that she needed to talk—I wished I had dropped everything and surprised her with fresh strawberries and champagne.

"On the radio they were interviewing a pilot who'd been in the air just northwest of Loowit. He told about seeing an avalanche of boulders and lava pour down until the lake and all its cabins vanished.

"Eventually I screeched up to the emergency entrance at Vanport Mercy Hospital and helped Jonas and Martin into the receiving station.

"In all that chaos, I didn't have time for my thoughts. Fortunately, the admitting personnel took minimum information and hustled the injured off to immediate care. I was grimy, ash in my hair, on my face and hands, but I wasn't burned. Half a dozen times while I was waiting to make sure Jonas and Martin were seen to, and, later, waiting for a pay phone to call Mrs. Fitch, I heard the same report: the lake was gone. Then, a spiffy-looking guy whose name tag identified him as the Mercy information officer went over the top.

"'You know how crystal clear that lake was? You could even see the bubbles the fish made,' he told an orderly. 'It's just a big mud pie now.'

"'How do you know, fool?' I growled.

"He looked me up and down before his expression changed into a smirk fit for some rude-ass dude.

"'Well . . .' he began.

"'Shut up, I don't want to know.'

"But no matter where I wandered, I heard *oohs* and *aahs* about the lake vanishing into slime. Two newsmen in the waiting room asked for an interview, and I found that talking about what it was like to be up there and drive out alive dulled the pain," Mick finished.

Driving along the Columbia River Highway, I veered between going out to Mick without reserve, comforting him with a respectful silence, or encouraging him to put his grief behind him. But I was a novice at consolation, and I could not separate his story from the work of politics that lay ahead.

"I'm sorry, Mick."

I reached over to touch his hand, and at the instant of contact, he clasped mine with conviction.

"That's why I told you," he said, the lines around his eyes retreating a little.

At the entrance to Timber Incorporated, I saw an enormous plaster-of-Paris logger in jeans and a flannel shirt, an immense ax poised in his hand above a log big enough to have put Paul Bunyan's mettle in doubt. Easing the car along a row of fifty-foot logs, I wasn't sure whether the statue was a welcome or a warning to visitors.

"Mick . . . " There was no time to try to say what I wanted to say, so I took a practical tack. "The only memorial to what you had with Rebecca is to make the fight. You two wouldn't have fallen in love if it weren't for your campaign."

Mick slammed his fist on the dashboard.

"That's what I fucking can't get out of my head."

I looked at him, taking my eyes off the road long enough to nearly run over the foot of the huge logger who hefted his ax above us.

"I'm not going to quit," he said, sensing my agitation. "Maybe running is the best punishment." He looked at me, his eyes burning. "You're my friend. I didn't want you to find out Rebecca Phillips was a volunteer in my campaign and try to use her," he went on, as if having told me their secret, he needed to make a promise to his dead lover. "If her name comes up, refer it to me. No one else touches her."

Hearing the tears in his voice, I reached over and rested my hand on his.

"Mick."

Now the force of his anguish poured over me like molten lava. We sat there for a while before I came back into time and space and remembered the campaign appearance. But he beat me to it.

"Let's go, Gabe."

As we walked toward the entrance, two law students with Whelan for Congress signs approached and raised a low cheer. By the time he reached the door, Mick was composed enough to clap one of them on the back, then walk a few paces ahead, while I brought up the rear.

CHAPTER 5

The television cameras began rolling the minute Mick Whelan walked into the cafeteria at Timber Incorporated. Two network stations had crews on hand, and so did two independents—unheard-of coverage for a speech in a congressional primary. In front of the rear wall on either side of the room were two professionally lettered Corbett Country signs, one held by a logger, a union pin on his overalls, the other by a midlevel manager in a polyester suit. On my way to sniff out the mood of the press, I encountered the law students with their campaign brochures and green-on-white Whelan bumper stickers and buttons.

"Mr. Bontempo." The unbearded one pointed to a short, stocky man in a red-and-black checked jacket. "That guy told us we couldn't put Whelan literature on the tables, but there's Corbett stuff right where the television cameras are pointed."

I put my arm around his shoulder. "Not to worry. People need to know who to vote against."

According to Bontempo's first law of campaigns, people new to politics see the closest tree, never the forest. It never occurred to this earnest young man that it was good luck for Mick Whelan to walk into hostile territory for his first speech since the eruption. Over the weekend, everyone had seen and heard him on television or read about him in the papers. Now there was the crackle of electricity in the room, an urge to see him in the flesh. So when the vice president of public affairs introduced Mick as a law professor from Connecticut come to learn about the timber industry in Oregon, there was an impatient murmur in the audience.

"Sit down and let the man talk," a grizzled lumberjack muttered, unwrapping the waxed paper from his bologna sandwich.

Whelan began by telling the crowd that, growing up in Connecticut, a state whose best-kept secret was its trees, he learned to tell the difference between maple, oak, elm, hickory, pine, beech—he kept the list going until snorts of laughter rolled through the room like runaway logs.

"Vice President Roberts is right—I'm in a good position to learn about Douglas fir, silver fir, and even noble fir here in Oregon."

Now the laughter became applause, as almost everyone in the room started to connect with this stranger who was prepared to take the company's man down a peg.

"There's a clue to Oregon's future in your company's name," Mick went on. "On Friday, nature yelled, 'Timber!' You didn't clear-cut that forest, the volcano did, but trees came crashing down just the same."

He stopped, a little uncertain as he looked from one logger to another.

"Loggers like you aren't out to get rich," Mick resumed. "You like to feel the wind and the sun—smell the weather, even the rain."

Guffaws came from two lumberjacks in the rear. From the gullies in their faces, it looked like they'd been working the forests longer than Mick Whelan had been alive.

"That's okay, sonny," called out another, this one with a red bulb for a nose, his Red Sox baseball cap turned backward on his head, "as long as you don't promise less rain."

Whelan held his right hand out flat in the man's direction.

"I've heard people say loggers don't care about the forest, or they wouldn't cut down a single tree. These people respect the Indians for putting every bit of the buffalo they killed to use—fur, hide, meat, and bone. But these same people live in houses made from wood, read books and newspapers made from pulp, and doctor their children with medicine made from bark and sap." Mick was slowly turning the loggers' amused attention into respect, and maybe a gruff affection.

"If this guy has horns, I don't see them," one said in a husky whisper to the man next to him.

The women who did clerical work and accounts receivable had wrapped their chewing gum into crumpled paper napkins and were also beginning to listen.

"I don't mean the timber industry is beyond criticism," Mick told them. "If you have any doubt that clear-cutting is wrong, go look at the desert left by the volcano. There's every reason for a company like Timber to be a friend to the trees. Jobs, safety, a reasonable return on shareholders' investments are all part of the good life. But sometimes timber companies get carried away with technology and short-term profit. The forces at work inside Mount Loowit also got carried away—whether we like it or not, nature keeps us honest."

Mick checked his watch.

"There's work to do. The blasted trees need to be cleared, their wood salvaged, and new seedlings planted. But if society expects you to risk working on the mountain, Congress needs to appropriate enough federal money so you'll know what's going on under the earth as well as on top of it. And we need seismic stations, like the one Congressman Corbett deleted from the Interior bill."

At Whelan's mention of Corbett, Vice President Roberts shifted uneasily in his chair.

"But I want to thank Mr. Corbett. A few weeks ago, in this same cafeteria, he called me *Earthman*. I take that as a compliment—we're all Earthmen and -women. And we're citizens. Whatever our differences, we should fight for the good life. I can't promise fewer floods, earthquakes, or volcanoes any more than I can promise less rain, but if you elect me to Congress, I promise to do my best for you and the Earth that's in our keeping."

Instead of ending with a conventional thank-you, Mick carried the audience back to what had been on their minds.

"Please join me in a moment of silence for the three loggers who were lost on Mount Loowit and all the others who perished or are missing."

Chairs were heard scraping across the rough concrete floor, and heavy boots thumped as the loggers rose. The coughing and clearing of throats lasted long enough for everyone in the room to imagine Loowit as it had been seconds before the volcano began its rampage. Then there was a general buzzing but no applause, and no one filed out.

As Mick moved among the tables, people surged up, clapped him on the back, and wished him well. At the back of the room, a knot of people surrounded the law students, grabbing buttons and bumper stickers.

As I waited for Mick, the anchor for ABC's Portland affiliate approached, a pert blonde looker with the voice of a spring bird.

"Is there time for a short exclusive?"

"I can give you five minutes," I told her.

There was time galore, but long ago I learned that the press gave you more attention if you played hard to get. Besides, after his press conference and now this speech, I had no doubt that Mick was the hottest story in town. After his snapshot was taken with a woman who worked in the plywood department, I steered him toward the reporter and her cameraman. The reporter flattered him breathlessly and shamelessly with questions that went from bad to worse.

"Do you really expect Congressman Corbett to debate you?"

"Maybe if you give him the message."

Mick smiled directly at the red light on top of the camera.

When he stepped back, she tugged at his sleeve and charged ahead after her scoop.

"Mr. Whelan, a human-interest question. Rebecca Phillips, the daughter of the congressman, is missing and presumed dead. Is it true she was a volunteer in your campaign?"

Mick looked hard at her.

"Yes."

"Have you been in touch with the Phillips family?"

"Yes."

Straining the leash of propriety to the breaking point, the reporter kept nipping at Mick.

"Is the congressman—?" She stopped in midsentence.

Whelan's eyes never moved from hers. He spoke with a fiercely bland expression I had not seen on his face before.

"I told the congressman how sorry I was and asked him to express my sympathy to Mrs. Phillips."

"Do you expect to speak with him again?"

Even the cameraman rolled his eyes at her chutzpah.

Unfazed, Mick ignored her question.

"Rebecca Phillips was a special person. I mourn her loss."

The reporter held her microphone closer to her mouth, giving her voice a brittle rasp.

"Mr. Whelan, there's a report that the *Vanport Statesman* is about to switch its endorsement from Congressman Corbett to you. There is speculation that perhaps Congressman Phillips—"

Mick held up his hand.

"He's grieving for his daughter," he said quietly.

On the way out, a bushy-haired logger who before the speech had been holding up a Corbett Country sign asked Mick for his autograph.

"Right there. See? Where I crossed out Corbett and wrote in Whelan? Put 'To Joe—From Congressman Whelan,' see?"

"Hey, it's too early for that," Mick said, shaking the man's hand after he signed his name.

"My congressman, see?" the logger said, holding up his sign.

One of the law students hustled over and gave the last Whelan bumper sticker to the departing logger.

"Great speech." The volunteer clapped Mick on the back. "I heard one of the toughest-looking guys say, 'Hell, I'm a loggerman, why shouldn't I vote for the Earthman?'"

In the car, Whelan slipped off his loafers and rested his stocking feet on the dashboard.

"Jesus, Miss ABC blindsided me in there."

On my left, a horn beeped—the law students were passing us in a Volkswagen bus with Whelan stickers plastered all over the trunk.

"She's a local looking for the silver bullet that will get her hired in L.A. or New York." I stopped, not sure how far to go. "But the way you handled it . . . Man, you've got ice water in your veins."

Mick pressed his foot against the glove compartment so his knee pointed at the roof of the car.

"Gabe, I'm going to run as hard as I can, but I won't deny Rebecca. When that babe did her party piece, I could see Rebecca swinging in the goddamn World War II hammock the Navy gave her old man after he steered a dry dock through the House Armed Services Committee." Mick put his feet on the floor and shifted sideways; he was almost always in motion. "Once when I met her at the cabin, she was so deep in her drawing, she didn't hear me row the boat through the reeds. I crept up from behind and covered her eyes. She didn't start or even blink. 'What took you so long?' she said. 'I thought one of those hippie chicks from the commune on the river had turned your head.' Before long, we were tumbling in the hammock . . .

"Anyway, when that silly blonde was snooping, I told myself, 'Get ready, man, this is how it's going to be.'"

He picked up a loafer with his instep and dangled it from his toes. "It's feeling her when I hear her name that's the hard thing."

Now he focused on me.

"Don't worry, Gabe, I'll give you the best I have. In a funny way, my heart's in it more now than before. I might just win this thing."

Ahead, the road widened into four lanes and an unfiltered view of the raw, scarcely built condominiums beginning to invade the barley fields below the foothills of the Coast Range. Off to the north, the Columbia flowed west to the sea in blue furrows flecked white by the wind, and in the east, Mount Loowit shivered in sunlight.

"Christ," Mick said.

I followed his eyes. The mountain looked like a woman's head. Whether a mother mourning her dead children or a hag grinning that a beautiful young rival was gone, I couldn't tell, but I was tired of coming face to face with what was left of that damn mountain. For the first time, Whelan had told me that he could win, but I was afraid that at the next sight of the mountain, he'd flinch and go through the motions. If that happened, he'd lose. His fifteen minutes of fame as the candidate who, caught in the wrong place at the wrong time, did the right thing was almost up. He was destined either to slip back into obscurity, his name the answer to a trivia question, or emerge as the guy with enough moxie and talent to take advantage of a break.

A sign on my right said Vanport 20 Miles. As I swung into the fast lane, the tires whined and Mick turned on the radio. Station after station scorched our ears with hard rock or country music until he found the Oregon Public Broadcasting spot on the dial just as the newscaster cut to a sound bite from Congressman Corbett in Washington requesting fifty million dollars of immediate emergency aid from Congress and the president.

"Son-of-a-bitching hypocrite," I said before the announcer quickened his pace and shifted to the campaign.

"Although Congressman Corbett acts the part of the incumbent in the nation's capital, there are indications he may be in for a fight here in Oregon. More on that from our political correspondent Al Diaz."

I moved to the right-hand lane to cut down the noise from the logging truck that I'd been about to pass. Whelan pressed his stocking feet forward against the dashboard and turned up the volume.

"Well, Ed, there are signs of trouble for Alexander Corbett in next Tuesday's primary. The *Vanport Statesman* has shifted its support. Though not an endorsement of challenger Michael Whelan, tomorrow's editorial calls both Corbett and Whelan acceptable choices for Democrats."

"Shit," I said. "Why can't the bastards ever go all the way?"

"Hang on," Mick said.

"The same edition of tomorrow's *Statesman* also has a new poll that's iffy for the congressman. Three weeks ago, Corbett led by more than three to one. The latest numbers gathered over the weekend have Corbett with fifty percent, Whelan thirty, and twenty percent are undecided."

"Closer, Al," the newscaster interrupted, "but if Congressman Corbett gets one undecided vote, he wins."

"That might be the case in most campaigns, Ed, but I'm inclined to believe these numbers aren't so easy to interpret."

Ahead, the sun had broken through, and in between banks of clouds, I could see bright clefts on Loowit's blackened skull. Here and there, ash showed through, but overall, it looked like an early-morning snowfall had fought the volcanic debris to a standstill.

"Al, can you explain what you mean for our listeners?"

"You see, Ed," Diaz continued, "the race is now volatile, and the valences all seem to be tilting in Michael Whelan's favor. The eruption and Whelan's rescue of the black father and son, together with the fact that Congressman Corbett recently moved on the House floor to kill seismic stations and also ridiculed Mr. Whelan's support for the environment— none of this helps the incumbent. I still pick Corbett to squeak through, but don't bet the farm on it. Last Friday, no one knew who Michael Whelan was, but now that people are seeing him on television, they find him an intelligent, attractive challenger."

"Twenty points is a lot to make up in a week."

The road was clear now, so I shifted into fifth gear and swung back into the left lane.

"Well, the firm number is Whelan's thirty percent. No one who's for him is going to switch. But some of Corbett's support is vulnerable. He's slipped fifteen points since the last poll—most of it since the eruption. His numbers could slip more as voters begin to compare him with Whelan. And I read the undecideds as people who haven't focused on the election yet. If Whelan runs an active, visible campaign, in the next week he can pick up the lion's share of the undecided vote. By Election Day, we may have the kind of horse race not seen in Oregon since the Morse-Duncan primary in 1968."

Mick snapped off the radio. I waited for him to speak, and when he didn't, I tossed my nickel into the pot. "That poll's perfect for raising dough. I'll get on the horn to the East when I get back to the hotel."

"Get the transcript," Mick told me. "And see if you can get Miles Stein to cut a television spot, but it has to hit the air by Thursday, or there'll be no debate."

"Let's get the pledges first, then make the commercial," I suggested.

Whelan shifted in his seat and leaned forward. "No, we've got to tease Corbett's gang into showing their hand, and assume the money will come."

It was after three when we passed the sign for the Vanport city limits. Driving along a flat stretch of road, I could see checkerboard hills rising gradually beyond the city. Through scattered clouds, Mount Loowit showed a pattern of gray-and-white cubes. The logging trucks were gone now, and because the view belonged to Mick as well as to me, it didn't take him long to roll the dice again in his mind.

"Goddamn it, Gabe, if I'd only told Rebecca to meet me in Loowit village last Friday morning." He looked straight ahead at the remains of the mountain, tears in his eyes. "We'd have been together," he said. "I'd have been with her."

Obeying Mick Whelan's law of underdog primary campaigns, I flew Miles Stein up from L.A. to do his magic tricks. In a thirty-second commercial, Miles could turn the moon into the sun and make you think you had a tan.

I'd met him in 1963 when he was with the U.S. Information Agency, and I heard him tell the attorney general that a ten-second clip of President Kennedy walking down the Mall during the March on Washington would do more for the country than all the state-of-the-art documentaries broadcast over the Voice of America. After the assassination, he moved to L.A. to freelance and make television commercials for a blue-chip agency. From time to time, he drifted into campaigns, usually for underdogs, usually at the last minute, and usually for expenses only. Two years before, he'd met Mick Whelan when he came up to Oregon for Wayne Morse. Picking up Miles at the airport, Mick found he'd locked his keys in his car with the motor running, then told him, "Fuck it, we'll just take a cab." His sangfroid impressed Miles, and now, in 1974, he was tickled that this young Irishman whose grandfather had driven trolley cars through Miles's old neighborhood in the Hill section of New Haven was running for Congress.

On Wednesday, he filmed a thirty-second spot whose grainy, muted, documentary look had the feel of news. Two images ran on a split screen: on the left, a wide-angle shot of a packed congressional hearing room preceded an unflattering close-up of Congressman Corbett looking perplexed while the committee chairman banged his gavel waiting for him to speak, while on the right, shots of Mick Whelan speaking to loggers at Timber Incorporated, voters in the street, and reporters at a press conference sped by. For the sound track, Miles cut from a voice-over announcing Corbett's vote against seismic stations to Mick challenging the congressman to a debate.

In the meantime, with the help of Congressman L. A. Jackson, whose Uncle Elijah had lived in Vanport before the flood, I raised enough dough to put the spot on the air over the next twenty-four hours. A quickie phone poll done Thursday put Corbett at forty-seven percent and Whelan thirty-five, with eighteen percent undecided.

The appearance of our ads on all four stations in the district and Corbett's shrinking numbers prompted his press secretary to announce in time for the Thursday evening newscasts that the congressman had accepted an invitation from KVPT, Vanport's independent television station, to appear on Sunday afternoon to discuss issues pertinent to the primary. He added that the congressman hoped his opponent would join him.

"Damn it," I told Mick, "it's all sleaze all the time from those bastards. They pick a station nobody watches except creatures looking for revival meetings, old Westerns, and the Jerry Lewis telethon."

"Gabriel, my man, the end run will piss off the other stations and their reporters. Before they're done, old Alexander Corbett will look like he said no for saying yes."

Mick was right. On television in the next few days, he was everywhere, Corbett nowhere. His handshaking at plant gates attracted television crews. So did an impromptu speech he gave to a union lunch, as well as the handshaking he did at the malls in downtown Vanport. Anchors introducing coverage of Whelan never failed to mention that with less than a week to go before the election, Congressman Corbett was absent from the state. To make matters worse for the incumbent, federal disaster relief was slow to flow, and Corbett could hardly denounce lack of action on a disaster he flatly predicted would never happen. For several days, he was the missing man, invisible except for the same—formerly bland, now somewhat ridiculous—"as-the-incumbent-I-can-do-more-for-you" commercials that were on the air before the eruption.

On Saturday, I had Mick barnstorm up and down the district, along the river towns from the coast, inland to villages in Corbett County northnortheast of Mount Loowit. Satisfied with the law students I put into the field as advance men, I stayed behind with Miles on Saturday morning to dub a fifteen-second spot scheduled to run at the top of the hour until the Sunday-afternoon debate. Footage of Loowit blowing her top dissolved into Congressman Corbett turning his back on reporters to board a plane, while a march-of-time voice quoted Lincoln's line from the Gettysburg Address about government of the people, by the people, for the people.

Slowing down the voice-over, Miles raised the volume on *for the people*. Then he cut to a tight shot of Mick inviting every Fifth District Democrat to hear him discuss the issues face to face with Congressman Corbett. By Miles's sleight of hand, the commercial seemed like a public service announcement. Few viewers noticed the Whelan for Congress disclaimer that flashed briefly across the bottom of the screen or heard it on the radio underneath the fade-out music—a single catchy fife whistling "Yankee Doodle Dandy."

On Sunday, while we waited for Miles in a dingy glassed-in editing room at KVPT, Mick picked up the shirt cardboards on which I had outlined talking points for the debate, dropped them on the desk, and fished something out of his pocket. In the bright halo from the spotlight above, I saw bits and pieces of glass—tiny blue waves surrounding a glass replica of Ship of Zion that rocked gently over the seven seas. At the service that morning, an old bluesman who also worked with glass had given the piece to Mick as a good-luck token. We were going over Corbett's votes in favor of clear-cutting in national forests when Miles blew in, his curly gray hair made more unruly by his windmilling arms.

"What's up, guys?" he asked, taking off his Burberry raincoat.

There was no point telling him that he was an hour late. No matter how good they were—and Miles was the best—media gurus were the same breed. Theirs was the only game in town, and there wasn't any other town. So Mick tapped his watch, as if to speed it up, and clapped him on the back.

"Put that stuff away," Miles said.

I fumbled for the glass miniature of the Ship of Zion.

"Not that—if there were more black voters, I'd put that figurine in a commercial—forget those issue papers. Let's check the setup. Don't laugh, guys. Once, when I leaned back in Vice President Humphrey's chair before the *Today* show, the seat collapsed." Miles kept talking. "I want your profile shot from the left in the close-up." Walking off, he muttered, "All I want is the profile shot. I'll give them everything else."

Sequestered in a windowless holding room with cinder-block walls, I looked sideways, fixing on the light and shadow on Mick's face. For an instant, wrinkles rippled out from his eyes like the cracks on the face of Mount Loowit. Suddenly, I remembered stumbling on a Quaker graveyard when I was a boy looking for acorns on Shelter Island. Letters slashed on the gravestones told the story of how grim Puritan magistrates hounded a small band of Friends out of Boston in the early 1600s, how they'd stripped the prisoners, set them in the stocks, cropped them of an ear, and cast them adrift in skimpy boats toward the devil's country in the North Atlantic before providential winds carried them to Shelter Island. In the trembling silence of that oak grove, I felt like a trespasser on the privacy of the dead, until a squirrel far above me dropped an acorn at my feet. Now, with talk dying between Mick and me, I wanted to make a gesture of luck, but when I thought to invoke figures from his private world, like Rebecca Phillips or Jonas Fitch, I felt like an intruder. I was still paralyzed when Miles cracked open the door.

"Let's go, tiger," he told Mick. "I got you the chair on the right. Remember, the camera's the people. Talk to it. Don't look at Corbett, even when he calls you a carpetbagging son of a bitch."

Mick stood up.

"One more thing, Whales," Miles urged, "you're first, he's last, so make your story Oregon's, not yours."

While Miles held the door and the station manager rushed up with an urgent question, I put my hand on Mick's arm.

"Win this one for Patrick."

The lines at the sides of Whelan's eyes flowed down into his grin.

"Old Patrick," he said. "He's the real reason I'm running."

Irritated that Mick and I were still in the holding room, Miles snapped his fingers, then smoothed his feathers before Mick noticed they were ruffled. He was a pro, and Whelan was his fighter, so keeping discipline fed the amplitude of Miles's ego. By the time Whelan caught his eye, Miles was kidding again, his jokes the resin a manager rubs on his fighter's gloves before the bell. I climbed up several stairs to the control room, where Miles and I could see both the set and the monitors whose images were about to fill voters' living rooms.

"Gabe," Miles said, sitting on the stool next to me, "I want footage for a last-minute spot. Hold my stopwatch. When I say *start*, write the time. When I say *stop*, the same."

On the set, Corbett sat propped up like a life-size replica of Smoky the Bear; Mick looked at ease. I had scoffed at Miles's impulse to put Mick on the right of the moderator; now I saw how the angle subtly counteracted a tendency to slouch away from the center of the action. Sitting up straight, he looked casual and comfortable in his own skin—before and after the cameras started running. From his opening to his close, he looked, spoke, and acted as though he was the congressman and Corbett the challenger. And once the cameras started shooting, Corbett didn't know what was happening. Clearly, his handlers had told him to come on as the stern but kindly incumbent so avuncular and committed to democratic tradition that he took pains to school a well-meaning, untried young opponent in the subtleties of government, a plausible strategy as long as Whelan did what Corbett's crowd expected him to do—attack. But, acting as though he was the congressman reporting to his constituents about the work and challenges ahead, Mick rattled Corbett until, with every repetition of "young man," the congressman looked and sounded more and more like a relic of fifties' small-town America. When Whelan showed just a touch of exaggerated patience, as if Corbett were a somewhat-addled great-uncle spruced up for Sunday dinner at an upscale retirement home, the congressman became angry.

"This young man," he thundered, "has the gall to tell Oregonians what they need. How in the world would he know? He hasn't been in Oregon long enough to pronounce the word. Well, I intend to tell the people who he was before he presumed to represent you in the Congress."

Red, blustery, and out of breath, Congressman Corbett paused and glanced offstage, as if seeking confirmation from his handlers that this was the moment to play his black ace.

"Start," Miles told me, pointing to his stopwatch. "Shit, what's the old coot got?"

"I've done some checking," Corbett continued in the smug, offended, inquisitorial tone of the Eisenhower years. "I have in my hands a photostat of the application this young Whelan filled out seven years ago for the Northwest School of Law."

He unfolded a document and held it lengthwise to the camera.

"No Young Democrats, no Lions, no Rotary. Not even," Corbett sniffed the air, "the Knights of Columbus or the Ancient Order of Hibernians. What's listed in this young man's handwriting is Students for a Democratic Society—the bunch of revolutionaries who shut down Columbia University in 1968."

"You know about this?" Miles whispered.

My gaze veered between the stopwatch and Corbett, while Miles scribbled a note on my yellow pad and chewed nervously on the top of his pen. From the control booth, I saw a tableau that included Corbett and the moderator, but in the monitor, Mick's close-up dominated the screen projected into the living rooms of those watching at home. I winced, afraid his face might break into a thousand fragments, but outside my mind, he sat cool and composed, his eyes steadily focused on the camera.

"Mr. Whelan," the moderator addressed Mick.

"Here goes." Miles pointed to the stopwatch and pad.

Before answering, Mick smiled and put his hand flat on the table next to Corbett's photostat of his 1967 job application.

"Sometimes what isn't said tells more of a story than what is. What Mr. Corbett didn't mention is that in 1966, the janitors at Georgetown University wanted to organize a union. To reserve a meeting room, they needed a student club with a national affiliation to sponsor them. So, yes, I joined SDS."

Upstaged, the congressman tried for the floor again, only to be told by the moderator that it was time for closing statements, the first of which belonged to Mr. Whelan. After the camera had shifted back from a shot of Corbett harrumphing to another close-up of Whelan, Mick leaned forward in his chair, as if resuming an informal conversation with a handful of voters in their neighborhood tavern.

"If politics isn't a force for good in ordinary times, we can't expect government to act well in times of crisis. Mr. Corbett called me *Earthman* because I proposed federal support for seismic stations and scientific research *before* a disaster."

The director interrupted his close-up of Mick speaking with occasional medium shots of Corbett opening and closing his mouth in response to points against his record. Meanwhile, Mick ignored his opponent and looked into the camera as if it were another pair of eyes.

"I run for Congress because the old politics are not worthy of this new district. Earlier, Mr. Corbett invoked the city on a hill—a metaphor for Massachusetts in 1630 but not Oregon's Fifth District in 1974. We are not members of a single sect. We come from every corner of the world. We are of every color, every background, every religion, and no religion. Our common creed is the idea of America." Mick cupped his left hand toward the camera. "And last but not least, we are a city *under* a hill. I was near Mount Loowit when it erupted. I felt the earth shake under my feet, and I trembled. I survived because two strangers took my hand. That makes me an Earthman."

My arm jerked as I felt Miles's elbow jab my upper arm, and he stuck up one finger, signifying that Mick had a minute left.

"Mount Loowit is a speck of rock and dust. But it's our world—its rivers and trees make us more alive. If my campaign has one theme, it is that we live with nature and each other as partners. If we show a decent respect for the ways of nature, we'll be able to keep faith with the inalienable American rights of life, liberty, and the pursuit of happiness."

Mick paused and looked into the camera. I couldn't tell if he was through or if he was waiting for a few telling last words before the red light flashed.

"If you elect me to Congress," he said, his voice a handshake, "I'll consider your support a provisional vote of confidence and look forward to your judgment of my record two years from now."

In the interval between Whelan's sign-off and Corbett's closing statement, I felt Miles's glance. Catching the wink, I turned my head back toward the set, where Whelan and Corbett sat motionless within the circle of klieg lights.

"Congressman Corbett, your closing statement."

Poor old Corbett's been dead and gone for years, but when I think of that debate, I remember him as one of those early personal computers that took forever to whirr into action. Called to deliver his climactic statement, his distress showed in tiny beads of sweat shining on his forehead. I could sense him scroll down the desktop of his mind before clicking on the one file with which he was familiar.

"I want to thank all of the voters in the Fifth District who have been so kind to my wife, Thelma, and me."

"Oregon hospitality," Miles whispered, and, sure enough, Corbett used the phrase in his next sentence, as if Miles had hacked his way into the modest database of the congressman's memory.

For a while, Corbett muddled through a canned closing statement until a power surge in his brain wiped out his programmed words and he lit up the blank screen with words different from anything he'd said during the previous hour, the campaign, and maybe his entire public life.

"When I think of Oregon, I think of a spring night when I was a boy walking along the Columbia River where the gorge is so wide, you can barely see the Washington side. I was with my mother's mother—my grandmother. She'd come west from Tennessee after the Civil War, a little girl in a covered wagon." Corbett's eyes glistened. "There was a sliver of moon so bright, I could see the shadow of the full moon behind it in the sky. 'Grandma,' I asked her, 'are there two moons tonight?' 'No, Alexander.' She leaned down and cradled me in her arms. She knew I was afraid."

By now, there was silence within the silence in the control booth as the technicians, Miles, and I began to pay close attention.

"'Hush, Alexander,' she said. 'That's the new moon in the old moon's arms.' Well, I felt better," Corbett continued. "And when I remember my grandmother's words, I feel better about Oregon."

The heat from the lights dried his eyes.

"There's still one Oregon, and like the moon that night, the new moon needs to rock a while longer in the arms of the old. Newcomers like Professor Whelan are bright all right, but their light comes from the old moon—those who led the way to where they are now. I'm proud to serve as your congressman in the spirit of that old Oregon. I'll always be proud of lighting the way for the new Oregon, like my grandmother did for me."

As Corbett finished, the red light on the camera went dark, and the lens zoomed in on the moderator, who thanked both candidates and, in a salesman's grating spiel, urged voters to "get your exercise by exercising your right to participate in the world's greatest democracy next Tuesday."

The set shone in the glare of the overhead lights like a boxing ring after the main event. Miles and I stood on one side, Corbett's men on the other, waiting for photographers to shoot the two candidates shaking hands. Corbett's handlers wore bland expressions, but I overheard vexed words as Miles and I walked by.

"All old boxhead's got to do is stay on the attack," fumed the one who, from the look of his tan corduroy suit against an open-necked fire-red velour shirt, appeared to be the guy in charge.

"Yeah, where'd he get that fairy tale about the moon?"

"Stuff it," the headman told his assistant as he realized that Miles and

I were within hearing distance.

The way the four of us made small talk, you'd have thought we were competing teams schmoozing at the United Jewish Appeal while we waited for the master of ceremonies to announce the totals. In television land, you kept your cool and spoke polite, meaningless words until the lights were turned off, the press gone, and you were alone with your candidate. To my surprise, Whelan and Corbett lingered, for a moment seeming to prefer each other's company to the custody of their managers and handlers. As the hubbub died down, Corbett left first, and Mick followed, smiling in response to our exuberant slaps on the back. On the way out, he shook hands casually but meaningfully with every employee he could find in the cubbyholes off the corridor leading to the front door of the station. At the information desk, he stopped, and when the receptionist put a call on hold to ask him for a button for her daughter, he took off his own and gave it to her. Just like the time at the Holiday Inn during the Kennedy-McCarthy primary, I thought, except now he was smoother. Only in the car did he let down his guard.

"High five, no jive!" Miles began.

"A knock out," I added.

"I had Corbett down for the count," Mick mused. "His eyes were glassy. Then he did his high-diddle-diddle act, and damned if he didn't jump over the moon."

As we passed Ship of Zion, Miles pointed at the church.

"Hey, Mick, you sure you didn't slip Corbett that little glass figure of the church?"

Mick turned sideways in the front seat.

"That good?" He clenched his fist.

"Damn good," Miles agreed. "Before the bit about Grandma Moon, you were as good as elected. That ending was the best homespun act I've ever seen. We're lucky the guys running his campaign don't get it."

Down a side street, on the way to evening services, a few black sisters swayed behind a little boy shaking his tambourine.

"Say, Mick," Miles said as an afterthought, "why didn't you tip us off that Corbett had that SDS smear up his sleeve?"

"I had no idea," he grimaced.

"Next time, give me a map of your closet," Miles said.

I felt like the guy waiting for his turn during a commercial.

"Look," I told them, "Corbett showed a human face at the end. But you made the case, Mick. You couldn't help it that the coin flip gave him the last word."

The Columbia rippled into view, and I pulled into the parking lot next to the Lewis and Clark Ferry Line. We were going to catch the ferry to York Island for an early supper at The Blue Hour bistro.

"Gabe's right," Miles said.

"I didn't expect Corbett to come back from the dead," Mick said quietly.

As we got out of the car, a cheer went up from the knot of people gathered outside the little brick building where they sold ferry tickets. A few held Whelan signs, hand lettered with Magic Markers, mostly in forest green. Those who showed up were a mix of young and old, white and black—a photograph of Vanport before and after.

"Hey, that's a good sign," I said before I saw Sarah rubbing her hands in the background and realized she had organized the demonstration, hoping to attract press as well as buoy her man's spirits.

"Yea, Mick!" she yelled, and as he worked the crowd, Mick gave her a big grin and the thumbs-up sign.

I moved ahead to the ticket window and felt a surge of electricity between Whelan and the people who came out for him. It wasn't the tumult I'd witnessed with Bobby K, but something was happening. Call it charisma if you want, but whatever you call it, Mick was beginning to catch on.

After huffing and puffing to catch up, Miles was beside me.

"Too bad this campaign is all but over," he said.

CHAPTER 6

When I picked up the phone in my hotel room first thing Monday morning, I heard the quick, urgent rhythms of Miles's voice.

"Rave, Gabe the Babe, rave. Final poll: Corbett: forty-eight; Whelan: forty-six; six percent undecided."

We're on the cusp, I thought, imagining Miles's index finger twirling a salt-and-pepper curl over his temple. Meanwhile, he barked instructions about Mick's constitutional-law class.

"Let the television guys set up early so there's enough time for the stations to edit a clip for the noontime news. And keep the Crazies for Whelan and their signs about herons, whales, and goddamn free pot outside. Inside should be quiet and serious—students listening to their teacher talk about that amendment—for Christ sake."

"The Tenth Amendment."

"That's what I said."

I could listen to Miles's staccato screeds by the hour, but this morning I needed to keep Mick on track and whip the volunteers into fighting trim for Election Day. So, before he snared me in a monologue about camera angles, lighting, the shape of the classroom, whether to go with a boom mike or attach a lavalier to Whelan's lapel, I disengaged.

"Miles, I've got to see about the candidate's shoes."

"Stay cool," he said. "Everything's under control."

In an uphill last-minute campaign, nothing is under control. But just because you're not in control doesn't mean things don't happen according to some sort of luck and logic. Mick Whelan knew this in his bones, so I wasn't surprised that while driving to the law school, when I asked him what he was going to say in his class, he opened the soft black-leather pouch he'd splurged on at the time of his appointment and removed a folder with his notes. Then he snapped the clasp shut.

"What's up?" I asked, downshifting behind a logging truck whose huge fifty-foot logs rolled from side to side, straining their ropes.

"Sarah tries to get closer, and I can't right now," he said. "Maybe it's better to lose. Then I'm not news anymore. If I win, I worry I'll keep things submerged."

The part of me from the days of the Sound Connection wanted to drive to the coast and get down like we used to do at the One Step in the sixties. But in my Bontempo-come-lately role as Head Nobody in Charge, my job was to keep Mick focused on getting elected and to discourage him from diving into undertows that could carry him out beyond the breakwater. As we got out of the car, one of the students waved a big Whelan sign.

"Cameras over here, Mr. Bontempo," he said.

As I turned my head toward the commotion, Whelan looked away and bit off a one-liner.

"If Freud were alive, he'd call American politics the superego of the late twentieth century."

"Tocqueville did, more or less," I said.

"No, he thought it was the id."

Mick lingered outside Frederick Douglass Hall with the volunteers until a guy with a portable camera and a network credential in his cap came toward him. Then, after a handshake here, a pat on the shoulder there, Professor Whelan headed down the middle of the sidewalk toward the cameraman, who had no choice but to back up and film a terrific shot of the candidate walking alone toward the entrance. Advancing Bobby

Kennedy, I learned that there's nothing like a television cameraman backing into a hall to stir an audience into applause. As Mick walked down the sloping floor to the podium, the clapping intensified. The moment he reached the front and the cameraman began to pan the crowd, students stood up in twos and threes and stayed on their feet, applauding with slow, steady force and duration. It was the last class before the final, and Mick was finishing up on the Bill of Rights.

"If Jimmy the Greek had been the bookmaker after the Constitutional Convention, he would have set the odds against ratification. What put the Constitution over was the Federalists' promise to introduce a Bill of Rights in the next Congress." Speaking more conversationally than professorially, Mick's eyes moved over the rows of students. "Thou shalt not, the Bill of Rights says over and over, but unlike the Ten Commandments, *thou* refers to the government, not the people."

Mick looked out at his students and settled on a sleepy-eyed guy with a blank look on his face and a Whelan button in his lapel.

"What's the Tenth Amendment all about, Mr. Guzzio?"

Guzzio pawed the ground with his sneaker and looked up, one hand touching his lapel, as if appealing his professor's decision to single him out after he had pinned his button to his jacket.

"Checks and balances?" he said finally.

"In a way, you're right," Whelan replied. "This last amendment is a boundary. Any powers not given to the federal government by the Constitution are reserved to the states and the people."

As I sat listening to Mick's case for the Tenth Amendment as a summing-up of the founding idea that America was a nation in progress, it hit me that he was also invoking an identity beyond assistant professor of law, political candidate, and, should lightning strike, congressman from Oregon's Fifth District.

"Remember," he told his students, "with one foot, the Tenth Amendment pivots back to the Revolution and the Constitution, and on the other, forward to the Civil War and the Thirteenth, Fourteenth, and Fifteenth Amendments on down to the twentieth century. None of it is self-evident."

He paused, and from the Irish wrinkles around his eyes, I knew he had found an ending. I was about to signal Miles, but in response to his gestures, the cameramen had already turned their cameras back on. Cyclopslike, each of the red lights protruded from the head of an identical unearthly twin—a cyborg able to turn circuits into flesh and flesh into circuits.

"Yes, young men and women of the law," Mick said with a twinkle, seemingly aware only of the young people slouching to attention before him, "there is life after Tuesday."

On Election Day, I was seized by the fear that Mick wouldn't make it, so one of the things I jotted down on my to-do list was a reminder to sketch out notes for a concession speech. In the meantime, I sat in the back room of the former water-bed outlet that was Whelan headquarters and passed the time by methodically crossing off item after item. As the day wore on, I listened to volunteers' stories of how responsive voters were when they were called and how more workers showed up at every storefront headquarters than had been expected. *Would I authorize a few bucks more for coffee and refreshments? I would. Would I shell out gas money for a few extra cars to drive people to the polls? I would. Would I see to it that there were chits for Whelan workers' drinks at the victory party? I would.*

When I arrived at the Vanport Arms a half hour before the polls closed, tally boards were set up for each county and two burly guys from the building-trades union were mounting television sets at the front of the ballroom. I finessed the reporters who were buzzing around looking for Mick by promising exclusive interviews. Soon they retired to the bar, and soon Mick, apologetic for going incommunicado, and Sarah, all smiles in a yellow sheath dress, showed up. Together they mingled with an expectant crowd pouring in to the strains of an incongruous medley of tunes—"Aquarius," "Give Peace a Chance," "Happy Days Are Here Again," and "We Shall Overcome"—played in rhythms that swung by a black and white jazz combo.

Election nights have different rhythms. In doomed campaigns, downing a few drinks before the polls close gives the faithful enough buoyancy to swim against the tide of bad news for an hour or so before the balloons begin to sag, defiant valedictory drinks are tossed off, the candidate concedes, and his supporters go home. Surefire campaigns are gatherings of the elect. The smell of success is an herb on the pâté, and, except among professionals, there's not a hint of apprehension, even in the instant of suspended animation before the first returns come in. But in close elections, no one, not the seasoned pro in his dark suit, the campaign girls in their sweaters, pleated skirts, and old-fashioned straw hats plastered with bumper stickers, the rummy who wanders in off the street for free booze, the savviest reporter, or the candidate, knows the result. In a real cliffhanger, victory and defeat make several visits before the certainty takes hold that nothing will be settled until the last vote is counted.

As the second hand on the ornate brass clock above the stage began its first revolution after eight o'clock, Miles gave me the high sign and I joined him in one of the few remaining congestion-free zones.

"Too close to call," he whispered. "Early returns a dead heat."

With the crowd's attention concentrated on television shots of the ballroom, Miles and I strolled over to Mick. Affecting nonchalance, along the way we gave the thumbs-up sign to curious volunteers. With a look here and a nod there, we nudged Mick into a private corner.

"Tough fight, long night," Miles told him.

Presently, we went our separate ways, Mick to mingle with the crowd, Miles to schmooze with reporters and media people, and me to keep the returns company in the back room. I was glad to get away from the noise and, worse, the communicable social disease of a political crowd—

anxiety. I'd been juggling figures in the stifling coffin of an office for more than an hour when I realized that the only pattern to this election was that there was no discernible pattern. The logic I was looking for couldn't be imposed reliably on the Fifth District's patchwork quilt of six counties. Miles and I had conceded the outlying towns to Corbett, except for pockets here and there, mostly on the coast, but we expected Whelan to win big in Vanport and the suburbs. Instead, Corbett, though losing, was doing respectably in Vanport, but in the river towns and rural areas along the Columbia, Mick was running him a close race. While I was trying to solve the equation of the election from incomplete returns, Miles came in, overheated and disheveled, tie loose, and swearing more than usual.

"Goddamn reporters," he said, as if continuing another conversation. "How the hell do I know? All I got is Mick and Corbett neck and neck. How about it, Bontempo?"

"That's what I got, too, but—"

"But, putt. Wait and see."

I smiled. Miles was a walking, talking incarnation of one of those state-of-the-art commercials that interrupts dull television programs.

"It's bizarre," I told him. "Corbett is doing well enough to win easily except for what's happening in the small towns."

"I can't figure it," Miles admitted, winding his index finger around a thinning curl of hair.

So we waited as the raw votes confirmed the topsy-turvy pattern of the election. By midnight, with eighty-five percent of the precincts counted, Whelan led by seventy-seven votes. He had taken Vanport, but not by as much as we expected, and he carried the suburban county east of the city, but he narrowly lost the western suburbs. In the two sprawling counties farther west, although the race was much closer than expected, Corbett was winning by several percentage points, with enough votes outstanding to overtake Mick in the districtwide totals. While I added and subtracted as new figures came in, Miles fumed and second-guessed. If he'd bought more radio time, if we'd sent Whelan into the western suburbs instead of keeping him in Vanport . . .

"Son-of-a-bitching 'new moon in the old moon's arms.'"

He stopped and looked at me, furious.

"Goddamn ancestral voices. I knew we should have answered that crap."

Miles was talking in riddles about an anomaly of a county whose returns we were sure would rub salt in the wound. Little Corbett County was the last to report. I say *little,* because although in square miles it was the district's largest county, it only accounted for some four thousand votes in the Democratic primary. The county wanders eastward almost thirty miles along the Columbia and south past Mount Loowit to the tree line on Mount Hood. Its citizens live in small mountain towns, half a dozen villages off the river, and, lately, in scattered farms, cabins, lean-tos, and A-frames inhabited by hand-to-mouth and well-off ski bums, freelance writers, artists, and others of more nondescript vocations who are glad to exchange the nuisance of commuting for the pleasures of the woods, as well as lots of retired people, many of whom had moved to Oregon since the late sixties. During the campaign, Mick worked the county some, but we conceded it to Corbett because his ancestors had settled there in the 1850s and given it its name. We figured to spot him a thousand votes and make up the difference in Vanport, the suburbs, and maybe a few of the little lumber towns where we sent Mick on walking tours after he'd done so well at Timber Incorporated. Before Corbett County reported, I told Miles to fetch Mick so he wouldn't hear the news cold turkey on the ballroom floor.

"Tell him I need to talk to him about his statement."

As luck would have it, the call from Corbett County came just before they walked in. Reaching for the phone, I remembered Mick telling me about the 1954 governor's race between Abe Ribicoff, an upstart Jewish congressman, and John Lodge, Connecticut's last Brahmin governor. As the grown man told the story, *twelve-year-old Mick listened to the returns with his father on a little kitchen radio in their Cape Cod cottage at the Branford shore. Although Ribicoff clung to a small lead, the smart money called it for Lodge. The challenger hadn't come out of Hartford, New Haven, and Bridgeport with enough of a plurality to hold on against the Republican votes trickling in from the bedroom towns of Fairfield County. Before Whelan's father called it a night, he told his son, "Abe gave it his best, but Connecticut's not ready for a Jewish governor." But his son disagreed. Mick noticed that Ribicoff's lead was shrinking very slowly, and it hit him that the Democrat was cutting into Lodge's margin among Jewish Republicans who worked in New York City and lived in Fairfield County.*

Now, in the drab, windowless office off the ballroom of the Vanport Arms, I brushed my hand over my eyes to banish the image of young Mick Whelan grasping what the professionals had missed. I sighed, pen poised above my pad, ready to record the bad news from the other end of the telephone. Like one stripped of all powers of ratiocination, I wrote down the numbers. The next sound I heard came from Mick Whelan, who, with Sarah and Miles in tow, had just opened the door.

"Tell Patrick not to worry. Life goes on," he said.

My eyes glazed, my mouth dry as dust, my mind whirled as I cleared my throat and read aloud what I had jotted down.

"Corbett County final returns: Corbett: 1,609; Whelan: 2,424," I said, my war whoop anticipating the thunder in the ballroom as the news flashed on the television screens and was announced at the podium.

"Congressman!" I held out my hand to Mick.

"Gimme the pad. You're mad!" Miles reached over Sarah's shoulder.

I obeyed him.

"Fucking transposition," Miles barked, blocking the doorway. "That's Grandma Moon's old homestead. How the hell could you carry that county when he beat you in the western suburbs, for Chrissakes?"

The phone rang. Miles grabbed it. It was Martin Fitch from his post at the AP election desk down at the *Statesman.*

"What's that?" Miles asked. "You sure?"

Suddenly seeing Mick, Sarah, and me, he began to repeat what young Fitch was telling him.

"AP projects it for you by three hundred votes," Miles said, his mouth curving away then back to the receiver. "Absentees all in? You're sure those goddamn Corbett County figures aren't a transposition?" He stuck his free thumb high in the air. "Swell. Listen, Martin, get down here so I can buy you a beer."

When he put down the phone, Miles told us that Corbett's guys had also been sure the Corbett County numbers were transposed. They had been counting on a plurality of nine hundred to a thousand. They'd sent a D.C. lawyer out to the elections office an hour ago, but the county clerk was a crusty old guy who lived on Lake Sacagawea until the eruption—when he returned from a trip to find the lake and his cabin vanished—and he was not about to be intimidated by a pinstripe suit from Washington with wavy black hair and wire-rimmed eyeglasses. He checked and rechecked the ballots and released the results only after the totals came out the same three times in a row.

"It's real, guys," Miles said, bear-hugging Mick, Sarah, and me.

While Whelan went back to the john to make himself presentable and Miles went out to talk to the press, I called the AP so I'd have final unofficial numbers for each of the six counties. Corbett's men were slick, and I didn't want a bunch of loose ends joining to form the noose of a recount. But the good news held. Final totals gave Whelan the victory by 313 votes.

"Isn't that a palindrome?" Sarah asked Miles, who was back.

"Drome, gnome," Miles grinned.

"My turn to give you a hug," Sarah said, her eyes tearing.

When the soon-to-be congressman emerged, he was shuffling two green campaign brochures. On the back of each, a few points were scrawled in black Magic Marker. I held out the county-by-county figures, but he didn't take them. Instead, he put his arm around Sarah.

"How can I miss after a night like this?"

In the ballroom, the din increased as Whelan made his way through a crowd that had doubled since midnight. As word spread, celebrants emerged from every nook and cranny of the sixties. Mick had campaigned very much in the contemporary moment, but now that he'd won—and won because of Corbett County—the political heads who'd gone underground reemerged, the sweet smell of their pot tickling my nostrils. Together they looked like a retake of Sgt. Pepper's Lonely Hearts Club Band, the Beatles' efflorescent album before they went their different ways. They came wearing bell-bottoms and tie-dye shirts, camouflage fatigues and army caps, miniskirts and maxi skirts, berets and bandannas. And they wore a profusion of fading buttons: Ben Shahn's dove or the peace sign; the clenched fist of the Black Panthers; the psychedelic waves of chemical liberation; one or two McGovern-Eagleton pins, a collector's item; and a sprinkling of McCarthy or Kennedy buttons, worn like military decorations under green Whelan buttons. Walking toward the front of the ballroom, Mick was a spot of forest green in his Italian-cut corduroy suit. Miles had urged him to wear navy blue, but Mick's green was of the Northwest, and the slender, tapered cut of his clothes fit the political transition under way that night. In choppy waves, friends, volunteers, contributors, and hangers-on broke toward him and receded according to his movements. Staying in character, he lingered with those who had worked for him, especially students and the middle-aged peace people he had met in Gene McCarthy's campaign. To those he knew only by their checks, he showed the cool deference of a chieftain.

Predictable as the light rain now tapping at the windows, Miles appeared, clearing a path for the television crews like a snowplow. Suddenly, klieg lights flashed on. Slight annoyance showed in the creases of Mick's eyes, and he ignored the microphones shoved in his face. But Miles was in his glory, nervously placing a reporter here, a camera there.

"Mick, over here."

"Are you surprised?"

"Is your victory significant for the peace movement?"

"The environmental movement?"

"Did you expect to win Corbett County?"

Like crows cawing from the same telephone wire, the media jabbered questions while Mick looked amused by the commotion. But as the crush separated him from the reticent, undemanding individuals with whom he wanted to savor the moment, his smile thinned.

"It's time," he told Miles, who was motioning one of the cameramen to shoot from Whelan's left side. "Set up a press conference for tomorrow."

At that, the reporters parted like the waters of the Red Sea, the sweating cameramen keeping their lights on and film running as Mick kissed Sarah, squeezed her hand, and made his way to the front of the ballroom.

Seeing no riser behind the podium, no Whelan for Congress banner on the wall, I rushed over to Miles.

"Where's the setup?" I asked him.

He was distracted. He looked toward Mick, who was standing before the noisy crowd, then at me.

"I thought you—"

"Me, you," I answered.

Over the suddenly deafening din, Mick looked good standing alone. With the moves of a natural, he walked back and forth along the warped boards of the stage, bending over to converse with people on the floor who he recognized, then back to the podium to adjust the microphone.

"Thank you," he said, holding up both hands.

"Whe-lan. Whe-lan. Whe-lan."

"The whale is in," shouted a big guy wearing love beads over a Nehru jacket whose buttons looked about to pop from the weight he had put on since his and his outfit's heyday in the sixties.

93

"Hey, hey," someone picked up the chant. "The whale is in."

"Wail, Whelan, wail! You're elected, baby!" the big guy yelled.

Grinning, Mick pointed down at Sarah, then at Miles and me, while the chanting kept going in strong, playful variations. Through long hours of waiting, the crowd had kept on drinking to ease the tension, and they were hell-bent on releasing it before letting Mick speak. At the podium, his hand went from one pocket to another and came away empty. For an instant, distress flashed across his face. Then he smiled.

"I had some notes," he began, "but I must have left them in the back room after I heard the returns from Corbett County."

Another cheer went up and became a roar, equal parts laugh and cheer, when Whelan pointed down at Miles and me.

"These guys said I needed two speeches: one if I lost"—good-natured *boos*—"and one if I won." More cheers. "I was afraid I'd get them mixed up."

In transition, he paused, and the room grew quiet. "But *I* is the wrong pronoun. This is our night. We won the election tonight."

He stopped and let the waterfall of cheers tumble over him. As he looked out, lifted by the warmth and affection of the crowd, the wrinkles around his eyes, the early lines faintly visible at the corners of his mouth, melted into the weathering landscape of his face.

"Standing here, I'm glad the election was so close."

Miles elbowed me. His job done at last, he inhaled slowly on his cigarette, exhaled, and chased the drag with a long swallow from his rum and Coke.

"Shit, what an election." He put a forefinger to his lips and inclined his head toward Whelan.

"Last Sunday, Mr. Corbett quoted his grandmother when he said that Oregon was the 'new moon in the old moon's arms.'"

A small cheer went up of the sort that escapes from those determined to cheer on every word lest they miss the cue.

94

"If you're like me," Mick resumed, "you wondered if the election was lost when everything was in except Corbett County."

Now, as the blood roar of victory drowned him out, he leaned forward in Sarah's direction until the din died down. "Television reception is bad in Corbett County, and I didn't camp out there. So why did I win? Did the voters resent the fact that Alexander Corbett's ancestors founded the county? I don't think so."

He stopped to catch his breath, and there were murmurs in the crowd. They liked a mystery enough to wait for its unraveling, but they weren't sure where their man was leading them. I wasn't either, and after a sidelong glance at Miles, I could tell that neither was he. Still, he was uncharacteristically subdued while waiting for Mick.

"But the people of Corbett County did vote for me," Whelan said. "Why?"

A raucous, good-natured chant began at the rear of the ballroom and worked its way to the front. "Whe-lan, why? Whe-lan, why?"

"You're a tough crowd," Mick laughed. Then, looking straight out into the crowd, he said, slowly and strongly, "I can tell you in three words why people voted the way they did. The first is *volcano*. Those folks live under Mount Loowit. They thought they were safe, thought they could count on the mountain. Before Mount Loowit erupted, Congressman Corbett told you he was proud of voting against spending taxpayers' money on seismic stations and research into the causes and timing of earthquakes and volcanoes. Then the mountain blew, and everything changed.

"That's the second word that explains the vote in Corbett County: *change*. Mount Loowit's eruption was nature's chaotic act of change. I was up there, and no man or woman could have stopped it. We can learn to read the signs—not always control them, but survive and thrive along with nature. But not in the old way."

By now, the ballroom was hot, especially on the platform, where Mick took the full heat from the television cameras.

"That's why Grandma Corbett's line of poetry is on my mind. Tonight the 'new moon *is* in the old moon's arms,' and the new moon is the society that's growing up in and around Vanport.

"And that's the third and last word that explains this election: *Vanport*. Twenty-five years ago, another violent act of nature destroyed Vanport City. The Vanport we gather in tonight is the new city in the arms of the old. Because of changes brought on by your vision and effort, a dream has become a city. It's the future of Oregon, because the old Oregon, like Grandma Corbett's old moon, takes its light from the new moon, not the other way around. So the vote in Corbett County is a beginning, not an end. It's an embrace of the new and a vote for change—the willingness of the people to cast their lot with an Oregon that looks to work with nature and acknowledge its chaos as well as its harmony and loveliness."

He glanced Sarah's way, then scanned the crowd.

"There's also a personal message in the votes of Corbett County. 'Young man, we'll give you a chance,' I hear its citizens saying, 'but we're as changeable as old Mount Loowit, and we can change just as surely as the moon. We'll give you a chance, but you better come through.'"

The exhaustion of Mick's private ordeal and the pace of the campaign began to show beneath the euphoria of victory in his eyes.

"I'd like to end by asking for a moment of silence in remembrance of those who lost their lives in the Mount Loowit eruption, especially Rebecca Phillips, the daughter of Congressman and Mrs. John Phillips, and a volunteer in my campaign."

Mick bowed his head, and everyone in the room, even the reporters, the cameramen who panned in on his face, and the political junkies who moments ago had been boisterous with the twin flush of drink and victory, bowed theirs. After he stepped down from the platform, it took Mick a while to work his way through those in the crowd who were eager to speak to him and shake his hand.

For a change, my mind was serene. I slipped back to the office to gather up my notes, but a moment later, the phone rang.

"Michael Whelan please," said a gruff voice.

"This is Gabriel Bontempo. May I have Mr. Whelan return the call?"

"Mr. Bontempo, this is Congressman Phillips."

Although I had met Phillips several times on the Hill, his let's-get-down-to-business tone did not allow for chitchat.

"I'm sorry, Congressman. Let me pry him loose."

Out in the ballroom, I craned my neck until I spotted Mick in the thinning eddy of celebrants determined to linger until the bartender poured the last drop from the last bottle of booze.

"Mick," I said. "Congressman," I tried again, giddy over knowing Phillips's call confirmed that my old friend Mick Whelan would be the next congressman from the Fifth District. "Call for you."

"Call, squall."

"Not this one," I said, looking at him as evenly as I could.

Mick had tossed down a couple of drinks, but he got the message and kept his cool until we were free of the hangers-on.

"Old Blackjack," he said, after I'd given him the word. "I thought I'd have to make the first move."

Inside the office, I closed the door, and Mick hoisted himself on the table and, after slipping off his shoes, picked up the phone.

"Congressman," he said. "Thanks for calling."

I put my hand on the doorknob, but Mick motioned me to stay, so I did, trying to imagine what the dean of the Oregon congressional delegation was saying on his end.

"I wasn't sure either," Mick said, once he was warmed up. "But I figured they'd make certain before releasing the figures."

He listened. After a while, lines creased his face. He rubbed his eyes and moved the phone away from his head. As he did, I heard the word *heartfelt* spoken as if underwater.

Then Mick looked at me and paused before wrapping up.

"I'm grateful for that. I'll be in touch, Congressman. And please give my regards to Mrs. Phillips."

Mick replaced the phone in its cradle, stood on the floor again, and stepped into his well-scuffed black loafers. "I guess it's real," he said, walking across the room. "Rebecca's death, too."

On our way back to the now-empty ballroom, he spilled the contents of Congressman Phillips's congratulatory call in dribs and drabs. Perhaps unsure of his own feelings, he referred to Phillips as *Judge Phillips*, *Blackjack*, and, simply, *the congressman*. In any case, John Phillips had praised his campaign, told him that he was amazed at the results in Corbett County, and admired the way Mick put his own twist on the "new moon in the old moon's arms." He called him a born politician, incubated in Oregon. But what meant the most was the congressman's gracious response to Mick's reference to Rebecca Phillips in his victory speech. As Mick was about to elaborate, Sarah rushed up, eager to hug him and go off together into the night. She was glowing, all traces of uncertainty gone from her face.

"Nighty night," Miles said. "Sarah, do I really have to call him Congressman Whelan?"

"You do, and I'll . . . he's got a big enough head already," she said, but her quickening eyes already seemed to see her man striding down the aisle in the House chamber for the swearing-in ceremony as the first congressman elected from Oregon's Fifth District.

"Bravo, Sarah," I said.

The four of us were smiling.

"Tomorrow," I said.

"Tomorrow," Miles, Sarah, and Mick repeated in unison before we left, just ahead of the janitor, who was flipping off the lights in the ballroom one by one.

CHAPTER 7

Twenty-five years later, on the Oregon coast, a stiff gale blew spray from the waves over the rocks along the beach road. I wanted to call Kiem, the Vietnamese American woman I'd been seeing in Washington, but my reverie had set the world whirling, so I settled for the CNN anchorwoman who jabbered like a petulant seabird about the on-again, off-again recounts in Florida.

A while later, the phone rang. I clicked the mute button on the television remote and heard Miles Stein's manic staccato voice.

"Miles!" I cried. "What's really happening down there?"

"Happening?" he growled. "*Recountus interruptus* is happening."

From his burned-out tone, I saw Miles in Florida winding an index finger around one of the now-sparse curls in his white hair.

"Listen, Miles, I've been going through some old Whelan files."

"Yeah." In his tone I sensed fatigue and a flicker of interest. "If he'd been the guy, we'd have won going away."

"Maybe Mick's run against Corbett then is a clue now," I replied, playing off his nostalgia. "Why not go after the votes you need up in the panhandle, on Bush's turf?"

"Manhandle the panhandle," he rhymed, and from Oregon I saw a smile break through the tragic mask of a man at his wits' end.

"Exactly. If we'd been looking for votes, Corbett County would have been the last place we'd have gone."

I'd gotten Miles all dressed up, but the only place I had to go was a campaign that once upon a time had been the start of something. But he thanked me, and brought up my health.

"Maybe what's happening to you is like Florida—symptoms in search of a diagnosis. Life goes back and forth," he said, and I felt him twisting his index finger. "I've been dreaming about Mick, too."

Before he could say anymore, a muffled voice hollered, "Miles, we're ready!" from what sounded like a control room, and I imagined him waving someone off as he said good-bye.

"What's new? Still a Jew. More slack if I were black."

Miles's sign-off from the Florida rabbit hole reminded me that campaigns are a time out of season. Being with people you hardly know twenty-four/seven has a Halloween effect: you wear a mask, and you're disoriented when someone remembers you from real life. Maybe that's why you become so attached to the candidate—he stands for life in between.

Back in Washington after that first Whelan campaign, a few cronies called me *godfather* and bent over as if to kiss my ring. But I made up for lost time at home and in the committee room of the House Judiciary Committee. After Nixon's resignation, the Republicans barely mounted a campaign in Oregon's Fifth District, so in the fall, Mick the insurgent became Michael the anointed.

In December, a Polaroid arrived of the congressman-elect and Sarah on a bone-white beach in Mexico, a Just Married decal stuck on his forehead like a bumper sticker. Then Alexander Corbett resigned just before the end of his term to enable Whelan to take office ahead of a long line of first-term Democrats, and when he was sworn in two days early in January of 1975, I was in the House chamber. The Cheshire-cat smiles of Phillips watchers widened when Blackjack let it be known that Mick would be assigned his committee of choice, Commerce, along with the Selective Service Subcommittee.

"A late wedding present," the dean of the Oregon delegation told reporters, "to go with the lucky couple's silver."

On a snowy evening in March, Kate and I tendered Mick and Sarah a celebratory dinner in the townhouse we'd moved into among sheltering elms across a ravine from Rock Creek Park.

"I'm eager for a look at Sarah," Kate told me while she set out the hors d'oeuvres and I filled up the extra ice tray. "She must have really wanted to be Mrs. Michael Whelan to settle for the Mexican-getaway wedding."

The doorbell chimed, and after the two women laughed over unnecessary introductions, I hung up the Whelans' coats and ushered them into the living room. Mick handed me a bottle of the dusty Andalusian red I'd introduced him to in the sixties while Patrick played peekaboo with Sarah from behind Kate's skirt.

"Kate," Sarah said, once Mick squatted down to engage Patrick, "you're probably deluged with stuffed animals, but we have one of those little black-and-white pandas for Patrick."

"Lovely," Kate said. "And thanks for asking first."

Kate hugged Sarah, something she rarely did with women, while I handed out flutes, then popped the cork on the vintage bottle of French champagne I'd been saving.

"To Sarah, to Mick." I held out my arm until the four glasses touched in a circle.

"To all of us," Mick answered. "That means you, too, Patrick," he added, hunching over to rub Patrick's head and tap his glass against the plastic juice cup that the little guy clutched in both hands.

The evening proceeded as if we were four old friends. After dinner, we settled down in the living room, looking out the French doors at snow dusting the trees outside. On my second cognac, I said that Mick and I were trying so hard not to tell war stories about Congress, we were in danger of becoming conscientious objectors.

"Listen to him," Kate told Sarah. "He thinks that because there's brandy, he and Mick should be in his study with cigars while we drink tea and crochet like some of the women still do in Georgetown."

"If Mick ever tries that, I'll send the press a video of him with the potheads on election night in Vanport," Sarah said, refilling her snifter. Her face lit up in a magnetic smile, and when she crossed her legs, her skirt flared briefly like a flag.

It was fun to take food and drink and talk about any damn thing. The two women knew that for a true foursome to emerge, they had to take the lead. They knew the times, the town, and their men well enough to know that if the first evening became the Mick and Gabe show, the pattern might be impossible to break. Although Kate could toss off an accomplished mean line in the best tradition of Alice Roosevelt Long-worth, she avoided the cutting contests that were blood sport at Wash-ington dinner parties. Nor did Sarah play the part of the congressman's wife, far from it; she performed like an equal. And after the good nights, Kate, temperamentally disinclined to give another woman the benefit of the doubt, praised Sarah in our postmortem on the evening.

"My Canadian cousins don't call me the American shrew for noth-ing," she said, leaving her nightcap unfinished. "I expected someone younger, someone happy just to be in the shadow of the emerging great man. Once she learns how to nurse a drink, she'll do him a lot of good."

"With women?" I asked, dish towel on my arm.

"Men, women, or children, it won't matter," she said, handing me a pot too big for the dishwasher.

"No?"

"It's him she has to keep."

"Well, she's woman enough."

"She's more than enough woman, Gabe. A couple of babies, and your friend Mick will walk through fire for her."

After we were done in the kitchen and I had turned off the downstairs lights, I gave Kate the credit for the evening.

"You weren't too bad yourself," she said.

My arms loosely around her, we went slowly up the stairs.

"But, Gabriel," she turned, putting her face close to mine, "why didn't you tell me she was so pretty—and sexy?"

"You didn't ask," I said in the upstairs hall, briefly measuring Sarah's quick smile and saucy green eyes against a lingering impression of Rebecca Phillips before turning around to touch Kate's nose. "Let's check on the Patrick bear and go to bed."

That May, after the last helicopter whirled away from the roof of the American embassy in Saigon, Mick invited me to lunch. We met in the rotunda of the Capitol, twisting our way through swarms of bubble gum–chewing teenage girls—pretty birds of passage dressed in the identical drab plumage of plaid parochial-school uniforms—*oohing* and *aahing* at the sight of the young congressman. Outside, the wind blew in spasms and the girls held their school berets on with one hand, their skirts down with the other. Viewing the Capitol Dome behind us and the Mall in the distance, Mick and I descended the long marble staircase. A few joggers toiled by, a far cry from the fitness party that would churn the loose pebbles on the paths into sand in the eighties and nineties. Distracted by cherry blossoms bursting in air between George Washington's obelisk and the distant dome of the Jefferson Memorial, we crossed Seventeenth Street before the Greek columns of Lincoln's temple caught Mick's attention and he realized he had gone too far.

"Funny how the memorials look like the presidents they're named after," he said. "Washington's the surveyor, Jefferson the architect, and Abe Lincoln a country judge holding court in the open."

North of Constitution Avenue, the White House came into view beyond the Ellipse. Soon, passing the Old Post Office on the corner of Pennsylvania Avenue, we turned back toward the Capitol. A few doors down, Mick stopped in front of a trattoria called Boccaccio's. Inside, before our eyes adjusted to the sudden dimness, a waiter appeared and showed us to an inconspicuous corner table. Before I knew he was gone, Anselmo reappeared, bearing bread so fresh the crust made my teeth ache and two glasses of his best Chianti. After looking over the menu, we ordered the special—rigatoni with fresh tomatoes, basil and garlic, aged Parmesan, and vodka. I waited for Mick to tell me what was on his mind, but he only leaned forward, chin on his palms, until Anselmo placed hand-painted bowls of steaming rigatoni in front of us with a Neapolitan flourish.

"*Benissimo.*" Whelan threw him a kiss with his fingers.

"*Ah, Congressimo,*" he looked from Mick to me. "*Italiano?*"

"Halfway," I said.

"*Ah, bene!*"

Mick told Anselmo to fetch two espressos, then turned back to me.

"It's some crew on Selective Service," he said, downing what was left of his second glass of dry, dusty Chianti. "When Henry Hart convened the subcommittee, he said he felt like Noah boarding the ark."

"Be careful," I said, telling him that Hart, who represented Lyndon Johnson's old district in the Texas hill country, had once ordered an assistant's desk bolted to the floor in the outermost room of his suite after overhearing the young man call him by his nickname, Have a Heart.

After looking for a suitable transition and finding none, Mick plunged ahead.

"The party hasn't floated major domestic initiatives in a serious way since LBJ let the Great Society go for Vietnam. Between now and January, I'd like to sketch out two bills—one on compulsory national service, the other a national network of high-speed trains."

Anselmo returned with our espressos. Mick stopped and bantered until the waiter departed.

"What do you think, Gabe?" he resumed.

I looked around at the thinning crowd in Boccaccio's.

"Too much, too soon."

Whelan tensed, but he extended his hand, palm down, in my direction. I'd been chafing under an endless round of conferences with chief majority and minority counsels to the Judiciary Committee and their insufferable know-it-all assistants from the Harvard, Yale, and Chicago law schools. Now I felt exhilarated.

"Imagine you're a ten-term congressman. You meet a promising newcomer. A month later, he wants to impose national service on the eighteen-year-olds in your district. Before the ink's dry on that bill, he wants billions for trains."

Whelan drummed his long fingers on the tablecloth and looked around to gauge how far out of range we were from the nearest person in Boccaccio's.

"I can't kick this around with anybody else, Gabe. Is there a way to crack it?"

"You're right to sound things out without sounding off," I said, remembering our Sound Connection. "Watch Hart's moves."

Anselmo bustled up with a small silver tray. Mick scrawled "M. J. Whelan" on what looked like a monthly tab but made no move to get up. He pushed his chair back and leaned forward, hands on his knees.

"I keep track of every word Hart and anyone else says about the draft, the volunteer army, national service, and Mrs. O'Leary's cow."

"Live inside their skins," I told him. "Their quirks are America's. If your first moves don't work, try something else. Lay the groundwork for your bill as honorable middle ground between those who want the draft strengthened and those who want military service with as many holes as a goddamn hunk of Swiss cheese. Come on like a pragmatist who wants to do something for the subcommittee as well as the country."

I took a last swig of the Pellegrino water in my glass.

"Mention your ideas in bits and pieces so nobody knows you're preparing to come out firing next session. When the time comes, let your colleagues dot the *i*'s and cross the *t*'s."

Whelan sat there smiling while I kept speeding.

"Everyone's a player, and Hart's the director," I finished. "He'll let you hold the cue cards as long as nobody else sees them."

Mick cupped his empty water glass.

"What are the chances?"

"You know the answer to that," I parried. "But it's why you came here."

Once we were in the street, the southern sun set the back of my neck on fire. Sirens died away in the direction of the White House, and we involuntarily quickened our pace. Except for a solitary runner, now sweaty as a marathoner, the joggers were gone from the Mall. As we approached the long flights of stairs leading up to the south entrance of the Capitol, the sun's glint died away from the Capitol Dome.

"You were right on, Gabe." Mick stopped and looked at me, his eyes blue as the sky. "You only left out one thing."

"More than that," I said, laughing.

"I can't do it myself. Or just with Hart." He flicked an unruly eyebrow out of his line of vision. "Will you come on my staff in January as top gun?"

I wish I could say I had smelled his proposition coming, but I hadn't—not during lunch, not afterward. Working on Mick Whelan's payroll was out of the question. He was able to ask me to advise him about his bills and stay for an answer because I did not depend on him for a single crust of bread. I'd watched more than one guy with his head screwed on right sign on to the staff of a good friend who was a congressman. Being an outsider who sees the inside of a politician's mind gives you a defense against his vanity—if you prick it and he stops calling, life goes on. But once you're on the payroll, it's different. First, you sense a coolness. Then, your advice begins to lose its sharp, fine point. Or you keep on keeping on, and the toadies on his staff start whispering. At first, the congressman or senator is too loyal to pay any attention, but once the others feed him enough raw meat sliced from your soul, his loyalty starts to go, or, before you know it, your sense of the truth deserts you.

Ahead, a Capitol policeman eyed Mick for a few seconds before he touched the bill of his cap.

"You with me, Gabe?" Whelan asked.

I pulled him over under the portico of the Capitol.

"Mick, I'm flabbergasted. I'm touched. I'm appalled! I'm your friend. I've got a job. Plotting with you is great. Working for a salary would jeopardize what we're fighting for. I can't do it. I won't do it."

I stopped to catch my breath, but I had said everything I wanted to say.

He looked at me for a long time before replying.

"That's why I didn't ask you before I was sworn in. But now I know that national service and high-speed trains won't happen without you and me working together."

"We'll do it . . . ," I hesitated, "unofficially."

We shook hands as we always did, Mick covering my right hand with his left. Then he walked into the Capitol, and I went toward the Rayburn building to face another interminable meeting about whether to issue subpoenas for certain tapes still in the possession of ex-President Nixon. I smelled the perfume of the cherry trees and tried to avoid stepping on the stray blossoms that had fallen to the sidewalk at my feet.

CHAPTER 8

During the summer of 1975, as the press and the American people began to absorb the magnitude of American defeat and disgrace in Vietnam, Mick Whelan bided his time. In the Democratic Steering Committee, Congressman Henry Hart argued that after Watergate, the country wanted more-open politics, in which leaders put an end to secrecy and discord and honestly debated difficult issues, such as military service. At his instigation, the Selective Service Subcommittee held hearings. For a while, there was reason to think that members might abandon the usual congressional grandstanding. Behind the scenes in the House, there were intimations of an alliance between those so weary of Vietnam's divisions and inequities they wanted to be rid of the draft for good and those who would turn military service from an albatross into an eagle. For the latter, Vietnam was a code word signifying the license and lawlessness of the sixties: draft cards burning, American flags flown upside down, scruffy Vietnam veterans camped out on the Mall. But the smart money on the Hill doubted that the coalition between hawkish partisans of a volunteer army unfettered by civilian intrusion and doves opposed to the draft would hold. So Whelan waited, hoping a deadlock would create the opening he needed to introduce compulsory national service.

Once the selective-service hearings were finished in late September, I strolled over to the House caucus room. Scanning the classical, vaulted room, I noticed high-ranking military men from each branch of the service—and, strangely, two women in full dress uniform, a colonel from the Army and a major in the Air Force, sitting in the front row. Behind them, I recognized lobbyists for several top-drawer defense contractors.

From his place halfway between subcommittee chairman Hart and the end of the row, Congressman César Rivera sought recognition. Baptized Caesar, when Mexican Americans became Chicanos, he became César. Rivera's new name gave him cachet in the barrios of San Diego that, combined with the megabucks of the aerospace industry, made him unbeatable. Paunchy in his polyester suits and always on the make, Rivera played the House Chicano so well that when he asked permission to yield to his Republican colleague from Oklahoma, Hart complied without thinking.

"The distinguished member from Oklahoma is recognized."

Hearing "Oklahoma," Congressman T. F. Randolph began to speak in rapid tones. His mother had been a Republican, his father a Democrat, so they named him Theodore Franklin. As a boy, young Randolph chafed under the name until his speed on the football field prompted a reporter to write that T. F. stood for Too Fast, and the moniker stuck.

"Mr. Chairman, every word spoken these last weeks has emanated from a momentous sense of patriotism and dedication to the national interest." T. F. Randolph enunciated his words in the precise, stilted accent of the King's English taught to black youngsters in segregated high schools by black PhDs before *Brown v. Board* changed everything in 1954. When it suited him, T. F. could slow down in order to speed up, and now a slow shake of his head signaled that he was about to accelerate.

"I represent a district in the former Indian Territory of Oklahoma that was the home of the buffalo soldiers. When this debate began, I was troubled by admonitions that the ranks of American volunteers are becoming an army of mercenaries. During the hearings, Mr. Chairman, I reminded my colleagues that a segregated army didn't stop my grandfather from charging up San Juan Hill to rescue Teddy Roosevelt. A segregated army did not stop my father from fighting at Palermo in

World War II. Mr. Chairman, in the Korean conflict, I served in President Truman's newly integrated Army as a *volunteer*. During the tragic Vietnam conflict, I was angry that black youth were drafted while white college students received deferments. When we debated the draft several years ago, I favored a random system—every young man eligible, every young man with an equal chance to be called. But *draft* was a dirty word, so in the end, I voted for a trial for the volunteer army."

The yellow light flashed, indicating that the congressman had thirty seconds remaining.

"Mr. Chairman, in the last two weeks I have become satisfied that all branches of the Armed Services offer equal opportunity to young men and women of all races, creeds, and backgrounds, and that the volunteer army enables those who join to reenter civilian society equipped with the skills to work at jobs becoming to their talents and dignity as Americans."

Hart raised his gavel but stayed his hand a little so that T. F. crossed the goal line before the reverberations died away.

"Mr. Chairman, I move that the volunteer army be the permanent means of constituting the Armed Forces of the United States of America."

Too late, an irritated Hart banged his gavel a second time.

"The time of the member from California has expired," Hart declared, ignoring Randolph and staring coldly at Rivera.

"If the chair please," Congressman Rivera responded, "I wish to second Congressman Randolph's motion."

"Whether the chair pleases or not, the motion is recorded as made and seconded," Hart responded peevishly.

From his knitted eyebrows, I could tell that Mick Whelan was stumped, barely able to keep his cool as he tried to read the face of the chairman and stared at the empty chair reserved for Congressman Louis Armstrong Jackson. Jackson played black and white sides of the House brilliantly, and I knew there'd be hell to pay if the other two minority members of the subcommittee had cut a deal without his knowledge.

While Mick's index finger remained poised in the air, several lights glowed red.

"The chair recognizes the gentlewoman from Connecticut."

Adjusting her microphone, Congresswoman Maggie Moxley leaned forward, her reading glasses dangling from a braided reddish brown cord that matched her tweed suit.

"Thank you, Mr. Chairman. In the spirit of bipartisanship so vital to national security, I would also like to yield to a colleague on the other side of the aisle, Congresswoman Atlady from Illinois."

Now the loose ends threaded into a single strand. Ordinarily, the two congresswomen's politics were like night and day, but on women's issues, they stood together, knowing the feminist movement would close ranks to protect them. Now, as Frances Atlady, no friend of the military, began to speak, the two women officers, one in Army gray, the other in Air Force blue, sat up straighter, uniforms starched to attention.

Heartland Bella, wags on the Hill called her. Usually her remarks were harangues, but this afternoon her voice was soft and controlled, and her thick eyelids fluttered like those on the Dolly Dimples doll.

"Thank you, Congresswoman Moxley. I was one of the first to worry that a volunteer army would be antidemocratic. Why, I was heartsick that the rights of the women of this country were ignored when Congress passed the original legislation. I have always believed President Kennedy had women's example in mind when he said, 'Ask not what your country can do for you; ask what you can do for your country.'"

After the bow to her feminist base, Atlady dropped the other shoe.

"The volunteer army is not my first choice, but I am willing to leave it in place, provided my male colleagues accept a friendly amendment that makes women eligible for service at all ranks in each and every branch of the Armed Forces."

As Congressmen Rivera and Randolph nodded approval, there was a smattering of applause among a row of civilian young women who were dressed in austere blues and grays.

The deal was done, but I couldn't tell whose deal. When I looked at Mick, I could tell he'd been caught by surprise, but before his instincts told him where to strike, the words "Will the gentle lady yield?" rang out from a member two seats away.

In the silence, Congressman Ted March stabbed his pencil toward Congresswoman Atlady.

"Will the gentle lady yield?"

"With respect, I ask the gentleman's patience."

In profile, March had the clean, sharp lines of a fox. He wore a neat, closely trimmed reddish blond beard whose bristles stood on end as Congresswoman Atlady denied his request. He was a physics PhD from Stanford who had started his own lab and made a bundle in Silicon Valley. He talked jock to the good old boys, books to liberal intellectuals who read *The New York Review of Books*, and he kept the National Institute of Health honest so the old farts in Congress would go along with him on research appropriations. Equally at home in rowdy bars, the Kennedy Center, and White House state dinners, March's diligent manners concealed a violent distaste for suffering fools gladly, ungladly, or at all. Though he supported women's equality on matters of fairness, principle, and self-interest—"I've been married to a feminist for ten years," he liked telling the old boys—he despised the huffing and puffing of Atlady and her allies. Now, as the congresswoman looked away, her large blue porcelain eyes narrowed to slits, a faint stain of red spread across March's face.

"Will the gentle lady yield for a point of information?"

Ignoring him, she clattered on like a freight train with just enough steam left to reach the next switchback.

This time, March put his mouth to his microphone and spoke in the sizzling voice of a working-class conductor calling out the stops on a commuter train.

"I appeal to the chairman on a point of order."

Henry Hart looked up and down the long table, chagrined that things were getting out of hand, annoyed that he had failed to smell out this suddenly sprung alliance of minority and women members.

"The gentleman from California is recognized."

"Congressman Hart," March began, "you have been fair to members in the other party and to the shifting winds in our own party. But I am compelled to raise a point of personal privilege."

Her microphone turned off, Atlady shouted at Hart in the voice of a barmaid announcing last call on Saturday night: "Objection, Mr. Chairman!"

March ignored her. Tapping his live microphone, he addressed Hart and his other subcommittee colleagues.

"Mr. Chairman, today's agenda consisted of discussion of testimony previously heard by this subcommittee. Both the motion and Congresswoman Atlady's amendment are premature and contrary to your goal of building consensus for a bill that can pass the House by a veto-proof majority."

Caught between acknowledging that he was in the dark about the moves of four members of his subcommittee or in cahoots with them, Hart looked like a grizzled old buck caught in the headlights.

"Mr. Chairman," Congresswoman Atlady interrupted in a half shout, "I object to the manner and timing of Mr. March's objection."

Hart's face changed as if the eighteen-wheeler had suddenly doused its lights and restored his view of the forest. He began to speak in his most courtly tones.

"I appreciate the distinguished lady and distinguished gentleman's attempts to focus the discussion."

He threw ironic looks at Representatives Atlady and Randolph.

"To my friend Mr. March, let me say that even an attentive chair does not always know the intentions of the members of his subcommittee. Did I know that Congressman Randolph intended to make his motion at this meeting? I did not. I would have preferred the courtesy of formal notification to the chair and to all the members of the subcommittee. But I am compelled to rule the Randolph motion and Atlady amendment in order."

The button in front of Congressman Whelan flashed red.

"The chair recognizes the congressman from Oregon."

"I appreciate the chair's response to Mr. March," Mick said, glancing at Atlady. "At stake are the vital questions of military service and collegiality within this subcommittee. Therefore, I request that Congressman Randolph and Congresswoman Atlady provide copies of their bill and amendment so that each member can prepare to discuss and debate the bill in an informed way."

Like children caught passing notes in school, Rivera, Randolph, and Moxley nodded in tandem. They ignored Atlady, who, smarting when no one came to her defense, sank from the garden-variety sulk of an egotist scorned into some private, blank world of hurt.

"Mr. Chairman," called Congressman Randolph.

"The chair recognizes the congressman from Oklahoma."

"The congressman from Oregon's suggestion is constructive. Accordingly, I move to postpone consideration of my motion. I assure the chairman that copies of the bill incorporating the amendment offered by the gentle lady from Illinois will be in the hands of the clerk by the end of the day. I intended no disrespect. I meant only to expedite consideration of the volunteer army. I hope Congressman Whelan and others will consider my bill on its merits without regard to the timing and manner of its introduction."

Chairman Hart lowered his spectacles over the bridge of his nose and looked out over the room, the hint of a twinkle coming into his eye.

"If I had better recall of Lyndon Johnson's stories about teaching school in south Texas . . . ," he chuckled. "Never mind. The subcommittee stands adjourned until two o'clock tomorrow." Then, like a judge to attorneys whose antics had turned his courtroom into a spectacle, he motioned Representatives Rivera, Randolph, Moxley, and Atlady to accompany him to an alcove off the hearing room.

Later, Whelan and I walked up Independence Avenue from the Capitol and the Library of Congress to the Hawk and Dove, a watering hole much in vogue since the sixties, where you could get a drink and good talk no matter what side of the fence you were on. Entering, we saw Ted March holding down a booth directly in the bartender's line of sight, off-line from the tables favored by congressional aides, who were fond of sitting near the windows.

"Payback time," he said as we slipped into the red leather seat across from him.

After snapping his fingers for a waiter to refill his Myers's dark on the rocks, March resumed spearing his lime wedge into an ashtray in order to blot out the etching of a hawk and a dove perched on the same branch. Like Whelan, he could sail under the silk flag of the Jockey Club, but when he wanted to let his hair down, he preferred a place with sawdust on the floor that reminded him of dives he'd frequented in East Palo Alto on the wrong side of the tracks from Stanford. On the basis of common sense and, often, the Constitution, March and Whelan were allies, but loathing for the cant of self-righteous ideologues of all stripes added an element of unpredictability, even perversity, to their politics.

"I cut the lady wrestler too much slack," March told Whelan.

As the waiter came up, Mick pointed to March's glass, gave the thumbs-up sign, and clapped his friend on the shoulder. I was still puzzling over the absence of L. A. Jackson from the subcommittee meeting when a huge brown hand pressed down on my shoulder.

"Lawyer Bontempo," boomed a voice that made the word flesh. He was wearing a powder-blue three-piece pinstripe silk suit obviously ordered during a junket to Hong Kong.

"Invisible man," I said, moving over two spaces.

"Watch your mouth, boy. Didn't your mama tell you white folks should be seen and not heard?" At six four, two seventy-five, Louis Armstrong Jackson cut a mean swath with his person, not to mention his evil, eloquent tongue. "I say, look, man, what went down? When a couple of pages saw me in the elevator, they looked at their shoes like a pair of deaf-mutes."

Jackson ordered a double Jack Daniels. It was utterly unlike him to be in on a fix and not blow lead trumpet. He was loyal to the "bloods," as he called his black colleagues, but he talked the talk and walked the walk of his own conscience in those days before identity politics. Now, as Whelan and March took turns briefing him, Jackson's eyes narrowed.

At first he was quiet, then he spoke with the nonchalance of a savvy man who has already lost what he has to lose.

"It's some wildcat shit," he said. "That Rivera's a slick cat. I bet he sweet-talked old Too Fast into believing it was his patriotic duty to save the U. S. of Army." Already he had us laughing, and before the waiter was within hearing distance, I sent him back to the bar by shouting over the increasing din for another round.

"When it comes to running with Rivera and the big boys, Too Fast is too slow," Jackson went on. "I mean, the dude's fast, but he ain't swift. You dig?"

"Pentagon?" Mick asked.

"Defense contractors, too. They don't want oversight from no goddamn peaceniks and beatniks like you and your boy with the beard here, never mind a blood from Brooklyn."

The more he talked, the more Jackson revved us up for a counterstrike. At first, March and Whelan favored an all-out assault. But Gene McCarthy hadn't been kidding when he said the real business in Washington gets done *after*, not before, the second martini.

"We don't have the votes to beat them in committee," Mick conceded at length.

"I say, look, man," Jackson went on, jabbing an index finger halfway between Whelan and March, "they figure us to be so hot and righteous, we'll play double or nothing. I'll let the blood go for now—that half-breed Rivera, too—but not the gray bitch."

On the wall behind me, a framed, autographed black-and-white photograph of Sam Rayburn, Dick Russell, and Lyndon Johnson looked down on the three congressmen. The signature scrawled across Rayburn's face made it impossible to tell if he was smiling or frowning at Whelan, March, and Jackson while they decided that Mick and L. A. would pay a call on Henry Hart in the morning, leaving March in the wings as Peck's Bad Boy, ready to cry bloody murder if a satisfactory compromise couldn't be worked out behind closed doors. Hart, they felt sure, would expect them to arrive hopping mad; instead, they would come offering a solution to *his* problem, rather than bearing a grudge.

When Mick and L. A. arrived at his office the next morning, Hart emerged immediately, then lingered, so the staff in his office would notice the friendly bantering conversation. Once inside his sanctum sanctorum, he declined to sit behind his immense mahogany desk and instead offered his junior colleagues easy chairs on either side of a low leather couch into which he eased comfortably.

"Louis," he said. "Michael."

Like other venerable committee chairmen, Hart could be more formal in an informal setting than he was in committee. But in its very formality, his use of full Christian names gave the meeting the quality of a tête-à-tête.

"What can I do for you?"

Whelan and Jackson smiled at each other. On the way down, they had speculated on whether he would recapitulate the committee's situation or put the ball in their court.

"Mr. Chairman," Jackson began, "we don't want a repeat of yesterday. We have a private suggestion."

Hart nodded.

Hart rather liked Jackson's flamboyance and respected his street smarts. But he knew the New Yorker was an operator and associated him with the characters Lyndon Johnson preferred to have inside the tent pissing out, rather than outside pissing in. Young Whelan he had heard about from his poker and bourbon friend Jack Phillips, and knew of his passion for compulsory national service.

"And you, Michael?" he asked.

"It's less the outcome than the way it was done."

"We don't want a street fight," Jackson added.

"Gentlemen," Hart said, "I appreciate that."

Mick laid out the compromise. At first, Hart balked at the subcommittee member Whelan and Jackson had designated to make the motion, but in the end, amused, he agreed.

At two sharp, I was in the front row when Henry Hart brought his gavel down soundly on the oak table in front of him.

"The subcommittee on selective service will come to order," he said as several red lights went on in front of the members arrayed on either side of him. Congresswoman Atlady's flashed first, and I detected a twinkle in Hart's eyes as he recognized Congressman March.

"Thank you, Mr. Chairman," March said. "Before making a motion, I would like to remind my colleagues and the American people that there are more young men and," he stared Atlady's way, "*women* serving in the military from California than any other state in the Union."

Except for Frances Atlady, the subcommittee members deferred to Hart's recognition of March by turning off their red lights. March, his incisors flashing, airmailed a try-me-if-you-dare smile in her direction until she swallowed the "Mr. Chairman" about to emerge from her open mouth.

"Mr. Chairman," March continued, "a number of us believe that the

122

motion made and seconded yesterday, though likely to pass in committee, might pass on the floor of the House only by a small margin after bitter debate." He stared at the red light still glowing in front of Congresswoman Atlady. "Until we resolve the meaning of the Vietnam War for America, the issue of military service will be a charged and moot question. Therefore, I would like to make a substitute motion."

"Will the gentleman yield?" asked Congresswoman Atlady, trying to keep dragon plumes of anger from spewing out of her nostrils.

"Mr. Chairman," March answered, "I yield to the congresswoman for thirty seconds."

Atlady made an effort at self-composure that even her enemies had to admire. But as the seconds ticked soundlessly away, her eyes clouded and her voice cracked as she thought of more things she wanted to say with every diminishing jot of time.

"Thank you, Mr.—I mean, Congressman March. I'm uncertain—I mean, I arrived expecting discussion to be on yesterday's motion, and my amendment to the main motion. . . . Will the gentleman yield for two minutes more?"

"I decline to yield further at this time," March replied.

"Please proceed, Mr. March," Hart said, then looked down his bifocals at Atlady. "I would remind the gentle lady that Congressman March intends to introduce a substitute motion. According to the rules, members of the subcommittee will decide if they wish to consider his motion or that motion proposed yesterday by Mr. Randolph and amended by you."

He banged his gavel sharply. "Congressman March has the floor."

Again, Congresswoman Atlady's light flashed. "Objection, Mr. Chairman."

"Will the congresswoman state the nature of her objection?"

"I object to the chair's ruling."

Hart took off his glasses and looked directly at the congresswoman from Illinois.

The hush in the room intensified. Congressman Hart prided himself on responsiveness to each member, no matter how difficult the personality. Ordinarily, he would have had an easygoing exchange with the unhappy member, yet now he played his high card immediately.

"Does the gentle lady wish to overrule the chair?"

His question took Atlady by surprise, and the silence from Randolph and Rivera was deafening. Worse, Maggie Moxley was scribbling a note on her pad, and when Atlady looked her way, Moxley fiddled with the turquoise bracelet on her arm.

"I can't help it—I've always been antiauthoritarian," Atlady said, invoking the refrain she dusted off on those occasions when she had the floor but lacked the votes. Looking around the room, she saw only one colleague prepared to meet her gaze: Ted March of California. Sensing a humiliating defeat if she challenged the chairman, she did her best to cut her losses.

"No," she said through taut, pursed lips. "I am reassured by your pledge to be nonprejudicial and nonauthoritarian in the conduct of subcommittee business."

As her red light went dark, the drama within a drama sent a clear message to the various factions. Subcommittee members not privy to the power play by Representatives Rivera and Randolph, Atlady and Moxley, who had wondered if the chairman had been in cahoots with the motion of the previous day, had their answer. And the four who had made the surprise move understood that by his recognition of Ted March, Hart was giving the devil his due. Observers such as the military brass, lobbyists, and reporters also knew that, however things might unfold, old Have a Heart had regained control of his subcommittee.

"The volunteer army is not my first choice," Congressman March continued, "but there is a disposition in this Congress to avoid stirring up the factions that polarized the nation during the Vietnam War and will again unless we sort out why and how the United States acted as it did in Vietnam. In the meantime, Mr. Chairman, I hope this subcommittee will take the lead in offering the country a democratic and effective way to provide for its military needs. My substitute motion will allow the volunteer army a full and fair trial and guarantee those with other ideas a time certain to present them."

The March motion authorized the volunteer army for four years. Characteristically, he included a reference to Title VII of the 1964 Civil Rights Act, which, on its merits and to rub salt in Congresswoman Atlady's wound, addressed gender. The motion's seconder, L. A. Jackson, praised with earnest, withering irony the initial efforts of Congressmen Randolph and Rivera. One by one, subcommittee members fell in line, and the rout was complete. Those who had sought to seize the brass ring of publicity and prestige saw the names of March and Jackson replace Randolph and Atlady on the markup of the bill. Henry Hart, looking like a baseball manager whose team has rallied to win in the bottom of the ninth, was deferential and courtly. Twice he asked the previous day's principals—Rivera, Randolph, Moxley, and Atlady—if they had any remarks. After the vote was taken, he kept the last promise he'd made to Jackson and Whelan.

"Before adjournment, the chair recognizes Congressman Whelan from the state of Oregon."

As the room buzzed, Mick nodded at Hart.

"Mr. Chairman, I voted for the March substitute motion because, at this time, it is a fair compromise for those favoring a permanent volunteer army, those who aren't sure, and those who seek another way of maintaining a strong military in a just and democratic society. Until it expires at the end of 1980, the authorization will meet the needs of the Department of Defense and allow members of Congress and the American people to formulate other options, such as compulsory national service, as the fairest, most patriotic way to meet our national priorities."

"Thank you, Congressman Whelan. The subcommittee stands adjourned sine die."

As consensus flowered on the floor of the House, colleagues from all over the country approached Mick to acknowledge his sense of principled compromise. Henry Hart commended him for putting party, country, and the art of legislating ahead of a doomed confrontation. And Melvin Israel, the perennially nervous ranking Republican on the House Armed Services Committee, told him privately, "One thing is certain, Mr. Whelan, this country will not return to the favoritism of the old selective-service system. Let the mercenary army have a trial. If it doesn't work, your scheme will be the first to come to the fore."

Incredibly, Mick hadn't even burned his bridges to Frances Atlady. She passed the word that she wished she had consulted him before plunging ahead with the likes of César Rivera.

Throughout the episode, Mick had been surprisingly cool. He had made the best of a bad deal, and he knew it. He had been blooded but not bloodied on the battlefield of congressional politics and learned that sometimes you win for losing.

CHAPTER 9

As the November days grew shorter on the Oregon coast, television reports from Florida were driven by partisan sound bites and confusion. When I called Kiem to check on her Thanksgiving flight to Oregon, she told me the Democratic National Committee was sending her to Tallahassee to monitor the counting of overseas ballots, especially those reportedly mailed from Ho Chi Minh City by Vietnamese who were now American citizens living in Florida. Bush's lead was down to some three hundred votes, and Kiem's assignment was to make sure the same standard was used for all overseas ballots, civilian and military alike.

"I miss you," I said. "I wish the recount were in Oregon."

"We'll be together the twenty-second," she said, melting my anxiety.

"Yes," I said, seeing Kiem as I had many times, swanlike, her lovely neck curving down while she bent over to stir a potage of leeks, carrots, and chicken on the old-fashioned gas stove in my Capitol Hill townhouse.

"I told your Mick Whelan the Pledge of Allegiance was a prayer," she was saying. "You remember, I told your Mick, when I was a citizen, he would be proud. You too, Gabe."

"I am," I said, cringing a little because I worried that Republican rabble-rousers who were shouting "Sore Loserman" at the Gore-Lieberman workers in Florida would mistake Kiem's soft-spoken manner for lack of nerve. I told her I'd heard that a plan was afoot in the Bush camp to disqualify as many civilian overseas absentees as possible, then cry foul over any Gore challenge to a military ballot.

"Oh, yes," she said. "Your L. A. Jackson told me if there's trouble, I should say to the cameras that Vice President Gore served in Vietnam, while Governor Bush stayed home in Texas."

"Good for you."

"And what else, Gabriel?"

I told her I'd meet her plane in Portland on the twenty-second, told her to be careful, told her I loved her. Only when her voice faded into the night and the foggy dark smothered the ocean, the rocks on the beach road, the trees outside my rented A-frame did I drift back to the turning point for Mick Whelan and me.

By late October 1978, my work for the Judiciary Committee had become so formulaic that when a top-drawer lobbying firm offered to make me vice president for congressional relations, I accepted, and invited Mick to lunch at the Monocle, a fashionable watering hole down the street from the Capitol. I waited behind a gilded rope while the French headwaiter bustled about, announcing the names of patrons at a volume befitting their place in the scheme of things. When Mick showed up, the waiter ushered us to a table adjacent to the swinging doors of the kitchen.

"Are you on the take already?" Mick joked as he recognized senators and lobbyists talking in hushed tones around the dark mahogany room.

Two bourbons arrived in short, thick glasses too wide to get your hand around. An *M* was etched in gothic letters, and the cut-glass surface felt as rough to my hand as the sour mash did to my throat. Mick rolled the ice cubes around in his glass as I explained that I was bored with supervising freshly minted, pushy young lawyers hell-bent on unearthing miniature Watergates.

"I thought I was part of something when I ran the first time," Mick said. "Now it's consultants, tracking polls, and blow-dried hair."

At a prime table a discreet distance away, a lobbyist was urging lobster tails on the portly white-haired southern senator who, despite decades of obdurate segregationist votes, had become a media darling during Watergate.

Sloshing the bourbon, I couldn't imagine playing the lobbying game without Mick Whelan around to justify the illusion that, even from K Street, I could contribute to the republic.

"Yesterday," Mick continued, "old Have a Heart pulled me aside outside the committee room—all hush-hush. I thought he was going to say the time was right to introduce my bill. Instead, he asked me if I'd taken the oath of the White House tennis court—even Henry's mocking Jimmy Carter."

He paused to let his words sink in, but I was in my incipient-lobbyist's world, wondering how much of me would be enlisted to cajole senators to indulge more than usual because the firm was picking up the tab.

The waiter brought two lamb stews. Fortified by another belt of bourbon, I speared the biggest hunk of lamb in my bowl and began to listen attentively as Mick made his case.

"There's no agenda. Carter's guys know they're going to lose seats next month. Their game is to brazen it out and run for reelection against the Republicans in two years." Mick attacked his stew, then looked at the platter of lobster tails on its way to the senator across the room as the waiter hustled up with two glasses of Cabernet Sauvignon and swept away our empty tumblers of bourbon in a single acrobatic gesture.

"There are worse games," I told him.

"Gabe, if I don't do what I came to do soon, I'll slide into being a professional congressman," he said, telling me he'd considered not running again, taking a job at George Washington Law School instead, and writing the book he had in his head about Abe Lincoln's principled sleight of hand with practical politics and the Constitution. "But I'm not a quitter. One way or another, next session it's time to introduce the legislation I've held back, on compulsory national service and high-speed trains."

After the waiter cleared away our empty bowls, lifting his nose in the air at our half-full wineglasses, he returned immediately and poured coffee.

"Is there a crackerjack on the Judiciary Committee staff?" I heard Mick say. "Someone who could go for broke and come on as my number one in January?"

Suddenly, he looked tired—no, fatigued, like I had come to feel during the months and years of jockeying for partisan advantage on the Judiciary Committee.

"I'll see what I can do," I said, keeping my counsel.

The waiter's arms swirled as he bent over and topped off our cups with steaming, dark coffee.

Meanwhile, Mick sighed and checked his watch.

"Commerce Committee at two."

After sitting down for a long talk with Kate that night, I stopped at Mick's office first thing the next morning. His private secretary, Marva Bradley, ushered me in without buzzing him. Marva was true blue. She had sung soprano in the Ship of Zion choir until Jonas Fitch introduced her to Mick as someone needing distance from her abusive, estranged husband and, not least, a person who knew when to talk, when to keep quiet.

"Mick," I said, after declining Marva's parting offer of coffee, "I've got someone for you—I know both his strengths and weaknesses."

His mouth curled into a smile.

"Anyone I know?"

"Me."

Whelan's smile widened, ran its course, and suddenly was gone, like a sunbeam erased from the map of his face.

"You sure, Gabe?"

"I'm sure."

"Kate?" he asked, knowing she had been juggling child care for Patrick in order to become an assistant curator at the Freer Gallery.

The instant he saw from my expression that family matters were sorted out, he jumped to his feet, put his arm over the desk to shake my hand, and shouted, "Long live the Sound Connection!" Grinning, I repeated his words, making the Sound Connection my oath of office.

Right after the 1978 midterm elections, I came on board as Mick's AA. He correctly assumed that the Democrats would lose seats, and prepared for recriminations between the White House and the House of Representatives, where many liberals considered the president a Republican on domestic spending. Most important, he figured a progressive initiative or two could fly under the radar in 1979 because the guard dogs monitoring legislation at the White House would be calculating odds for the primaries. Because Mick expected a serious challenge to Carter from the left in 1980, his ploy was to set compulsory national service and L. A. Jackson's railroad bill on parallel tracks at the same time—like a split in blackjack.

"L. A.'s like me," Mick mused as we sprawled in easy chairs in his office on a darkening afternoon in early January. "He's a seventies' congressman with the energy and baggage of the sixties, so when he gets bored, he veers off the main track and derails."

From the windows of Mick's office on the fourth floor of the Rayburn building, I saw government employees trooping toward the Metro while a few last tourists stared wistfully at the purple clouds billowing above the Capitol Dome.

"L. A. is L. A.," I said, lighting a cigarette. "You've got to win over a bunch of old pols who grew up with trains but made their careers by going along with the oil companies, the automobile industry, and the airlines," I finished, flicking ashes over the Oregon state seal on the bottom of the ashtray.

"Jackson will shame the bastards," Mick continued. "The minute his eloquence gives them pause, I come in with the Golden Spike and link the roadbeds with compulsory national service."

Outside, the winter dark fell so suddenly over the Mall that by the time Mick and I quit, I could no longer make out faces above the long coats and collars pulled up against the wind.

He and I were a good team. Only rarely did he have to ask for something. Usually, if it was a memo, I'd already started it; a phone call, I'd tried once and jotted down a note to call back. If he noticed that sometimes I played congressman instead of the congressman's right-hand man, he didn't let on.

In the meantime, a once-promising congressional session slowed to a crawl because of gridlock between the Democratic congressional leadership and the White House. Oil prices crept up. President Carter turned down the heat and spoke to the American people from the Oval Office in his cardigan sweater. But PR gimmicks only exposed fissures in the party between those favoring all-out drilling for oil and natural gas, and those who wanted to seize the day for conservation and the environment. Off to the side of the legislative road, unnoticed by the congressional hares of high policy, Mick Whelan inched along, tortoiselike, until the Easter recess, when he invited Congressmen March and Jackson to lunch at Boccaccio's. Conscious of protocol, even with Ted March and L. A. Jackson, I didn't show up until the three congressmen were settled in conversation, their topic Washington's usual: the outlook for peanut ventures in 1980.

"In two years, one call from the White House; ten in the last three months," L. A. was telling his colleagues as I sat down, and Anselmo, now the maitre d', filled my glass from the carafe of Chianti on the table.

"Same old, same old for me," March said. "Zero."

"Listen, March, before I walked over here, I stopped a young thing's heart when I picked up the phone and said, 'Congressman Jackson.'" L. A. lifted his fork and held it like a telephone receiver next to his ear. "Her voice rose an octave, and I could hear the chair scrape as she retrieved her script. 'Sir,' she stammered, 'Sir, I . . . I was calling your appointments secretary.' 'Miss,' I told her, 'calls from the White House, I take personally.' Personally. Hear that, March?"

Though he had built up a head of steam, L. A. held his mimicry until Anselmo moved out of earshot.

"'Congressman Jackson,' that sweet, black-eyed Georgia pea cooed, 'President and Mrs. Carter request the pleasure of your company and Mrs. Jackson's at the George Washington Carver Symposium on the role of the peanut in contemporary America . . . '

"Look here, you white boys are spared this nonsense," L. A. went on, polishing off his Chianti and refilling our glasses while Anselmo returned and set down four chafing dishes of piping-hot lasagna. "Massa Jimmy may not know much, but he do know he be one dead goober man without black folks and black votes come 1980."

After lunch, March lit up a Camel and exhaled two jet streams of smoke through his nostrils. Then his eyes glinted on Mick's.

"Now that we're all dressed up, is there someplace to go?"

Whelan picked up his tin of brown pencil-thin cigars, shook one loose, and lit up. Exhaling, he blew a trail of smoke straight and strong enough to have come from one of the old Silver Zephyr locomotives and began to lay out his plan. L. A. would strike first. At the beginning of vacation season, when oil prices were high, he'd make the case that a high-speed rail network should parallel the interstate-highway system and ease airport congestion.

"Hell," Whelan's voice grew more intense, "the CIA is bugging the FBI about hijackings, and I hear Aviation is doing the numbers on what it would cost to have federal checkpoints at every airport.

"Gabe will funnel you the research, L. A., so you'll be armed when the oil and automobile companies and the airline and aircraft industries perk up their ears and see your bill as a catastrophe for the free-enterprise system."

Miming Mick's sense of motion, Anselmo swooped down to sweep away our plates.

"Gentlemen, four espresso, no?"

"Maybe I should get that dude on the railroad subcommittee," L. A. said once the waiter tore off for the kitchen, his silver tray gleaming above his head.

"Anyway," Mick kept on track, "the trick is having a couple of Selective Service Subcommittee members think the connection between high-speed trains and national service is their idea."

The espressos arrived, along with a glass of ruby port for March, and Mick offered his tin box of cigars all around.

"This must be the free lunch I've heard about," March said.

"Hell, no. You're the set-up man for national service and the draft. You pry T. F. Randolph away from the Pentagon and keep watch on impressionable new members."

At that, March blew smoke in my direction while Mick kept the train rolling down the main track.

"Keep the committee loose so that the bill I introduce gets center stage. And figure out who should second it."

"Not sweet Frances Atlady?" March needled.

"Do that," Mick replied, "and you could write the stories about what I did in Illinois to line her up."

"I'd like to read them," he deadpanned.

Realizing that March had been kidding to ease the tension associated with the point of no return, Mick relaxed.

The grandfather clock with its brass pendulum, which Anselmo had retrieved from a town near my grandfather's village in the Italian Alps, struck two long chimes, six short: two thirty. The restaurant was almost empty. Automatically, we checked our watches, moved our chairs back with scraping sounds, and the lunch was over.

When Mick and I were alone, I told him that we didn't have a reliable enough reading on what to expect from the new members of each committee.

"You're backup to March," he said. "And don't forget, that woman from Virginia I campaigned for is on Armed Services."

"Regina Warren?"

"She's the leadership's third woman. She holds her cards close. Keep an eye on March. I don't want the congresswoman to have any excuses."

"All cherry blossoms, all the time," I said.

Mick clapped me on the shoulder, and we walked the rest of the way back to the Rayburn building, admiring the trees in silence.

Even in an inner circle of three, I knew you had to be attuned to human weakness. Ted March had a catholic eye for women, and L. A. Jackson lapsed into occasional grandstanding and self-promotion. But fortunately, even with his tendency to overreach and his sudden fits of guilt over Rebecca Phillips's death, Mick Whelan was low maintenance. I liked to think my going to work for him had cut him the necessary slack to overcome his sophomore funk, but, in any case, he cut a figure combining a veteran's poise with the dash of a newcomer. At home, Whelan seemed grounded by his marriage to Sarah and by fatherhood—he had a two-year-old daughter, and Sarah was due later that summer. Like my Kate, Sarah had ambitions of her own; like me, Mick sometimes forgot that his political vocation engendered jealousy as well as loyalty from his wife. But other women out for kicks with an up-and-coming congressman sensed a magnetism between Sarah and Mick. They had to, for I saw a few of them eye Mick, waiting for a gesture that never came. Mick held his charm in check, all right, and perhaps not just for Sarah's sake, but also from a loyalty to the love he had had for Rebecca.

On July second, in a timely improvisation, L. A. Jackson introduced his bill in Congressman John Phillips's subcommittee on railroads. Months earlier, Phillips had run for party whip, implying he would step down from the chairmanship. But when he lost, he clubbed to remain chair over a fellow senior colleague who sought to divert Amtrak funds to subsidies for the trucking industry. To break the lingering tension on the subcommittee, L. A. presented Blackjack with a silver replica of the Little Engine That Could molded from ore mined in Phillips's eastern Oregon district, and Phillips responded in kind.

"Some say," he began, holding up the little silver engine, "that the name of this body should be changed to the Pullman Car Subcommittee." Everyone laughed, and Phillips rolled the toy engine up and down until it came to rest in the middle of the sign bearing his name and the word *Chairman*. "Well, I'm here to tell you that the Little Engine That Could is now the official mascot for this subcommittee. Therefore, I recognize the distinguished representative from New York."

Louis Armstrong Jackson removed his black horn-rimmed glasses from the bridge of what he called in proud, private jest his distended African nose and held them at half-staff.

"Mr. Chairman, I intend to heave on as much coal as it takes to move this train."

Years later, I can hear L. A. highballing through that congressional committee room, the clickity clack of speeding trains in his voice. He had heard so many stories from his Uncle Elijah Jackson about huffing and puffing and highballing up and down the Rockies, and streaking along the Mississippi as a Pullman porter on the City of New Orleans that he could draw a map of the United States marked with cross ties. As he spoke, the Little Engine That Could became a passenger train with Jackson as its conductor, solving each passenger's difficulties with tickets, baggage, or destination. Beginning with the impersonal, driving riffs of his namesake's trumpet, L. A. Jackson soon crooned in that same man's warm, gravelly voice. He sang a song of the open road, and the train's implacable speeding motion gave his fellow subcommittee members a sense of being at home in the world. He knew more about the past and present of railroading in their respective states than they did—a gambit African Americans had mastered long ago with white folks. Addressing the representatives from Pennsylvania, Ohio, Illinois, and Missouri, he rehearsed the history of the Baltimore and Ohio, observing that 150 years ago, dreamers brought rails to the Ohio River and beyond to Saint Louis and Chicago. To Representative Horace Fogdall, Republican of Utah, whose aversion to federal expenditures mottled the man's very skin, Jackson directed words of praise about completion of the original coast-to-coast tracks nailed down with the Golden Spike at Promontory Point in 1869. Mopping his brow with a polka-dot handkerchief, Jackson called national networks of transportation a form of equal protection, noting that 1869 was the year after ratification of the Fourteenth Amendment guaranteed every American citizen equal protection under the law. Soon, his colleagues were leaning in his direction. But he did not end with a call to arms. Instead, he posed a set of rhetorical questions calculated to move the elected representatives to act as guardians of the commonweal.

"Shouldn't we take the interstate-highway act of the fifties with its network of roads as our example for the eighties and beyond?" he asked. "Shouldn't we act now as legislators, in the open, to mandate a level of national commitment and support for rail travel equal to what has enabled the aviation industry to thrive? Should we not act now to take pressure off construction and maintenance of interstate highways and slow traffic and pollution? Should we not act now to prevent airport congestion from increasing to where air-traffic control is stretched past the danger point and major airports are located farther and farther and more inconveniently from our cities? Do we dare not act now to link the potential of the railroad to the potential of the inner cities in our great metropolitan centers?"

L. A. paused and once more drew his black-and-white handkerchief across his face.

"When the Barbary pirates threatened the United States, the cry went up: 'Millions for defense, not one cent for tribute.' In our time, the federal government spends billions for highways, little or nothing for the tracks and roadbeds required for fast, efficient, and safe rail travel, billions to subsidize airports and the airline industry, little or nothing for state-of-the-art trains. I believe it is this subcommittee's charge to stop railroad travel from being held hostage to the vested interests of other forms of transportation."

After a brief, comfortable silence from those gathered around the crescent-shaped table, a gradual buzz rose to a small crescendo. Several members nodded in Jackson's direction; others made approving noises.

"The chair thanks Congressman Jackson for his fine remarks and recognizes the distinguished ranking member Congresswoman Frei." Blackjack Phillips banged his gavel to assert a touch more authority over the work of the subcommittee.

Connie Frei was a no-nonsense moderate Republican from the Philadelphia Main Line in a district Democrats had lately come to contest vigorously as the suburbs turned more liberal. She suspected that the Democratic leadership, in cahoots with conservative Republicans who held her unreliable on social policy, had shunted her off to an irrelevant sideshow of a subcommittee.

"Thank you, Mr. Chairman," she began. "I want to commend you and Congressman Jackson. Before today, I feared the cloakroom gossips were right and this would be the sleeping-car subcommittee. I don't know what you intend to propose, Congressman, and I'll not jeopardize my reputation for independence by promising to support additional federal subsidies. But although I'm not against jetliners and automobiles, from my point of view, Philadelphia was a more livable city when railroads were in their heyday and the Main Line set a national example with a station in every village."

Other members spoke in a similar key. No one made a commitment, but one after another spoke as if engaged in a vital national debate.

Presently, Chairman Phillips relinquished the floor to Congressman Jackson. Once again, I underestimated L. A.'s discipline, for he gave credit where no credit was due and resisted the urge to move the subcommittee a giant step toward his proposal.

"Mr. Chairman, let me thank the members of this subcommittee. Like several of you, when I was appointed, I thought I'd been railroaded." He paused, then joined the round of laughs. "I had," he added, "and I'm glad."

His colleagues putty in his hands, he reversed his field.

"I got some things off my chest this afternoon," he told them. "And as you've made your comments, I see a bill taking shape. It's not there yet. I need your help. But if Chairman Phillips is willing, I would ask for two to three weeks, by which time I will have something to offer the subcommittee."

Again, there were murmurs, this time against the grain of his suggestion. The first light to flash belonged to Congresswoman Frei.

"Mr. Chairman," she said, "I appreciate Congressman Jackson's humility and courtesy. I wish these virtues were in more abundant supply in the Congress. But as my sons tell me too rarely, Congressman, you're on a roll."

Murmurs rose again. Taking in the sudden consensus, I realized that L. A. Jackson had tapped into feelings of resentment against the leadership of both parties for treating members like stray cattle whose duty to the republic was to stand and wait mutely in bunches until their betters summoned them to fall pell-mell into a stampede.

When the chamber was quiet, Congresswoman Frei continued.

"Why not come back in ten days or, if the chairman sees fit, in a week, with your best thinking?"

After Congresswoman Frei finished, members turned the subcommittee into an amen corner.

"Congresswoman Frei," the chairman took charge, "I am going to interpret your suggestion as a motion and ask for ayes and nays."

The chorus of ayes reverberated long after an undercurrent of one or two nays subsided.

"This subcommittee is adjourned until a week from today."

Phillips banged his gavel. After adjournment, he and almost every member of the subcommittee lingered to pass the time with Louis Armstrong Jackson. As I walked toward the swinging doors, I heard Democrats and Republicans from Utah and Florida, Pennsylvania and California playing Huck Finn to L. A.'s Jim as they swapped stories about riding trains in their youth.

Outside the committee room, Mick and I waited for L. A. to send his legislative assistant on an errand.

"Skin, Michael J. Whelan, skin," L. A. said.

Mick slid his palm across Jackson's, and, savoring his own performance, L. A. manipulated a return slide of his fingers and Mick's into the brothers' handshake.

"On the case," Mick said, looking up at L. A. "On the case."

The three of us walked over to the Rayburn building, raising our nostrils in homage to the sweet fragrance of full summer.

Inside, before L. A. left us to go to the elevator, he turned and spoke to Mick.

"This could be some fucking country, brother. Know that?"

"Later, L. A., later," Whelan replied. "In every sense of the word."

Later turned out to be sooner. Now that the Jackson Limited was speeding down the track, there was no choice but for Whelan's national-service legislation to depart the station in rapid succession on parallel rails. So, late one afternoon, Mick went to see Chairman Hart.

"Michael, sit down."

Hart indicated the largest of three amply padded leather easy chairs, but Whelan chose the second best.

"Afraid I'll ask who's been sitting in my chair?" Hart laughed.

Crossing his legs, Mick offered Hart one of his little cigars.

Hart shook his head. Instead, he went to a cupboard and placed a bottle of Jameson's, two glasses, and a bowl of ice on the table. "Best of both worlds, Michael—good Irish whiskey that I don't have to drink with the lobbyist who paid for it."

Mick let Hart pour him a good-sized drink and put up his hand to decline the ice cubes the chairman held out on a spoon.

Hart sat down, and the two men clinked glasses, then savored the sharp, pebbly whiskey.

"Michael, I suppose you're here about your national-service bill."

Mick put his glass of Irish down on the silver coaster with the initials *HAH*, noticing the acronym for the first time.

"I got caught off guard last time, Henry."

While Whelan placed his mini cigar in an ashtray cut in the shape of the Lone Star State, the older man bent forward in a confidential way.

"Charlie Armstead goes in for colon cancer surgery next week."

Armstead was known in the cloakroom as the congressman from the Pentagon. He wangled more than twice as much military spending per capita for his Georgia district than any other in the country. He had bushy white hair, which he ran his fingers through before and after he spoke. Gentlemanly Henry Hart barely maintained a civil working relationship with the man who had passed over him for the chairmanship of a watchdog subcommittee Hart coveted and assigned him to Selective Service instead. So he hurried past Mick's expressions of sympathy.

"Even if the surgeons get all the cancer, Charlie will have to step down for the rest of the session. In the meantime, Michael, I'm to be chairman of Armed Services."

As the news sank in, Whelan took a deep breath and leaned closer to Hart.

"Michael, I've been looking for a way to repay you for helping me out of that embarrassment a few years back. I've decided to place your bill directly before the full committee."

Hart stood up, went to the sideboard for the whiskey, and poured Whelan another drink, half as large as the first.

Looking over the mantel at the black-and-white photo of Hart between Speaker Sam Rayburn and Senator Lyndon Johnson, Mick took Hart into his confidence.

"Henry, as soon as Louis Jackson's legislation passes the Railroad Subcommittee, I'd like to introduce my bill. I'll argue that rebuilding the roadbeds would be a terrific way for young people to fulfill their year of national service."

Hart rolled the ice cubes around in his glass, then took a long swallow of whiskey.

"Michael, I'm having a hell of a time squeezing out a few dimes to upgrade the airport in my district. I'll help you get the timing you want, but tell Louis he's got a lot of persuading to do before I'll vote for King Railroad."

Mick stood up and buttoned his jacket.

"Henry, if you can resist L. A.'s golden tongue, you're a hard man."

Afterward, Mick came directly to my office. There was work to do on compulsory national service, but L. A. Jackson's presentation of his bill was only three days away. On cue, the buzzer squawked on my private phone.

"Congressman Jackson, Mr. Bontempo."

Mick grabbed the phone.

"I know *L* stands for locomotive," he said. "I haven't figured out the *A*."

For sport, Mick held the phone at arm's length. As he did, a shaft of sunlight poured into the room and lit up the map of the projected high-speed transcontinental-rail network on my wall.

"Kiss my ass!" sailed loud and clear from L. A.'s end, and he proceeded to break us up with a repeat in which the three words were given a quarter note, half note, and whole note, respectively.

Then L. A. got serious. He had been making the rounds of subcommittee members. Predictably, once he appeared, railroad cap on his head, they tripped over their feet to make him welcome. And he acted as if he were not quite comfortable—*Race matters. Yeah, it do.*—until the conversation turned from cocktail chitchat to expressions of support, at which point he projected a palpable ease.

Presently, L. A. took Mick up on his offer to put me at his service until he had a final draft of the bill. At first, I was wary, but working at close quarters with Louis Armstrong Jackson soon became a high point of my years on the Hill. In the next few days, the man's focus and discipline were so intense, you'd have thought his life (and mine) depended on getting the smallest detail right. From the endless charts I fed him on rail connections and points of terminus, he created a potential network that seemed more real than virtual. And his strong aptitude for numbers put me to shame. That didn't take much, but when L. A., Mick, Ted March, and I held our council of war before the decisive subcommittee meeting, March, who had breezed through advanced calculus at Stanford, now whistled in admiration at how Jackson had taken the mean speeds attained by the best passenger trains in Europe and Japan, calibrated the effects of the terrain between key cities in the United States, factored in the travel time by air, by car, and by bus at peak hours, and estimated the average speed required to make rail travel an attractive option for American consumers spoiled by cheap gasoline and the low airfares that followed deregulation.

"Amen, my man. Amen," was all March said.

"One more amen, brothers," L. A. exulted, "for Massa Jimmy Carter and the fifty-five-mile-an-hour speed limit."

L. A. was right. The energy crisis had slowed down auto traffic and sent more and more Americans into the crowded skies.

"Tomorrow I'll sketch out the parameters," L. A. promised. "Gabe, make sure you get the backup materials so you"—he pointed at March—"can tear into my logic like you're CEO of General Motors and United Airlines."

L. A. broke into a grin so wide and arresting that I noticed a small gap between his front teeth—pronounced only when the light was right, but a liar's gap nonetheless.

We shook hands all around. To my surprise, and much to my delight, L. A. was drawing us into a circle of hip brothers. With one of his grins doing duty for more than words, he guided me beyond the basic brothers' handshake, turning his fingers and mine ninety degrees and sliding thumbs skin-on-skin into a closing connection like the out chorus winding down one of Duke Ellington's swing tunes.

At two o'clock the next afternoon, Congressman Blackjack Phillips gaveled the Railroad Subcommittee to order. L. A. had paid a solo call on the chairman, who grew nostalgic as he remembered the boy standing hypnotized at a lonely crossing in Prineville, Oregon, until the wail of an approaching train pierced the darkness and the red light of the caboose disappeared into the night. As he listened to L. A., Phillips reexperienced his boyhood yearning for a larger world, and soon his professions of neutrality yielded to intimations of outright support when the time was right.

"The clerk has passed out copies of the Jackson bill proposing that the Ninety-seventh Congress authorize creation of a national network of high-speed passenger trains. At this time, I recognize the honorable member from New York."

From an inconspicuous folding chair behind Mick Whelan, I tried to size up the mood of the members. I feared L. A.'s words might fall short of last week's political and emotional high. I also feared that half the committee would be on guard, especially Republicans. Worst, I feared that one or two, after telling colleagues outside the subcommittee of the brotherhood they'd felt while listening to Jackson, would have encountered good-old-boy snickering. *Why, if I'd only known your fondness for black preaching, Congressman, I'd have given you the address of the black church in my district—yes, sir, fine preaching, only two collections, and some fine, fine women in the choir.* But L. A. struck a diminished chord.

"Mr. Chairman, I have put the markup of the bill in front of you and the members. Therefore, I move passage of HR 1369 and reserve the balance of my time to answer any questions."

Again, I underestimated Jackson. If *I* could imagine a scenario of resistance, how much more would he have calculated and put a human face on just such a possibility? I jerked forward in my chair as Blackjack Phillips's gavel struck like a judge's verdict, subtly reinforcing the authority implicit in L. A.'s remarks.

"Questions for Congressman Jackson on the bill before you?"

Phillips looked around, then banged his gavel a second time.

"Congresswoman Frei."

"Congressman Jackson," she began, "your proposal is well and good. Like many American cities, Philadelphia's roads and skies are more and more congested and polluted. But is there evidence that our roadbeds and tracks can be made to absorb train speeds of 150 miles an hour or higher?"

L. A. bowed his head, as if praying for an answer. "France and Japan have done it, Madam Congresswoman, with economic aid from the United States, I might add. My bill presumes American ingenuity can do other nations one better."

"Congressman Fogdall," Phillips announced.

"My constituents in Utah want to know how your bill's enormous outlay of federal dollars would benefit them."

L. A. wiped his brow and took a healthy drink of water.

"The energy crisis has lowered the speed limit to fifty-five miles an hour. If passenger trains ran east from Salt Lake City to Denver or Chicago, or west to San Francisco or Seattle, averaging 130 or 140 miles an hour, your constituents could get from downtown Salt Lake to their destination in half the time and see the countryside without worrying about other drivers on the road, including the state patrol."

Congressman Fogdall hid his umbrage behind a chuckle.

"I take your point, sir. And may I say, a law-abiding citizen like yourself has nothing to fear from the Utah State Troopers."

One by one, members of the committee threw questions at L. A., some soft, batting practice pitches, others more difficult, but not as tough as those already hurled his way by March and Whelan. One came from Lillian Grillo of Ohio, a former social worker who was angered by the Carter administration's fiscal tightfistedness and the rise in interest rates, inflation, and unemployment.

"Congressman, I salute you for your vision, but I have to weigh priorities. Honestly, at a time when federal programs that you and I support and our low-income constituents depend on are underfunded, where is the money for a national rail network on the scale of the interstate-highway system going to come from?"

I watched L. A. keep his face expressionless.

"Congresswoman Grillo, no great nation stands still. Even in this economy, there are ways to fund the rail network." He took a drink of water and looked toward Mick, whose hands remained cupped in front of his face. "In the fifties, Congress and President Eisenhower used government bonds to fund the interstate-highway system. Why shouldn't a penny or two of the federal tax on a gallon of gas go for railroads? Airports are built off that tax, why not a network of fast trains that can improve the life of the nation?

"In 1946, Congress passed the full employment act, but today, almost ten percent of the American workforce is out of work. We extend unemployment benefits but don't create jobs. Imagine the jobs that would be generated in every state of the Union from a program to repair the tracks and rebuild the roadbeds. Imagine the capital investment that would flow into manufacturing the equipment and amenities needed by a national high-speed rail network. Imagine the future. Do we want to stagger into the twenty-first century twenty years from now under the weight of two overburdened, ailing transportation systems when the railroad could mean three healthy ones? Congresswoman Grillo, cities building light-rail systems now wish they'd started ten or fifteen years ago."

After answering colleagues' questions for over an hour, Jackson stopped and drew his red-and-black polka-dot handkerchief across his brow. Then one, two, three red lights flashed on before John Phillips stepped in to direct traffic.

"The chair recognizes the distinguished ranking member."

"Congressman Jackson," Connie Frei began, "may I make a personal comment? I won't say you've persuaded me completely, but you've brought me most of the way. I'm thankful one of us in this room has a dream."

"Congresswoman Grillo is recognized," Phillips said.

"My sentiments, exactly," she said, flipping off her light.

"The chair recognizes Congressman Slattery of Florida."

"Mr. Chairman, my commitment to transportation systems able to serve Americans of all regions—not just the northeast corridor—is second to none. I have several questions for the congressman from New York, a state where many of my constituents reside except for the winter months, when they sojourn in the Sunshine State."

The laughs James Slattery waited for came in the form of a weak chuckle from fellow Republican Fogdall of Utah.

"Congressman Jackson, you've made much of the Congress working with President Eisenhower on the interstate-highway system. Before anyone is premature enough to second your motion, I would ask if you have enlisted the support of the White House," Slattery said, pointing a finger at Jackson. "And if not, why not?"

A gasp escaped from the throats of several spectators. But L. A. Jackson knew about transplanted New Yorkers, and he delayed long enough for everyone in the room to know that he was keeping Slattery waiting on purpose.

"Let me assure the congressman from Florida that the White House Congressional Liaison Office has copies of the bill before you."

"No further questions, Mr. Chairman," Slattery responded, as if he were dismissing a witness rather than addressing a fellow congressman.

Chairman Phillips broke the muggy silence.

"Is there is a second for Congressman Jackson's motion that HR 1369 be sent to the full Transportation Committee?"

Half a dozen red lights went on.

"Congressman Inada of California."

"It is fitting that members from New York and California should move and second this bill. Congressman Jackson, I know what the black people did to build the railroads. I want my colleagues on this subcommittee to know that in the West, the Chinese had help from the Japanese building the great transcontinental railroad. My grandfather died while blasting tunnels through the Sierra Nevada. In his memory, I second the motion."

The red lights went off. Then the one in front of Mick came on.

"Congressman Whelan of Oregon."

Mick looked from Inada to Jackson to Slattery back to Jackson.

"Mr. Chairman, instead of singing that nineteenth-century Irish ballad 'Paddy on the Railroad,' I call for the question."

In the midst of laughter, Blackjack Phillips recorded a roomful of ayes on the question and announced the vote on the Jackson bill.

"By a vote of eight to two with two abstentions, HR 1369 goes forward to the Transportation Committee for consideration." He banged his gavel. "We stand adjourned."

To the initiate, Congressman Phillips had signaled that he intended to see that HR 1369 received full and fair consideration. As the second-ranking Democrat up the line on the parent Transportation Committee, he had carried buckets of water for Chairman Jimmy Starks, a wily, crusty Democrat from Davenport, Iowa, a quad-cities' railroading town on the Mississippi. For Starks, elected on Harry Truman's Midwestern coattails back in 1948, when played both ways between a congressional committee chairman and a president of his party, loyalty was the highest card in the political deck. So, with irritation, he told Blackjack Phillips how, last month, after trudging to the White House to brief the president, he'd been shunted to a young aide who took half a dozen phone calls during their meeting. Phillips stoked Starks's anger and encouraged the chairman to schedule an early vote on L. A.'s bill. For over an hour, the usual small questions and quibbles were followed by set pieces in which members went on record in favor of help for the railroads *in principle*. Then, his motion again seconded by Inada of California, Jackson settled back, almost relaxed, as he saw the red light flash in front of Congressman Slattery.

"The congressman from Florida," Starks boomed.

"Mr. Chairman, I, too, could pull out the conductor's cap I wore long ago as a model railroader, but the time has come for frankness about the Jackson bill," Slattery said, then took an audible drink of water. "Ladies and gentlemen, I want a bill that can pass on the floor of the House and the Senate and be signed by the president, so this afternoon I will be the messenger who bears the bad news. About the price tag, we know only that it starts high and goes higher; we know that the bill would fatten the federal bureaucracy; and we know it would compromise the efforts of the automobile and airline industries to meet our nation's needs."

Slattery put down his water glass and wiped his mouth on his cuff.

"Yesterday, while I was at the White House," he directed a serpent's smile at L. A. Jackson, "I brought the president fully up to speed on the bill before us."

Again, Slattery paused, and when L. A. still did not move a muscle, he tried again. "Congressman Jackson, I challenge you to stop and consider how much the citizens of my district and others like it subsidize the people you represent in New York." Now the grimace turned into a grin. "I ask you to withdraw your bill and join me in proposing regional railroad networks under federal authority but with each state controlling specifications for right-of-way and maintenance of tracks and roadbeds, provided that access is granted to Amtrak on select interstate routes. In exchange for your cooperation, I would agree to designate the city of New York, my former home, as the headquarters of the northeast regional network."

Slattery looked around the long table at faces whose expressions ran a gauntlet of emotions, before dropping the other shoe.

"Therefore, I move to table consideration of HR 1369."

"As the congressman well knows, a motion to table is not debatable," Starks declared after L. A. Jackson's red light flashed on.

"Point of information, Mr. Chairman," L. A. called out.

L. A. sat stretched to his full height and ignored Slattery in favor of the rest of the committee.

"I have two points of information for the congressman from Florida. First, I will not withdraw my motion. Second, it is the constitutional responsibility of the Congress to propose, and the president to dispose, once the legislative process has concluded, and the will of Congress is known."

In response, there was a collective sigh punctuated by the flat, no-nonsense voice of James Starks.

"All in favor of tabling HR 1369?"

Before the smattering of ayes died down, he spoke again.

"Opposed nay."

An immediate crescendo.

"Nays have it," Starks said and banged his gavel to quiet the hubbub.

One by one, members of the committee spoke up for L. A. Jackson and his bill. Some agreed with him; others dissociated themselves from the remarks of Congressman Slattery. Of those who announced their intention to vote against the Jackson bill, most voiced the hope that, if defeated, the bill would come before them again in different form. Slattery alone vowed to defeat the bill on the floor of the House. At length, the red lights went dark, and even Slattery lifted up his hand and let it rest upon the dead microphone in front of him.

"Will it please the clerk to call the roll?" Starks thundered.

The members voted, the ayes speaking loudly and distinctly and, except for Congressman Slattery, who bellowed, "No!," the nays answering in whispers, as if paying homage to Congressman Jackson with their low-key dissent.

"The vote is twenty-two ayes, ten nays, two abstentions. Accordingly, the clerk will forward the final write-up of the bill to the clerk of the House. This committee is adjourned sine die."

Again, I had underestimated the man named for Louis "Satchmo" Armstrong, jazzman who'd blown the meanest trumpet in the land. Moreover, just now it was best to let others share his time in the sun. L. A., too, acted this out by keeping Mick waiting to shake hands and quickly turning his head to give full attention to one of the four Republicans who had voted for his bill. Mick and I maintained poker faces of pleasure as we walked along the path that led through the cherry trees from the Capitol to the Rayburn building. Only when we were in the elevator did we break discipline.

"Presidential timber," said Whelan.

"The Senate, anyway," I replied.

An hour later, Mick and I met L. A. on the Capitol lawn.

"You buying?" L. A. said without preliminaries.

"Hell, no," Mick said, pointing at me. "He is."

Like Roman senators returned from a triumphal tour of newly conquered provinces, Mick and L. A. walked in front, arms around each other's shoulders, enjoying the barberries blooming gently underneath twin birch trees on the path leading away from the Capitol.

In the meantime, Ted March commandeered a booth at the rear of the Hawk and Dove sheltered from other patrons by an empty table whose tilted chairs proclaimed the spot off-limits to wayward drinkers.

"Leave it to Massa Jimmy's boys to dream up *regional* networks," Mick delivered the first gibe as a tray of drinks was set on the table.

"Some states-rights shit dressed up in balance-the-budget clothing," Jackson added.

L. A. took a swallow of his double dark Myers's on the rocks. Not until a couple of drinks were downed did Mick ask March to calculate the chances of national service in the Armed Services Committee.

"Up in the air," he said. "Maybe we should hold off. L. A., maybe you should sing your railroad song in the full House first."

"L. A?" Mick said after a sudden awkward pause.

"Hell, no!" L. A. turned to March, who was checking the view as the waitress bent low over a table on a diagonal line from ours.

"If we stall on the national-service bill, the jackals will figure we're scared—they'll play divide and conquer. Don't sell yourself short, March. You might just pick off Randolph. That self-help patriotic old black Republican likes national service, and you sure been sweet-talking him about making the Army everybody's thing again. But let Rivera go—even LBJ would rather have had that dude outside the tent, 'cause inside pissing out, he's liable to move his dick and piss on his own folks."

March lit a Camel and held his empty glass high over his head toward the waitress.

"Grit out both bills. It's the only way," Jackson continued. "You're Hart's boy, Mick. Yeah, and you got Frances Atlady so deep in your pocket, you need a tailor. Besides, I'm signed on to the program. Ain't gonna let nobody turn me around."

The waitress reappeared at the table to check our drinks. Ted March didn't say anything, just handed over his glass.

"No more for me," Mick, L. A., and I said in turn.

"Good," said March. "I always say your best friends are the guys who let you drink alone."

Mick tapped his tin of little Dutch cigars on the table until four were showing. He offered them around, and there were four takers. Even March stabbed out his half-smoked Camel.

"I'm game," Mick said. "I'll see Hart first thing and find out how soon he'll put the Whelan bill on the calendar."

"And I say, look, man, you're an honored guest at the gig a week from Friday at my place. You, too," he looked my way. "And March, don't forget to bring your old lady."

"She'll be there," March said, his drink having vanished without any of us noticing the glass pass to or from his mouth.

Chapter 10

I looked forward to L. A. Jackson's party as a welcome midsummer break and maybe a chance to do business outside the stifling ways of Capitol Hill. Driving watchfully down Kearny Street in northeast Washington to an address not far from Howard University, I tensed as clouds of smoke swirled above the curb, while on the sidewalk a contraption like a portable traffic signal flashed from green to yellow to red.

"There's some kind of trouble ahead, Gabe!" Kate cried as two black teenagers sprang to attention, one at my door, the other next to hers.

She clicked the lock button on the passenger door, and I lowered my window a crack and did the same. Grinning, the boy on my side stepped back and cupped his hands to his mouth.

"All aboard for Congressman Jackson's!" he shouted.

Spotting the Amtrak logo above the bill of his cap, I relaxed.

"It's okay," I told Kate. "Just one of L. A.'s railroad capers."

Perched above a high terrace, the Jacksons' two-story house belonged to a neighborhood mostly built up by black professionals before Washington was segregated in the wake of Woodrow Wilson's pre–World War I decision to cleanse the federal government of blacks, mostly Republicans, who had held civil-service jobs since Reconstruction. As the boys tipped their caps and went to park the car, we mounted the steps to the beat of Marvin Gaye's "What's Going On?" blasting through the window screens.

Inside, the sounds of the party took their cue from the easy black greetings exchanged at the beginning of Gaye's signature tune.

"Hey, Gabe, what's happening?" boomed L. A., standing in the door-way, dressed in a beige linen suit and a forest-green lightweight-cotton mock turtleneck that understated his midriff. "Where you been keeping this fine lady?" he said, measuring Kate until, suddenly conscious that she might take his words the wrong way, he tried to compensate for any real or imagined gaucherie. "Excuse me, but now I know for sure why this dude sneaks out of committee meetings early."

I could have kicked him.

"Congressman Jackson, a pleasure," she said, then in went the sharp, slender knife. "Gabe didn't tell me you were dipping into the pork barrel to fund an old-fashioned train station out here."

"I'm lucky you're not on the Transportation Committee," he laughed. "And I'm L. A. to you."

Her silence gave him leave to continue.

"If you'd been sitting in the spectators' section, I wouldn't have got-ten away with the shaky stuff I was putting down."

Acknowledged, Kate let him off the hook.

"Congratulations, Congressman."

"L. A.," he repeated.

"L. A. then," she smiled. "Gabe told me he's never seen anything like what you did—even during Watergate."

"Watergate was a tougher nut."

"Not at all," she countered. "Even the most tongue-tied politician could have found words on that. To turn a committee around on the railroads takes something special."

I admired Kate. She had made peace but on her terms. L. A. put an arm around each of us and led us to the spot where a woman who had to be his wife was talking to Mick and Sarah Whelan.

"Shug, meet the Bontempos."

Shug was short for sugar. Her name was Yvonne, and if L. A.'s complexion was the color of black coffee touched with a spot of milk, Yvonne's was coffee lightened to a delicate tan with a sure-handed tablespoon of the freshest cream. She had a charming way of speaking and acting as if L. A., her hero, needed the love and advice she gave him from intimate knowledge of his foibles and weaknesses as well as his strong points. But if the party put the Jacksons on display as a couple, the guest list paid a palpable tithe to what would soon be happening on the Armed Services Committee with the Whelan bill on national service and the draft, and in the full House on Jackson's bill to create a high-speed rail network.

Henry Hart was there with his wife, a thin, sharp-featured, graying woman whose enjoyment seemed to be heightened by her making mental notes to share with her friends of the goings-on at a *black* party.

There was also a smattering of other members from Armed Services carefully chosen by L. A., perhaps after consultation with Mick—Randolph but not Rivera, for example; Connie Frei, who could one-up her sons with descriptions of a hip party; but not Frances Atlady. (After campaigning for her the previous fall, Mick had decided to work her privately and not risk a public indiscretion on her part.) Ted March and his wife, an elegant, almost stately woman, much closer to a looker than to his stock image of a feminist, were there, moving easily between knots of men and women wearing Afros as painstakingly, expensively coiffed as Malcolm X's conk had been in the forties. One or two good old boys were also there with their starched and painted formidable wives, whom one imagined dancing with a certain desperate devil-may-care courage in immense hoopskirts at cotillions to keep up Confederate morale during the doomed, waning days of the Civil War. Different as they were, none of L. A.'s guests displayed the least squeamishness about attacking the ribs and greens with their fingers when knife and fork failed.

Congresswoman Warren was there, too, with a man acting half like her husband, half like a bored old flame. Trying to be inconspicuous, I watched March, for, as I had been tracking the tremors, political and otherwise, among various members of the Armed Services Committee, I had sensed him eye her without eying her. Now I heard Regina Warren introduce her husband to the Marches, not by his first name, but as the "tall, dark, and handsome man I keep out of sight." The male in question said nothing, only preened, trying to look the part as he made his excuses and circulated among several stunning black- and brown-skinned women in vibrant, slinky African-print dresses. He was an export banker, sheltered and foolish enough to assume, even in Washington, a colonial impunity with black women.

While I was kibitzing in a circle that included the Whelans, Marches, and Kate, I caught wind that something was stirring. I noticed March's eye shift from a rear view of Regina, abruptly on her way to the powder room, to her husband and two svelte African American women in the little group next to ours. "I don't believe that," he said, to no one in particular. Then he pointed toward two angry faces and a third face in shock. As I followed March's decisive finger, I heard Regina's consort blurt out a question.

"Excuse me," he said as he turned, raising his hand in the air.

"Excuse *who?*" the lovelier and darker of the two women demanded. "Where you get off rubbing your hand down my back?"

Warren mustered a practiced look of disbelief, as if to say, "This, too, is part of the game." And his expression changed to a smirk so brazen, the offended woman drew back her hand and prepared to slap him, until her friend intervened.

"Quincy," she called to a man a few feet away. "Quincy Parker, you get over here. There's a sure enough dumb northern cracker mashing Althea."

As Parker approached, the competing cliques of voices hushed, and suddenly the entire room, including Regina Warren, stopped in her tracks on the way back from the john, focused on the contretemps by the butcher-block coffee table.

Parker, whose light-heavyweight muscles rippled under his dashiki, stepped between his wife and the now-red and relenting Mr. Warren.

"Honey, what's going on?"

"This honky don't know where to put his hands and where not."

"Hey, Jack, what you putting down with my wife?" Parker asked, giving Warren a withering glance.

As Regina's other half shrunk back, L. A. Jackson came up and put his arm around Quincy Parker's shoulder. But Parker shook him off.

"L. A.," he said. "You gonna put this white-trash tomcat somebitch out your house or am I?"

L. A. led Quincy away to an empty corner, while March, standing next to me, moved to put the best face he could on things with Regina, who, walking with the tiny, awkward steps you take if your shoes are too small, now stood at the edge of our group. Shielding her now-wild, now-tame face, March removed a flowing handkerchief from his jacket pocket and dabbed at a white spot above her upper lip, as if he were a physician removing a speck of dust from her eye. Only he smiled, and she returned the look.

Soon, L. A. beckoned Regina and her husband, caught Quincy's eye, and, for a few minutes, conversed with his trio. Then he deftly squired Regina's husband over to where Althea Parker stood, remaining a tactful but intimidating few steps away until Warren apologized, not once, but twice, and rejoined Regina.

"L. A. wants those bills," March told Mick, "or he'd have let old Quincy tee off on that fool."

March was right, and he knew it. Quincy Parker was nobody to fool with. He'd been one of the movers and shakers in SNCC who had chosen black power in 1966 and soon after become top staff man for Mayor Gibson in Newark. As a consultant on urban affairs in the seventies, he became an unpaid advisor to the Congressional Black Caucus, all the while maintaining excellent connections with various Black Muslim mosques and the well-funded think tank that monitored black voting patterns. Black members of Congress preferred not to cross him for solidarity's sake, and because of the power he had to recruit insurgent candidates to challenge insufficiently militant black congressmen and -women in primaries, as he had done successfully in Detroit and Chicago.

The party was almost back in full swing. People danced, the booze flowed, and now, thanks to the efforts of L. A. Jackson and Mick Whelan, who were at opposite ends of the room, groups that had shifted along racial lines were once again salt and pepper.

Later on, Mick kept a judicious eye on the front door, and when he saw Henry and Mrs. Hart, and behind them the two Warrens, approaching Yvonne Jackson to say good night, he hustled over and asked them to wait. I obeyed his whispered command to sneak over and turn off the stereo, and before anyone sensed what was coming, Whelan, tapping his fingernail, made his wineglass ring.

"Friends," he called out in a voice that carried pleasingly, "I'd like to offer a toast. We've all heard L. A. recommend Adam's Rib as the best joint in town for soul food, but until tonight, I didn't know his point was to keep us off the scent of Yvonne's cooking."

On the far wall behind Whelan hung a painting from the *Sharpeville Series* whose abstract reds, blacks, and greens flowed into riverine images testifying to the struggle in South Africa.

"L. A., as I'm sure Congressman John Phillips would have said if he'd been able to make it, you've brought the underground railroad above ground tonight."

Mick looked toward the Jacksons and the Harts at the door.

"A positive vote in the Transportation Committee doesn't make a bill law, but if we follow L. A.'s lead, his bill will pass the House and Senate, and we'll have a great American railroad system again. We see tonight how much of that is Yvonne's doing. So Yvonne, keep him strong for all our sakes—and our gratitude and friendship to you both."

Shouts of "right on!" drowned out the sounds of "hear, hear!," and plenty of rhythmic handclapping moved L. A. to step forward.

"I got two things to say about all this signifying. One, the railroad bill is soul brother to the national-service bill, so we got one almost down and one to go. Second," he sent such a wide grin my way, I could see the liar's gap from across the room, "Bontempo, you set Whelan up for his Irish blarney. Go turn that box back on."

Among the last to leave, the Whelans, Marches, and Kate and I lingered on the front porch with the Jacksons while, at a sharp, prolonged whistle from L. A., three boys with Amtrak caps jumped up from the still-flashing traffic sign on the sidewalk below and hustled after our cars. With L. A. as escort, we walked down the steps from the terrace, March and I fishing in our pockets for a tip for the boys, Whelan coming up empty.

"Never mind no dollar bill, Whelan," L. A. said. "Just credit the cat fetching your car with a month toward his national service."

A few days later, Henry Hart told Mick he would put the Compulsory National Service bill on the docket in the Armed Services Committee before Labor Day. Although Hart would not bend any rules, to Mick the warmth of the older man's lingering handshake augured well. But for the bill to have a chance, Mick had to create a constituency of conscience independent of the usual alignments. Whether they were trusting or skeptical of the military, members of Armed Services tended to be ambivalent about both the draft and the volunteer army. Each constituency had a foot in the opposite camp. Those who wanted an invincible all-purpose army feared that volunteers would fall short, especially in prosperous times, and they considered a random draft an incentive to enlistment. Those who wanted the military under the unambiguous control of civilian authority disliked state coercion of young people by the draft but resisted a volunteer army because of its inevitable wayward tendencies.

In the memo Mick asked for, I addressed him directly.

"Why not couch your bill as an appeal to everyone's patriotism? In the aftermath of Vietnam, the right distrusts young people and the left indulges them. During the sixties, and now in our time, the right argues that hippies, peaceniks, potheads, and draft dodgers and their apologists don't know working kids or poor or minority kids, and don't want to know them. They have a point. Many on the left belittle young Americans who salute the flag, sing the 'Star-Spangled Banner,' and volunteer for the Marines. Compulsory national service would throw everyone together for a year after high school or age eighteen. No deferments—the only exceptions on medical grounds."

Then I reminded him of connections I'd heard him make many times.

"The model is Roosevelt's CCC. Cite the building of dams like Grand Coulee, lodges like Timberline in Oregon, and the cleanup of national forests during the Depression. Touch the railroad issue—but lightly. Mention roadbeds in a list of possible projects. Then include a provision for military service as an option whereby able-bodied eighteen-year-olds fulfill their national service. What hangs it together is the common denominator of being an American. Make young people's voter registration contingent on registration for national service. (Because national service will be compulsory for young women as well as men, there'll be delicate issues of housing—leave those for later.) Along the way, if you play your cards right and simply act as ventriloquist for an idea that's in the hearts and minds of Americans, people will come out of the woodwork to help."

I tagged off there. Over and above its specific provisions, Mick's legislation imbued national service with the same idea of public happiness that Adams, Paine, and Jefferson found in American experience back in the Revolution.

When we talked the next day, Mick focused on the practical.

"Keep me honest, Gabe. Cough if I head into the clouds."

Then he remembered the name he had forgotten when we went down the list of committee members.

"After the other night, how does March read Regina Warren?"

"Nothing yet. Look, she's a Navy brat. She represents Norfolk and Newport News. Besides, she's been told she's attractive so often, she thinks she's smarter than she is. I wouldn't count on her."

I didn't tell him that a few days before, on the way out of a stylish bar on upper Pennsylvania Avenue, I went back when I realized I hadn't left a tip and noticed Ted March sitting off in a corner, smoking.

He waved me over. "Gabriel, my man."

Obviously waiting for someone, March was dawdling over his drink. He was in a fine mood. I sat down for a minute and debated whether to order something. I wasn't in a rush, but when March didn't summon the waiter, I stood up. March had stayed seated, then abruptly rose and looked past me. Turning around, I saw Regina Warren tentatively picking her way toward our table like a doe in an unfamiliar wood. Seeing me, she looked flustered, but recovered after March moved the chair I had been in toward the table and pulled out the one across from him.

"Just leaving," I said.

March eyed her without eying her, then addressed me.

"Committee business," he said. "It never ends."

When Mick inquired after Warren's vote, I meant to tell him that March might be doing a bit of national service, but, instead, remembering a once-vivid dalliance of my own, I did the splits on a tightrope of values and kept quiet.

As the hearings began on the Whelan national-service bill, there was the expectant feel of a Fourth of July softball game with hot dogs and hamburgers sizzling on the grill to be followed at nightfall by patriotic fireworks. Between them that high summer afternoon, Henry Hart and Mick Whelan created a sense of occasion, where memorable things could happen if the individuals present yielded up their fixed positions and personal preferences to the unforeseen. For a while, though, the members paddled around in the shallows. Mick, too, held back, until curiosity and pedantry brought Congressman Daniel Israel, the ranking Republican, to the rescue.

"Mr. Chairman," he said after opening statements, "I would like to address a procedural question to you and several substantive questions to the chief sponsor of the legislation."

"The ranking member will proceed," Hart said.

"In my mind, the proposed legislation overlaps the jurisdiction of several House committees: on spending implications, the Appropriations and Ways and Means Committees; on interface with public lands, the Interior and Insular Affairs Committee; and, finally, because of its potential impact on patents and inventions, the Science and Technology Committee."

Inaudibly, I groaned. Henry Hart suffered pedants as gladly as he did fools, but from his expression, you would have thought that the angels Israel had placed on the pin of his question were an array of fascinating creatures that Hart had never seen before and would never see again. The chairman nodded two or three times and, when Israel finished, very deliberately scribbled a few notes on the pad in front of him.

"I would like to thank the honorable gentleman from New York for raising a question germane to this committee's deliberations in the coming weeks. I assure my good friend that I consulted with the chairs and ranking members of the committees he mentioned. Each acknowledged the ambiguity of jurisdiction, but each felt that, given the bill's proposed restoration of the draft, the House Armed Services Committee is the appropriate point of origin."

Congressman Israel looked around to gauge how closely the twenty-odd Democrats and fifteen Republicans around the horseshoe table were following his colloquy with Hart.

"I appreciate the distinguished chairman's attention to the protocols of the House of Representatives. I now look forward to an informed, constructive debate."

Hart waited until he was sure Israel had finished.

"The chair appreciates the clarification by the ranking member. You have eight minutes remaining, Congressman Israel."

Israel opened the blue folder in front of him. "Now, Congressman Whelan, any consideration I give this bill would follow from a provision that eighteen-year-olds' registration for the draft could not be set aside by the president without the express will of Congress. Second, I would have to have something written into the bill to provide the secretary of defense with explicit authority to allocate manpower as needed among the three services. Finally, your bill would need to specify a pool of military reserves sufficient to protect this nation in a national emergency."

Israel took his assigned time and then some after two other Republicans and Democrat César Rivera gave him liens on theirs. Thus, it was soon clear that Mick Whelan would not be responding to a single pedantic ranking member, but rather a treacherous potential coalition that could defeat his bill. He needed to be deferential to Israel without pandering to a man whom some found insufferable and others found a guided missile practiced at shooting down bills he disliked.

Into the breach once again stepped Henry Hart, who knew the ropes better than those, like Israel, who thought they held them, did.

"I take it, Congressman," Hart said in a voice that tactfully but firmly reminded Israel that he intended to exercise his chairman's prerogatives, "I take it you are asking that Congressman Whelan respond to your several questions."

Nor did Hart stay for an answer. "If there are members of the committee prepared to relinquish some of their time to Congressman Whelan . . . "

Red lights flashed in front of Jackson, March, Atlady, and several others, mostly on the Democratic side of Hart, but significantly Connie Frei at the Republican end of the table.

"The chair recognizes the congressman from Oregon, whom, I trust, will not avail himself of the time offered by all seven members whose lights I see turned on."

Mick laughed at the chairman's double purpose.

"Congressman Israel, I agree no president should have the authority to suspend registration for the draft without the consent of Congress. Your second and third points pertain to Article I of the Constitution, which empowers Congress 'to raise and support armies' and 'to provide and maintain a Navy,' and Article II, which names the president commander-in-chief and authorizes him to spend monies appropriated by Congress. Finally, yes, the bill should direct the president to allocate manpower appropriately and adequately among the services."

Mick scanned the faces of the members seated around the horseshoe table, lingering on the Republican members on his right. Then he looked directly at Israel.

"Congressman, if you are willing to supply some additional language, I will try to incorporate it."

Having disposed of Israel's queries more swiftly than anyone expected, Mick shifted gears while he had the committee's attention and goodwill.

"I'd like to say a word about how restoring the draft is related to requiring a year of national service from every American man and woman as they assume the rights and duties of citizenship. Often we speak of the rights of citizenship, rarely the responsibilities, almost never the duties. But the first premise of a true republic is citizen participation, beginning with the responsibility to defend the state. Presidents come and go, urging their fellow citizens, especially the young, to give something back to their country, and Congress passes resolutions designating National Citizenship Day, but otherwise we act as if the duties of citizenship are someone else's business. National service should be compulsory for the same reason the income tax is mandatory—for the good of the republic. Compulsory national service would further the social and moral welfare of the nation as well as its material well-being."

Mick looked up and down the table at the different hues and features of his colleagues.

"As a nation and a people, we've made progress breaking down artificial racial lines, lines of gender, and even region. But fault lines are growing between rich and poor in America. A year of national service after high school would throw young Americans together, working for their country on an equal basis. The first national need addressed would be military service. For the last half dozen years, the United States has had the all-volunteer military force. The young men and women in the ranks have performed admirably. The volunteer army has provided young people who often have no options except the lowest-paying jobs or lives of crime or on the street a way out and a way up. 'Fine,' you say, 'a good democratic trade-off.' But is it fair for the country to entice its least well off, least mobile young people to defend it year in, year out, and be the only ones in harm's way in time of war?

"My friends, the word *volunteer* is misleading. Our volunteer army is really a hired army. Some sign up because they want to be soldiers, some because they want to carry on in their fathers' and grandfathers' footsteps, many because no other option is open. But the volunteer army is not a citizen army. The volunteer army is a version of the warrior class in Plato's *Republic*. I cast no aspersions on the individuals who join and serve, but the volunteer army *as an army* poses threats to a democratic society and to the integrity of this Congress."

Christ, I thought, hearing undertones of disapproval, he doesn't have to tell it exactly like it is.

"Today, if the president wants to take military action and comes to Congress for authorization, we don't weigh the request as gravely as we might if it meant that our sons and daughters would be drafted. But if a draft were instituted as the first priority of compulsory national service, it would affect every young person in America. There would be no deferments. If able-bodied and of sound mind, those who are called would serve for a year. Only rarely will the nation be at war. The proposed draft would make military service, like national service, the responsibility of every young American. And therefore, under this legislation, every American citizen would have reason to be informed and vocal about what the country is fighting for."

Mick looked toward Frei and Israel on the Republican side.

"I'll close by reminding you of President Lincoln's appeal in his first inaugural. Southern states were seceding, but he still imagined mystic chords of memory swelling in a chorus to summon the better angels of our nature on behalf of the Union. Today, there is no Civil War, but who is to say the bill before us won't put Americans in touch with the better angels of our nature and make this a more perfect Union?"

Whelan paused, looked from colleague to colleague, then up at the portraits of nineteenth-century senators on the wall, so alert in their frames they looked poised to join the discussion.

To the accompaniment of approving murmurs, Chairman Hart adjourned the committee until after the Labor Day recess.

Mick's brief for his bill had been more than the pair of jacks he needed for an opening hand in the high-stakes poker game to come. Afterward, March and Jackson congratulated him; so, more circumspectly, did several others, including Dan Israel, who, conspicuous as always, lingered in hushed discussion long enough for me to slip out alone.

Stealing along the corridor, I heard a Texas voice crack the air behind me in surefire tones. I turned, and Henry Hart took my arm and guided me quickly down the empty hallway.

"Michael did well," he said.

In the light, natural from the windows, artificial from fluorescent tubes above, Hart's eyes were the intense rinsed blue of the skies that preside over cloudless days in the Texas hill country.

"Tell Michael no fireworks."

Hart disengaged my arm and walked briskly down the corridor.

Half an hour later, when I passed along Hart's words to Mick, he looked out of his office window at a long line of tourists snaking patiently around the entrance to the Capitol hoping for a glimpse of the great rotunda.

"Hart's testing me," he said softly. "The demon in me wants to shoot off fireworks. He's willing to work behind the scenes if he can trust me to trust him." He kept on talking. Though Mick knew how to listen, like most politicians he was reassured by the sound of his own voice. But now, when I didn't speak, he broke into an Irish grin that promised a renewed covenant of friendship.

"Gabe, thank God for the old Sound Connection. If Hart hadn't heard that briny rock music, he wouldn't have sidled up and confided in you."

No phone calls followed to Ted March or L. A. Jackson, no celebratory drink at the Hawk and Dove. Without another word, I returned to my office, and Mick went around to the business side of his desk.

CHAPTER 11

After the Labor Day recess, Henry Hart abruptly urged the Democratic leadership to move the Jackson railroad bill to the floor of the House. In the ensuing days, the imminent bailout of the Chrysler Corporation, and rumors that the Carter administration was encouraging the airlines to queue up for similar help if oil prices kept rising, drove moderate Democrats and Republicans to take a fresh look at the state of the nation's rail travel. Afraid of offending liberal Democrats on what looked like the eve of a challenge by Senator Edward Kennedy to President Carter's renomination, the White House stayed neutral. In the end, so many members rose in support of his bill that in his closing remarks, L. A. waxed poetic. He called the high-speed passenger train modern technology's version of Walt Whitman's body electric—a force traversing the continent according to the rhythms of every individual, every group. His last words were Whitman's call to arms:

Arouse! Arouse—for you must justify me—you must answer.

Hurrahs rocked the back benches of the spare old House chamber like responses shouted out in the ramshackle eighteenth-century black churches of New England.

The next day, a cartoon in the *Post* showed the House chamber morphing from a huge pork barrel into the Little Engine That Could led by L. A. Jackson in an Amtrak cap, while behind him members of Congress waved at the public from the windows of the train.

Now, as that old owl Henry Hart had intended all along, members of the Armed Services Committee began to push for action on the Whelan national-service bill. So it was no surprise when he paid an unannounced call one afternoon in early October while Mick and I were huddled, counting likely ayes and nays.

"Congressman." I stood up to leave.

"Gabriel, stay there. I want to talk to both of you," he commanded, his eyes lit by a silvery twinkle. "Michael, I intend to bring your bill up next week. That doesn't mean your colleagues don't have serious reservations. But the bill deserves a full and fair hearing, and I came down to see if you would be receptive to a suggestion." His voice had become low and intense.

Once Mick had each of us settled in leather chairs, Hart took a stylish ballpoint pen from the outside pocket of his jacket and tapped it on the coffee table. "I've told Dan Israel you are as approachable as any man in the House, but he shies away."

Hart uncrossed his long legs and looked at me as if he was deciding whether or not to treat me like a fellow congressman he could count on to observe the code of silence. "Gabriel, I've heard it said that on Tuesdays Israel talks like a schoolteacher turned lawyer and on Thursdays like a lawyer turned schoolteacher."

Then he took pains to address both of us.

"Dan learned his way of speaking at the knee of an uncle whom GIs liberated from Dachau in 1945—an uncle who saw his father and mother selected for the gas chambers. After the war, he learned English by reading law books."

Hart fiddled with his pen.

"Israel fears a mercenary soldier class could grow up in America. Putting his name on your bill would be a personal thing for him and good politics for you. I know he's a pedant in his bow ties, horn-rimmed glasses, and prosecutor's tongue, but the Republicans you need think he keeps the liberals' schemes honest."

Beyond the windows of the suite, leaves on the oak trees overhanging the walk to the Capitol were turning red and brown.

"Why don't I ask Israel to coauthor the bill?" Mick asked, as if he were suddenly one of the pigs in Gene McCarthy's story who, seeing the stock pen for the first time, thinks he discovered it and goes in.

"Michael, I never have to explain the universe to you." Hart stood up somewhat stiffly. "I'll take the bill up—the Whelan-Israel bill, perhaps—next week. Let's see, Halloween's not a bad day for a vote. What say, Gabriel?"

Old Have a Heart passed out of the outer office speaking different words of farewell to each of the secretaries, while Mick asked me to spell him with a group of high-school students from Scappoose who were expected in ten minutes.

So, while Mick trooped off to Dan Israel's office, I was left to entertain the future voters of America. As surely as you can tell the age of an old-growth redwood by counting the rings in its trunk, administrative assistants reveal their time in grade by how they handle high-school visitations. Newcomers act as if they're the congressman, and grizzled types develop routines tinged with ambivalence.

I came by my sense of irony honestly. Several years back, when the Republican incumbent announced his retirement from my old district on eastern Long Island, I jumped into the Democratic primary. I was the favorite until two hacks from the state legislature dropped out in favor of the crusading district attorney from Suffolk County, a cult figure to the locals for getting a court order restraining New York City from dumping sewage into Long Island Sound. That bicentennial year of 1976, Denny Donovan ran as if I were an insider in the pay of King George and he a ragged soldier in George Washington's army. The day he dressed up in a Revolutionary War uniform and rowed up and down a stretch of coastline fouled by sewage from the city, I knew I was in trouble. And sure enough, I lost so badly that in Washington, no one slapped me on the back and said, "Wait till next time."

Now, in an ambivalent gesture, I titled my talk to the kids "A Day in the Life of a Congressman." I ended with the old rhyme "A man works from sun to sun, but a woman's work is never done." Usually the line drew sighs from the girls, but instead of clucking like junior mother hens, these young hussies chewed their bubble gum and made cow eyes at a pair of smart-aleck boys.

"So, Bontempo," asked an unprepossessing kid with glasses and a crew-neck sweater, "when does Congressman Whelan do the important stuff?"

"Like writing laws," added his sidekick, a burly guy I imagined sitting at a truck stop in twenty years, his varsity-letterman sweater stretched over a bulging gut.

I gave the question the back of my hand, looked at my watch, and ended the meeting. Staring into the daggers masquerading as eyes on the face of the group's chaperone, I told the new Whelan intern to take the students on a tour of the House chamber. As the delegation filed out, the girls popping immense bubbles instead of saying thank you, Whelan appeared. Grasping the situation, in three minutes' time he undid the damage I had done the previous hour.

"Sorry, Gabe," he said once we were in his office. "An AA's work is never done."

Embarrassed, I refused to be jollied, until Mick gave me chapter and verse of his meeting with Dan Israel. Far from wrapping himself in the white flag of gratitude, Israel chose Joseph's coat of many colors. He acted suspicious, modest, high and mighty, and ingratiating by turns—had Mick approached him without Hart's coaching, I'm sure he would have left. But armed with Hart's inside dope, Mick acted as if Israel were the big one he was not going to let get away. At first, when he moved to reel Israel in, the congressman swam off in another direction, but as Mick lessened the tug, Israel wheeled about, as if to lead the fishing boat to his mating ground. In the end, the joyous expression on his face belied his reluctant words of assent.

"So, Mick," I said, no longer feeling used, "if Dan Israel were prime minister of Israel, there'd be a tree with your name on it planted on the Avenue of the Righteous in Jerusalem."

"Avenue of the Righteous? Hell, we're talking Elders of Zion."

True to his word, Hart set Halloween as the date for a vote in the Armed Services Committee. Abetted by the subtle ways of his chairman, Mick sought to kill the other side with kindness, making fence-sitters loathe to side with a disagreeable minority.

Two hours into final debate, T. F. Randolph signaled that he wanted to address the committee.

"Mr. Chairman," Randolph began, "as I left home this morning, my wife asked if I would be taking our son, Dwight David, trick-or-treating tonight. I said that I would, provided my colleagues and I reached a decision about whether to give the author of this bill, my friend Congressman Whelan of Oregon, a trick or a treat."

Behind the horseshoe table, three female aides dressed up as the witches in *Macbeth* shook their broomsticks, mumbling, "Fair is foul and foul is fair," until Hart's gavel restored order.

"Mr. Chairman," Randolph said, "when this debate began, despite my high regard for the distinguished congressman from Oregon, I was opposed to the measure before us. In these austere times, when a Democratic president is holding down domestic spending and deficits continue to grow, sympathetic as I am to the idea of every young person in America doing a year of national service, I decided that legislation should wait for a stronger economy. Also, because of my respect for the joint chiefs who have made the Army, Navy, Air Force, and Marine Corps a model of an integrated military, I intended to oppose this bill."

Randolph looked out at the front row, where four men and two women from the Pentagon sat, medals flashing and buttons sparkling on their full-dress uniforms. Uncomfortable standing on the bridge he was about to cross, Randolph summed up honorably, looking straight at the high-ranking officers before him.

"But I have since concluded that compulsory national service is an idea whose time has come, an idea in need of prompt, full, and fair implementation if the United States is to remain a great and well-defended nation. I remain uneasy about reinstituting the draft. That provision of the bill may not have received the scrutiny it deserves. However, pending debate on the floor of the House, I intend to give the Whelan-Israel bill the benefit of the doubt."

Whelan's red light flashed. From where I sat, I saw Henry Hart hesitate, then smile with confidence.

"The chair recognizes the congressman from Oregon for the purpose of responding to the member from Oklahoma."

Whelan turned over several pages of the text, found the section on the draft, then looked straight at T. F. Randolph.

"Congressman Randolph, I'm grateful for your question on how the bill reconstitutes military service."

He paused, and I understood Hart's smile of a moment before. Mick intended to use his answer to Randolph as touchstone for a few last words and with the hope that one of his allies on the committee, perhaps with a nudge from Hart, would follow by calling the question.

"Congressman, the tradition of a strong patriot army goes hand in hand with the Constitution and the American body politic. It was the earliest form of national service back in the Revolution. Provision for a draft, supplemented by enlistees, is now the first mandate of the legislation."

Congressman Randolph nodded and looked around, clearly pleased, and, in return, Mick was ready.

"I'll close by assuring my friend from Oklahoma that Congressman Israel and I want the strongest possible bill, a bill that does not invite challenge in the courts."

Hart banged his gavel.

"Are there questions or remarks from other members?"

Two or three seats away, the light in front of Congressman Rivera of California turned red. Ever since Rivera pulled the fast one on this issue four years ago, Hart had rebuffed his efforts to swivel back into his good graces. Today, Rivera had been quiet. So the chairman yielded to the procedural fairness in his bones.

"Does the congressman wish to speak before the vote?"

Rivera smiled the sly smile of one who has been found out but has the right to do his business. "Yes, your Honor, I mean, Mr. Chairman."

"That was in another country, once a republic, Congressman—the state of Texas—and the defendant is long since deceased."

Even diehards like Homer Fogdall laughed at Hart's sally. I saw L. A. Jackson's face darken, but other members' glances at Rivera mingled exasperation with curiosity.

"In this morning's *Washington Post*, a member of this committee was quoted as saying she supported the Whelan-Israel bill because it would replace the mercenary army."

Mick Whelan looked my way. He and I had discussed the article in question—a routine piece profiling the bill except for a quote, tucked away in the story, attributed to Congresswoman Frances Atlady, disapproving of mercenaries masquerading as democratic volunteer soldiers. "With friends like her . . . ," I had told Mick, remembering the surreal, rollicking day and a half he had put in out in Illinois rescuing her from defeat the previous November. "Frances Atlady and I haven't always agreed," he'd said into the cameras at O'Hare Airport with the straightest of faces, Frances beside him wearing a heavy orange turtleneck sweater, a plaid skirt with safety pins in the pleats, and bobby socks, "but, like you, I always know where she stands." There was the hint of a wink as he spoke, and even that pleased the congresswoman. The one agreed-to appearance multiplied into a church breakfast, a brunch at the Kosiusko Society, a walking tour of the Frances Atlady bird refuge on a slender finger of marshland where Lake Michigan dipped briefly into her district, a noisy rally held without a permit in a northwest Cook County mall, and, finally, an early supper for get-out-the-vote workers at Atlady head-quarters. Afterward, Mick said he'd felt like Simon the Cyrenian helping carry the cross up the hill to Golgotha—a blasphemous image until you understood that Atlady was the cross.

But on election night, when she was losing, Frances called to tell Mick she would never forget his support: "If the people send me back, I'll be with you." So, after reading the *Post*, I suggested he talk to her.

"If I do, it will only stir her up," he told me. "Let's get through the vote. If it looks like anybody's paying attention, I'll have her put out a low-key correction."

Now, the eyes of most committee members were on the congress-woman from Illinois. She wore earrings with large silver hoops inside of which dangled peace symbols fashioned from pink and lavender quartz. She was looking Mick's way with an expression that said both "Oh my God, what have I done?" and "This is nothing, everything is perfectly all right." Like everyone else in the room, she waited for Rivera to strike.

Finally, disappointed that his quarry refused to bolt from cover, he did. "Would the congresswoman from Illinois care to explain her remarks to the effect that the dedicated men and women defending this country are mercenaries?"

The officers in the front row sat up straighter as Rivera spoke, and the members of the committee, no admirers of Frances Atlady, gasped at the blunt force of his accusation. Again, the congresswoman summoned an unwonted discipline, and waited patiently for recognition.

"If the congresswoman from Illinois desires recognition, the chair is pleased to extend it," Hart offered graciously.

Conscious she was onstage, Atlady nevertheless leaned toward Henry Hart as if theirs was a private colloquy. "Thank you, Mr. Chairman. I have no wish to expand on remarks I may or may not have made. But let me say I am deeply offended that Congressman Rivera would take words a reporter misquoted and put them further out of context."

As Frances Atlady warmed up, I looked around at the faces of the members I knew well. L. A. Jackson reminded me of those statues of two-faced African gods, one side ready to intervene while the other looked on in sphinxlike impassivity. Ted March was amused. There was nothing constructive he could do, so he sat back and watched, self-satisfied, from one of the best seats in the house. I was sure Mick realized that César Rivera's move had been carefully timed and calculated by the opponents of the bill inside and outside the committee. The lines that creased his forehead told me he second-guessed his decision not to address the mercenary issue earlier. During the few seconds it took me to read the faces on the dais, Atlady paused, and a wild hope possessed me that her pause was not a pause. She had told Rivera and her colleagues how she felt, neither affirmed nor denied the exact words attributed to her, and linked the *Post* reporter's opportunism with Rivera's. Just when her pause became a finished silence, another red light went on.

"Will the gentle lady yield?"

The voice belonged to Congressman Israel.

Now Frances Atlady was confused. Her eyes widened and narrowed as she sought to have it both ways.

"I will," she said, "provided the chair allows me to reserve the balance of my time."

I saw Mick look hard at Henry Hart.

"Madame Congresswoman," Hart said, "the chair recognized you for the purpose of responding to Congressman Rivera's question. You may yield the floor to Congressman Israel, but if you wish to further pursue the matter raised by the question, you must request recognition after Congressman Israel is finished speaking."

"Thank you, Mr. Chairman," she said, uncharacteristically relieved to have someone else dictate a way out.

God, I thought, seeing Mick relax, money can't buy having the chairman on your side.

"Mr. Chairman," Israel was saying, "if I may, I would like to respond to Congressman Rivera's remarks."

Mick did not have a good angle. Short of sprawling forward on the table, he could not thrust his face directly into Dan Israel's line of sight. Even if he could have, there was no guarantee Israel would heed his signal, and if he did, the entire committee would see idealistic Michael Whelan as Slick Mick, a puppeteer in the tradition of Lyndon Johnson. So he tried to will Israel to turn his gaze in his direction. Eventually Israel did, with a smile that said, "Don't worry, my boy, I'll clean up this little contretemps good and proper."

Sensing Israel's conviction, Mick tried to set up roving eye contact with Jackson and March: Mick at second base, the keystone sack; Jackson at third, the hot corner; and March, tall and rangy, at first, ninety feet from home, where catcher Henry Hart stood guard over the plate, hands taut, mask down over his face.

"Certainly," Hart was saying. "But may I remind the congressman from New York that the hour grows late. If, as you and Congressman Whelan indicated earlier, you desire a vote this afternoon, brevity would serve that purpose."

I did not see then, and I do not see now, in the millennial year 2000, while crude partisan sallies fill the airwaves like artillery shells in the battle for Florida, how a politician could act as signalman to his cause and party and still keep faith with the politics of fairness any better than Henry Hart did on that Halloween afternoon.

"As always, Mr. Chairman, I appreciate your counsel," Israel said. "In my judgment, the congressman from California confuses things. No supporter of the Whelan-Israel bill casts aspersions on the men and women who wear the uniform. But the mercenary issue is real. Many who volunteer do not do so for purely patriotic reasons. If that were so, why would this Congress authorize so much money for recruitment bonuses to those who volunteer, not to mention the benefits offered after their tours of duty?"

Whelan sat stock-still—how could he interrupt the Republican coauthor of his bill? L. A. Jackson's hand twice moved to the switch that controlled his recognition light, then he withdrew it.

"Mr. Chairman, the Armed Forces provided for in the bill I am coauthoring will be a mix of draftees chosen fairly and at random from all young people in American society and those who choose to extend their tours of duty or sign up after their national service is done."

With friends like that, I thought, avoiding Mick's eye as Israel finished and Hart recaptured the floor.

"Does the congresswoman from Illinois wish to add to her earlier comments?" the chairman asked, gavel raised and poised in his right hand.

Frances Atlady paused. "Not at this time," she answered as red lights glowed on either side of her.

From their respective positions in Whelan's infield, Jackson and March spoke briefly and well before another light came on.

"Congressman Randolph is recognized."

"Mr. Chairman, fellow members of this committee, I hope the author and coauthor of this bill will hear me out when I say that I am disturbed by the comments made in response to Congressman Rivera's question. Not by Congresswoman Atlady. Who in this room has not had his words taken out of context? But I am surprised and distressed by the statements made by Congressman Israel. As coauthor of the legislation, he should know the intent behind the bill that bears his name."

Randolph stopped and looked down the row of members.

"Much as I appreciate the good-faith efforts at clarification by

Congressmen Jackson and March, this legislation is vital to the national security of the United States. For it to deserve the benefit of the doubt and have a chance of passing the full House and the Senate by enough of a majority for the president to sign it, there must be bipartisan agreement about its rationale. Earlier, I said that I had decided to support the bill. Despite questions about how a mix of draftees and volunteers—volunteers, not mercenaries, Congressman Israel—would function in the field, the philosophy expressed in the bill is a noble one consistent with the patriotic traditions of enlistment and the willingness to be called to fight and die for one's country."

Randolph looked pained, for now his code of honor compelled him to look at Mick as if they were the only two persons in the room. Hiding his disappointment, Mick met T. F.'s eyes as if he were a proud enlisted man facing his superior officer.

"Mr. Chairman," Randolph went on, "I am confused about whether this bill's purpose is to destroy what some insist is a mercenary army posing a danger to the republic or to protect this nation's security through two exalted traditions. From what I have heard this afternoon, I fear that the authors of the Whelan-Israel bill are fuzzy on this point."

Now Randolph looked at Hart as if at a fair and principled commanding officer.

"Mr. Chairman, without satisfactory clarification once the authors have considered what has been said this afternoon, I will, in good conscience, have no choice but to vote against the bill in committee and, should it pass, oppose it vigorously on the floor of the House of Representatives."

Approving murmurs spread across the room from the declared opponents and enough undecided members to turn a decisive victory into a nail-biter. In the meantime, the red lights in front of Whelan, Israel, Rivera, Fogdall, Frei, Jackson, March—the whole damn committee—flashed on.

This time, Mick took a chance and did not wait for recognition.

"Mr. Chairman," his voice broke the silence.

"The chair recognizes the author of the bill."

"As principal author of the Whelan-Israel bill, I thank my friend from Oklahoma. Congressman Randolph, you could have kept your counsel and simply voted against the bill. Or you could have spoken in opposition and called for the vote. But instead you did what a man of principle and conscience would do. You announced your intention to vote against unless—*unless*—further exchange of views inside this committee should again persuade you that the bill's principles and practice are consistent with your own."

Mick paused and looked around the room, lingering on the faces of the Republican members he needed if his bill were to have a chance on the floor of the House.

"My friends, I intend to keep faith with Congressman Randolph and every one of you. Therefore, I move to table the motion . . . "—there were undertones of surprise and irritation around the room—"until the next scheduled meeting of this committee, on November sixth."

Several voices, male and female, Democratic and Republican, shouted, "Second."

"A motion to table is not debatable," said Chairman Hart.

He looked at Israel until the New Yorker switched off his light.

"All in favor of the motion to table say aye."

A chorus of voices boomed aye as if the result were in doubt.

"All opposed, nay."

Several nays scattered their sounds upon the air, among them Fogdall, Rivera, and a female voice I couldn't quite place.

"The ayes have it," Hart boomed. "The committee is adjourned until two o'clock one week from today."

Broomsticks in one hand, committee documents in the other, the young women in witch costumes mugged for the cameras.

They say the Lord giveth and the Lord taketh away, but sometimes the process works in reverse. The combination of Frances Atlady's blunder in the press and Dan Israel's in committee all but torpedoed passage. But the timing of the faux pas turned a trick into a treat. Between Halloween and the November sixth reconvening of the Armed Services Committee, all hell broke loose. Far away from Capitol Hill, fanatic Iranian clerics and students seized the American embassy in Tehran and took sixty-six Americans hostage. Closer to home, Senator Edward Kennedy announced for the Democratic nomination against President Carter.

For his part, Mick went to work on T. F. Randolph and other possible Republican votes on the committee, persuaded Dan Israel that the bill's fate was more important than the word *mercenary*, and secured a pledge from Frances Atlady that if she opened her mouth in the forthcoming meeting, it would be only to praise the men and women ready to step into harm's way and rescue the American citizens held hostage in Iran.

In the end, T. F. Randolph moved to take the Whelan-Israel bill off the table. Doing so, he spoke for passage on the twin grounds that Congressman Whelan and the Ayatollah Khomeini had tempered his misgivings. He ended with a line that drew applause from every corner of the room. "Mr. Chairman and colleagues, there is an eighteenth-century English saying appropriate to our situation: 'Nothing concentrates a man's mind more than hearing himself sentenced to be hanged in two weeks.' We have clear evidence that in this world there are those prepared to pass such a sentence upon the American people. Now is the time to stand united in our constitutional responsibility to provide for the common defense. The Whelan bill will do that by combining our best military traditions: enlistment and a fair and inclusive draft."

César Rivera switched on his light and was recognized.

"Mr. Chairman, in deference to its authors and to the chairman of the Armed Services Committee, I call for a vote on the motion. But in the name of national security and for the sake of the good names of our men and women in uniform, I urge you to reject sending such dangerous legislation to the floor of the House."

Chairman Hart acknowledged the several cries of "second" and waited a little before banging his gavel and calling for order.

"Are there any other members who wish to speak before I call for a vote on the motion?"

He held his gavel high in the air like a club.

"Hearing none, the clerk will call the roll."

By a vote of twenty-three to thirteen, Regina Warren voting present while looking straight at Ted March, whose expression acknowledged her neutrality, the motion carried.

In the aftermath of the Whelan-Israel bill passing out of the committee on Armed Services, newspapers and newsmagazines took tentative note. Although Michael Whelan was a liberal Democrat, he was not considered doctrinaire, and because patriotic fervor was at fever pitch in response to the hostage crisis in faraway, fanatic Iran, the opposition shied away from attacking national service and the draft.

About a week after the bill's passage in committee, Henry Hart asked Mick to come to his office and bring me along. It was Veterans Day, I remember, because Hart, a man who didn't wear his love of country on his sleeve, had pinned a red poppy to his lapel next to a tasteful silver version of the tiny plastic American flags rushed into production and circulation in the days after Americans were taken hostage in Tehran.

"The House leadership is interested in your bill," he told Mick. "They're not for it—not yet," he paused, choosing his words carefully. "There's no confidence President Carter's going to get those people out of Iran quickly and safely, and the Republican presidential candidates, especially Reagan, are calling the hostage-taking the worst humiliation for America since the Barbary pirates."

"Maybe it'll get Carter Reagan as his opponent," Mick said.

Hart frowned.

"They're laughing at Reagan at the White House too, Michael, but I'm not so sure. Thirteen years ago, Pat Brown thought Ronald was a joke in California and lost to him by a million votes."

Hart pushed his chair back from the desk and swiveled to the side closest to where Mick and I were sitting.

"At any rate, the leadership thinks your bill might counteract the line that Democrats are soft on terrorism as well as Communism. They'll bring it up first thing in January."

Whelan's expression changed from one of sobriety into a grin.

"Gabriel," Hart continued, "if Michael is agreeable, I want you to sniff out any amendments from Democrats that might compromise the bill's principles, especially on national security."

I kept quiet, and Hart put his hand on my shoulder. "I'll let you go. I want Michael to march with me in the Veterans Day parade that starts at the Washington Monument in twenty minutes and ends up standing at attention before President Lincoln."

Hart chuckled as he walked around to the front of his desk.

"Abe Lincoln may not have been a commander in the field like George Washington, but he was just as smart a general."

We walked to the elevator together. After riding down with the two congressmen, I walked back, taking the stairs two at a time, and asked Marva to type a triple-spaced list of the members of the House of Representatives by state and by party.

CHAPTER 12

On Christmas Day, while Patrick patted the miniature leather camels on the tree and asked me about the three men in richly dyed robes holding tiny chests marked *gold*, *frankincense*, and *myrrh*, the radio blared news of the Soviet invasion of Afghanistan.

"Maybe the wise men have come back as Afghan chieftains," I told Mick on the feast of the Epiphany as we sat calculating the votes for and against his bill. We laughed, but in the early days of the congressional session, the American eagle seemed to descend from the great seal of the republic and swoop through House and Senate chambers screaming for retribution against the Russian bear.

As the spirit of the Cold War revived, L. A. Jackson's network of high-speed trains languished in the Senate. Now, senators displayed maps of Iran and Afghanistan and vied with the president and each other over who could talk toughest to the Soviet Union. And in the House of Representatives, many argued that the Whelan-Israel compulsory national-service bill was urgent. On both sides of the aisle, members suspected that the American people would hold them accountable if Congress dithered away its practical patriotic opportunity.

Before the vote, Mick Whelan rose to say he was proud to be in the people's House, whose members belonged to that necessary third party, the party of hope.

After the bill passed easily—251 to 179, with 5 abstentions—Mick told reporters clustered in the rotunda that the support of almost 60

Republicans augured well for the bill's chances in the Senate. Standing next to him, a beaming Dan Israel observed that with the Whelan-Israel bill and the Jackson railroad legislation on its docket, the Senate had a historic opportunity to change the face of America.

Nevertheless, after several months of deafening silence, Mick and L. A. paid a call on Henry Hart, with me along for the ride.

"Ah, the Senate," Hart rested his hands behind his head. "Michael, Louis, when Lyndon Johnson was president, he picked me to run for the Senate from Texas. I won't lie. I was flattered. I lined up commitments. I talked to my wife, talked to some other people . . . " Hart stopped and looked up at the framed photograph of himself, Lyndon Johnson, and Sam Rayburn that was hanging above our heads. "Then I remembered old Sam saying that before buying a ranch, a man should walk every acre and look in every cow's mouth. If he's running for office, he should put his feet on the ground in every county. Well, I did, and Texas was too big. Good God, I went from Mexico to Oklahoma, Louisiana, all the way to New Mexico." Hart sighed a sigh of relief and regret. "With the seniority I had, I knew I could do better for my district, for Texas, and the country in the House than the Senate."

"I wish you were there now," Mick said, and Jackson nodded.

"That's kind of you." He chuckled, naming each man again. "But there's another thing, and it brings me back to your predicament—*ours,* because I'm with you on those bills."

Usually Henry Hart was laconic to a fault; today he had stepped out of character, so now he pretended to search for a word when in reality he was checking to see if Mick and L. A. were still with him. "The other reason I didn't run for the Senate was vanity. Don't take this wrong—the two of you may wind up in the Senate, and the House is a stepping-stone to the Senate, but in many a senator's mind, the Senate is the threshold to the White House—I lacked senatorial vanity."

Now that Hart was through with his monologue, Mick looked at L. A.

and passed around his tin of little cigars. Finding no takers, he put the box back in his pocket.

"What should we do, Henry?"

"What you're doing."

Hart was back on his laconic frequency. He felt awkward about having spoken so much. To pick his brain, Mick and L. A. needed to shift into a fighting mood.

"Twiddle our thumbs?" L. A. challenged.

"Defer to the Senate's procedures. Louis, Michael, House leaders talk to the Senate leadership, and there's sympathy with your predicament."

Unconvinced, L. A. puckered his lips.

"Louis," Hart shaded his eyes from the midday sun pouring into his office and, for a second, the back of his hand became a yellow eyeshade and his eyes narrowed like those of a blackjack dealer in a psychedelic casino, "I wouldn't be surprised if you and Michael wound up on the conference committees."

L. A. drummed his fingers on the arm of his chair.

"How do we keep the bills from being bottled up?"

"You don't. But with a little help from your friends . . . "

"You know, L. A.," Mick said sarcastically, "the senators who are always calling."

"Ah, Michael," Hart wagged a bony finger. "I'm surprised at you, forgetting your Constitution. Appropriation bills initiate in the House. Some of these senators—I won't say how many—have pet projects they want funded for their states."

"That's why we came to see you, Henry," L. A. said.

"And all this time, I thought you missed my company."

As we stood up, Hart remembered something and turned his hands palms down to indicate he wanted us in our chairs again. "Louis, there's something else I want to bring up." Hart twined his hands together on the back of his head. "Now that the governor has pulled out of the Senate race up in New York, the party is frantic. Yesterday, your name came up at a Congressional Campaign Committee meeting."

Hart stopped to blow his nose.

"I'm a Texan a long way from New York, but I butted in. I told them I didn't see how the Democratic Party could do better than Louis Jackson. I don't know a damn thing about New York politics, but I know you'd make a hell of a senator."

"Senatorial vanity, right Henry?"

"Now, don't hold that against me, Louis. You're fast on your feet. You have energy, savvy, a sense of the big picture."

Mick had trouble camouflaging his worried look, so he leaned over and put his hand on L. A.'s arm. "Sorry, L. A., I was thinking about the two bills."

"So am I," Hart agreed. "I'd hate to lose you on my committee, Louis. And I've watched gifted congressmen run for the Senate and lose every-thing because they didn't send a hanging judge out to take a reading," Hart considered. "About your bill and Michael's . . . if you win, twenty senators perk up. If you lose, twenty will use your defeat against the bills. The Republican incumbent is a tough cookie. Beatable, but no sure thing, even in New York in a presidential year."

L. A. sat back a minute.

"Henry?" he finally asked, question marks forming in his eyes.

"I told you what *I* did, Louis, but I'm not you—you're on the grand scale. Your speeches prove that. And no hypothetical is worth a damn."

"Mick?"

"You'd be a great senator. But if you lost . . . "

"Yes," Henry Hart and L. A. said an instant before I did.

Outside the mahogany French windows installed at taxpayers' expense by Hart's predecessor, countless cherry blossom buds were poised to burst into bloom. The question marks in L. A.'s eyes became exclamation points that pointed down to a grin that spread across his face, exposing his liar's gap. As he tried to read Mick, the telephone console flashed red and rasped three times.

"One short, two long—serious," Hart said, picking up the receiver. "Yes, Miss Stack. No, don't tell him that." He wrinkled his nose and winked at us. "I've just now gone out the door."

By the time he put down the receiver, we were on our feet, and L. A. had his hand on the doorknob.

"Be talking to you," Henry Hart told us as he led the way out.

From May until August, Mick and I kept one eye on the Senate, the other on New York. In Washington, sitting senators began to make favorable noises about the legislation mandating high-speed trains and national service, while up in New York, L. A. Jackson's competition for the Senate nomination consisted of former congresswoman Lillian Brodski, a kosher Frances Atlady, and Secretary of State Nicholas Valeri, a brash, ambitious pretty boy favorite of the bosses. In a July poll, Jackson had forty-five percent; Valeri: twenty; Brodski: fifteen; with the rest scattered between undecided and the right-to-life candidate. And when the Republicans nominated Ronald Reagan for president, L. A.'s backers clapped their hands, convinced the stars were aligned so that 1980 would be the year of the first black Democratic United States senator. Key Democratic senators also passed the word to Mick through Henry Hart that the railroad and national-service bills might be just the right mix of progressive patriotic legislation to bring up for a vote when the presidential campaign heated up in October.

Up in New York, L. A. Jackson declared formally for the Senate nomination in August the week before the Democratic Convention. For a day or two, his face was on the television channel you were watching and the station you switched to. On NBC's convention preview, he and Mick Whelan touted their pending bills on the high-speed rail network and compulsory national service as a contemporary American revolution. But the fratricide between the Carter and Kennedy partisans at the convention eclipsed L. A.'s fifteen minutes of uncritical fame. Some New York pols whispered that a black Senate candidate might swell the Reagan vote, and from his aerie in Washington, Henry Hart huddled with the Democratic Senatorial Campaign Committee.

"It helps the party to have a strong black candidate running for the Senate in New York," his emissary told party bigwigs in Albany, "and we like L. A. Jackson."

The word that came back astonished Hart. "Jackson for Congress in Brooklyn, the Bronx, Manhattan, we don't care—the Senate statewide, we care."

Then came the teeth: "You pick the national ticket, fella, we pick the state—everybody's happy."

Three days after the convention, Brodski and Valeri made their candidacies official in well-orchestrated serial press conferences. Valeri's marching orders came from party bosses upstate and a triumvirate of oil, airline, and automobile lobbyists; Brodsky's from a dormant messianic complex activated when she led a doomed last charge against Carter's renomination.

But L. A.'s luck held into September. He was a street fighter, yet he didn't break discipline—not once. I know. I advanced his trip by train up the Hudson to Albany. On the way, he diverted to Catskill—his father's birthplace—where he spoke to the Rotary Club. He told them that in 1915, after seeing *Birth of a Nation*, a mob of masked townsmen came to his grandfather's porch waving torches and guns and threatened to burn him out. His hunting rifle at his side like a shillelagh, Grandfather Jackson faced them down, and no one belonging to Catskill's three black families was bothered again. After the talk, a dozen Rotarians led L. A. on an unscheduled walking tour of Main Street behind a vanguard of white and black schoolchildren and tossed their hats in the air outside city hall.

Ten days before the primary, the *Daily News* poll put L. A. at forty-one percent; Valeri: thirty-one; Brodsky: sixteen; the rest split between undecided and right-to-life.

Then, the weekend before the election, Nicholas Yale Valeri's campaign stumbled on the kind of carny shtick that sometimes turns elections in America. The New York Mets were locked in a pennant race, with the hated Los Angeles Dodgers coming to Shea Stadium for a four-game series the weekend after Labor Day. Valeri was scheduled to attend the Saturday afternoon game, and, scouting things the night before, his advance man noticed a chant go up and build to a high-pitched roar: "New York, Yes! L.A., No!" until his ears ached. Next morning, according to a post-primary story in *New York* magazine, the advance man pleaded with the campaign manager for permission to hand out signs reading N.Y., Yes! L. A., No! at Shea Stadium.

"Fuck the Mets, for Christ sake." The irritated honcho in the back room looked up from his eyeshade. "I got an election."

"But Mr. Esposito, doesn't Valeri's middle name begin with *Y*?"

"Yes, schmuck, Yale—Nicholas Yale Valeri. You won't have a name you don't beat it."

Like a taxi driver stiffed on his tip, the advance man advanced on his boss, shouting, "New York, Yes! L. A., No! Mets and Valeri, Dodgers and Jackson."

The campaign manager's scowl became a beatific smile.

"That's it!" he yelled. "I'll get the printers' union to print signs. Call some volunteers. What are you waiting for? Beat it!"

In a flash, Esposito got on the horn to the big boys in Albany, who told lobbyist connections in D.C. to find two hundred thousand for last-minute radio and television. Before the umpire hollered, "Play ball!" on Saturday afternoon, Valeri's workers had given away five thousand signs—N.Y., Yes! L. A., No!—and were waiting for a second truckload. When the seventh-inning stretch rolled around, a third and fourth batch of signs had been gobbled up by Mets fans, the game was tied, and a made-for-television wave erupted from the left field foul pole, surged past home plate, and rolled out past the right field line in Shea Stadium. "New York, Yes! L. A., No!" roared fifty thousand fans holding their signs. In response, the Mets rallied, won that game and a doubleheader on Sunday, and Nick Valeri, now known as New York, became a feel-good icon destined for fifteen minutes of fame.

On a tip from Ted March that L. A.'s nemesis César Rivera was channeling aerospace money to Valeri, Mick Whelan commandeered Miles Stein to produce and put on the air a spot of L. A. speaking from the well of the House. After a voice-over by Mick, the camera panned around the chamber, showing lawmakers rapt with attention, some with their hands over their hearts, as L. A. chanted Walt Whitman's lines of praise for America.

On Sunday night, Mick appeared side by side with L. A. at Irish clubs in Queens and out on Long Island. "I'm a black Irishman asking you to vote for my friend L. A. Jackson. He's got grit, he's got wit—he's as much a Mick as I am."

Standing on a makeshift dais, Whelan belted down a pint of Guinness. "You New York Democrats will be proud when Louis Jackson represents you and your state in the Senate of the United States."

Monday, I advanced Mick and L. A. as they took the A train from Battery Park uptown for a walking tour down 125th Street.

Jackson's bringing an Irish American congressman into Harlem the day before the election drew front-page photos of the two congressmen wading into jubilant crowds in front of the Apollo Theater. But the back pages of the same tabloids crowed about the Mets winning three in a row, and every headline writer seized on the Valeri campaign's "New York, Yes! L. A., No!" stunt. In both the *News* and the *Post*, the *N.Y.* was followed by an exclamation point, whereas *L. A.* had a red slash through it.

On Election Day, statewide polls showed L. A. ahead by three or four points. Instead of heading the stories "Jackson Holds Narrow Lead," the dailies screamed that Valeri was closing the gap and the race was too close to call. Even the good gray lady published a highbrow piece in the sports section comparing Valeri's surge to the Mets' capture of first place.

Election night, Mick and I joined the faithful at the Americana for the Jackson victory celebration. The first rush of votes eased our anxiety—L. A. jumped in front, forty-two percent to thirty-three percent for Valeri, twenty percent for Brodsky, and five percent for the pro-life candidate. While we waited, an old black man, yellow smears of jaundice in his eyes, mounted the stage, removed his trumpet from its case, and played Armstrong tunes accompanied by a young piano player in a stovepipe Afro with deft tapered fingers and melancholy minors reminiscent of Thelonious Monk. A little before one, they played "Round Midnight," then, while L. A. Jackson strode through the crowd to the platform, broke into "Mack the Knife." L. A. was resplendent in a chocolate pinstripe suit with a pale-green tie the color of Yvonne's dress. Seeing him, the crowd roared. Next to me, an elegant woman in a black dress that didn't miss a curve said, "Mmm, that is one handsome brother," to which her companion responded, "He a baaad motherfucker, baby—and you know what I'm talkin' 'bout."

L. A. took the mike in his hand as if it were the bat Hank Aaron used to break Babe Ruth's record. "Brother, is that song for me?" L. A. pointed down and to the right. "Or *Mick* the Knife here, my friend and comrade in the fight for high-speed trains and a military that's fair in this country?"

The sight and sound of the two friends trading riffs had been the buzz of the campaign during Mick's four days in New York. Acknowledging L. A.'s compliment, Mick gave the thumbs-up sign.

"I saw a man going round taking names, but when the returns started coming in, he blew the joint," L. A. resumed his riff.

The crowd roared again. It was Jubilation City.

"Folks, it looks like a long night, but we've had long nights. Long nights don't bother me. I came up here to thank you and tell you that to be for L. A. tonight is to be for New York. And to be for New York is to be for every New Yorker as an American, whether African American, Jewish, Hispanic, Irish, Italian, Polish, or," he paused and licked his lips, "white Anglo Saxon Protestant."

L. A. mopped his brow, the green polka dots of his handkerchief matching his tie. "Keep the faith, and we'll celebrate a great victory."

After L. A. made his way through knots of well-wishers, Mick approached him off to one side of the ballroom.

"Can I call you Senator?"

"Depends which votes are out. I've slipped a point or two."

I wondered. I knew that L. A.'s lead could melt away if Valeri had carried the expanse beyond the city convincingly. At one thirty, L. A. was up forty/thirty-six/eighteen with the city eighty-five percent counted, suburbs seventy-five percent, upstate sixty-five percent. An hour later, the city's votes were ninety-five percent in, suburbs eighty-five percent, upstate eighty percent, and he led by two. For an hour, the numbers held steady, and in one of our brief confabs, L. A. clapped Mick on the back and told him he had run almost even on Long Island. "It's those black Irish out there." Even tiny Shelter Island with its handful of Democratic votes handed him a thirteen-vote plurality. But few votes from New York City were left, and we watched L. A.'s lead melt, excruciatingly, to nothing, as the tally seesawed back and forth. By three in the morning, the city's precincts were all in and the suburbs were complete except for scattered absentees. With L. A. leading unofficially by just under one thousand votes, there were some twenty thousand votes to come in from towns northeast of Niagara Falls near Lake Ontario, villages between Potsdam and the Canadian border, as well as Plattsburgh near Lake Champlain and some tiny hamlets west of the Green Mountains.

While L. A. was talking to Mick, someone on his staff handed him a piece of paper. He looked down, then broke into a grin so wide his gold crown shone.

"Kiss my ass," he said. "Grandfather Jackson's watching over his grandson tonight."

In the ballroom's dim light he held out a paper on which the Catskill returns were scrawled in a hurried hand: Jackson: 303; Valeri: 230; Brodsky: 34; pro-life: 55. But the next hour revealed that Catskill was an aberration, not a bellwether. When they were heard from, the out-of-the-way places went forty-nine percent for Valeri, thirty-six percent Jackson, six percent for Brodsky, and nine percent for the pro-life candidate, whose name I could never remember. The unofficial final totals gave Valeri thirty-eight percent and change; Jackson: thirty-eight percent; Brodsky: sixteen percent; pro-life: seven percent. Valeri's plurality over Jackson was a hair under 2,500 votes, tantalizingly close, but not close enough for a recount to turn things around.

The foregoing was clear at four in the morning. Three hours earlier, L. A. had urged his supporters to go home, but they had followed the old adage Do as I say, not as I do. So when the votes were in and Valeri was declared the winner, there were still several hundred people in the ballroom drinking, talking, dancing, and hoping against hope. When Nick Valeri appeared on the overhead television and did a little stutter step of a jig while proclaiming, "New York, Yes!" Jackson's supporters booed and began a chant that grew in volume and intensity as L. A. made his way to the platform.

"Jackson, yes!" they shouted. "Valeri, no!"

L. A. pointed toward the edge of the stage, where the old jazzman mounted the stairs, golden trumpet in hand. The youngblood had stayed at the piano, and now splayed his fingers over the black keys, striking the familiar fortissimo chords of "When the Saints Go Marching Home." People began to clap and cry until the trumpet man held his hand up to the piano player. In the silence, he lifted his trumpet to L. A. in salute, then put the scarred horn to his lips and, without accompaniment, began to play the classic tune "What Did I Do to Be So Black and Blue?" The clapping continued, and a few of those listening sang the lyrics. When they reached "I'm white inside / But that don't help my case," most trailed off, humming the tune instead. And the trumpet player didn't pause, only accelerated the velocity and bite of the notes.

For a minute, L. A. stood there, nodding his head, hazel flecks burning in his brown eyes. Then he grabbed the mike, caught the beat, and waited until the offending lyrics came round again. This time, the man on trumpet slowed down and tilted his horn toward L. A.

L. A. shut his eyes as he began to sing.

"I'm *black* inside, and that *do* help my case."

Without prompting, the trumpet man deftly inserted a repeat, and everyone in the hall sang L. A.'s improvised line.

"I'm *black* inside, and that *do* help my case."

A hush fell over the ballroom. The battle-scarred trumpet glinted in the single spotlight, the soloist drew near to the end, and L. A. remained transfixed at the podium. As the trumpet blared out Louis Armstrong's restless, plaintive last question—"What did I do to be so black and blue?"—Jackson nodded to the trumpet player.

The old man responded by playing the last bar again, this time in a piercing, defiant blast. He held the last note an impossibly long time, allowing L. A. to breathe, then respond to the song's last brooding words in a tenor voice deep in the lower register.

"What did *I* do to be so black and blue?" L. A. sang the signature line. "Nothing at all," he answered in words all his own. "Not a blessed, solitary thing."

Although they'd never been a duo before, L. A. and the trumpet man finished at the same instant. Then L. A. stepped back and indicated the main man with a sweeping gesture.

"Let's hear it for Brother John."

The crowd had swelled. Hearing music coming from the ballroom, busboys and waiters had strolled over from the kitchen to check things out.

"Now, brothers and sisters, especially my wife," L. A. began.

Her disappointment palpable, Yvonne Jackson turned a proud face to her husband, then to the crowd. Tears shining on her cheeks, she hugged L. A. He took the rumpled polka dot handkerchief from the upper pocket of his suit jacket and wiped his forehead, passing the cloth quickly over his eyes.

"All we needed was a third of one percent—less than 2,500 votes," L. A. resumed. "But that's all right, we'll keep the faith and hold Nicholas Yale Valeri accountable."

There were boos and cheers from the crowd.

"We'll hold him accountable on the high-speed rail network and the national-service bill proposed by Brother Mick Whelan. Most of all, we'll keep faith with each other on what's been the heart and soul of my campaign, and that's our commitment to make this nation the 'more perfect Union' aspired to in the Preamble to the Constitution but not a reality in the United States of America."

L. A. paused, and the crowd leaned forward.

"In 1915, the people of Catskill tried to burn out my grandfather after seeing a movie celebrating the Klan. In this campaign, I went and met the citizens of Catskill face to face. Tonight, they voted to send my grandfather's grandson to the United States Senate. So keep the faith, brothers and sisters, keep the faith."

The cheers made fatigue palpable on Yvonne's face and began to bring ashes of roses to L. A.'s bronze complexion, but the Jacksons lingered. This was the hour of New Yorkers whose souls were wrapped up in L. A.'s run, so Mick and I hung back, waiting for a tactful moment to say good night.

"L. A.," Mick called as he sidestepped into the space between his friend and the knot of people a few feet away.

"My man," L. A. said, folding him into an embrace.

"I'm proud you're my friend," Mick said, his eyes glistening. "I wish I'd come up earlier and walked the Irish wards in Buffalo and Albany."

L. A.'s grin changed to a frown.

"I say, look, man, you're the one guy who came up and stayed."

Whelan slapped him on the back.

"We'll get them next time, L. A."

L. A. dropped his hands and raised them to grasp Mick's shoulders.

"No next time—this time. We got to pass those bills this time."

He grinned, and, after a moment, Mick did, too.

Back in the street where skyscrapers obscured the dawn's early light, Mick and I walked past dark blotches of homeless people huddled on the scraggly grass that in daylight had been the tip of the slender green finger of Central Park. Too tired to quit, we found a quiet bar and dulled our disappointment with an Irish whiskey before walking the six blocks to our hotel.

I didn't know it, but the midnight hour at L. A.'s election-night gathering in September of 1980 turned out to be the political apogee of Mick Whelan's years in the House. Two days later, Congress reconvened and things slid downhill fast. First, the Jackson bill on high-speed trains was tabled in the Commerce, Science, and Transportation Committee of the Senate on the grounds that further study was needed. Then word was passed to Whelan that the votes were not yet there to deliver the national-service bill from the Armed Services Committee to the full Senate. The message implied that patience on his part might incline the committee chairman to call for a vote immediately after the November elections. Mick bided his time, but on Election Day, the president went down to a smashing defeat. More incredibly, in the last-minute Reagan sweep, the

Senate changed from a fifty-eight to forty-one Democratic advantage to a fifty-three forty-six Republican majority. During the lame-duck session of Congress, by a one-vote margin, the Senate Armed Services Committee sent the Whelan bill to the floor, where, on a motion made by the reelected Republican senator from New York, it was referred back to committee. The vote was close, but in the end, too few moderates of either party were prepared to stick their necks out, particularly when the incoming White House made it clear that passing legislation before the swearing-in of the new Congress would be interpreted as a hostile gesture by the president-elect.

On the evening of the vote, L. A. Jackson, Mick Whelan, Ted March, Henry Hart, and I sat in the Senate Gallery. Afterward, we were too dispirited to do anything other than wish each other Merry Christmas and trudge into the night.

Of the five of us, L. A. Jackson made the gamest effort to keep his chin up.

"I say, look, man, I learned something in those upstate Dutch villages," he told us as we stood shivering in the snowy dark. "I mean, if you're a young cat in America and you're bad, you might not get anything for Christmas. But if you fuck up in the old country," he said, sneezing, "some dude crawls down the chimney—an Anti Klaus—puts coal in your stocking, and gives you an ass whipping."

He stopped to blow his nose.

"You know what they call that dude?"

He inhaled a few snowflakes. "Black Peter," he snorted. "If I'd had the balls, I would have dressed up as Black Peter tonight, gone around with a whip, and put coal on some of the desks in the Senate. Know what I'm talking about?"

He sneezed again.

"Yes, Louis, I do know," Henry Hart answered. "And come January, more than a few of those senators will wish they could exchange a whipping for some coal on their desks."

L. A. gave Hart a muffled clap on the back with his gloved hand and called out, "Later," with a snuffle as, heads down, we went separate ways in the fast-falling snow.

CHAPTER 13

I rubbed my eyes and closed the Whelan file. Outside the A-frame, snow was beginning to stick to the deck. I wouldn't be able to walk the beach before dark, so I flipped on the television. There I learned that Kiem would have blue skies on her flight from Florida to Oregon for Thanksgiving, and that the canvassing board in Miami-Dade County was poised to recount its presidential ballots.

The next day, I awoke anticipating my first sight of Kiem. Before I left for the airport, I remembered it was November 22 and switched on CNN in homage to Jack Kennedy, patron saint of close presidential elections. The dateline was still Miami, but the live shots showed a mob of Republicans—some of them congressional aides from my time on the Hill—pounding on the glass behind the table where the canvassing board sat in front of stacks of ballots.

A Riot of Suits, I thought, wishing I could tell Mick. Although he'd been clubbed during the police riot at the 1968 Democratic Convention, the Riot of the Suits was worse because it had stopped the counting. Shaken, I picked the 1980 folder off the coffee table and wrote Louis Armstrong Jackson's name on the tab alongside Mick's. When I went outside to brush last night's film of snow off the windshield, I imagined Kiem in the air, somewhere over the Mississippi. I knew I could not forget the past of Mick Whelan and L. A. Jackson any more than the Riot of the Suits would forever obscure the votes cast and miscast, counted and uncounted in Florida in the year 2000.

Twenty years before, the interval between the Ninety-sixth and Ninety-seventh Congress had been a hiatus of helplessness for Mick Whelan. When Henry Hart informed him that Charlie Armstead would return as chairman of the House Armed Services Committee, Mick saw the handwriting on the wall. He accepted the chairmanship of a feasibility task force on national service and authored a report admired by the few who read it. He told the press he felt like the little boy who held up a page of writing for his father to read. "You wrote it," his father said, "you read it." Whereupon the boy looked up and replied, "I can write, but I cannot read."

More and more, Whelan's life in Washington flowed according to clock and calendar, but out in Oregon, space held time hostage, so it was no accident that he returned home more often. So did Congressman John Phillips, and, before long, each man looked to the other for company on the long transcontinental flights. Turning the corner into his late sixties, Old Blackjack was fit and restless. He kept on rock climbing and chopping wood and disdained the sit-down life of the nation's capital in favor of the mountains and high desert of central Oregon.

Discovering that his younger colleague also had trouble sleeping on airplanes, Blackjack opened up to him.

"The damn House is like a run-down old homestead. I've lived in it too long to fix it up, but I'd rather not die there," he said on a delayed, bumpy flight to Washington from Portland, and added a wish to end his political life in the Senate. "You understand—no one will arrange things for me like I did for poor old Corbett."

"The old man is serious," Mick told me the morning after Blackjack spent the flight bending his ear about the 1982 Oregon primary.

My prolonged chortle drew a rebuke.

"Lesser men have become senators, Gabe."

206

"I'm laughing at you," I said. "Of course he's going to run. If you're Blackjack and there's one guy could take the Senate nomination away from you, he's the guy you confide in."

Mick straightened the knot in his tie.

"If old Jack wants a run for the Senate, let him have it."

On one cross-country flight, the plane was diverted to Dallas and delayed. Walking through the concourse to an ostentatious airport restaurant, the two congressmen passed booths advocating sterilization for gay men, the death sentence for doctors performing abortions, and Senator Edward Kennedy's arrest in the Mary Jo Kopechne case of a dozen years before. Once they had been seated—by a waitress in cowgirl boots who bent over twice to show off her Texas cleavage—Phillips moved his water glass back and forth in agitation.

"There wouldn't be a Constitution if those right-wing kooks had their way. I see them and think of my boy—the hell of a time he had in Vietnam." With an effort, Jack composed himself. "I said Vietnam, but damn it to hell, Michael, I gave him my name, expected him to outdo me, then never gave him the chance."

As his father talked, young Jack Phillips no longer appeared as the Technicolor apparition that Mick had seen through his sister's eyes. He now saw a young man turning from a caterpillar into a butterfly whose damaged wings bore markings of the bloody landscape he'd stumbled upon in Vietnam.

"What's young Jack up to, Judge?" Mick managed to ask.

"This and that."

The margaritas arrived, and Phillips looked away.

"My God," he told the waitress, "the rims on these glasses could pass for the salt lick on my ranch."

"You ranch in Texas, honey?" she bent low over the table.

"Far away, thank God," he said.

When she lingered, ostensibly to move his glass, Phillips drew the curtain. He waited until the young woman left, her silver spurs jangling behind her, then, once he had a clear track, like an engineer on those nineteenth-century trains with cowcatchers, he pulled the throttle all the way out to make up for lost time.

"Damn it to hell, I've gotten little Jack hired at I don't know how many federal agencies since his sister's death."

Mick imagined the vigorous old congressman broken up over his daughter, squiring his son to one of the better restaurants in Washington, where he sought to comfort and be comforted. On guard at first, young Jack slowly began to believe that he was consoling his father, only to see the other shoe come clunking down on the tablecloth from the chandelier as, with husky awkwardness, his father told him what he'd told him so many times: forget the goddamn son-of-a-bitch little Mex who had fallen on the grenade and saved his life and shape up.

The waitress returned, and with a flourish Mick associated with the Dallas Cowgirls, clattered down a huge tray on the empty table opposite.

"What are young Jack's interests?" Mick inquired matter-of-factly.

"One, the environment. Two, the environment. Three, the environment."

Mick put his hand on the older man's arm.

"Maybe I can help."

Phillips's eyes glistened. Clearly, he thought his son beyond reaching.

After a silent interval, Mick leaned over his barbequed ribs, closer to the judge.

"Extra money's appropriated for the seismic station on Mount Loowit. They'll hire at least one more field person . . . "

Phillips cut him off.

"Can't ask it of you," he growled. "Of course Jack would be interested. He wants to work *in* nature. What's your man's name? I'll call him as soon as I get back to Washington."

Suddenly hearing his own voice, Phillips knew he was blundering.

"Forgive me, Michael. I've set young Jack up so many times . . . ," his voice trailed off.

"Maybe if he got a job he wants on his own," Mick said, and paused. "Judge, let me have a crack."

Later, when Mick told the story, his voice shifted into the urgent key I remembered from his story of Rebecca Phillips.

"Young Jack's all yours," Judge Phillips responded, waving his wallet, but Mick's credit card was already on the table.

On the way back to the gate, the judge seemed almost happy, as if seeing the scrubbed young Texans peddle their scurrilous wares closed the door on the conversation he had just had about his son.

Back in Washington, Mick had me draft a letter to John D. Phillips Jr. informing him of an opening at the Mount Loowit Seismic Station. He also called Scott Gore, the man at the Interior Department in charge of Oregon.

Two days later at nine o'clock sharp, a young man in his mid-thirties bearing an eerie resemblance to the late Rebecca Phillips lounged uncomfortably in the outer office of Congressman Whelan's suite. Fearing his face might unsettle Mick, I tried to usher young Jack into my office.

"I'll wait for Congressman Whelan," he said, his eyes wheeling, as if uncertain whether to put up his dukes or flee in terror.

Afterward, Mick told me that young Phillips had looked over the photos on the walls first thing.

"Don't see a picture of Dad."

Mick smiled and waited.

"My sister worked in your first campaign," Jack said. "They never found her. The lake just sank in the mud."

His eyes were glazed and miserable, and Mick cursed the impulse that had made him rush into a situation avoided by even the most exalted angels. But he plunged ahead, more to get it over with than from any illusion of a breakthrough.

"Mr. Phillips, Scott Gore's having a hell of a time finding good people for the seismic station near Mount Loowit. Some find the work too hard, others are really after a desk job in Washington."

Young Phillips snorted in disgust.

"I worked my tail off in Mount Hood National Forest before going to Vietnam. Desk jobs since," he stopped. "But, Congressman, how did you find out about me? Did my f-father ask you?"

Whelan looked straight down at his visitor.

"Mr. Phillips, I wrote several letters," he said out of the corner of his mouth.

Young Phillips's face fell.

"I didn't . . . ," he stammered.

"Yes?" Mick pressed.

"I m-mean, thank you for thinking of me."

"Mr. Phillips, I was thinking of the Mount Loowit wilderness. You seemed a good fit. But your father, the congressman, has more national forest in his district than I do, and I have no intention of poaching. Please make that clear when you tell him about our conversation."

Mick stood up from behind his desk and put out his hand.

"Congressman Whelan," Phillips stayed in his chair, "my f-father tries to help without telling me. I've walked into situations before . . . They never w-work out."

Jack half stood now because he was afraid he would queer the whole thing if he did other than Mick expected. Mick started to reassure him, then thought better of it.

"Mr. Phillips, I'm a go-between for the environment and the government," he moved out from behind his desk.

They shook hands, Mick covering young Phillips's right hand with his left before breaking the clasp.

"Give my regards to . . . ," Mick paused. "Scott Gore," he said with the straightest of faces.

Within the week, Whelan received a short, obviously much-worked-over letter of thanks from John Phillips Jr. informing him that he was leaving the next day for the Mount Loowit Seismic Station. Late one afternoon, Blackjack Phillips came by unannounced and stood in the doorway until Mick emerged, and Blackjack thanked him for helping with a delicate constituent problem.

Then, as the judge-turned-congressman disappeared down the corridor, Whelan slapped me on the back.

"Must have been the prose in that letter you drafted."

Knowing Blackjack's struggles as a father led Mick to appreciate him more as a politician. Blackjack's lair was the center, and he was a stubborn, independent cuss. Perhaps because his district was conservative, he fought extremism from the right more fiercely than he did folly on the left. So it did not surprise me that when Phillips declared for the Senate nomination, Mick assigned me to liaison duty during the primary.

One soft spring night, as I drove from Vanport in shirtsleeves toward the high-desert country of the Metolius, clouds broke over the Santiam Pass unleashing a sudden blizzard. Hearing my tires spin angrily up the road to his compound, Blackjack appeared in parka and goggles behind the wheel of a jeep with a small plow attached to the front. He ordered me to twist my steering wheel this way and that until he cleared enough of a path to set me free. After the snow stopped, he tossed a pair of boots my way and took me on a walk. The compound had a bunkhouse and a small art studio formerly used by Rebecca. Not far from the churning river was a large A-frame made entirely of unfinished logs. The house looked like one of those cabins you run across in Mathew Brady's pre–Civil War photographs.

"They don't call these Lincoln logs for nothing," Jack boasted, schoolboy-pleased that on the outside all you saw were logs with a layer of bark still on them, whereas inside were lovely mosaics of laminated wood chips. They kept out the wind and rain, but also had the look of lacework patterns that had been cut out on dark winter nights while the woman of the house waited for her man.

Outside, the air was cold and windy enough for the breath to rise above our heads in frosty plumes. To the east and west, snow was falling, but overhead, a patch of dazzling sky appeared whose stars were dense as snowflakes.

"Here's the Metolius," Phillips told me, pointing to where I heard water rushing but saw only blackness. "I'll take you to the headwaters tomorrow!" he shouted. "Took Mick a couple of months ago in the dead of winter."

Ever since the job had come through for his son, Phillips never called Whelan anything but Mick.

"You'll have trouble believing all this water trickles out from a few rocks."

We walked upriver until there were absolutely no lights. Along the bank, the air was clear and cold, and gusts of wind blew white water from the rapids high enough that now and then it looked like fragments of the Milky Way tumbling between heaven and earth.

"That Mick Whelan's not as much of a city slicker as I thought," Phillips said. "I can't tell Mrs. Phillips, but it's an easier thing taking him around this part of the country than young Jack."

I didn't say anything. I felt a little embarrassed, and I envied Mick Whelan becoming the beneficiary of Blackjack's narrow, fast-running mountain stream of paternity. So when Mick called and asked me to stay in Oregon until the primary, a week away, I hemmed and hawed but inwardly jumped at the chance.

"On second thought . . . ," he said, teasing, and I was quick to remove any doubt. "The old man's half-ass sweet, taking me around to some of the spots he showed you."

"Maybe it's the Oregon connection," Mick said before giving me my marching orders. "I'm going to barnstorm the state with Jack while you run things at High Desert Central. He wants you to advance the rock-climbing event at Smith Rock. You know the drill: he and I take a puddle jumper from Portland to Redmond and afterward leave for Klamath Falls, then to Medford and Ashland for evening speeches."

I wrote off the rock-climbing stunt as an old man showing off, maybe dangerously, at one of the most difficult sites in the world. On the other hand, Jack's age was beginning to have legs as an issue, and I knew shots of him scaling a forbidding precipice would be a great photo op for the closing week of the campaign. So I kept things humming at headquarters—formerly an old saloon and hotel in Sisters—while Mick did Rotary and Lions Club luncheons and impromptu drop-in interviews with Phillips at lonely radio stations up and down the Willamette Valley. In Sisters, there was local history galore, but the echoes of gamblers, gunslingers, and madams paled before the snow-covered crags that loomed nearer and nearer. On blue days, driving from Bend to the Phillips compound on the Metolius, I passed a crooked line of mountains—Bachelor, Broken Top, Three Sisters, then sporadic, dazzling sightings of Mount Jefferson, until, on the last stretch along a black ribbon of road whose shoulders were red as blood, the snowy knuckles of Three-Fingered Jack were raised in warning.

The dedication of the national park at Smith Rock by the congressman from the immense Second District the Saturday before the election featured Olympic-class climbers, but Blackjack Phillips rappelled an almost-sheer cliff with the best of them. He persuaded Mick to put on a pair of crampons, then led him up a sloping twenty-foot rock open to conquest by anyone with moderate balance between the ages of seven and seventy. The Phillips-Whelan two-step led to a terrific Associated Press photo of candidate Phillips, who looked less than sixty and fit, showing (and literally throwing) the ropes to his much younger colleague. The camaraderie between the two men was contagious, and showcased Mick Whelan as proof of the older congressman's rapport with the younger, progressive wing of the Oregon Democratic Party.

Blackjack Phillips was certain to be the Democratic nominee, but if he mustered only fifty percent against two forgettable state senators, the press would decree him a weak candidate for the general election. If he broke fifty percent, say, fifty-three or higher, the commentariat would anoint him even money in the fall, and, at fifty-five percent, he might become the favorite. Don't ask me why, except that politics is a blood sport, its handicappers as ruthless and shady as racing touts or the wiry, gap-toothed characters who hold the stakes at cockfights. In the end, Blackjack received fifty-six percent and was promptly designated a slight favorite over the lackluster Republican incumbent.

The day after the election, the weather turned summertime hot, so the victory lunch at the Metolius compound was served at three long tables under a stand of ponderosa pines higher, Phillips insisted, than the cliffs at Smith Rock. When Mick and I arrived, Blackjack hugged Mick and gave me the tight-gripped, slightly formal handshake a rancher might tender his foreman.

Perhaps because of that, Mrs. Phillips, who was in the receiving line with her husband, went out of her way to greet me.

"Gabriel," she said, as she took my arm, "I will miss seeing you."

She made a little motion to take me aside, but the crush of people kept me in line, so she paid her compliment in public.

"Two of the ladies in the quilting store in Sisters loved your Washington stories. One of them even voted for Jack." She eyed her husband keenly. "They're strong peace people," she went on. "They were put out with Jack's support for the Vietnam War."

Behind me, I heard Phillips tell his wife to thank Mick.

"Congressman," she said, finally, "thank you for everything you did for Jack—and our family."

"For God's sake, Elizabeth," Jack butted in, "call him Mick. He's practically family."

"Yes, dear," she said, and shook Mick's hand a second time before the line pressed him forward.

"My friends, a toast," Phillips said as he took off his soft, white cowboy hat and waited for the conversation to subside along the immense board of food and drink. "Here's to Congressman Mick Whelan, my friend, friend to the Phillips family, and, someday . . . "

There were cheers and a few shouts of "Yahoo!" by cowpokes from the former Phillips' cattle ranch in Prineville.

"Be careful, Mick," young Jack Phillips warned, "Dad's got rope in the shed. He's liable to sucker you into climbing one of the pines."

After lunch, we left old Blackjack swapping barnyard stories with a couple of rancher friends, and Whelan went through the motions of looking for Mrs. Phillips, then told me we needed to make tracks if we were going to catch our plane.

"You're the boss," I said, and, waving, we left the three Jacks behind—father, son, and mountain, its three stubby fingers glistening in the distance.

After I raved about the Oregon high-desert country, Kate, Patrick, and I packed up and went off to hike the trails to various lava beds, waterfalls, and mountains in the vicinity of the Deschutes. Hoping to do Blackjack Phillips's campaign a spot of good, the last Saturday in August we met Mick and Sarah Whelan and their two young girls, Molly and Maud, in Sisters, where a herd of Kiger mustangs, a breed descended from the steeds of Spanish conquistadores, now in the wild on Steens Mountain, were about to strut their stuff in the annual Parade of Horses. Old Jack Phillips was grand marshall, set to ride down Main Street with his son, Jack, astride one of the mustangs. A little before noon, young Jack hurried up, too upset to give our families even perfunctory nods.

"Where's Dad?" he asked Mick, then me.

"Parades always start late," I told him.

"Not this one, guy," he said, his anxiety turning to anger.

He wore loose trousers that bore a resemblance to jungle fatigues from Vietnam.

"Has your mother seen him?" I asked.

When his hand veered uncomfortably close to my face, Mick stepped between us.

"Was he coming from home or somewhere else?"

"He was going to breakfast at that b-boys' ranch. I had to curry my horse—I told him I'd meet him."

"Where?"

"I told you—here."

"No," Mick said softly. "Where was the breakfast?"

"I told you—Redmond," he glowered. "Where is he, motherfuck?" he lunged at me.

I sidestepped, and Mick slid over in front of me.

"Gabe, call Mrs. Phillips. Jack and I will wait by the Redmond road."

As I hustled off to use the phone, a large man I recognized from Blackjack's congressional staff came out of Phillips for Senate headquarters. Perspiring heavily, he advanced at a clip halfway between a walk and a jog.

"Clay," I hailed him. "Where's the congressman?"

Clay had a blood feud with verbs. He spoke in nouns, throwing in an adjective when he got desperate.

"Smith Rock. Accident. Bad news. John Jr."

I stopped and put my hands on his shoulders. "Jack's over there with Congressman Whelan," I said as meaningfully as I could.

"Hospital," he said. "Bend."

Finally, I grasped that the panting aide's errand was to inform young

Jack that his father had had an accident. As I considered what to do, a deputy sheriff rushed up.

"Mr. Cheeks," he said to Clay, "Mrs. Phillips is on her way. You're not to tell young Mr. Phillips."

That struck me as less likely than a blizzard on this ninety-degree August day.

"Gabriel Bontempo, officer," I said. "I work for Congressman Whelan." I pointed to Mick and to young Jack, who was pawing the ground. "I think the congressman can keep him steady if you commandeer a trooper to drive them to the hospital."

The officer rubbed his hands on the polished-brass belt bisecting his paunch and looked down the street at Jack, who, flecks of foam at his mouth, stared at Mick like the villain in a silent movie.

"Got it. I'll take them," he told Cheeks, then turned to me. "Mr. Bontempo, I'll radio the officer driving Mrs. Phillips."

While I waited, Mick and the deputy eased young Jack into the state police cruiser. The officer did not turn on his flashing lights until he was past the knots of onlookers gathered for the parade, and I didn't hear the sound of the siren until he was beyond the line of mustangs waiting to gypsy their way down Main Street.

After he stopped for me, the state policeman driving Mrs. Phillips chafed to turn on his siren until I told him he might trigger a stampede.

"Roger," he said, while in the backseat Mrs. Phillips tried to talk to me over the squawk of the radio.

"Jack will be sorry to miss the parade. He was so looking forward to leading the mustangs, having young Jack beside him."

As the captain nosed past the posse of waiting horses, one of the mustangs broke away from the others and frisked along the side of the car. The young colt looked like no other horse I had ever seen. His mane was blonde-black and hung down the front of his head, accentuating the black pools of his eyes. The hair on his legs was so smooth, it seemed an extension of his skin, and, like his mane, went from blonde to black as if the two were a single color. As the patrol car slowed, his eyes caught mine, telling me the spine of his back would be freer and more comfortable than my seat belted perch in the squad car. I swear he winked as if he knew I would refuse his invitation to ride free.

"When he was a boy," Mrs. Phillips interrupted my reverie, "young Jack had a Kiger—a foal separated from his parents one winter. We named him Metolius. He got so he let me feed him, and his tongue felt like velvet," she said, then, realizing she was talking to a tenderfoot, smiled indulgently. "When you feed a horse, Gabriel, you hold your palm up so you won't get bitten. He rolls his tongue over your hand—some horses have sandpaper tongues, but not mustangs. Not Metolius."

She and I looked out our separate windows, she north toward Smith Rock, me south over fields that rolled toward Broken Top. Silently, I repeated the old nursery-rhyme line "Jack fell down and broke his crown."

Tumbleweeds drifted past, accelerated now and then by gusts of wind. As Awbrey Butte loomed close at the Bend city limits, the state policeman turned up his two-way radio.

"Car two," an official voice squawked.

"Roger," the captain said.

"Patient en route from Smith Rock admitted to emergency."

Reacting to the normalcy implied by the rasping message, Mrs. Phillips suddenly began to talk to me again. "The call from emergency rescue said Jack fell from a cliff. He never could resist showing off at Smith Rock."

At the door to the emergency room, the captain turned off the cruiser's siren and its flashing red and blue lights.

Inside, there was an aftermath of frantic activity. Nurses rushed around or stood off to one side, talking in hushed voices. A man in a leisure suit approached Mrs. Phillips, followed by a doctor in a freshly starched white coat.

"We're doing everything we can, Mrs. Phillips," the man in polyester said on that frequency of concern once reserved for undertakers and now the province of public-relations officers.

She ignored him.

"Doctor?"

Practicing a different, more humane craft, the doctor moved Mrs. Phillips into a corner away from the other man. In soft, sure tones, he explained what had happened.

Congressman Phillips had driven the back way from Double D Ranch, forded the creek, and met the boys at Smith Rock, where they refused to believe that "a white-haired fogy"—Jack's moniker for himself—could be a rock climber. Below the cliffs, the boys turned pale at the sheer face of the rocks, while Jack borrowed some of their equipment to show how it was done.

"He was careful," the doctor took pains to say. "The boys and their case manager agree on that, Mrs. Phillips."

When Jack mounted the neck of a face that looked prehistoric, he stood up straight.

"Man, this gringo's like one of those alien dudes on TV, only Wild West," riffed a Latino kid from Los Angeles, while below, a couple of the boys whistled when the sun turned Jack gold and he took off his soft, white ten-gallon hat, swept it up at the sun, and down toward the boys.

After a while, Jack motioned for quiet and prepared to come down. As he reached a bolt about ten feet from the top, the spike jiggled loose.

"Hey, watch out, amigo," Jack's LA admirer called out, but the bolt tore loose from the rock. The rope holding Jack went slack until his legs churned in thin air. In an instant that lasted for hours, he fell straight to the ground and lay there, crumpled. Fortunately, the case manager was trained in first aid and did not move the congressman. Instead, he sent one of the older boys for help, applied compresses from his kit, and waited.

Mrs. Phillips knotted and unknotted the fingers of her two hands while the doctor told her that her husband was going in and out of a coma. Only if he survived the first twelve hours could he be airlifted safely to the head-injury unit at Oregon Health and Sciences University Hospital in Portland.

In the elevator on the way to intensive care, he told Mrs. Phillips she was lucky that her son and Congressman Whelan had arrived so swiftly at the hospital.

"They were at his side as soon as we wheeled him in. You can never be sure in these cases," he added, wincing as he heard his last word. "The congressman hasn't been able to speak. But his right eye shows tremors and his hand has twit—" he caught himself, "has shown spasmodic motion. By the way, the congressman is right-handed, isn't he, Mrs. Phillips?"

"No, left-handed, very. Why, doctor?"

He pursed his lips.

"Knowing helps us keep closer track of the vital signs."

I could barely make out Judge Phillips through the tubes and machines hooked up on all sides of his body. Mick and young Jack stood on opposite sides of the bed, each holding one of his hands. Reaching for his mother while holding his father's fingers, young Jack shook loose one of the tubes.

"Careful," the doctor said.

To make up for the upset, Mick stroked the top of old Jack's hands, and when things settled down, he and I made the best transition we could to the door.

"Mrs. Phillips, I'm so sorry," Whelan said.

When we were alone in the hallway, Mick spoke quietly.

"Damned if the case manager wasn't Martin Fitch. He heard the crack when Jack hit the ground."

In the meantime, young Jack and Mrs. Phillips stayed with the congressman. Spooked at being alone with his father when the specialist took his mother down the hall for a conference, Jack asked him to send Mick in. Manic by now, young Jack began to talk to his father about his Senate campaign, and the judge briefly blinked out of his coma. His left eye flashed and three of his fingers jerked. Still dressed for the parade, young Jack wore a T-shirt with "Phillips for Senator" in huge black letters. Suddenly, he stopped pawing the floor and leaned over in front of his father's face, pulling on the shirt so that "Senator" stretched tight before the old man's eyes.

"You're the next s-senator, Dad."

At that moment, Mick believed the congressman's eye became mottled for the first time. But young Jack could not stop. Mick's quiet pleading seemed to make him more intense. After a couple of his son's exhortations, sparks flickered in his father's eye, and his fingers sought the word *senator* on his son's chest. Twice, he touched the letters, and with an effort moved his crooked fingers in Mick's direction. At first, young Jack was buoyed by his father's animation, then he broke down sobbing.

"No!" he cried in a hoarse, desolate voice. "Dad, d-don't die."

"Jack," Mick said, coming around the bed to embrace the son, "your father's delirious, but there's vitality—that's a good sign."

At that point, Mick pushed the button for a doctor or nurse, and Mrs. Phillips came in. Surprised to see Mick Whelan, she went about comforting her son and resumed her vigil on the near side of her husband's bed.

Once Mick was in the hall, the trauma specialist told us that Congressman Phillips's vital signs were beginning to fluctuate wildly. His heart was fibrillating at an alarming rate. Hours passed and there was no improvement. Instead, John Phillips slipped deeper into the coma, and his heart beat more and more erratically. At midnight, the family minister was summoned, and, an hour later, while his wife and son held tightly to his hands and each other's, Jack's heart beat for the last time.

After speaking to the minister, Mick and I left notes for Mrs. Phillips and Jack expressing our sympathy and our readiness to do anything we could.

The next morning, the judge's lawyer telephoned.

"Congressman Whelan, Thomas Burns. The family wishes me to thank you for all you've done."

After clearing his throat, he continued, crustily.

"I've been Jack Phillips's lawyer since before he became a judge more than thirty-five years ago. Now, you were his friend, so you know he was a loveable old bastard. But he could be cantankerous—I wager you know that."

He stopped, as if waiting for protest at the other end of the line, but Mick was silent.

"Now, the family has decided to have a strictly private burial service— no press or politicians, no one except family and a few of his and Elizabeth's oldest friends."

"Certainly," Mick said.

"Well, now, Congressman Whelan, you know that's not why I'm calling at seven thirty in the morning," the old lawyer harrumphed.

Again, Mick kept quiet.

"I'm calling because the old man changed his will right after he won the Senate nomination—I told him to stay in the House, he'd been content there all these years, but that's neither here nor there. He knew there'd be some public ceremony, but he didn't want it controlled by politicians he considered fools. So he specified what he wanted in black and white: three speakers at his memorial service—he wants it in the legislative chamber in Salem. You're to be the last speaker. Young Jack, the second, if he chooses— what the old man meant is if Junior can stand on his feet long enough to string five minutes' worth of sentences together. That's neither here nor there. The governor speaks first—if Jack hadn't respected protocol, that double-crossing son of a bitch wouldn't get within ten miles of him."

Mick started to speak, but Burns cut him off.

"I assume you'll speak. Jack knew men. I wager he didn't guess wrong in your case."

"I'd like to. It's an honor," Mick said. "How is Mrs. Phillips?"

"She got your note and your man's. Bowtimely? That his name? Said to thank him for her."

The night before the funeral, camping on the Deschutes River, we told the children that Congressman Phillips's body would lay in a silver coffin in a big round room, surrounded by marble statues.

"Is dying what happens to an animal?" Patrick asked, remembering the yearling white-tailed buck with the beginnings of antlers he'd seen Mick and me move from the middle of Route 20 outside Sisters.

"Yes and no," we told him, taking turns preparing the children for the sight of the dead man lying in state in an open casket.

"People's families dress them up before they go back into the ground like the animals," Kate said.

"Animal man," piped up Patrick.

"Congressman Phillips to you, Mister." I rolled my eyes while Mick gave each of the kids a last marshmallow before we tucked them into their sleeping bags.

The next morning, the governor sent a limousine to take the Whelan and Bontempo families to Salem. The giant-finned fifties' Cadillac lifted Patrick and Molly and Maud Whelan into seventh heaven as they crashed like kamikaze pilots against the deep, soft black leather cushions. In Salem, the limousine driver freshened his morning clothes with spray from a water bottle and led the seven of us up the steps to the rotunda, where we took places at the end of the line filing past the open casket. Dressed in black, on the edge of fatigue, Mrs. Phillips stood beside her son, whose pinwheel eyes spun wildly until he caught sight of Mick and hugged him with sobs that brought tears to Mick's eyes. Otherwise, there were handshakes and tentative pats on the arm. Mrs. Phillips twice told Kate how much she appreciated my good work in her late husband's campaign, while Mick and Sarah, Maud and Molly, Kate and Patrick clustered around young Jack. Passing the time of day with Mrs. Phillips, I felt the line of people exert an invisible pressure from behind. As one, the four Whelans slowly moved past the casket where John Phillips's body lay dressed in one of the dark-blue pinstripe suits he favored along with a tie the shade of burnt sienna his skin sometimes seemed to absorb from the earth of the high desert that he loved. As I took a last look, little Maud Whelan dropped Sarah's hand and scooted back to the casket. I patted her head and tried to take her hand. Shaking me off, her round face shiny and red and very serious, she looked down at the dead man, pointed her finger at his face, and said in an awed voice of sudden revelation, "Aahmull mahn!" We pretended not to hear until Mick came up and took her hand, walking her forward while Mrs. Phillips took an involuntary step back.

Precisely at noon, the governor, Mick, and old Jack's third-grade teacher, a tiny octogenarian named Mrs. Badger, emerged from the supreme court chambers and took their places on either side of the rostrum while the boys' choir from the Double D Ranch sang a piano-backed jazz rendition of "Amazing Grace."

The governor's speech was mercifully brief. He compared the late judge and congressman with the bronze statue of the mythical Oregon frontiersman atop the golden dome of the state capitol, associating Phillips with the push to the Pacific despite the dead man's love for the mountains and high-desert country of the interior. He also elevated him above partisanship, which must have been news to those among the mourners who bore scars of Blackjack's reputation as a take-no-prisoners political infighter.

When her turn came, Mrs. Badger noted the presence of the boys from the Double D. "It is fitting that Jack's last hours on Earth were spent with you," she said, looking down at them. "Whether as Master Phillips, never quite well-behaved enough to be a third-grade monitor, or a judge tempering justice with mercy to boys in trouble, or a congressman passing laws in our nation's capital, the boy in Jack never left him."

She told of his love for the Metolius wilderness. "His favorite tree was the ponderosa pine." But her voice had small range and little carry, so, in spite of the affecting simplicity of what she was saying, before long, there was the rustling of programs. With a nod to Mrs. Phillips and blowing a kiss in the direction of young Jack, whose place she had taken at the last minute, she placed a spray of vivid green needles from a ponderosa on the casket and took her seat, unobtrusively, on key, as she had taught generations of third-graders to do after their party pieces at Prineville Elementary School.

Mick looked down at the outline he'd scribbled on a single folded sheet of congressional stationery and then out at the crowd, searching for a point of reference. At first, his voice sounded in need of a tuning fork. "The Honorable John Phillips; Master Jack Phillips, the little boy; the Jack Phillips I knew," he began, and I followed his eyes as he scanned the rows of faces. His wife, Sarah, his girls, Molly and Maud, and his friends Kate, Patrick, and I were his safe harbor, but I could tell he was seeking contact beyond us in the open sea. He lingered over Mrs. Phillips and young Jack. Sensing his gaze, Elizabeth Phillips looked down at her feet, but Jack's eyes were those of a zealot determined to lock Mick into their orbit. Finally, Mick's gaze came to rest on the dark blur of Martin and Jonas Fitch at the rear of the chamber.

"With his restless walk, his weathered face, and spray of white hair, Jack reminded me of a sturdy ponderosa pine," Mick said, picking up where Mrs. Badger left off, his voice now full and natural. "Like the ponderosa, he was a sheltering force. Like the ponderosa, Jack was native to Oregon. Born and raised in Prineville, he met and married his wife, Elizabeth, in Sisters, sired and raised his son and daughter in a grove of ponderosas along the Metolius. Like the landlocked kokanee salmon of the Metolius, he was a man of the interior."

As he spoke, Mick's finger moved in a downward arc until Mrs. Phillips and young Jack were in its path. Mrs. Phillips kept time by fanning herself with her program. Rigid beside her, fixed on Mick's every word and gesture, if the spell held, young Jack looked like he'd make it through the service. Like Mrs. Badger, Mick praised Jack's connection with the boys at the Double D Ranch, and to show how far Jack had moved beyond the insularity of old provincial Oregon, he wove Martin and Jonas Fitch into his eulogy.

"When I was a young congressman, Jack Phillips took the time to show me the ropes. 'Young man,' he told me when I complained about the way things were, 'what goes around comes around.' Standing in this chamber today, I see the young Double D caseworker who comforted Jack when he fell from Smith Rock; without him, the doctors say Jack wouldn't have made it to the hospital to say good-bye to his wife and son."

Mick had hit his stride. From the quick gesture of his hand, I could tell his page of notes had become a distraction.

"That young man, Martin Fitch, is here with his father, Jonas, who came to Vanport City from Oklahoma to build Liberty ships. Half a dozen years ago, Jack Phillips made common cause with a delegation from Vanport before a congressional committee considering federal aid. I remember Jack and Jonas, one a native Oregonian, well known, well off, and white; the other a settler, a working man, unknown, and black. Although he had a reputation as a congressman who was frugal with taxpayers' money, Jack Phillips listened to the arguments and went against the grain of Oregon's rural-urban split. He brought along enough skeptical colleagues to pass the appropriation, and this year the Fitches and many others in Oregon's cities reciprocated Jack's trust by supporting him for the Senate.

"Yes, Jack Phillips was a man of politics. But late in his life, I knew him as a private person, a whole man. In the last week of May, he took me all over the state. He liked to campaign, to meet people, to tell stories between stops, to laugh at human foibles—including his own. In Roseburg, he arrived late for a speech because he took me to the courthouse and showed me the ballot box he claimed some feuding Democrats had stuffed for Republican Abraham Lincoln during Oregon's first presidential election, in 1860."

Mick looked out at his two girls and Patrick. They were looking up at him beaming, with only an occasional fidget.

"The man and the boy in Jack had two wishes that tell us about the human being we mourn. The man wanted to be a senator from Oregon; the boy wanted to carve his initials in the same Senate desk that that other little boy—the late Wayne Morse—carved his in years ago. That won't happen, but Jack Phillips did carve his initials in our hearts."

Mick stopped. I don't think he saw faces anymore. Now he was breathing mountain air.

"Jack Phillips was a man who did good for his state and his country. He was a man you respected, a man you admired. And there is something else. I grew close to Jack as a politician but closer as his friend at the end of his life," Mick's voice quavered a little as he finished. "So I know from experience that Jack Phillips was also a man you could love."

As Mick took his place between the governor and Mrs. Badger, a small organ filled the crowded chamber with chords of the formidable, abiding Lutheran hymn "Ein Feste Burg." People stood, listening, some eyes dry, others wet.

As mourners surrounded Mrs. Phillips, young Jack disengaged and rushed up to the platform, forgetting to shake hands with the governor and give Mrs. Badger a kiss on the cheek. Turning to Mick, his eyes were steady, his bearing manly and untroubled for once, as he looked straight at Whelan.

"I'm proud of you, and my father would have been proud."

Then his eyes began to wheel out of orbit.

"You know what he wanted. You were there. Y-you saw him."

Mick looked puzzled for a moment, then he understood.

"Jack," he said, "No, Jack."

Mick hugged him a long time until a crush of people surrounded them, expressing an awkward mix of congratulations and condolences. My job was to ease Whelan out by inches and feet, like an old advance man who seizes every opportunity to gain a bit of ground. Mick would want to give Sarah and his two girls their due, and I needed to steer him to Jonas and Martin Fitch. But I needn't have worried. The Fitches were waiting on the steps of the capitol, a strange, knowing look on Jonas's face.

"Mick Whelan, listening to you brought back that morning under the volcano."

I felt a tug on my sleeve. When I looked around, the undertaker motioned that the procession of cars was ready to leave.

"Congressman," I said to Mick, but he ignored me and leaned over to Jonas. All I heard was a last scrap of words.

"About time you let us change that title of yours," Jonas said, Martin grinning beside him.

On the way back over the mountains, everyone dozed or fell so deeply into reverie that I was startled when the driver slowed and turned left off Route 20 down the thinly paved narrow road that led through Camp Sherman toward the Phillips compound.

I tapped Mick on the shoulder.

"What's with old sport?" I said, nodding at the driver.

Mick considered.

"Cars ahead and cars behind," he said. "We'll have to sort it out when we get there."

Sarah looked at Kate and saw that she, too, caught the drift.

"Surely, Mick, after your eulogy, not to mention Kate and I dressing up the children and taking a day out to pay our respects, surely, we're welcome at the burial."

"It's outrageous if we're not," Kate agreed.

I looked uncomfortably from one woman to the other.

"We'll sort it out," Mick answered flatly. "I'll sort it out."

The undertaker had forgotten to tell our driver that his passengers were not invited to the private service. We were standing around awkwardly in a clearing when lawyer Burns appeared and folded us into his commodious arms.

"Mistake," he said. "Glad you're here. After that eulogy, I want you here. Jack's glad you're here—both Jacks."

The burial consisted of prayers from the Anglican *Book of the Dead* read by the family's ecumenical Congregational minister who favored the prose of Elizabethan England along with the music of Bach. Off to one side of the family cemetery were gravestones bearing spare inscriptions, such as Abraham Phillips, Died of the Fever, Spring, 1853; Young Josiah, Died of Rattlesnake Bite, July 4, 1877; and Beloved Ruth, Died in Childbirth, January 23, 1899.

Close by the Metolius, in one of the plots reserved for the immediate family, John D. "Jack" Phillips was laid to rest. Nearby, I noticed a plaque that read, simply, In Memory of Rebecca Ruth Phillips, Beloved Daughter and Sister, June 1, 1948–May 17, 1974.

After the service, I obeyed Mick's signal and our two families declined the invitation to stay for cold cuts and cider. We paid our respects a last time to Mrs. Phillips and young Jack.

The undertaker's driver had started to pull out into the reddish dirt road when Mrs. Phillips, now in her apron, rushed up and handed a bulging napkin of cookies through the rolled-down rear window.

"You can't expect those children to behave forever," she said to Sarah and Kate, a smile breaking through the shadows on her face. "I know," she added, looking at Mick, "I've raised two."

Chapter 14

Driving Kate and Patrick to the Portland Airport the next day, I explained the whys and wherefores of choosing a new candidate for the United States Senate. Under Oregon law, when a candidate nominated in a statewide primary dies within ten weeks of the general election, the chair and vice chair in the state's thirty-six counties choose a replacement, each county casting a percentage of the vote proportionate to its number of registered Democrats. Quickly tiring of my technical prattle, Kate flipped on the radio to see if we were far enough out of the mountains to bring in a station. Soon the battle between static and language tilted in favor of a soft-rock station in Vanport whose deejay interrupted his retrospective on the Beatles to read a news bulletin.

"Is Congressman Michael J. Whelan of Vanport the Sergeant Pepper of this political season?"

Trying to improve the reception, Kate lost it entirely.

Coming to the rescue, I wet my fingers and played with the knob like a safecracker.

"Tomorrow's *Vanport Statesman* will carry an exclusive interview with the son of deceased congressman John D. Phillips revealing his father's deathbed choice of Whelan to succeed him as the Democratic candidate for the United States Senate seat held by incumbent Republican—"

Suddenly, power lines in a grid stretching as far as the eye could see drowned the voice in static. This time, Kate's touch fought the feedback until the buttery tones of the deejay came back in over the noise.

"In an intriguing footnote, John Phillips Jr., who holds a federal post in Congressman Whelan's district, told reporter Harry Hacker that the Vanport lawmaker was present in the intensive-care unit when Congressman Phillips signaled his endorsement."

"Fucking media!" I yelled.

Kate put two fingers over my mouth.

"A spokesperson in Whelan's Vanport office declined comment. In the meantime, the two state senators defeated by Congressman Phillips in the primary, Edith Meyers of Portland and Brot Warren of Medford, told KVPT radio that they intend to step up efforts to secure the nomination at the Democratic State Central Committee's meeting in Eugene next weekend."

Hand on the dial, I heard John Lennon's voice sigh, "I read the news today, oh, boy . . . ," then I snapped off the switch.

"Gabe," Kate threw down the gauntlet of exasperation, "when were you planning on telling me?"

"When someone told *me*, Kate."

I survived as Whelan's top gun by sometimes holding back how I felt as well as what I knew, but in this case my wife touched some not-entirely-atrophied nerve. When I made a funny face, she looked at me as if I had just offered to sell her the Brooklyn Bridge. Her eyes flared, and she turned around toward the backseat and pulled Patrick's seat belt tighter.

"In the chaos, Mick didn't tell me the whole story." But the more I said, the deeper I sank into quicksand, and the sensation numbing my thighs told me that if Kate is suspicious, the other candidates and the press would flay Mick alive. I imagined rumors flying from one county chair to another about Whelan working old-man Phillips while he was still warm, and young Jack when the body was cold. To make amends, I reached over and covered my wife's hand with mine.

"Better call that reporter," she said.

Ahead, garish billboards advertising car rentals, fast-food joints, and cheap motels replaced the stands of Douglas fir. In front of me, planes ascended and descended, while in the rearview mirror, I saw Patrick trace the path of a jetliner on the car window with his finger, and in the distance, Mount Hood loomed like the shorn wing of a jumbo jet, its silver tip glinting in the sun. Loowit, too, looked dusted by an early snow. Even from forty miles away, its collapsed west face remained a tragic mask.

At the airport, I double-parked, left the motor running, and lugged the suitcases to the baggage stand. As I leaned over to kiss Patrick good-bye, he kicked up a fuss about his travel bear, insisting it should ride on his lap. That problem solved, I hugged my wife, my son, his battered brown bear, and watched them disappear through the revolving glass doors before I hopped back into the car and drove to Whelan's district office, where the staffers were buzzing around referring to "the senator."

"Cut that out," I ordered, and they scattered like birds seeing an advancing cat. I whipped through the messages on Mick's desk until I found one with Harry Hacker's name on it. Wary of the hired help, I picked up the phone. "Harry? Gabe Bontempo here."

"I left word for the congressman," he said in a monotone.

Harry was old school—a hard drinker who relied on his notes and a built-in shit detector to do duty for a tape recorder. People liked the taut style he cribbed from Hemingway and Stephen Crane with twists of syncopation from the days when he played a mean honky-tonk piano. If you gave him a false lead, Harry would hunt you down as mercilessly as a backwoods-Kentucky sheriff tracking a moonshiner who'd welshed on a payoff.

"Got time for a drink at The Blue Hour?" I asked.

"Seven sharp," he replied.

Iceberg Harry, I thought. Seeing the tip of his agenda, I sensed the bulk of it looming underwater. At first, in 1974, he had dismissed Mick Whelan as an arrogant kid who cut his eyeteeth in Gene McCarthy's campaign and thought he could skip the state legislature and run for Congress right out of the chute. Mick's upset victory over Corbett made Harry sit up and take notice. From then on, he'd been fair—and then some. But Hacker was a climb-the-greasy-pole guy, and I worried that Mick falling into the Senate seat would revive the sense of privilege he'd resented in the first place. In any case, Harry's barbs were better directed at me in person than Whelan in print, so I caught the ferry to York Island.

At The Blue Hour, Harry was sitting in the shadows. I no sooner eased onto the neighboring stool than the bartender set down two double Jameson's.

"Compliments of the house?" I asked, recognizing the same lean, athletic man with the elegant pencil-thin gray moustache who sang tenor in the choir at Ship of Zion.

"This man's house, Mr. Bontempo," he said, pointing at Harry.

"Irish, in honor of the luck of the Irish," Harry muttered, clinking his glass against mine. "So, your boy's off floating the Deschutes with a fishing pole and a straw hat."

"Drop-dead whiskey," I said.

"It's from the stream that runs past Lord Blarney's castle."

Just to the left of an enormous mirror behind the bar, French doors opened on the Columbia. A long barge slid toward us along the river. At the last minute, the man in the pilothouse turned the wheel and angled the flatboat west toward the Vancouver side of the island.

"Driving over, I heard a radio report quoting you," I said, my teeth shivering from a swallow of Irish.

Harry stirred his drink. "So?"

"Something about old Jack anointing Whelan from the hospital."

The waves churned up by the barge disappeared from the surface of the river leaving shimmers of heat turning orange in the last glare of sun.

"There's a rule," Harry said, motioning to the bartender, "that no one gets more than one free ride in politics."

"Two more?" the bartender asked before he took our empties.

In the nick of time, I remembered his name. "Horace," I said, "Harry thinks Mick Whelan got his seat in Congress handed to him."

Horace held the two glasses by the thumb and forefinger of one hand and with his other wiped the counter like he was shining his Sunday shoes. "No sir, Mr. Hacker," he said. "You must be thinking of that Corbett fellow. He was Judge Phillips's horse, but Mick Whelan came up on the outside and nosed him out down the stretch."

Horace started down the bar, then turned around.

"Mick Whelan had help from lots of us at Ship of Zion back then. I reckon you can put it in your paper that we'll be with him again."

Horace's words stopped Harry's line of attack so cold, I was able to seize the reins of the conversation.

"Harry, I'll see to it you're first in line for an interview as soon as Whelan gets back."

The second round arrived, singles this time, and Harry looked at his glass distastefully before taking the first belt. "I knew your boy was running when I heard his eulogy for old Blackjack."

My job was to humor Harry. I was ahead on points, but I needed to get away before he turned our conversation into a story.

"Don't play dumb, Bontempo," he needled me, and in one swallow drained his tumbler of Irish. "Whelan went to the edge with that stuff about Blackjack wanting to carve his initials in Wayne Morse's desk."

He held up his glass. "Two for the road, Horace."

Horace glanced at me. I nodded.

"And he had one foot dangling in the air with that last line—'a man you could love'—or was it loathe?"

Horace placed two more singles on the bar, mine directly in front of me, Harry's more than an arm's length away.

Seeing a dim reflection of my face and my no-longer-bushy, sandy hair in the whiskey glass, I could not let Harry's taunts go and still use a mirror when I shaved.

"So we're all shits, and politicians the biggest shits of all?" I paused for a sip of whiskey, saw my eyes dimly reflected in the bottom of the glass, and kept going. "Damn it, Harry, Whelan was giving a eulogy. Did Blackjack Phillips have faults? You bet, but Mick meant what he said—by the end, the old man had more than his share of crust and courage."

Harry rolled his index finger around his glass and carried on as if I hadn't spoken.

"You better be glad Whelan said 'could' or I'd have to crucify him after Junior's little deathbed revelation."

He tossed off his drink and snapped his fingers. "Horace!" he shouted after a few seconds.

I put down a ten and a five.

"What's that for?"

"My half."

"Drinks, yes. Tip, no," he laughed, pushing the five back at me. "But remember what I said."

Outside the bistro, Harry turned left toward the independent bookstore that specialized in mystery novels.

"Tell himself he'll get a fair shake; tell him it was the 'could' that did it."

Harry bowed with vaudevillian flourish, then departed.

On the flight to Bend, I looked over the packet prepared by the Whelan staff to make sure there was an enlarged map of Oregon color-coded according to county population along with thumbnail biographies of every chair and vice chair. While the single-engine prop plane rock and rolled through a sudden squall, I made illegible notes of combinations that would give Mick enough votes for the nomination. In his district, he could count on eighty percent. By mending a fence or two, he could make it unanimous. Properly touched, the chairs in Blackjack's Second District would support him. Even if the Wild West characters saw him as a city slicker, he had been a friend of their friend. I conceded southern Oregon to the local state senator on the first ballot but scrawled "get toehold in Coos County" on my legal pad. Senator Warren's backers knew he couldn't win, they simply wanted Democrats in Portland to hear the blood call of the Fourth District. If it came down to Edith Meyers or Whelan, I was sure they would go with Mick. But if the feminists supporting Meyers got a whiff of a deal, they could retaliate by sitting out the election, or even supporting the pro-choice Republican. To win cleanly and decisively, Mick needed half the votes in Portland's Multnomah County and the metropolitan suburban counties of Washington and Clackamas. In either scenario, he had to have Eugene's Lane County, whose block of Democrats was the second largest in the state.

Checking into the Whitewater Motel, I found a message from Mick inviting me for a drink as soon as his girls were bedded down. Once settled in my room, I sat down at a small round table overlooking the river. As the willow trees tacked in the evening breeze, I sketched out a schedule for the next week, and a plan. Hearing Mick's knock, I put on my jacket, tucked the pad in a folder, and followed him outside. At the Whelans' suite, Sarah had her feet up on a nondescript couch and was leafing through a glossy coffee-table book whose cover was a luminous photograph taken at sunset with Smith Rock in the foreground and the Three Sisters in the distance.

"You don't look like the wife of a man mulling a run for the Senate," I said as she held out her cheek to be kissed.

"Maybe the decision's made," she said with the rapier thrust of a wife who knew her husband's political plans ahead of his staff.

"Young Jack's called a couple of times," Mick said, riffling through the pink squares of messages. He poured three Irish whiskeys into water glasses and used their plastic tops as coasters. "What else?"

I told him and Sarah about my meeting with Harry Hacker, and walked them through the selection process. "Your two opponents are ripe to cancel each other out, but you've got to announce soon."

"If he's running," Sarah said, her smile as cool and transparent as the shivers of ice in a dry martini.

"I just work here," I joked.

After almost a decade, her oblique sallies still took me by surprise. Now, she raised her water glass of Irish whiskey and held it out for me to clink. "To the almost unflappable Gabriel."

"The announcement's a tricky call," I said.

Mick and Sarah smiled at each other.

"Sarah's found another option."

"No, Gabe." She stretched her stocking feet across the entire length of the heavy oak coffee table. "A little old lady found me while we were rafting. Her sister's the Deschutes County chair. Next thing we know, Isabel O'Day called Mick, begging him to speak at her Labor Day picnic on the Bend riverfront."

Mick uncapped the whiskey bottle and dripped a little more into each of our glasses. Sarah waited until our attention was on her, not the whiskey.

"Labor Day weekend's a terrible time for a press conference. Why not declare in your talk?"

"Gabe?" Mick asked. "Can you hold off the press with a release that says I'll be speaking at the Deschutes County picnic?"

"Have it come from Mrs. O'Day," I said.

"Perfect," the Whelans said at the same time.

"As long as the release goes out tomorrow morning," I cautioned. "You can't play it cute. I'll start returning calls in the afternoon, tell reporters you're wrapping up your vacation on Sunday and you'll do interviews after the picnic."

"Sweet," Sarah said, taking a sip of whiskey.

"Young Jack?" Mick inquired.

I looked at the bottle of Irish, then my watch.

"Arm's length," I advised. "The Forest Service operator's gone for the

237

weekend—so call Jack. The day after Labor Day, I'll tell him you couldn't get through. Till then, he's missing in action."

I moved my glass to a far corner of the coffee table and reached for my folder.

"One other thing, Mick. To keep my reputation in show business, I'd like to give Harry Hacker a heads-up."

Before I finished, Sarah was on her feet.

"I'm going to leave you two," she said. "Those girls have their father's metabolism. They'll have me up before six."

Mick picked up my empty glass, went to the sink in the kitchenette, rinsed it out along with his, and put the glasses down on the coffee table.

"Let's have one more, Gabe." He poured two goodly drinks and put them down on the coffee table.

I rolled the whiskey around in the glass and drank.

"What do you think?" Mick asked.

I picked up my folder and detached several sheets of paper clipped to the yellow pad.

"I've got poop on the various county chairs and vice chairs and the percentage of votes for each county."

"I mean, what do you think of me running for the Senate?"

My face colored.

"There's nobody better," I said quickly. "You won't get the nomination free, but next weekend's meeting is as close as it gets. No one can beat you but you."

Mick gathered up the notes I'd given him. "Bedtime reading," he said before telling me to stay in Bend, take soundings in as many counties as I could, and set up calls to Democratic warhorses back in Washington.

"Bottoms up," he said, rising from the couch. "I'll bring your notes to Lost Lake tomorrow."

"Mick, if I were you, I'd check out the fossil beds over at Painted Hills."

We said good night. The traveling and the Irish had caught up with me, so when the bedside telephone jangled at quarter of seven, I felt like I had just fallen asleep.

"Gabe," a voice as familiar as my own said. "Can you drag yourself to the coffee shop?"

"Sure, Mick. Seven thirty okay?"

"I was thinking seven—before you start making calls to the East."

"Yeah, I'll be the guy with his shirttail out."

Mick sat at a window table, oblivious to the river foaming over a boulder so weathered and worn that it had more perforations than one of those oval specialty sponges. Through his reading glasses, he was studying the page of Oregon election law that I had clipped to the folder. He looked up only after I coughed a before-coffee smoker's cough.

"Hearing you reminds me to quit those damn little cigars," he said as I pulled up a chair.

He cleared away the notes, maps, and biographies I'd given him the night before and slid my empty coffee cup back where it had been in the first place.

"Change of plans, Bontempo."

The black coffee that arrived was hot, but that wasn't why I spilled my first mouthful over the saucer.

"Easy," Mick handed me his napkin. "Reading your memo told me we're approaching this the wrong way."

By now, my coffee was flowing where it was supposed to.

"The vacancy is an emergency that state law turns over to the county chairs and vice chairs. They sort it out and pick someone, like the founders intended with the Electoral College."

"Where you going, Mick?" I asked, stirring my coffee to mask my frustration at his academic turn of mind.

"I shouldn't declare my candidacy—no one should. And I won't," he said, reading my mind. "But I'll make sure the chairs and vice chairs know I'm available."

Our asparagus and Tillamook cheddar cheese omelets arrived, presented by a waitress who lingered and fussed over our plates long enough to make me suspect she was listening for gossip to carry back to the kitchen. Mick slowed down but did not change the subject or fall silent, as was the custom in Washington. Out of habit, I jumped in at the first pause to cover him with small talk.

"It's okay," he told me when she was out of earshot. "In these parts, waitresses have better things to do than listen in, and they resent being treated like informers."

He stopped long enough to eat a few forkfuls of omelet.

"If the state committee decides to pick me, I'll accept as long as there's a united party behind me."

"Makes sense," I said as the waitress returned and refilled our coffee cups. "What can I do?"

Mick smiled at the waitress.

"Thanks for making the second cup better than the first," he told her, then turned back to me. "Call D.C. and see what kind of money is loose. Sweet-talk Hacker. If county chairs pester you, tell them I'm speaking to the Deschutes County Democratic Labor Day picnic," he poured a splash of cream into his coffee. "I'm willing to run, but Christ, Gabe, after your memo, I couldn't sleep, imagining those state senators chasing my ass from Portland to Medford, Salem to Lincoln City, Eugene to Vanport and back. Besides, campaigning openly like that puts young Jack's story front and center. I can hear the one-liner now: 'From Bedside to Roadside: M. J. Whelan's Traveling Medicine Show.'"

The check came and Mick signed his room number.

"The law doesn't intend a mini primary," he finished. "The chairs and vice chairs need to step up and make their call."

"And when they call about that call, will you talk to them?"

"No, you will," he said, that grin of his breaking out like summer sun through an overcast sky. "And I'm available."

Passing the front desk, Mick told the clerk that calls for him were to be forwarded to my room. Outside, he scanned the sky, shading his eyes from the formidable early-morning sun.

"All right, Gabe, we have a campaign without a campaign," he told me before going off to collect Sarah and the girls.

"Mick," I remembered to say, "head for the Painted Hills. You won't be sorry."

He chucked me under the chin.

"No wonder Hacker's scared of you—you don't quit."

I went back to my room. Too wired to sleep, I thought about Mick. I'd always considered him a natural, but maybe with the same hint of condescension I remembered from baseball writers who used to rave about Willie Mays's instincts and miss his comprehension of the game. Most politicians would have taken overnight polls and gone into meetings with tiers of advisors. But not Mick Whelan. After reducing the calculations to a simple equation: on one side, his availability, on the other, the authority of the State Central Committee, he was off hiking—not running, hiking. No wonder I was so keen on the fossil beds, I thought, reaching for the phone.

Labor Day dawned so bright and booming that when I arrived at the dining room, Mick handed me a traveler's Styrofoam coffee cup and suggested we walk along the river. Ahead, the straggler from a flock of Canada geese flapped his wings and flew in a small circle back to the others, who rested unperturbed.

"Looks like Brother Goose isn't sure which way to fly," I said.

"Maybe he wants to feel the sun on his wings," Mick observed as he picked up a crust of bread and tossed it toward the bird, now floating alone at the edge of the river.

As we broke from the shade of a huge spruce, I shielded my eyes from a blast of early-morning sun.

Mick rolled up the sleeves of his blue button-down shirt.

"This morning, I woke up from a dream that it was Labor Day and I was back in Connecticut trying to defy the cliché that time and tide wait for no man. I was having one last swim, and my father hollered to come in and get changed. But I decided I'd stay in the water until the waves reached a long piece of red seaweed at the tide line. So I turned over on my back and kicked out from shore, feeling the sun come closer."

Shading his eyes, Mick looked out over the river.

"When I closed my eyes, shapes and colors came and went in amazing patterns. All the greens and blues, browns and reds, yellows, blacks, and purples I'd seen somewhere in a photograph of the Great Barrier Reef. My skin felt cool, everything went dark, and when I opened my eyes, the sun was in bits and pieces behind a long gray cloud. On the shore, wave after wave ran up the beach, way past that piece of red seaweed."

Aware he'd gone far afield, Mick tried to make his monologue a conversation.

"Anyway, Gabe, when I looked east toward Long Island, I'd lost my bearings in all that color. I couldn't separate the blur of land from the horizon. Coming out of the water, I was cold, and my father was standing with his hands on his hips, shouting at me from the lawn above the beach."

Next to Mick on the river path, I kicked a smooth gray stone off the path to see if the fuss would scatter one or two of the geese.

"I remember Labor Days over in that blur," I told him. "I wanted the haze to come in early so I could sneak off with a girl before dark."

"Old Gabe," Mick said as we passed a couple of geese who were sunning away from the rest.

"Labor Day was the last chance to make something happen," I said.

Mick stopped and looked at me.

"You were lonely back then?"

For a minute, I teetered between phases of my life.

"I wanted something to happen," I told him.

Perhaps sensing that I had momentarily lost my balance, Mick guided the conversation back in a straight line.

"How about Labor Day present?"

Overhead, the sky was absolute blue without a trace of haze.

"I hope you knew what you were doing when you turned down Miles's offer to come out and film your speech," I said, grateful for his call back to the present.

We were walking in the open just before a footbridge that crossed the river. Mick stopped and looked above at the vapor trail crossing the sun.

"Your drink with Hacker cinched it. He'd take one look at Miles sweating over his camera and run the photo under the headline 'Whelan Not Running, Whelan Available.'"

We walked to the middle of the footbridge and stared at the river as it disappeared around a bend leading upstream to some rapids. Doubling back, we headed for the motel. Usually Mick tried out his lines on me, but today he was noncommittal, almost evasive about his speech. Only when I teased him about having a secret speechwriter did he give me a hint.

"You were right about the Painted Hills."

By early afternoon, the sky had deepened to the blue of the patriotic bunting draped over the speaker's platform. In the middle of the river, a stray Canada goose drifted over a patch of sunlight and honked at the dark shallows where a family of domesticated swans floated beneath the willow trees, oblivious to the human commotion on the riverbank.

I arrived ahead of the Whelans and told Mrs. O'Day's volunteers from the community college to point their video camera at the images of an old-fashioned picnic: hot dogs and hamburgers sizzling on six-by-ten grills, tubs of beer and soft drinks laid over slabs of ice. I told them not to miss the makeshift corral off to the side, where two frisky young donkeys took turns ferrying kids around a miniature roped-off circle of grass.

In politics, you never know if or when the press is going to cut you some slack. I was intent on having Mick mingle with the local Democrats, make his speech, and give reporters their pound of flesh afterward. I recognized television stations from Medford and Eugene, Portland, Salem, and Bend, half a dozen radio guys, and political reporters from the major dailies, including Harry Hacker. They played the protocol my way, reporters taking up positions at the foot of the platform while television cameramen filmed cameo shots of geese, old folks in folding chairs under the cottonwood trees, fanning their faces with their straw hats, kids squealing, donkeys braying, and, best of all, Mick Whelan passing the time with local Democrats before Mrs. O'Day mounted the platform and presented a boy and girl to sing the "Star-Spangled Banner" backed by an acoustic guitar.

"Americana all the way," Hacker said in a stage whisper.

I nodded. Long ago, I learned that the same reporters who laugh at one-liners directed at local goings-on think nothing of having their laugh and printing it, too—with attribution. The trick was to signify without signifying, and this time it worked. While Mrs. O'Day plowed on with her labored introduction, old Harry laughed and slapped me on the back as if we were in cahoots.

"I won't keep you in suspense any longer, and I hope our speaker won't either," she plodded over the finish line. "Fellow Democrats, Congressman Michael Whelan."

Mick vaulted onto the stage and, as he passed Mrs. O'Day, shook her hand and added the affectionate but not too familiar gesture of holding his left hand under her elbow as he said something that made her smile. Once at the microphone, he did what Mrs. O'Day had been too mesmerized by the cameras to do.

"Fellow Democrats and friends, let us observe a moment of silence in memory of our late friend and congressman, the Honorable John D. Phillips."

Ladies touched their sun hats and men took off their caps while, here and there, coughing and throat clearing sounded an out-of-tune accompaniment. Mick scanned the crowd and a spot of river so smooth and silent, you would not have guessed that a single bend away it would shatter and rush pell-mell over a pile of bone-white boulders.

"Yesterday, driving east with my family to the fossil beds, I remembered that Jack Phillips promised to take me to the Painted Hills."

Mick shaded his eyes as he turned his head and looked out toward the sagebrush country beyond Pilot Butte. "'We're all fossils,' Jack told me once, "and I wondered what he meant."

He took a sip of water from the Dixie cup at his side. "Maybe he meant that most of us don't know how we change or why. But Jack did, and he was glad it had taken all the leaves in a prehistoric forest to paint those simple stripes of red, yellow, and black on the hills."

Mick looked out at the faces of the crowd decked out in summer colors before him. Two thin worry lines appeared beneath the wrinkles at the corners of his eyes. "Deep down, that's why Jack Phillips was a man of politics. He knew that like the leaves of those tropical forests from thirty million years ago, no one leaves a mark without help." He gestured toward the river, where a sudden breeze broke the glassy surface and stirred the water into little waves that rode north in perfect time to the surging current underneath.

"There's the Deschutes winding toward the Columbia and eventually the Pacific. In that spirit, I will answer Mrs. O'Day's question." His eyes fixed on at a point just above the eyes of the crowd.

"I am not here to declare that I am a candidate for the Senate."

He stopped and looked down at the reporters, whose drawn pencils scratched the pages of their notebooks in desperate unison. Unlike Harry Hacker, whose hands stayed anchored to his pockets, their faces wore looks of surprise and disquiet.

"But I am here to tell you that when the county chairs and vice chairs gather this weekend, I am available, as every Democrat should be, to carry our party's ideas and spirit and program to the people of Oregon over the rapids of a tough campaign. And whoever is chosen will be a fossil."

Some of the older Democrats in the crowd looked tired, trying to follow Whelan's references to fossils. Gradually, they had ceased waving their Victory in '82 donkey fans. Mick sounded flat, perhaps deliberately so, I thought, waiting for him to rouse the crowd.

"The success of whoever is chosen will depend on the slow, patient motion of many others," he continued. "God knows there's work for all of us in '82. For too long the Democratic Party has not offered the American people foreign- and domestic-policy initiatives responsive both to change and to the timeless founding principles of this nation. In 1980, we lost the presidency and the Senate. In the last two years, we've lost the initiative to the Republicans. This fall, the battle for the Senate is the principal test."

There was applause and several shouts as the donkey fans waved in Mick's direction.

"In our time, life, liberty, and the pursuit of happiness include the right to a decent job, a home in a true community, a becoming education, and what the Declaration of Independence calls a 'decent respect to the opinions of mankind,' which, along with a vigilant national defense, can create a peace that holds our lives and the lives of the people of the world in high esteem."

Mick held up his hand to acknowledge, then quiet, the rising applause, and, pointing to the river, swept his arm in an arc from south to north.

"John Phillips once told me that in pioneer days, this town was named Farewell Bend because the wagon trains stopped here on the Deschutes. Before some of the pioneers went in one direction, others in another, they said farewell on the riverbank where I stand. Soon, those first Oregonians came together again and secured statehood for the Oregon Territory. On this Labor Day, you and I will also go separate ways. As good Democrats, we know the road. Whether it winds east to the Painted Hills, west over the mountains into the Willamette Valley, south to Crater Lake, or north to the Columbia River, the road leads to the good life. Let's follow that road and show the way to achieving a more perfect Union."

Applause muffled his words as he leaned forward.

"It's time for me to let you have another crack at the beer and burgers and Mrs. O'Day's Irish potato salad. So, like the Oregon pioneers, I'll say farewell until we meet again."

While knots of well-wishers clustered around Mick, I escorted the press into the shade of a large gray boulder, keeping an eye on Harry Hacker. He hung back, an expression halfway between a smirk and a frown playing over his face until Mick approached, a step ahead of Mrs. O'Day and her entourage. In earshot of reporters, local Democrats half teased, half cajoled Mick until the more high-spirited of Mrs. O'Day's teenage sons came up and chucked him on the shoulder with his baseball glove. That morning, the boy had pitched a two-hit shutout in the state finals of the American Legion tournament. Now, he elbowed aside his younger brother, who was holding a makeshift, hand-lettered Whelan for Senator sign, and taunted Mick good-naturedly.

"Say it *is* so, Mick. Say you're running."

Mick stepped between the two boys and rubbed his hand over the heel of the baseball mitt.

"Have to get you some Neatsfoot oil," he told the older boy, then turned to his younger brother. "Same colors I picked out in my first campaign," he said, touching the boy's Whelan sign. "White letters on forest green."

The boy smiled up at Whelan, and obedient photographers snapped pictures of the boy gazing at Mick the way every father wants to be looked at by his son.

The scene was too much for Hacker, who put his hands on his hips and asked the first question.

"Congressman," he began, "why not just say you're running?"

Whelan scuffed his shoe on the base of the boulder and looked at me briefly before fastening on Hacker, his smile fading.

"Harry, in an emergency Oregon law leaves the choice of a nominee to the Democratic county chairs and vice chairs."

Harry took a step that positioned him directly in front of Mick.

"Congressman, a candidate is a candidate by any other name. Why not go through your paces like anyone else—like the two state senators, for example—instead of playing hard to get?"

A drop of sweat tickled my back between the shoulder blades. I had the same helpless feeling I'd experienced before when Mick was in a tough spot. But he was stubborn and practiced at the art of holding back for the right words. He never forgot that reporters interrupt one another as a matter of course, so he waited, pretending to be absorbed by Harry's question until he allowed another reporter to sidetrack him.

"No, Harry," he began in a direct, strong voice before inclining his head toward the woman from Bend's flagship radio station.

"When will you announce your availability, Congressman Whelan?" she asked, shoving her microphone close to his face.

"Natalie, I'll answer your question as a follow-up to Harry's."

Hacker leaned forward to object.

"Just a minute, Congressman . . . "

Mick smiled, a sign he had figured out where he wanted to go and how to get there on the wings of the two questions.

"In my view, there is only one candidate, and that's the person chosen by the men and women on the State Central Committee."

Listening across the boulder from Mick, Mrs. O'Day perked up and moved in between the two closest microphones.

"Congressman Whelan is right," she piped up. "We know his record, and on that basis I intend to work for his nomination."

Just like that, the reporters, like proverbial blackbirds, lighted on the invisible wire occupied by Mrs. O'Day—all except Harry Hacker, who, though outmaneuvered, stood his ground.

While he waited for the buzz to subside, I sidled up to him.

"Harry, I haven't forgotten your exclusive."

From my point of view, there were more things Mick didn't want than he wanted from the press coverage. Certain headlines—"Whelan Labors Not to Declare at Labor Day Picnic" or "Whelan Eyes Draft for Senate Nomination"—were poison. But I gambled that Harry and I had enough of an inside-outside kinship for him to seize the interview, and that Mick, having bested him in the press conference, would offer him a choice tidbit or two.

I was right.

Before Harry could ask, Mick offered him two exclusive interviews, one before, the other after the State Central Committee picked the nominee. And in Tuesday's *Vanport Statesman*, he reported Mick's speech with only a sardonic reference to an urban congressman's sudden interest in the flora and fauna of central Oregon. He pitched his story to the resemblance between the deliberations of the State Central Committee and those originally meant to take place in the Electoral College. And smart, economical reporter that he was, he touched enough bases—the two declared candidates, the Phillips-Whelan connection, the diverse profile of the State Central Committee, the uncertain outcome—so that he could report the end of the story next, then write a third piece that pointed ahead to the general election.

"If I had press credentials, maybe I could get in touch with you," Kate groused when I called to tell her that while Mick went back to D.C. for a few days, I would be his eyes and ears in Vanport.

"That's why you didn't call for two days," her voice flared.

"No excuse," I said, realizing I should have seen her anger coming.

Formerly, I loved to amuse Kate with long-distance tales. Now I lacked the energy and imagination to brighten the brown and gray shades of my work, and the daily phone calls I used to make first thing from the road I made late or not at all.

"So," she interrupted, "what's going on?"

"Same old, same old."

"Gabe!" she cried, alarm in her voice. "How in the world is working to get Mick the Senate nomination the same old, same old? And while I'm at it, I don't need an exclusive on the carpools, soccer pick-ups, and homework while you're out there kvetching in some godforsaken motel." She stopped long enough for her voice to descend an octave. *"Gabriel, what's the matter?"*

"I'm just low—it's the lot of the second in command." I hesitated. "I swear the best thing was Mick working the fossils into his speech."

Three thousand miles away, she laughed.

"You're an old fossil," she said.

Outside the window, a flash of white water leaped above the motel's shadow and became a sudden rainbow in the setting sun.

"I don't qualify, Kate. These fossils are amazing bands of color from millions of dead leaves," I told her, beginning to think that maybe, even if I was a drab spot of beige between the streaks of color, I could still be a bit player in an inspiring landscape.

She listened, not sure where I was going, and then spoke.

"It's called *compost*, Gabriel." Then her voice came closer, descending into a lower register. *"And what else?"*

Wary and now in a hurry, I told her I would stay in Oregon until the State Central Committee chose a nominee, and then fly back to Washington. She handed the phone to a clamoring Patrick, and I talked to him in much the same vein, failing to find a common wavelength. After a minute or two that seemed to last forever, I hung up. But the shortfall of intimacy left a flat taste. I backed up my intention to be in true touch by sitting down to write separate notes, which I signed *Your loving fossil, Gabe.* and *Your favorite fossil, Dad.* Checking out of the Whitewater, I gave the desk clerk a five and asked him to make sure that my letters went out first thing in tomorrow's mail. Then I hustled out to the airport shuttle to join the Whelans on their flight to Portland.

CHAPTER 15

While Mick was in Washington, I negotiated a truce between two squabbling staff members, reassured young Jack Phillips that Mick didn't hold his indiscreet comments against him, smoothed the feathers of several county chairs who were upset that Mick was not campaigning, and declined to add Congressman Whelan's name to a telegram to the Democratic State Central Committee from state senators Meyers and Warren calling for a debate among likely Senate nominees. Finally, on Thursday, I went to Eugene, where that evening the buzz in the bar was that the two state senators, together with uncommitted rural chairs and vice chairs, had enough strength to force the contest to a second ballot.

After the state committee's organizational meeting Friday evening, Mick and I met Mona and Mario Goode for a nightcap in the bar of the Eugene Hotel. The Goodes were chair and vice chair, respectively, of the Lane County Democratic Central Committee. Of the two, Mario was a perpetual wannabe, Mona the natural. Twice defeated for the state legislature, Mario taught political science at the university, long since persuaded that he was too smart and sophisticated as well as too principled to be elected to public office. Mona had charm, savvy, discipline, and crackerjack organizational skills. She lacked only ambition and a mate able to see her as the politician in the family. Sitting in the hotel bar, I did a slow burn as Mario indulged his penchant for interrupting then charging ahead with tedious hand-me-down expositions masquerading as stories.

"What's your poison?" he asked me in poor imitation of a drinking buddy.

"Double Jack Daniels on the rocks," I replied, and when the drinks arrived, I kept on. "Here's to Blackjack Phillips, sour mash kinsman to Tennessee Jack Daniels."

From then on, it was a one-legged race between me and my shadow. With one ear, I listened to Mario butt in whenever Mona attempted to give Mick her take on the chairs and vice chairs. With the other, I heard a voice in my head urge me to say good night on the grounds that I was tired and wanted to keep a promise to call my wife. After a while, I felt the toe of a shoe bite one of my shins. Looking up, I saw Whelan's smile refract off Mario's glistening forehead, and I became suddenly inquisitive about the nominating procedure at tomorrow's meeting.

"Is there precedent?" I asked. "Or is it seat of the pants?"

"Both," Mario said with the world-weariness of a man in the know, unappreciated by his inferiors. "The need arose after the Seventeenth Amendment provided for direct election of U. S. senators and Oregon established the primary."

I took a swallow of my second double, and began to relax. "Sounds like the parliamentarian's in the catbird seat," I said.

On my right, Mona brightened and rested her hand lightly on my arm. "That's Mario," she said, "elected by acclamation tonight."

Before I could think of a question or two about possible sticky wickets in tomorrow's order of the day, Mrs. O'Day approached with the Coos and Douglas county chairs. Mick stood up and I tried to slide out of the booth, but Mona wouldn't hear of it, so I sat down again across from Mario. While Mick kidded about the meaning of "available," Mario, scorning such small talk, held me captive with his opinions about what a principled Senate campaign should look like in the year of our Lord nineteen hundred and eighty-two. His principal reason for backing Mick Whelan, he told me in an annoying confidential tone, was bound up with issues of peace, disarmament, and the imperative to cut defense spending.

"Whelan will need help," he added, and I gritted my teeth, expecting a pitch for a staff position.

Hoping to satisfy him with polite noises, I nodded, when suddenly I caught a different drift.

"As a freshman senator," Goode went on, "Whelan's going to need a mentor, someone people respect."

"Hell, Mario, the Senate's not Cardinal Newman's university," I said, then tossed back a swallow of Jack Daniels.

"I have someone in mind, Gabe," he said, still smiling.

Not this clown, I thought, while he began to speak in tones just this side of a whisper.

"Suppose I told you I see Mick Whelan walking down the aisle in the Senate chamber being sworn in along with Eugene McCarthy?"

Only a snort of bourbon rescued me from breaking into snorts of laughter at Mario's image of Clean Gene returning to the Senate with a respectful, filial Mick Whelan in tow.

"I'm serious," he repeated.

The Coos County chair had called for another round of drinks, and just as I was downing the dregs of my second (or was it my third?) double, another arrived. As I cupped both hands around the fresh glass in thanksgiving, Mario picked up his warm gin and tonic and set it down next to the wall. By the time he arrived at the punch line, I was halfway through my tête-à-tête with Mr. Daniels.

"I keep in touch with McCarthy's people," he told me in the voice of an oracle. "They tell me Gene's coming up fast."

I listened deadpan. I knew McCarthy had been spending time in Minnesota. I also knew that the Democratic establishment had lined up behind a neophyte whose assets were a family fortune, no enemies, and no unsettling ideas of his own. This I resolved to confide only to my friend Jack Daniels.

"Is that right?" I said to his prediction of a McCarthy victory.

But my grace note was off key, and he caught the scent of condescension.

"Why do you hired guns think you know it all? You experts said Gene didn't have a chance in New Hampshire in 1968."

I shook the ice cubes around in the bottom of my glass, then broke off my conversation with Mr. Daniels long enough to let Mario have it.

"This is 1982, not 1968," I said. "Look, Mario, there was an issue then—Viet-fucking-nam."

Although surprised by my vehemence, he didn't fold.

"There are important issues today, Gabe," he retorted. "Otherwise, why all the fuss about the Oregon Senate nomination?'

I drained the last drops of bourbon from my glass before replying. I also stole a glance at Mick. He was in the midst of telling a story, and I was sure the sparring match between Mario Goode and me was not even a blip on his screen.

"In 1968, Gene McCarthy was the white knight," I said.

"Yeah, and in 1982 he's still got more to say than anybody else. Who else goes after the defense budget by saying it's not the fat but the lean that should be cut?"

"Maybe so," I agreed, with grudging admiration for Gene McCarthy. "Jesus, Mario, it's too bad, but no matter how right he is, regular Democrats won't forgive him."

He moved his hand dismissively in retort, and before I knew what I was doing, I grabbed his fingers and pressed his hand to the table like an arm wrestler.

"Have you been to Minnesota?" I asked, my voice rising. "Christ, the labor guys are still so pissed about McCarthy not helping Humphrey in '68, half of them cross the street rather than speak to him. And he endorsed Hubert, for Christ sake!"

At the other end of the table, more than one head was tuning in to our channel, but I had the pedal to the metal.

"Look, in 1980 McCarthy endorsed Reagan. The man in the street forgets that, but the pros don't. Not with Ronald sitting in the White House and Democratic job seekers holding their hands over their asses at the Brookings Institute. If Gene had gone to Minnesota and said a few nice things about Mondale two years ago, he might have had a game. As it is, he's history."

Talk about Pyrrhic victories. By now, the whole table knew I had given the vice chair of the Lane County Democratic Party a dressing-down. Only Mick and Mona cared about the substance of the argument, but Mrs. O'Day and her fellow county chairs were aghast that Congressman Whelan's man Friday would tear into a party official so publicly. Through the bourbon haze it occurred to me that even if they counted Mario a fool, they would wonder when I might turn on them. I was stuck. All I could do was emulate a Victorian child and be seen and not heard.

Just then the waiter appeared, and along with everyone else, I declined another round despite Mona Goode's pointed question, "Are you sure, Gabriel?" Her use of my full Christian name was a shrewd reminder to those at the table that, although I had misbehaved, I was Whelan's man and, therefore, deserving of reprieve, if not slack, because Mick was her man.

"Mario," Mick said, "I hope Gabe's wrong and you're right." He leaned forward and looked past Mona to her husband. "I keep in touch with Gene. He says things are tough."

"If Bontempo's got it right, why is he running?" Mario asked.

"Good question," chimed in Mrs. O'Day, who, as a Whelan supporter, was doing her bit to keep Mario in the fold.

"Well," Mick hesitated. "Gene thinks that if he can get past the primary, he can take the seat back for the Democrats."

"A kind of atonement for being right about Vietnam," Mario sneered.

Mick looked at the glasses on the table, his gaze lingering on my empty, then rapped his knuckles on the pine.

"To Mario being right and Gene McCarthy being back in the Senate."

"Hear, hear!" the company responded, rapping with their tongues instead of their knuckles.

There were animated good nights all around. I thought about taking Mario aside to apologize but decided to let well enough alone. He had it coming, and, besides, Mick was my principal. His intervention had either restored Mario's pride of place or it hadn't. If so, there was no good left to be done; if not, there was no good this side of Plato's cave that I could do.

In the elevator, Mick waited until the last of the others had stepped out and the door thumped shut before speaking.

"It's not like you to lose your cool."

The elevator stopped at the tenth floor. I got out first and made sure we were alone in the corridor.

"No excuses," I said.

His room was first, two doors before mine, and I lingered as he fished for his key.

"Why not let him have his dream?" He turned over the key in his hand.

"Old Jack Daniels played me false." I patted him on the shoulder. "Don't worry, Mick, you fixed it."

Mick turned the key and opened the door.

"I'm worried about *you*," he said.

"I'm all right," I said. "Let's get some sleep, and get you through tomorrow."

"You sure?"

Involuntarily, I lifted up one shoe and pointed it down at the floor like a ballet dancer, scuffing the other to keep my balance.

"Appreciate it, Mick, but if I don't get some sleep, I'll be roadkill in the morning."

"Let's have coffee before my breakfast with those suburban chairs. Call you at quarter of seven."

I heard his door close as I zigzagged along the carpet to my room. Twice I dropped the key while trying to introduce it to the lock, but on the third try I opened the door like a second-story man. Inside, I banged around and bumped my head before my hand found a switch along the wall. The sudden light stung my eyes and the room whirled while I took off my clothes, tossed them on an imitation-leather easy chair, and shook on the monogrammed white terrycloth bathrobe the Eugene Hotel had hung in the closet for guests to wear and perhaps purchase come check-out time. After opening the curtains to let in the shine from the sparse lights twinkling in the hills west of the city, I turned off the lamps on either side of the bed and stood by the window. The dark oblong scar of the Willamette River loomed north of the hotel, where the descending moon, formerly a thin white fingernail, now looked jaundiced and swollen like an infected finger. Turning away from the window, I snapped on the television, then sprawled on the king-size bed and peered at the clock radio on the nightstand. The ghost-green digital numerals flashed eleven forty-four.

I picked up the phone to call Kate. *No, too late. Why too late? When the flame was white hot, no hour was late. It's two thirty in the morning, you'll wake up Patrick. No, his door will be closed, and after two or three rings, Kate will reach over for the princess phone next to her night table.*

I pressed nine for an outside line and heard the dial tone click in. Other nights I'd had things to tell her; tonight, she'd be awakened to hear that I drank too much and lost my cool with a poor sad fuck like Mario Goode.

"Why, Gabe, a couple of years ago, you'd have flicked him off like a piece of lint." I dialed half the number and stopped. *"Is that why you called, Gabe? Are you drunk?"* I hesitated.

"If you'd like to make a call, please hang up and try again," instructed the bright, brittle voice on the recording.

I hung up all right but left the receiver in its cradle. Curled up with one pillow bent around my arms, the other between my legs, I tried to imagine Kate all soft and warm in bed but only heard her voice speaking harshly. Images of other women glided through my mind and beckoned—before going on with that, I threw off the pillows, rooted around in my toiletry bag, and found the silver flask of Irish whiskey I kept for occasions like this on the road when, the later it got, the farther I drifted from sleep. I measured a finger of Irish into the water glass on the spare white plastic nightstand, took off the robe, hung it in the closet as if it were my best suit, and flopped into bed.

In the dimness, I sipped the whiskey slowly and let my eyes wander to the pinpricks of light flickering beyond the window. The Irish went down smoothly, and when it was gone, I had no craving for more. From bed I hit the remote, switching off the television, and before I knew it, the objects in the room began to dissolve into shapes as fuzzy as those I used to tumble through before falling asleep as a little boy. For a while, the world melted into a beige shadow the consistency of tapioca. All through my body I felt the tingling sensations of childhood accompanied by the old dread that I would not rise from the soft abyss into which I had fallen . . .

Sitting on a beat-up couch, I flipped from channel to channel with the remote before pausing at familiar documentary images that flashed on the screen. Shots of Robert Kennedy's jubilant advisors in a penthouse suite alternated with images of Gene McCarthy's volunteers, whose faces drooped under snazzy straw boaters, then cut to a vivid, weathered Bobby Kennedy speaking to a mob in the hotel ballroom, his right hand raised in the thumbs-up gesture.

"So, my thanks to all of you, and it's on to Chicago, and let's win there."

The network film clip yielded to a wobbly handheld camera's black-and-white images of Bobby and Ethel pausing at a swinging door leading to a stainless-steel kitchen, then doing an about-face to walk through a short corridor to the street.

Outside, a neon sign flashed red, white, and blue as Bobby and Ethel fought their way through a clutching, boisterous mob and disappeared under the discotheque's psychedelic marquee. I drank a beer as a series of small explosions popped through the heavy air, and there were gasps from the bug-eyed crowd until smoke rose from the tail of a Chinese dragon and Peter, Paul, and Mary began singing "Puff, the Magic Dragon."

I walked from the concourse at Los Angeles International Airport straight into the terminal at JFK. The dingy stairs down to baggage claim were slick with cold water. Candy and cigarette wrappers swirled against miniskirts in the windy heat.

Dragging my bag through the revolving door, I was blown to the curb by a terrific wave of hot air. A familiar-looking actor, whose name I couldn't remember, wearing a snappy red cap, escorted me to the head of a long queue, opened the door of a Yellow Cab, and ushered me in next to a young woman in a peppermint-striped mini miniskirt . . . her bare brown thigh touching my seersucker trousers. During the ride to midtown Manhattan, I told her I was on Robert Kennedy's staff, in New York to instigate defections from Eugene McCarthy. She fingered my Kennedy button.

"What's the trouble?" I asked.

"You," she said playfully. "Didn't you see the papers?"

I covered her hand with mine as we crossed the Triborough Bridge.

"Bobby's lead in California is down to a single point," she told me. "Less than thirty thousand votes, with absentees to go."

"Jesus."

Her perfume was an aphrodisiac in the stifling, soul-crushing heat seeping into the cab through sealed windows. Her head rested on my shoulder. All the way down FDR Drive she hummed the chorus of "New York, New York" close to my ear.

"Dinner?" I asked her. . . . "My name is Gabriel Bontempo."

I waited. Once the cab came to a stop at her hotel, she reached out her hand to shake mine.

"Do you always invite strange women to dinner?"

"Don't we know each other?" I answered.

"Busy," she said. "Besides, I didn't think you Kennedy men bothered with women on the other side."

She picked up her tote bag, turned it over, and slapped the dark-red fabric. There, large as life, was plastered one of those maddening blue-and-white McCarthy daisies. As she walked away, she turned and gave me a jaunty wave. "Maybe we'll meet again, Mr. Bontempo."

The back of her miniskirt flashed a figure-ground print showing a photograph of a smiling Gene McCarthy when she swung her hips left, and the words McCarthy for President when her snug bottom swished to the right. . . .

"RFK Lead Melts in California: McCarthy within 5,000 Votes in Unofficial Final Count" screamed the headline on the front page of the Daily News *for Thursday, June 6, 1968. On the hotel television, I saw a montage of Gene McCarthy arriving, waving, shaking hands, being hugged and tugged at a subway stop at 145th and Broadway, speaking to black people jamming a city block, others in dashikis and negligees hanging out of upper-story windows. Then images of McCarthy on the screen brightened to shots of Bobby K mobbed at the UN, at Yankee Stadium, on the Lower East Side, in Hell's Kitchen, on Wall Street. In Technicolor as bright and washed as the sky after a hurricane, Kennedy stood in an open car, grinning, propelled through a vortex of black and white hands and faces by the windmilling arms of bodyguards. Then another cut, and McCarthy loped through waves of people who parted to make way for him. Between two mounted policemen, Mick Whelan led Senator McCarthy up some steps to a platform, his back to the Hudson River. "The final citizens' right is the right to a decent house—not a house in a ghetto, but a house in a neighborhood that is part of a community that must be a part of the United States of America . . . " McCarthy's words were distorted into a louder and louder hum until he tapped the mike away from his face and smiled.*

"We may not make it to the moon if I'm elected president, but we will

have public-address systems that work in the United States of America."

The image shimmied, then came back into focus before McCarthy wiped a bead of rust-colored sweat from his forehead.

"The Vietnamese poets have said that in the name of humanity, this war should come to an end. The time has come for us, as citizens of the United States, to say, 'In the name of America, and all that it stands for, this war must be brought to an end.'"

Then Kennedy, again whirling from borough to borough, people wearing fedoras, yarmulkes, baseball caps, babushkas, scarves, and no hats at all, grabbing at him, and Bobby reaching out with the touch of a prince, people's cheers mingled by an astute sound mixer with snatches of Kennedy, right thumb in the air, denouncing "inexcusable and ugly deprivations in Mississippi and Watts, in the hills of eastern Kentucky, on Indian reservations," then, hand flat, fingers spread apart, appealing to an American spirit of optimism and uplift: "We are a great country, an unselfish country, a compassionate country."

The screen went black, and I was guiding Bobby through the police line to his convertible.

Unable to remember where I was as the screen glowed into life again, this time displaying row upon row of 1982 red, white, and blue Cadillacs, followed by a close-up of a car dealer spieling about making room for the new models, I broke into a sweat and shuddered . . .

There was a blankness before Tuesday, June 18, 1968, *rolled across the screen below split shots of the candidates' headquarters then extended shots of McCarthy supporters cheering and Kennedy partisans groaning as delegates pledged to McCarthy were declared the winners in one congressional district after another. On enormous screens reduced to tiny squares on the television I was watching, a very New York commentator announced the results. "Eugene McCarthy has done what he predicted he would do: beat Robert Kennedy in his own backyard."*

A composed, smiling Eugene McCarthy suddenly filled all the screens.

Cameras panned to a crowd hanging on his every word. The senator wiped away a drop of perspiration that glowed red on his forehead.

"My campaign—really, your campaign—has set America free."

Now the din became a roaring concentration of the blood. Against my will, my throat strained in response to McCarthy's words. On the screen, wide-angle shots of the shouting, stomping crowd changed to a medium close-up of McCarthy giving the peace sign, the thick farmer's fingers of his right hand held in the air, then to a tight close-up of his face. As McCarthy waited, a loud clap fractured the cheers. His expression changed from exhilaration to amazement to a hurt, stymied look. Then his head sank, his shoulders crumpled, and he collapsed to the floor. The report came again, muffled this time, and the ballroom whirled as the television cameraman could not hold his shot steady, and the next sound was that of breaking glass as his camera thudded to the floor. Shattered images filled the screen. Screams broke from those in the ballroom, but the most anguished cry came from my throat as I watched block letters march across the broken images of the scene: "Eugene McCarthy Assassinated." The words rolled across the screen several times before the documentary surrendered to another commercial, this one a procession of military jeeps, machine guns mounted on every roof.

Brrring, brrring, brrring.

On the third ring, the reel of film from my dream snapped and began to flap in the darkness. Briefly, my mind went blank before focusing slowly on the phone and the bedside clock, which read twelve forty-six.

"Hello," I said into the apparent nothingness of the receiver.

"Say, Gabe, Mario Goode here. We were having a nightcap, Mona and me, and I decided to call to tell you there are no hard feelings."

"Uh-huh," I managed to say, trying to keep from drowning under the furious waves of my dream.

"Maybe we can talk it over tomorrow—Gene McCarthy going back to the Senate, I mean."

Beyond the hotel window, a few lights were on in the hills. I tried to

263

imagine which ones belonged to the Goodes, and whether there was a shit-detecting laser-guided bomb that would immobilize Mario and leave Mona untouched.

"You there, Gabe?"

"Uh-huh."

"Talk tomorrow?"

"Uh-huh."

The phone fell against my flask of Irish and dangled free halfway to the floor. I leaned over, happy to hear the dial tone, replaced the receiver in its cradle, and, as a reward for my woozy discipline, unscrewed the silver top and tossed down a goodly jot of Irish. While there was still a glow in my gut, I tucked the flask safely behind the clock radio and flicked off the light. Soon the semidarkness dissolved, and once again I hovered between sleeping and waking, grieving all over again for Bobby Kennedy and Gene McCarthy, for the country and my own lost youth.

To hasten sleep, I began to count votes in the coming election I was sure would pit Mick Whelan against the incumbent Republican senator from Oregon. Before the virtual votes were counted, I fell asleep in *fields of sepia full of fast-growing patches of wild strawberries. Dreaming again, I turned on the remote, and when the same test pattern appeared on every channel, I lit up a joint and then another . . . From Bobby Kennedy's New York headquarters, I heard church bells toll nine.*

"Take that stuff down," I heard Kennedy's press secretary command an eager young man who had unfurled a roll of black crepe over the podium where Kennedy was to speak.

"I—we thought," the young man stammered.

"Don't think," he was told. "Make that McCarthy poster on the back wall a little crooked."

"How about the inscription?" asked a young woman.

I flinched. The voice belonged to the woman in the cab with Gene McCarthy's image silk-screened on her shapely ass.

"Fine," the press secretary said. "Perfect, Margo."

She had created a border at the bottom of the poster of McCarthy stand-ing alone in a cobblestone courtyard, and printed in black block letters: Eugene McCarthy, Warrior for Peace: R.I.P.

I turned away, sweat running down my forehead into my eyes.

All around me, Kennedy people fought to control their excitement at the imminent arrival of our man. Every once in a while, someone called out, "The senator's coming," only to be shushed by more-professional heads. I decided to clear my mind by running cold water on my face. Looking for the men's room, I saw Mick Whelan come through the front door of the Fifth Avenue storefront. He was crying. I formed his name on my lips, but no sound came. He took out a handkerchief and silently blew his nose.

"Hey, Jude, don't make it bad.

Take a sad song, and make it better."

"I promised I'd be here if anything happened to Gene."

I put out my hand and wrapped his in both of mine. "Mick," I said finally. "I'm so sorry."

As he took in the headquarters' bustle, he grimaced. He wore a McCarthy button in his left lapel, a Kennedy button in the right. My eyes roved from one button to the other. McCarthy's had a star for Minnesota, the North Star State, above his name; Kennedy's was a flashy affair made of scrimlike fabric whose images changed according to the light. A television camera turned in our direction, and on the Kennedy button Bobby's face changed into the font used for the logo of The New York Times. *My head snapped to attention as the words and image hit me upside the head: "Fuck Your Dead Brother" was superimposed on a photo of President Kennedy and Senator McCarthy on the White House lawn. I strained to see what I'd seen, but the camera swung away, and once more I was looking at a smiling Bobby Kennedy on the face of the button.*

Outside, there was a sudden commotion. Trembling, I looked for Mick. Sirens rose and fell.

Inside, the crowd fell back, and Mick Whelan, growing larger, his face fiercer, receded toward the door, then vanished into the glare of the street just as Senator Kennedy, not smiling or reaching for any of the hands stretched out to him, strode through the room, becoming smaller and more and more out of focus the closer he came to the podium.

CHAPTER 16

"Gabe. Gabe."

Where had Whelan gone? I felt someone grasp my shoulder, repeating my name. Shot out of the deep like Jonah, as I came to, I heard Mick's voice. Slowly it dawned on me that when I had not responded to his wake-up call, he'd come to fetch me. Abruptly, I sat up and rubbed my eyes.

"Jesus," I said, "I overslept."

"How about a couple of Tylenol?"

Still raw and bleeding inside, I chased the pills with a glass of ice water.

"Get yourself together and join me for some coffee."

"You're on," I told him, fumbling for the sheet with one hand while I pulled a monogrammed bath towel around my waist.

Mick gone, I tried to shake off the double cobweb of Jack Daniels and my nightmare by turning the shower knob back and forth from hot to cold quickly enough to administer a jolt to my nervous system.

On the way down in the elevator, I rubbed my eyes to banish the image of Mick's button morphing from a smiling snapshot of Bobby Kennedy into Fuck Your Dead Brother against the background of Jack Kennedy and Gene McCarthy sharing a joke at the White House.

Dazed, I approached the farthest corner of the hotel restaurant. My mind hovered between the image from my nightmare and the consoling human being who had awakened me a short time ago.

"Gabe," Mick motioned me to his window table.

Seeing him close-up, I was relieved to find the driven, melancholy, facsimile black Irishman I had encountered at the end of my dream vanished. Moreover, Mick drank his black coffee with a tranquility that belied the fact that in a couple of hours, his fate would be in the hands of three score and twelve virtual strangers.

"Please bring this man the same cup of joe you brought me," he told the hovering waitress.

"Sorry I missed the wake-up call," I said after I turned the menu face down and ordered the healthy breakfast—oatmeal with blueberries and skim milk.

"Man, were you checked out."

He laughed.

His cheeks were the ruddy color of Indian summer, eyes keen and warm, hair alive with highlights from the sun. He pushed his newspaper toward my plate, pointing to a small item about Gene McCarthy's also-ran status in the upcoming Democratic primary in Minnesota.

"Looks bad for Gene, so let Mario down easy."

"What's another loss when last night I dreamed McCarthy was assassinated instead of Bobby?" I said, then took a quick gulp from the mug of steaming black coffee. "You were in the dream, too."

He had a Senate nomination ahead of him, and he wanted to go over the drill before working suburban county chairs over breakfast, but he looked at me with a flicker of curiosity, his expression at once guarded and intimate.

"You didn't kill me off?"

"You were larger than life at the end," I told him. "That's what was so scary."

"You okay?" he covered my hand with his.

I fiddled with my coffee spoon.

"You and Kate?" Mick asked, looking through my eyes.

Still no words formed from my welter of feelings.

"How about the little guy?" Mick frowned. He was so fond of Patrick, he couldn't imagine things getting to a point where my son was in jeopardy.

"To be honest, sometimes I'm neither here nor there," I said, pushing away my half-eaten bowl of oatmeal.

I looked at my watch, and he did the same.

"You're my main man, Gabe. Better take care of business—you won't during the campaign."

Mick laid aside the newspaper with the story on Eugene McCarthy's fading hopes tucked under the fold. Out of the corner of my eye, I saw the two suburban county chairs enter the dining room. Like a good aide, I swept up the newspaper and left, letting a big wave and an index finger pointed in Mick's direction do duty for a formal greeting.

Back in my room, I dialed Kate several times before remembering it was Saturday morning in the East and she would be at Patrick's soccer practice. After a while, I sat down at the little half desk to calculate the vote. I figured Mick would win narrowly on the first ballot, and that switches would give him a strong majority.

I was wrong.

From the roped-off spectators' section on the ballroom floor, I heard a motion made and seconded that the three candidates be invited to address the convention, then a crusty old sheep rancher, whose ancestors had settled Wheeler County, ask for recognition.

"I'm against the motion," Sam Wheeler called out in a growl heard over the bleats of a few stray delegates. "We're here to pick a sheepdog to protect the Democrats of Oregon. Speaking for myself, I don't need to hear any of these dogs bark." Wheeler coughed a chain-smoker's cough, took out a large red-and-black-checkered handkerchief, and spat into it noisily.

"Beg your pardon," he said, folding the handkerchief in three corners, like a flag. "I knew Jack Phillips when there were spittoons at meetings like this. Now it's our business to pick someone to run in his place. No one is sorrier than I am that we have to do it."

Wheeler coughed lightly enough so his handkerchief stayed put. "Madame Chairman, I don't want hard feelings connected with the name of the man we can't replace but have to replace. So I won't speak against the motion made by my two fellow chairs."

Wheeler paused long enough for smiles to break out on the faces of the maker and seconder of the motion.

"But with due respect for the good intentions of the Democrats from Multnomah and Jackson counties, I move to table the motion."

After a murmur of seconds, Sam Wheeler sat down, and smiles vanished from the maker and seconder. At the behest of Mrs. O'Day, the parliamentarian stepped to the podium.

"A motion to table is not debatable," Mario proclaimed in a reedy voice. "Each county will have voting power proportionate to its number of registered Democrats. The secretary will call the roll."

Wheeler took supporters of the motion by surprise. They had forgotten that his years of friendship with Jack Phillips included two terms in the state House of Representatives, where the two men had worked their will in the chamber through superior knowledge of parliamentary procedure. I heard scattered shouts of protest and the words "point of personal privilege," but there was no formal call for recognition, so at the sound of Mrs. O'Day's gavel, the clerk called the roll. Delegates who could not have voted against a motion to have prospective nominees speak and returned home with their reputations intact recognized the ploy for what it was—an attempt by two candidates to forge a coalition against the third. When Wheeler's motion to table carried by a sixty–forty margin, it was clear that state senators Meyers and Warren lacked strong support beyond their own delegations.

During the fifteen-minute recess that followed, I rushed to a house phone in the lobby. Explaining old Sam Wheeler's gambit, I told Mick to shake a leg, that the nomination would soon be his.

Back on the floor, after speeches for state senators Warren and Meyers, Mrs. O'Day nominated Congressman Whelan, and, in a fast shuffle, Jonas Fitch, who had been designated alternate vice chair from Vanport County, rose to second the nomination.

"Madame Chair," he added after his brief speech, "it is also my honor to introduce state senator Edith Meyers of Portland."

There was a stir as tall, horsey Senator Meyers cantered to the podium, a red rose for the Rose City smartly pinned to the lapel of her loose-fitting lavender pantsuit.

"I rise to withdraw my name and second the nomination of our eloquent congressman from Vanport, Mick Whelan."

Cheers interrupted her.

"I also rise to introduce my friend and colleague state senator Brot Warren of Medford."

Senator Warren walked to the platform, turning a face florid from too much sun and too much bourbon toward the delegates in a broad smile. The telltale bulges in his brown, wide-lapeled, seventies' polyester suit revealed that Warren was a man too vain and foolish to see that the fit of his suits was a road map to the very precincts of flesh he was trying to hide.

"Like Edith Meyers, whom I esteem, I am grateful to have had my name in nomination. As such, it has been wonderful for my wife and me to meet so many supporters I didn't know we had. Maybe if she had been the candidate . . . "

He paused for laughs that didn't materialize.

"As such, I also rise to withdraw my name and to move that Congressman Michael Whelan's nomination be unanimous."

Finally, Warren had his cheers. His cheeks took on the glow of a substitute Santa Claus who polished off every glass of Christmas cheer left on the mantels along his route.

As Warren left the stage, a delegate moved that a notification committee be formed to inform Congressman Whelan of his nomination and invite him to address the delegates. Giddy with pleasure, I didn't see Harry Hacker until he was already bending to sit in the empty chair on my right. After my dustup with Mario Goode, I needed no reminder to watch my mouth, but I also knew the surest way to arouse Hacker's suspicion was to act like the cat had my tongue.

"Bontempo, what would your boy have done if that motion passed?" Hacker asked me, raising his bushy salt-and-pepper eyebrows.

"Addressed the delegates," I told him.

"Look," he said in his best Falstaffian voice over the commotion, "if it ain't Congressman Consensus himself."

Up the middle aisle strode Mick Whelan, led by Mrs. O'Day, flanked by Edith Meyers and Brot Warren. As more and more delegates and alternates stood, Whelan began to reach for the hands stretched out to him, first on his left, then his right. As he approached the Vanport delegates, he embraced the chair and vice chair, lingered with Jonas Fitch, and on impulse motioned Jonas to accompany him. Once the procession slowed, the clapping became cheering until the motley gang of five arrived at the platform.

"Fellow Democrats," Mrs. O'Day held up her hand for quiet, and provoked another round of cheers, "the man I am about to present needed no campaign, and he needs no introduction."

Mick slid behind his former opponents and held their hands over his head in a victory salute. Anticipating Mick's nomination, Mrs. O'Day, Mona Goode, and the Vanport delegation, with a little help from the eager beavers on Whelan's staff, had prevailed on about a hundred spectators, mostly students, to scrawl and hold aloft Whelan for U.S. Senator signs in the rear of the ballroom. Mick gave this contingent a quick half wave, then grasped the lectern and leaned forward so the microphone would project his voice without distortion.

"I accept your nomination," he began, and, as applause and cheers rolled toward him, he turned sideways and stretched out his hands long enough for the two state senators to stand, acknowledge a ripple of applause, and sit down again as if they were on a trapeze bound together by an invisible wire.

"My thanks to all of you, especially Senator Meyers and Senator Warren. And to my wife, Sarah, and my daughters, Molly and Maud, who will be out campaigning soon. Fellow Democrats, I want to acknowledge the late Jack Phillips, who taught me many things about Oregon's history and its people, and another man maybe not known to many of you."

Again, Mick pivoted.

"Eight years ago, I was driving straight into the volcano. But Jonas Fitch saved me, and you ought to thank a man who saves your life whenever you can."

Jonas took a small step forward as a smile played over his brown face. Mick motioned to the microphone. Jonas shook his head, then changed his mind to a flutter of applause.

"This is your day, Mick Whelan," he said, standing on his toes. "But I'm up here taking names."

They embraced, and Mick waited for the older man to reach his chair before turning back to the crowd.

"When I first ran for Congress, there was talk about two Oregons. But what we have now is one Oregon—old and new, rural and urban—a different state, a changing state."

By now, Mick had received more than enough cheers for the weekend newscasts and the Sunday papers, and he moved easily into his speech.

"Oregon's problems are America's problems. The Republicans say we should have hundreds of millions for defense, little or nothing to reduce unemployment. They say we should have tens of thousands of troops stationed in Germany and Japan but not have our young people on the front lines of our cities or up and down and across this country rebuilding the roadbeds and laying tracks strong enough to support a network of high-speed passenger trains that would diminish congestion and pollution."

Mick chopped the air with his left hand.

"They say we should have tax write-offs for the second and third homes of the rich in America but not spend a billion dollars for low-cost housing beyond the slums and ghettoes of our cities. Oil companies should receive tax breaks for exploration but not be held accountable for stewardship of the environment. Auto companies should receive billions in bailout money but not design engines to reduce emissions to improve the air we breathe. The Republicans believe corporations should have the rights of citizenship without the responsibilities."

Flying high, Mick soared higher on the wind currents of cheers from an aroused crowd. His exposition of a set of rights implied by the inalienable rights of the Declaration of Independence owed something to Franklin Roosevelt and also to his man Eugene McCarthy, but his personality and presence jolted even someone as jaded as me to stand at political attention.

"During the term of the senator elected in November, the Constitution will turn two hundred years old. Instead of a commission decreeing the celebration, let's remember the Preamble of the Constitution, and let's, 'we, the people,' carry on the unfinished work of the nation."

The audience sat up straight and a dozen necks arched in the air.

"Now is the time 'to form a more perfect Union.' Now is the time 'to establish justice, insure domestic tranquility, provide for the common defense, promote the general welfare, and secure the blessings of liberty.' Now is the time to embrace the good life for each and every citizen as individuals who give our state and nation its character. Now is the time for the citizens of Oregon to embrace the revolutionary spirit of 'public happiness.'"

As Whelan finished, the applause accelerated. The audience rose by ones and twos, and they seemed to stand up for each other as well as for Mick Whelan. Around me, the people standing divided their energy

274

between clapping and mulling over what they had heard. But soon, a bony forefinger poked my shoulder.

"Text!" Harry Hacker demanded.

"Harry, you saw the notes scribbled on an envelope. That's the text."

"Too bad," he said. "Some of it was good, rousing stuff."

In his gruff way, Hacker was telling me that Whelan had passed his first test as a Senate candidate.

"Harry, I'll get you some time with him before your deadline."

Hacker grunted. The stairs to the platform were clogged with delegates and press, so, using my right hand for leverage, I vaulted up to the stage and swiveled next to Mick.

"How about if I give a couple, three reporters twenty-minute exclusives in time to meet their Sunday deadlines?"

"Give me a chance to talk to the television and radio people," he told me, sliding the notes for his speech into the inside pocket of his suit coat. "And see if the KEZI guy will make a dub of his tape."

"That good, huh?" I kidded.

In my free time before putting on my press secretary's hat, I went to my room to freshen up and check messages. Kate had left a breathless message about seeing a CNN clip from Mick's speech. Just before I picked up the phone, it rang. Expecting her voice, at first I thought the wires were crossed and I was listening in on someone else's call.

"Busy, busy, busy. No phones in O-ray-gone?"

"Miles!"

"Even a lousy speech, if I tape it, it's good for a thirty second."

Miles was hurt at not being asked to come to Oregon to film Mick's speech. At the other end of the line and the country, he riffed about how to jump-start a campaign that on its first day was already in its eleventh hour. Listening, I remembered that the first reporter was due at Whelan's door.

"Miles, I gotta go play press secretary."

"Tell Mick not to get a big head and stiff his old friends."

I hadn't returned Kate's call, but now I straightened my tie, slapped hotel cologne on my face, grabbed my jacket, and headed for Mick's room. I resolved to call my wife between interviews, but I was kidding myself. Once a round of interviews starts, there's no break, although on this day things were natural and easy with the press. Except for Harry Hacker, the reporters were of Mick's generation, and they admired him as a fellow professional who had played one card—availability—and won the pot.

Afterward, Mick told me we'd leave for Vanport in an hour.

"The Goodes want me to have a drink with a few of their friends."

"I'll give you half an hour lead time," I said.

"No more," he said. "By the way, while I was waiting for news from the floor, I booked us on the red-eye tonight."

Back in my room, I called home, and the phone rang and rang like it does sometimes when you call a number that's no longer in service but not yet connected to a recording. I packed up, tried again, and this time a busy signal squawked—two shorts, one long, like Morse code. Going out on the balcony, I watched a sailboat bob past a curve in the river, then came inside and tried again. I heard the squawks again, as if a brazen crow had tapped into the line somewhere over the Great Plains.

"Jesus," I said, starting for the bar, where Mario Goode had seized the limelight after downing an uncharacteristic second single-malt Scotch.

"So, Gabe," he handed me a drink, "you getting the car reminds me of one of Gene McCarthy's lines."

Poor Gene, I thought. Long after 1968, every political groupie who ever wore a McCarthy button still dined out on his jokes.

"'Press secretaries are expendable,'" Mario quoted McCarthy. "'The hardest thing is to find a good man to drive your car.'"

Mario laughed so loud and long, a knot of drinkers turned their heads and fell back against the bar.

I sipped my drink, trying to decide whether the Meyers's I was drinking was watered or if the bartender had slipped me bar rum.

"Another?" Mario leaned forward and asked.

"I'm driving."

"See," he said, looking around for an audience he didn't have, "even an old Kennedy hand takes Gene's line to heart."

Wincing at Mario's slap on the back, I spotted Mick at the bar. He caught my eye and put his glass on the polished wood. As I sought a quip to extricate myself from Mario, Mick moved into the light, where he had a good angle facing the cluster of people in the party.

"Before I go—and I do have miles to go before I sleep."

There was *oohing* and *aahing* from the women and a smirk or two from the men as the line's provenance sunk in.

"A good end to a good day," Mick told the people crowding closer to him.

Those with glasses raised them.

"To the next United States senator from Oregon."

"Go Mick!" shouted a couple of students standing next to the ubiquitous staffers egging them on.

"This will be a hard campaign. Help me keep my balance and keep the Republicans off balance. I'll see you in a couple of weeks."

He shoved off from the bar using the elbows, shoulders, hands of those who reached out to him for leverage, never coming to a complete stop. While Whelan was making his way out, I circled around the edges of the crowd, picked up the tape of his speech from the front desk, and had the car waiting when he appeared in the midst of a small entourage.

Heading out of town, I turned on the radio, and when a Beethoven symphony came crashing out of the speakers, my hand hesitated.

"As long as it's not the Fifth—Bum-bum bum-bumm," Whelan said, approximating the arresting opening beats.

Soon I recognized the defiant chords of the *Eroica*.

As we took the beltway out of downtown Eugene for Interstate 5, Mick grew expansive. He was proud of sticking to his guns, declaring availability and letting others squash the Meyers-Warren axis.

"Sly old Sam Wheeler," he said, reclining in the bucket seat. "Those bastards had no idea who they were up against. Jack used to regale me with tales of the two of them tying the legislature in knots."

"You mean . . . ?" I looked at Mick.

But he was pointing at the sign for the northbound Portland exit just ahead. "It's on the left," he warned before returning to my implied question. "I didn't know what Sam was up to until you told me, but he's the only one able to carry something like that off."

Yellow splashed the western sky as the sinking sun came up for air between two lavender cloud banks. Looking forward to a long slow dance in the sky from sunset to twilight, I relaxed into the drive, accompanied by Beethoven's epic galloping.

"How'd the interviews go?" Mick broke into my reverie.

"You're the only game in town." I hesitated. "By the way, Miles called. He's hurt you didn't have him out."

Mick's face changed.

"I took the rap," I told Whelan. "Promised him the raw footage."

Now I drove into a sky whose horizontal lines of pink were disturbed by jagged streaks the purplish color of bruises.

Mick yawned and sat up.

"I thought we'd eat in that bistro on York Island."

Soon, all the king's horses and all the king's men enlisted by Beethoven to put the world back together again finished their labors, and Mick dozed. Overhead, the sky darkened. Angry reds drained into a monochromatic gray. By the time I saw the lights of Portland blinking west of the Willamette River, rain pattered on the windshield, and Mick stirred in his seat.

"Next stop, L' Heure Bleue," I said. "It's French for martini."

It was not quite eight-thirty, so there was time to freshen up, dine, and dump the car at the airport in time to make the red-eye.

Over dinner, Mick resumed the conversation we'd started at breakfast about what was turning me against myself.

"A man never knows about another man's house," he said without prompting, and I felt free enough to respond.

"Ordinary days are okay," I told him. "It's the highs and lows that leave me empty. Days I want to go home and say, 'To hell with the Hill or Mick Whelan's office, *this* is what it's all about—*this* is where I live.'"

I nudged the lemon peel from the side of the glass into what was left of my Prohibition-dry martini.

"Instead, Kate has her world, I've got mine, and we tug at each other. When I question one of her opinions, the rap is that I don't take her seriously."

When Mick's profile caught the light, wrinkles appeared and disappeared down the side of his face. The waiter came up to see if we were ready to order. By the time he left, the open-ended fluid mood was broken, and Mick Whelan the problem solver was front and center.

"Take a few days off, Gabe. Take Kate to the Dolley Madison, in the Blue Ridge Mountains."

When I started to protest, he waved me off.

"Self-interest. How the hell am I going to win this election if my main man is off his feed?"

He clapped me on the shoulder, reached for one of his little Dutch cigars, and when he leaned over to light it from the candle, furrows creased his forehead and deep wrinkles highlighted his keen blue eyes.

"I had a bad moment up there this afternoon," he said after the waiter had taken our orders.

Through the uncurtained French doors beyond the table, a pleasure boat grew larger. Moving down the Columbia, its paddle wheel churned the black water white, and on the deck couples danced to the music of a calliope.

"I grabbed Jonas Fitch as a lark, but, boy, up there on the platform, I needed that man."

His head jerked as if he had a sudden crick.

"Rebecca?"

Mick stabbed his cigar in the ashtray.

"I was on that damn mountain seeing her again. Jonas saying he was taking names saved my life."

Our dinners arrived, Mick's poached salmon with asparagus, mine, New York steak, rare, with green peppercorns over wild mushrooms.

"She's never gone entirely."

The waiter poured the wine, bowed, and left.

"Eight years isn't long, Mick. I mean, it is and it isn't."

We broke the silence by speaking of our children, as if to fill empty spaces Mick and I, in different ways, shied away from. Neither of us wanted to be the first to change the subject back to politics, and so we simply had dinner together, cutting each other the slack old friends expect from one another. Only later, when the attendant at the airport gate recognized Mick, did we reenter the big world.

"Congressman, the bad news is, I couldn't put you and Mr. Bontempo together in coach."

The man liked to smile but had the kind of teeth and breath that landed him the late shift.

"The good news is, I bumped you to first class."

He handed over our boarding passes and waved us through.

"In the old days, you'd have had a McCarthy button on him by now," I told Mick while we walked down the ramp to the plane.

Mick sat by the window so he wouldn't be a target for every passenger coming down the aisle into coach. Once the doors were closed, the svelte, savvy stewardess assigned to first class returned with two flutes of champagne on a sterling silver tray.

"Congratulations from the crew, Congressman Whelan."

During the all-night flight, Mick and I plotted the campaign along easy, complementary frequencies of conversation and silence—a media campaign with press coverage and free television highlighting the messages of Miles's commercials.

"You'll travel with me," Mick told me as the plane steadied at thirty thousand feet over Hell's Canyon and we reclined in our seats. "We hit the road Thursday and go flat out until it's over."

Then he turned his head toward the window and dozed while I kept calculating. As I saw it, Jack Phillips had reached his high-water mark in early August when the polls showed the race neck and neck. Old Blackjack played well in eastern, central, and southern Oregon, but his voting record on social issues was to the right of his Republican opponent's. I figured that by the time the Republican media consultants got through with him, his support in sparsely populated sections of the state would have been more than offset by Republican inroads among new-to-Oregon Democrats and Independents in greater Portland and the rest of the Willamette Valley. Mick would start behind, but he had the sweet smell of a winner. Things seemed to go his way—from the Mount Loowit eruption eight years before to the sudden death of Jack Phillips to yesterday's nomination by acclamation. And his statewide reputation, although vague, was that of a fighter. His stands for compulsory national service and high-speed trains had won him the hearts of activists throughout the state, particularly against a Republican who trimmed his sails to suit every shift in the wind and whose campaign had made the mistake of running a mocking negative spot against Judge Phillips two weeks before his death. I was jotting these thoughts down as background for Mick and Miles when the stewardess asked passengers to fasten seat belts and bring their seat backs to an upright position on the final approach to National Airport.

When the landing gear came down, Mick buzzed the stewardess and ingratiated his way to using the men's room before touchdown. While he was gone, I scooted into the window seat and accepted a glass of orange juice. In the dim light, my watch, on Pacific Time, read nine after five. Still dark, I thought, until I pulled up the shade and morning sun splashed into the cabin. Now the juice looked more yellow than orange, and it occurred to me that Mick was freshening up in case an early-bird reporter turned up at the gate. As the plane taxied to the gate in a bright wash of sunlight, Mick said something to the stewardess, and when the door swung open, he had our shoulder bags on the floor and was the first passenger through the door. Halfway down the tube leading inside, he turned and waited.

"Never know who you'll find waiting at the gate," he said, motioning me ahead.

In a minute, I understood his deference. Kate and Patrick were inside the rope, the little guy clutching his battered bear in one hand and pulling his mother toward me with the other. Behind them stood Sarah Whelan and, next to her, jumping to see who could spot their father first, the two girls, their four pigtails swinging up and down in time to squeals of glee.

"First, first class, now this. What's next, Mick?"

"I try harder," he told me as our families reached us, Kate and Sarah trying their best to embrace us as the children grabbed the legs of the appropriate father.

"Surprise, Daddy! Surprise!" the three children cried in unison.

Bearing bags, briefcases, and stuffed animals, the seven of us piled into the Whelans' station wagon parked close by in a VIP space. Sarah insisted on driving, and pretended to be lost until she pulled into the parking lot of a restaurant that looked down the Potomac toward the monuments of Washington. The reservation was in the lesser-known Bontempo name, and the heads that turned while we marched in disorderly single file to a window table sought a better view only of three handsome, excited, scrubbed children.

"What a relief—a world outside politics," Mick said.

Sarah ordered mimosas, and Mick and I toasted our wives and children. Once the thrill of homecoming passed, and the children were busy making love to three enormous chocolate croissants, Kate and Sarah peppered us with comments from the home front.

"I loved you repeating, 'Now is the time,'" Kate told Mick.

"God, Mick," Sarah said. "On the news, there you were with that Fitch guy. He's the good-luck charm for your speeches—whenever he shows up, you're terrific. Good thing he's not a woman."

The brunch bantered on like that until the children became restless.

Outside, we walked along the river. Mesmerized by the Potomac shimmering in the milky pastels of late summer, the children pleaded with us to rent paddleboats.

"Another time," Sarah said, lifting her head to heaven as if praying not to be judged by the patron saint of small children.

At home that evening, after Patrick was in bed, Kate and I talked over cognac and coffee.

"Mick said you might have a surprise," she said when I broached the idea of going off alone for a couple of days.

"It's kind of between you and me."

"Gabe, I'd love to. And God knows we need it."

Ignoring the *but* in her voice, I proposed dates. But between a meet-your-child's-new-teacher night, Patrick's soccer, Kate's duties at the Freer, and other commitments in the round of daily life, nothing worked.

"We won't have another chance till after the campaign," I persisted.

She smoothed her hair and faced me cross-legged on the couch. "Oh, Gabe, don't spoil it."

She leaned forward to reconnect on my turf.

"I've been dreading Mick's Senate run," she confessed. "But from what I heard of his speech—especially the stuff on the good life—I'm excited."

She hesitated, hovering between wanting to be honest and fearing to offend. When I leaned closer and touched her cheek, she sat up straight and looked at me knowingly.

"Seeing how much Mick needs you and how good he would be in the Senate may take away some of the hurt from that primary you lost."

"What?"

"Deep down, you're not over it, Gabe."

I felt like Humpty Dumpty. Losing the congressional primary six years before had been a small fall but a fall nevertheless. Now I felt pushed off the wall all over again by Kate's offhand comment, which in my mind hinted I was a wannabe, a me-too guy. If I had been comfortable in my skin, I simply would have been glad that my wife considered me indispensable to my old friend's run for the Senate. But I was neither comfortable in the old skin nor ready to slough it off. Instead of telling how I felt, maybe talking about Mario Goode, my nightmare, my feelings about Mick's campaign, or about us, I applied the tiger balm of denial to the sore spot.

Later, in bed, I told Kate she was right about postponing our escape to the Blue Ridge Mountains. Instead, I told her that I'd make time and take Patrick to see the pandas at the zoo before I went back West.

"He'll love that," she said, her breathing easing before we curled away from one another into the separate planes of our bodies.

CHAPTER 17

Now, many years later, on the Sunday after Thanksgiving, I put Kiem on a plane back to Washington. Waiting for takeoff, I watched CNN in the airport bar. Her four days on the Oregon coast had been so close and cosy, I felt my equilibrium returning. After we walked two miles from the A-frame to the town of Manzanita and back on Friday, the next morning, at Kiem's suggestion, we climbed half-way up Neah-Kah-Nie Mountain. In my preoccupation with the tides of my blood, it hadn't occurred to me there was a god of the mountain. But Kiem told me that the place of Kani was a sacred spot where in ancient days young people had gone to cleanse their spirits.

"That lets me out," I said.

"No way," she said, smiling shyly.

The pleasure she took mastering American idioms made me want to live a long time. Nursing my drink at the airport, I hoped that her plane would be diagnosed unfit to fly so that she could stay another night. On the overhead screen, Secretary of State Katherine Harris was certifying George W. Bush as the winner of Florida's twenty-five electoral votes, while beyond the picture window Kiem's plane finally rumbled down the runway.

When I arrived back at the coast, the sky was still creased with pale light. Rummaging through my files, I found an undated folder from Mick Whelan's 1982 Senate run, identifiable because of a photo of Patrick in profile staring at two Chinese pandas eating bamboo leaves on the captive side of a stone wall. My eyes stung at the sight of my son's clean, utterly composed eight-year-old's face, and again I felt the surge of the past. . . .

The day before we returned to Oregon in mid-September of 1982, Mick and I met with Miles Stein in a House caucus room. Miles needed a haircut; wild tufts of unkempt gray hair curling from his ears to the dome on top of his head together with his wire spectacles suggested Benjamin Franklin. He was a shy man who overcompensated by speaking in tongues unconventional and indecipherable enough to rub a stone the wrong way. He showed up overprepared—deliberately, he said, while unpacking the storyboards he'd prepared for each of five commercials—because he wanted Whelan to feel free to nix a spot or two without hurting his feelings.

Preparing to make his pitch, he dropped a thick storyboard straight down on Mick's instep.

"Jesus, Miles, you trying to get me the invalid vote?"

"FDR won in a wheelchair," he said. "Four times."

"Don't worry, Mick, we can recycle the damn things as sandwich boards."

"Listen, guys," Miles went on, undeterred, "I want to go on the air at the end of the week."

Often Miles was brought in like Saint Jude, the patron saint of hopeless causes. Now pumped by the chance to design spots that would be road signs for an entire campaign, he presented outlines and rough footage for an overlapping sequence of spots. He led off with "Passing the Torch," a sixty-second biographical montage.

"How'd you get that?" I asked, whistling at the sense of motion in shots of Whelan and the crowd during his speech accepting the Senate nomination. "The stations just showed tight shots of Mick."

"The lord of media works in mysterious ways—splice twice, splice thrice."

In the second spot, "The Party's Choice," Miles fast-forwarded old photos of jawing Democrats intercut with still lifes of portly cigar-smoking Republicans guffawing at the opposing party's dissension. Then he faded to a shot of Mick's unanimous nomination, the announcer's voice-over yielding to Mick's appeal to the spirit of public happiness. So far, so good. But we all knew that, without compromising Mick as a positive, smart, honest politician who never shrank from a fair fight but didn't play dirty, Whelan's advertising had to tar the Republican incumbent.

Two years back, a photograph of workmen extricating the Oregon senator from the revolving doors of the Russell Senate office building had appeared in the inside pages of several Oregon dailies. So Miles created "Revolving Door," where, caught by a tourist's amateur footage, the incumbent boiled over with frustration, pain, and humiliation until his face exploded into the foaming snarl of a trapped wild animal. Miles cut from the captive incumbent to Mick Whelan passing smartly through an open doorway on his way to a committee hearing at the Capitol, the dome looming serenely in the background. Miles wanted to burn an image of the incumbent as a comical but fearful figure into voters' minds so that when his negative ads against Whelan went on the air, fair-minded Oregonians would see the attacks coming from the same desperate, intemperate man they'd seen thrashing in a revolving door.

"Brilliant," I said.

"I'd like to check the finished version." Mick rubbed his mouth. "I don't want a backlash for kicking someone who's down."

"That's right, you're bright," Miles replied.

The fourth spot would be snappy testimonials from prominent congressional Democrats and, if we could shake one loose, a Republican, interspersed with clips of Mick Whelan speaking in committee and on the House floor for his national-service bill. Miles knew if he exaggerated Mick as the "Congressman Who Gets Things Done," we would be vulnerable to a counterattack asking why such an effective congressman would abandon the House of Representatives for the Senate. Was Michael Whelan really Slick Mick driven more by personal ambition than the public good? To head this off, Miles wanted a fifth spot with voters in Mick's congressional district praising him. The spot would also have the heads of a man and a woman from outside the Vanport district on opposite sides of the screen listening to Whelan's constituents, then saying, one after the other, "I wish we had someone like that."

His curls damp with sweat, Miles put his pencil back over his ear. "I've reserved time for one more, which I'll shoot when I know how you want to end the campaign." He checked his watch. "And, guys, remember to avoid amnesia, drink milk of magnesia," he said and was gone.

The next five weeks sped by like a newsreel. Once his television and radio spots began running during the first week of October, Mick was down by five points in one poll, six in another, with fifteen percent undecided.

"You don't need fireworks," I told him. "Just run in place, slowly pull even, then surge, and cross the finish line two or three lengths ahead."

For the rest of the campaign, Mick's rhythms in geographical space fused with Miles's in virtual space.

Mick Whelan was a born campaigner, but the first time I dared think he might have the stuff for a leading role on the national stage was at the annual dinner given in honor of the late Senator Wayne Morse at the end of October. For sentimental reasons, the affair was put on at the shabby Portland hotel Morse had stopped at for three decades. Its small mezzanine ballroom was dingy and uninviting—ill lit, paint peeling from the walls, and thick red curtains suggestive of a burlesque hall. But on this night, the Morse people, helped by Whelan's staff, gave it the feel of its glory days in the late thirties and early forties when capacity crowds paid twenty-five cents a head to dance to music of the big bands and drink from bottles stowed under the tables. On the afternoon of the banquet, tall floor lamps were placed at regular intervals on opposite sides of the ballroom to illuminate the life-size posters of Senator Morse from his twenty-four years in the Senate glaring down between high rectangular windows. Bisected by a podium, the head table looked out at diners from the old bandstand in use during the swing era. Across the proscenium arch hung an enormous green banner: Wayne Morse: Tiger of the Senate, 1900–1974.

On my strict instructions, Mick's staff made sure the ballroom stayed bare of Whelan paraphernalia. The only sign that a campaign was on came from the smattering of Whelan buttons worn below faded Morse buttons dug out of drawers and placed on lapels by Oregonians who revered Senator Morse. Once the table d'hôte specialty of roast beef, mashed potatoes, and hospital green peas was more or less consumed, a half dozen speakers offered meandering tributes. By the time master of ceremonies Mario Goode strode to the podium to introduce Mick, my aural faculties were so diminished, I relied on my eyes to track Mario's progress. He repeated the name Whelan so many times, I didn't spot the end of the introduction until he stepped away from the microphone and began clapping. To get his bearings, Mick opened with lines meant to be funny but not entirely a laughing matter.

"Friends of Wayne Morse and my fellow Democrats—not always the same thing—standing up here, I feel intimidated. I'm afraid Senator Morse is listening, looking for an excuse to come down and address you in my place."

Mick paused to let the laughter roll gently through the room and warm an audience grown as cold as the banquet food. He focused on a white-haired old man at one of the front tables whose shaking hands were wrapped around an oak cane with a long silver handle.

"I remember hearing Senator Morse speak at a lunch in 1970 after President Nixon's invasion of Cambodia and the National Guard killings at Kent State."

A murmur passed through the crowd at Mick's mention of names unredeemed and unrehabilitated, outrages unforgotten and unforgiven.

"The lunch was in this same old hotel for a young man running in the congressional primary against an incumbent Democrat. Wayne Morse knew that the challenger didn't have a chance, but the incumbent was drifting closer and closer to Nixon."

I poured more coffee, hoping the caffeine would sharpen my concentration so that I could tell if Mick was improving lines I'd heard him deliver before.

"Through open windows, we heard protesters shouting, 'Peace Now! Peace Now!' as they marched in the Park Blocks below. I think Senator Morse caught a whiff of disapproval from those listening in the comfort of the hotel, because he departed from his remarks to tell us that the 'tramp, tramp, tramp of marching feet' might be all that stood between 'we, the people' and 'this unconstitutional war waged by Nixon with the complicity of the Congress.'"

While applause broke out, Mick looked from left to right at the Morse posters along the walls.

"Then Senator Morse turned to the business at hand. 'I'm satisfied,' he said, 'that if Carroll Healy had been in the Congress of the United States in 1968, he would have voted with me against supplemental appropriations for the war in Vietnam.'"

Whelan paused, a smile breaking through his deadpan expression. "I remember young Healy beaming as Senator Morse kept going. 'I'm satisfied that if Carroll Healy had been in the Congress,' the senator repeated, his voice booming as he counted off congressional vote after vote against the war that had failed to carry. 'And I'm satisfied that if Carroll Healy had been in the Congress in 1964, he would have voted with me against the Gulf of Tonkin Resolution.'"

At that, Mick pointed to the poster on the left wall showing a stern, schoolmasterly Wayne Morse.

"The audience cheered. But a sheepish expression came over Healy's face because in 1964 he had been too young to serve in the House. But

Wayne Morse kept going. 'I'm satisfied,' he said until he reached the Quemoy-Matsu crisis in the late fifties and even Dien-Bien-Phu in 1954. 'I'm satisfied that Carroll Healy . . . ' The old warhorse finally stopped, but not until some of us feared the senator from Oregon might go back before Healy was born."

Now those in the crowd who had loved Wayne Morse for his peccadillos as well as his principles began to laugh warmly as if Mick Whelan were perhaps that rare younger politician the tiger of the Senate might have taken into his lair.

"Now that story gives a side of Senator Morse that's serious as well as funny, for he had a patriot's devotion to the Constitution and the Senate's constitutional duties in foreign policy."

By this time, most in the crowd had pushed away their coffee cups and dessert plates and were leaning forward in Mick Whelan's direction.

"Tonight I'd like to tell you about the first time I heard Wayne Morse—a rainy November Sunday evening in 1967. I could have heard him in Washington. I could have gone over to the Senate where he spoke to an empty chamber on many a Friday afternoon, but somehow I never did."

Frowns creased a few brows.

"But when I was out here interviewing for a job at Northwest School of Law, there was a notice in the Sunday paper that Senator Morse was speaking that evening at the First Congregational Church."

Mick's voice was suddenly full of wonder at all that had passed and passed away during the intervening fifteen years.

"His topic was the rule of law. When he was done, a man, who is here tonight, stood up and thanked him for his work in the Senate on behalf of international law,"

Mick indicated the man whose hands shook on his silver-handled cane.

"At first, the applause came like a fine rain. Then, when the gentleman said, 'and especially for your courage on Vietnam,' applause poured down until Senator Morse stepped back into the pulpit and held up his hands. Right away the church hushed, and he said what I'm sure he'd said a hundred times before and what most people listening had heard him say a dozen times."

At tables here and there, gray heads were nodding as Mick drew them into his story.

"But it was my first time hearing Wayne, seeing his owlish expression, watching those seething salt-and-pepper eyebrows move up and down as he said, 'I won't have the blood of a single American boy on my hands. Oh, I'm targeted for defeat. I know that. And I know they'll tell you my votes against this war would leave American soldiers defenseless.'"

Not a cough or the scrape of a chair traveled through the ballroom to impede the flow of Wayne Morse's words on Mick Whelan's tongue.

"'They're lying,' Senator Morse said that Sunday night fifteen years ago. 'There's enough materiel in the pipeline that not a single American boy would be deprived of a single pair of boots. They won't tell you that, and they deny it when I tell you.' The senator moved his hands as if to wipe clean a blackboard chalked with obscene scribbles. 'Oh, they say, "Senator Morse is violating national security." But as your senator, I have a sworn obligation to defend the Constitution of the United States—and I intend to do just that.'"

Mick lowered his voice to its usual level.

"Afterward, I was too shy to break through the crowd gathered around him. I later came to know him . . . But I'll never forget feeling ten feet high walking out of that church in November of 1967."

Mick paused to gather his thoughts for the close as memories of that time scrolled across my mind.

"There were two men in Wayne Morse. One might have been a Supreme Court justice writing learned opinions, persuading, cajoling, sometimes browbeating his colleagues over constitutional principles. The other—'the senator from Oregon'—was Tom Paine in a dark-blue suit, sometimes walking a tightrope between the indignation of a patriot and the accusations of a demagogue."

There were a few resisting murmurs, but Mick did not retreat.

"Yes, once in a while Senator Morse approached demagoguery because he was so used to standing alone to defend his principles—the principles of constitutional law and republican government. And there will never be another Wayne Morse. No one will ever be 'the senator from Oregon' in the same way. Wayne's territory was like the Oregon he loved—an ideal place, always sought, always missed, but always there."

Mick half bowed his head, focused his eyes on his place at the head table, and returned to his seat. Although the applause rose to the point where the audience stood almost as one, Mick stood next to his dinner companions and made no move to return to the podium, despite the windmilling gestures of Mario Goode. Presently, he raised his hand in a half salute to remind people that they were standing for Wayne Morse. Afterward, the faithful surrounded him to say thanks and tell him they were helping him as they had Senator Morse so many times. As I eased his and Sarah's way out of the ballroom to the car outside, I heard Mario's presuming voice.

"Just right, Mick. You left politics and philosophy alone. You just told a story. Mona and I would be glad to buy you and Sarah—and," he paused fractionally, "Gabe, here, a drink in the bar."

I moved in.

"Mick and Sarah would love to take you up on the offer, Mario—I certainly would—but tomorrow starts at five thirty."

Mario wagged his finger at Mick.

"Half an hour later than Senator Morse's days."

Whelan pressed a hand down on Mario's shoulder, shook hands, gave Mona a quick kiss on the cheek, then took Sarah's arm and escorted her into the night.

First thing the next morning, the Saturday before the election, Mick, Miles, and I held a council of war. Three public polls showed the race a statistical tie—the incumbent up by two in the first, by one in another, even in the third—but there were whispers that Republican internal numbers had him up four points among likely voters.

"They're coasting," Miles said, unpacking a cardboard mock-up of two potential commercials. "Unless the sky falls between now and Tuesday, you're gonna win it."

The first, a montage of the five spots that had been running for a month, turned the viewer into a participant in a fast-moving, exciting, public-spirited world, where something significant seemed about to happen. In the alternative spot, Whelan spoke directly into the camera and was shown against a background suggesting a senator's office. On the wall, the American flag and the Oregon state flag framed portraits of past great senators. Gradually, the camera retreated from the medium shot of Mick to reveal the Capitol Dome through a window, dazzling gold in the sun.

"You talk about the Senate and what you'll do as senator from Oregon," Miles told Mick, then took a swig of the grapefruit juice still on the coffee table of the suite. "I want to take incumbency away from the incumbent. Like you did with Corbett."

Mick drummed his fingers on the table. "The montage is a great setup, but it doesn't go anywhere. How about ten seconds worth, then me talking about public happiness and the good life?"

Miles disentangled his finger from a wayward curl, scribbled and drew images on his spiral notepad.

"Gabe?" Mick addressed me.

I hesitated.

"I like the montage feel, Miles, but you need Mick talking. Otherwise the images disappear into the void like the Pepsi generation ads."

"Void, schmoid. You drink the stuff," Miles countered, winding a tuft of hair around his pencil as a keen look took possession of his eyes. "I knew something was missing—I didn't know what."

After Miles left, Mick and I went over the day's schedule. He had a union breakfast in half an hour, four appearances in and around Portland, the taping session with Miles, then a black-tie benefit dinner for the Greater Portland Urban League at which the Honorable Louis A. Jackson was to be principal speaker, introduced by his friend Congressman Whelan.

That's the other thing I remember from the 1982 campaign—L. A. Jackson swooping into Oregon just before the election. After beating a cancer rap, he had become a consultant and a prominent speaker about employment, race, and the cities on the national circuit.

In the meantime, Miles cut a beautiful spot. Like those commercials where the whirl of music and handsome, dancing, laughing, and talking twentysomethings draws you to the right girl and the beer of choice, Miles's action shots prepared the viewer to swear allegiance to Mick when he spoke to the camera. Because the assistant editor had another commitment, I played grip to Miles until the sausage was made and the cutting room floor tidied up. Campaign chores forced me to miss the Jackson-Whelan show, but Miles and I watched the coverage on the late-night news. Two of the three networks sent their lone black reporter. Unlike the young blond woman for the third station, who covered the event like a fashion show, they stressed the Vanport angle. Their pieces had excerpts from Mick's introduction noting L. A.'s Uncle Elijah Jackson's connection with the old Vanport, and L. A.'s remarks praising Mick and others in the audience for making the dream of a resurrected city a reality.

"Coverage money can't buy," Miles said.

Around midnight, after Miles left, the phone rang.

"I say look, man," the caller said. "What's this about you boycotting the Urban League dinner because you didn't like the speaker?"

"L. A.! How the hell are you?"

"My health is back and my face is black."

"Miles is pissed he couldn't make a spot of you," I lied.

"Spot, blot. Where is he?"

"Late news over, Miles done gone," I said.

He laughed, and I imagined that gold crown of his flashing.

"Miles is insane, you know that. But look, man, I'm not coming and going from this burg without seeing you."

"I'm game."

"And I'm trashed. It's past three Eastern Standard. Lord knows how late on this man's Colored People's Time."

I was quiet.

"I say, look, Gabe, you a church-going man?"

I remembered that, since his first run for Congress, Mick's custom was to attend services at Ship of Zion the Sunday before Election Day.

"I'll be there with your boy, the next senator from Oregon."

Unlike Mick, I wasn't comfortable at Zion. Going got his juices flowing, and the fix lasted, but I felt so out of place among all those gussied-up black folks that the high took a while to kick in, and wore off fast.

I went.

Almost twenty years later, the sermon and the congregation are a blur. I see Ship of Zion better when I look at the little ship in blown glass that Brother Blue gave Whelan in 1974 than I do the real thing. But I remember the music. No, I remember one piece from the half a dozen belted out that day. The night before, the choir had brought down the house at the Urban League dinner. The singers blackened a chorus of Handel's so that "The Lord gave the word, great was the company of preachers," became "The Lawd *give* the word, great *be* the company of preachers" in a stirring reversal of the convention of Anglicizing the black speech of the spirituals.

I knew none of this before the performance at Ship of Zion. And performance is the wrong word, because Deacon Jonas Fitch decided everyone would sing. To make his word law, he designated Michael Whelan and Louis Jackson as leaders of the tenors and basses. And that was a sight to see—Mick on one side of center aisle, L. A. on the other, both looking sideways at one another, furtively, then with downright pleasure. I heard strains of wonder in L. A.'s voice when he put Handel's line into black vernacular. "Kiss my ass," he seemed to be saying, "I come to Oregon, and this Mick, this Whelan, in cahoots with bloods I don't know, puts me in a trick." He loved every minute of it. And on Mick's face I saw an expression that said, "This may not be the promised land, but it's a new day, damn it, a new day."

Grins spread across the faces of the two men—L. A.'s revealing his gold crown, Mick's expanding until the wrinkles around his eyes were as numerous and stark as mountain gullies in the dry season. Mick took his cue from his friend and didn't stop or slur "Lawd." And when the singing ceased, as it did when each of the sections uttered the last repeat of "preachers" in perfect unison, I was sure the old master Handel would have been delighted at the black American variation on his sacred chorus. All that remained was for Jonas to say a word of thanksgiving—his brown face so full that I couldn't tell how much of the brightness came from sunlight pouring through the stained glass, how much from the tears holding steady in his eyes.

"Brothers and Sisters," he began, "I been carried back twenty years to the March on Washington, and Dr. King's 'I Have a Dream' sermon—they call it a speech, but I'm telling you, it was more sermon than speech. But that's not all I'm remembering this morning. I'm remembering that the two men who led you in Handel's chorus, the Honorable Louis Jackson and the Honorable Michael Whelan, were there that day, and so was Mr. Gabriel Bontempo, who's been singing in the back pew this morning. Yes, Gabriel, you were there."

I turned red. I had been at the march, and I remembered the father and son who were there. And Jonas was right about that Sunday morning, too: I had joined in, lip-synching at first, but by the end, I belted out the line with everything I had. Now, tears flowing down my face, I realized that Jonas had taken down my name and put it in his book of life.

Steadying the ship of his emotion, Jonas continued.

"This morning, we are blessed to live in the shadow of that great gettin'-up morning that was Dr. King's dream and is our dream," his brooding expression gave way to a radiant smile. "Yes, and come Tuesday, brothers and sisters, you take your souls to the polls."

"Our souls to the polls," echoed every voice, including mine.

Afterward, I lingered. For once I felt comfortable speaking with people I knew and people I didn't. For once I was not a stranger.

But at this remove of years, that's also a blur, and so are the hours between that Sunday morning and the election on Tuesday. Miles's last spot, run over and over on Sunday and Monday, gave Mick a boost. I'm sure of it, because the other side held a press conference Monday afternoon and dredged up several minor officeholders to proclaim it would be a disaster for Oregonians to toss out a sitting senator who had brought federal largesse to the state in favor of an unknown congressman, a carpetbagger who, after four terms, had nothing to his credit but a failed piece of tax-and-spend liberal legislation.

Election night had none of the tension and drama of Mick's first run in 1974 or L. A. Jackson's losing primary battle in New York in 1980. Whelan jumped out to an early lead that never dropped below two or rose above four percentage points. In the wee hours, it settled at fifty-one percent to forty-eight percent and held there until the last votes were counted.

I left the celebration early, but not before I fielded a call to the senator-elect. The caller refused to leave a name or message, and when the volunteer operator said the congressman was unavailable, the person on the other end insisted on speaking to me.

"Yes?" I said into the phone, exasperated at the never-ending maintenance work.

"You mean *yeah*, boy!"

The heavens opened, and I saw L. A. Jackson's liar's gap and gold tooth through his wide-as-the-ocean grin.

"L. A., for Christ's sake, why didn't you leave your name?"

The connection crackled with intermittent static.

"I got my reason."

I pressed the hold button, located Mick, and he almost ran into the holding room. By the time I parried a question from an eager-beaver staffer about jobs in the Whelan Senate office, the receiver was back in its cradle and Mick was walking away.

"Wait a minute!" I hollered. "Don't I get the word?"

Whelan delivered a mock tap to my cheek with his fist.

"He didn't say much." Mick could not keep from breaking into a big grin.

I waited, savoring the moment, glad he was taking his time.

"He said, 'I say, look, Mick Whelan, you be a great preacher.'"

CHAPTER 18

Mick Whelan might have been a great preacher, but Senator Whelan soon learned that the Senate was no Ship of Zion. On the Interior Committee, he minded his p's and q's, spoke with enough authority to double the appropriations for seismic stations and volcano research, and won approval of a new federal center for the environment near the site of the Mount Loowit eruption. Also a member of the Judiciary Committee, he impressed colleagues in both parties with his knowledge of the Constitution. And keeping a promise from his first campaign, he authored legislation friendly to Vietnamese refugees. And when the Senate came back into Democratic hands in 1987, he became chairman of a subcommittee charged with redefining existing immigration quotas.

So it went until the summer of 1988. Mick was up for reelection that fall, and because the Republicans had torn each other apart in a nasty primary, there was every reason to put pleasure over politics.

Kate and I had drifted into a state of peaceful coexistence, deriving enough sustenance from work and raising Patrick to keep ours a marriage if no longer a love affair. To my surprise, she agreed that a vacation in Oregon was just the thing. At my insistence, she chose our destination, and picked Crater Lake, the bluest, deepest lake in captivity. I did a quick study and discovered the lake was a caldera, or cauldron, that had slowly filled with clear, clear water after Mount Mazama vanished in a titanic eruption some seven thousand years ago. Our second day, fourteen-year-old Patrick laid eyes on Isabel Riggs, a drop-dead beautiful girl from

Vanport, and the two became inseparable. How inseparable I learned one morning when, hearing the sound of a violin in the meadow beyond the lodge, I spied Patrick steadying Isabel's music stand while she practiced her scales.

One afternoon, cooling down after a hike along the immense rim of the lake, Patrick explained to me with touching seriousness that Mazama was a name imposed on the ancient mountain by some mountaineers at the turn of the century. Isabel told him that, according to Klamath Indian legend, the eruption was the climax of the struggle between two gods, one chief of the Below World, the other of the Above World.

"And, hey, Dad," he told me with the earnest, equine look of Picasso's early boys, "a beautiful Klamath princess started the whole thing."

I recounted Patrick's tale to Kate one evening as we sat on the porch watching the light slowly fade from black volcanic rocks high on the rim of the lake. Presently, Kate pointed to a stand of trees and handed me the binoculars. Adjusting them, I spied Patrick and Isabel swaying out toward the lake on a rope swing attached to two cedars in the woods beyond the lodge.

There was an ease watching Patrick spread his wings beyond our shadows. Kate relaxed. She and I were closer than we had been since he was a little boy when, hearing him coo in his cradle, we raced upstairs, each trying to be first to lay eyes on him. . . .

Then, in the middle of our second week, the curator of the Freer Gallery asked Kate to spell him at a Computers and the Arts workshop at the Whitney Museum in New York. The evening before she left, we dined with Isabel at Crater Lake Lodge. In front of her parents, the girl told us that next week her older brother, a Mazama mountaineer, was leading an all-day hike along a newly opened trail around Mount Loowit. Could Patrick come along?

Later, in private, Kate ticked off her misgivings: an untested trail, a young, inexperienced Mazama, and her absence. Sitting on the overlook,

I put her hand in mine and assured her I would go along and that we'd turn around if the going got too rough. In the indigo lake below, ghostly reflections of clouds advanced across the water. After a few minutes, Kate squeezed my hand, said she was being silly, and that it would be good for Patrick to go on the hike.

The next afternoon, Kate was slow getting out of the car when I pulled up at the curbside baggage kiosk.

"It's been good," she said.

"Yes." I rubbed my hand along her bare arm.

"You're sure you don't mind going on that hike?"

"I told you, I want the whole week with Patrick."

The redcap handed Kate her boarding pass. She thanked him, and, raising my index and middle fingers, I held up a five-dollar bill like the peace sign.

I kissed Kate good-bye and told her to play hooky long enough to sample a couple of good New York restaurants.

"Remind Patrick to call," she said before disappearing through the revolving doors into the airport.

The day before the hike, Mick Whelan called from Seattle, where he was holding hearings with his immigration subcommittee. In response to accusations of unfair labor practices against Vietnamese truck farmers in Corbett County, the ranking Republican was pressing for a day of public testimony in Vanport.

"I authored the amendment enlarging the Vietnamese refugee quota," Mick reminded me. "If I don't hold a hearing, I'm stonewalling; if I do, that wolverine of a senator will try to foul my traps and make me vulnerable in the fall. Will you staff it tomorrow?"

Mick had a double-digit lead over his Republican challenger, a plodding state senator running on a promise to bring federal dollars to Oregon instead of concentrating on national issues, as he accused Mick of doing. Still, I'd learned enough from Miles to know that a split-screen television spot could show a flustered Senator Whelan presiding over a nearly empty hearing room on one side and a mob of angry constituents shouting that they had been ignored on the other.

"Mick, I swore a blood oath I'd go hiking with Patrick tomorrow."

"That's all right. I'll sort the thing out."

Half an hour later, he called back.

"What time you setting off tomorrow, Gabe?"

"Half past dawn."

Mick hesitated. "Listen, I've got the morning session staffed. Kiem Phuong's coming up from San Francisco to coordinate witnesses. How about hiking till noon, then showing up for the afternoon session?"

I waited, and Mick's follow-up was softer than I expected.

"If you don't show at the Civic Center by one thirty, I'll know you couldn't make it and I'll muddle through."

From the balcony of our small suite at The Blue Hour, I saw the York Island Ferry chugging across the Columbia from Vanport. Patrick stood at the front, hands on the railing, hair in the wind. He looked older than fourteen. While I listened to Mick, the ferry docked and Patrick was the first one off. Once both feet were on land, he broke into a run up the path to the hotel.

"It's a deal, Mick," I said.

"Terrific," he said. "And let's you, Patrick, and I grab a bite at the bistro afterward. Tell him to bring his girlfriend. Something tells me I better get a look at her."

Patrick burst into the room, so I put him on the line, and Mick gave him the word about dinner.

"Hey, Dad," he said when he hung up, "Uncle Mick wants me to bring Isabel to supper tomorrow. Does he mean it?"

"Sure."

I didn't tell my son about my contingency plan, but I called New York after dinner, eight thirty my time, eleven thirty Kate's. The phone in her room rang and rang, so I left a message with the desk.

In the meantime, Patrick and I laid out our things for the morning. His two-minute call to Isabel lasted over an hour, reminding me of the old teenage custom that the closer you were to seeing your girl, the longer you talked on the phone. In bed, I read for a while and must have drifted off, because when I woke up, the lights were off in Patrick's bedroom and there was a note on top of my backpack: "Dad, you were zonked. I set my alarm for four thirty—Patrick." Under his name he had drawn his signature bear. I checked the clock. Eleven twenty. Slightly miffed, I decided Kate would think me a damn fool for waking her up at two thirty in the morning to clear a plan I was perfectly capable of executing. I spread out my hiking shorts and kneesocks alongside a shirt and sweater. Then I packed a dark suit, television-blue shirt, red polka-dot tie, and my oxblood loafers neatly into a carry-on bag. Finally, I shaved.

The next morning, Patrick was whistling in the other room, and when I emerged, he had the balcony door open and was pacing back and forth into the small living room.

"There's coffee and hot chocolate in the lobby, Dad."

Waiting for the elevator, he noticed my suit bag, and I told him I might peel off early and work Mick's subcommittee in the afternoon.

"That's cool. You'll be there for the rad part, when the sun comes up over the mountain."

"And the best part, when you first feel the sun burning your neck," I said, clapping him on the shoulder as we headed to the ferry.

At the ticket booth, I remembered I hadn't reached Kate.

"What's the matter, Dad?" Patrick asked me as we went through the turnstile and boarded the first ferry of the day.

"Nothing, Patrick bear. I was going to call your mother."

"Call later."

Driving toward Mount Loowit, we watched the mountain turn from blue-black to lavender and the sun curl through volcanic gaps in the peak with the purple majesty of the song. Finally, the sun lit the mountain on fire before craning its neck into the blue sky beyond the summit.

At the trailhead, Isabel and Jeremy were waiting for us along with three or four others. While Patrick and Isabel fussed over who had the strongest sunscreen and tightest water bottle, her brother handed me a walking stick.

"This is not mountain climbing," he told us soberly, "it's hiking."

We hadn't wound very far up through stands of cedar and fir before I gave Jeremy his due. He spotted a beaver everyone else thought was part of the small dam across a creek, and explained why certain birds nested on the south side of cedar trees, others on the north. But in an hour or so, the charm of the woods wore off enough that I was thinking of Mick's hearing. Besides, I caught no whiff of two young people scheming to make a break from the others. Every time I met Patrick or Isabel's eye, they waved. Behind me, Jeremy kept pace a half step to my left so I could talk without having to slow down or turn around. He told me his ambition was to rise high enough in the Forest Service to put his ideas about national forests into practice. His questions prompted me to tell him my dilemma about Mick's immigration and refugee subcommittee meeting.

"Mr. Bontempo, that Patrick is a born woodsman. Go ahead and help Senator Whelan. And maybe . . . "

"Shoot, Jeremy."

"Maybe you'll introduce me sometime."

"With pleasure," I said, planting my staff against a rock. "Listen, Jeremy, I'm going to pick up the pace so I'll be more than halfway up the mountain before I turn back."

A new spring came into my step while I moved as stealthily as an Indian over the needles on the forest floor.

Above the trees, the fog burned off, leaving a booming blue sky that reminded me of the Labor Day six years before, when Mick Whelan brought his dream of the Senate within his grasp. Hearing Patrick and Isabel's voices echoing from the stand of cedars around the next bend, I looked forward to Mick's impression at dinner that night. His older daughter, Molly, was on the cusp of adolescence. Suddenly, I looked forward to the two of us coming out on the other side of raising our children. For now, I felt light and free in the wilderness. The higher I climbed, the more vivid and subtle the leaves and bark, sky and clouds, peaks and streams. Soon I lost track of time so completely that the next sound I heard was Jeremy clearing his throat behind me.

"Excuse me, Mr. Bontempo. It's after nine thirty. Going down's faster, but it'll take you a good two hours to reach your car."

I stopped and pointed the staff he'd given me toward a break in the thinning trees.

"Even if I use this as a pogo stick?"

I shook hands, then pole-vaulted to where Patrick stood pressing his fingers into the gouges woodpeckers had made in the trunk of an old-growth cedar.

"Look, Dad," Patrick said. "The pulp sticks."

His fingers were red as war paint.

"Just a flesh wound," I told him. "These trees have been taking punishment since before Lewis and Clark."

Obeying an impulse, I drew the two kids out of earshot, held their shoulders, and hugged them.

"Don't turn your backs on any woodpeckers. See you at The Blue Hour between six and seven."

"Love you, Dad."

I could feel the two of them looking at me as I reversed course and began to wind down the trail. For a while, I felt a glow from my son and also *the* sun, as, continuing its ascent, it brought serious heat to bear on my neck and shoulders. Still feeling the red flesh of the old-growth cedar from the print of Patrick's hand on my palm, I heard no voices or footfalls, and saw no forms except for the trees. Suddenly, beyond a clearing I saw the remains of Lake Sacagawea—a vast, bleak plain of mud with only stray reeds breaking the plane. Uphill to the right, where Patrick was heading, an overgrown, rutted path led through a graveyard of trees to the former lake.

My God, that's the logging road Mick Whelan was on when Loowit erupted fifteen years ago.

Walking downhill, I needed Jeremy's staff to keep from stumbling as I imagined Mick driving into the fury. In the sun's bright ten o'clock halo, the spots before my eyes gave way to the shimmering shape of Lake Sacagawea in those afternoons Mick whiled away with Rebecca Phillips before she and the lake were swallowed up by an avalanche of fire and ash. Overhead, clouds stampeded over the top of Mount Loowit, blotting out the sun like a herd of albino buffalo. Chilly, I hurried on to the trailhead and the road to Vanport, eager to put a spit shine on Mick's immigration hearing.

At the Vanport Civic Center, I ran into my old sparring partner, Harry Hacker.

"The angel Gabriel to the rescue," Harry greeted me, pointing to the Republican vice chair huddled with an aide outside the hearing room. "Election-year shenanigans."

Apparently, the witnesses had alleged conspiracy by Vietnamese truck farmers to undersell their American competition by using undocumented refugees as laborers. When the farmers showed proof that every last worker was a legal alien, the lead witness charged that the farmers were spies aiding Marxist liberation movements in certain unnamed Latin American countries.

"Went nowhere," Hacker told me. "So bad the ranking Republican apologized and agreed to support putting negotiations between the

Republic of Vietnam and the U.S. of A. on the afternoon agenda."

On my way to the hearing room, I ran into Kiem Phuong, the lovely Vietnamese American who, after entering the United States under the pilot program, had become congressional liaison person at the Center for Vietnamese Refugees. For the past couple of years, I'd worked closely with her as Mick drummed up support in the Senate for higher quotas for Vietnamese.

"I help Senator Mick stop lies about American Vietnamese," she told me after inquiring politely about my hike with Patrick.

Presently, Kiem left, Mick turned up, and he and I strolled around the garden of the Civic Center.

"All's well?" I asked. "Even with the Red Scare?"

"Better than well." He grinned. "The old wolverine forgot I'm chairman of the Latin American Affairs Subcommittee, with access to all the current dope on subversion."

Turning a corner past huge ceramic pots of cosmos and nasturtiums, we stopped before three sculptured panels depicting the phases of Vanport: a foreground of Quonset huts against a World War II background of black and white Americans on the docks building Liberty ships; undulating brown lines of aluminum representing the swelling waters of the 1948 flood; and a rainbow of faces arching over the steel, glass, and wood of the new city. North of the Civic Center, two ferries passed to and from York Island and lovers walked hand in hand along the riverfront.

"Nudge the television reporters to interview Kiem," he suggested, waving at several Vietnamese approaching behind a monk in saffron-colored robes.

"The way she looks and acts, I won't have to. She's living proof that Vietnamese are good for America."

"I'll try to wrap this up early so we can catch up before meeting Patrick," Mick said.

Senator Whelan did just that. By four thirty, he was calling on the

State Department to open talks with the Vietnamese government on the trade embargo, American MIAs, and eventual diplomatic recognition. It was going so well, I held off announcing that there was time for only one more question.

As the reporter from a Portland weekly launched into a long reprise of United States military atrocities in Vietnam, I saw Kiem glide swiftly into the room from the side door and place a note on the lectern in front of Mick. He froze, and when he recovered, he apologized and left the dais.

"Let's go, Gabe."

When I didn't move, he took my arm and, hardly breaking stride, led me from the room. In the corridor, I broke free.

"For God's sake, what's wrong?"

"Patrick's hurt," he said, looking from me to the door at the end of the empty corridor.

"Hurt? How? What happened? I mean, where?"

Outside, I caught up and ran for my car.

"An accident on the mountain. He's at Mercy," Mick said.

I ran faster, and had the motor running and the emergency brake released by the time Mick opened the door to the passenger side. In traffic, I swerved in and out, passing everything on the road like I used to do on Shelter Island over black ice.

"Kiem took the message," he said. "The dispatcher told her the medics were giving him oxygen on the way to the hospital."

"Why did I leave him? Oh, God!" I cried.

The stained-glass windows of the hospital lobby glowed in the sun as I shot into the driveway and double-parked. Slamming the door, I realized I had locked the keys in the car. For a minute I stood paralyzed in the middle of the service road.

"Never mind," Mick said, and led me into the foyer of Mercy Hospital.

A doctor and a priest standing next to the information kiosk approached.

"Mr. Bontempo?" the doctor said to me. "I'm Doctor Hadden."

"Where is he? What happened?" I demanded, my voice bringing everyone in the lobby in range.

"Mr. Bontempo, Senator Whelan," the priest said, "let's go where we can talk."

He led us to a small sitting room. As I followed, I saw Isabel and Jeremy huddled together in a corner of the lobby, Isabel's face smudged with tears. When she saw me, new ones began running down her cheeks.

"Where's Patrick?" I shouted.

The doctor closed the door.

"Please sit down, Mr. Bontempo."

The priest arranged four chairs. Mick waited, and I sat down in the chair next to his.

"We did everything we could to bring your son back, Mr. Bontempo."

I looked around wildly.

"Mick, please find Patrick!"

Mick put his hand on my arm.

"Doctor, the message said Patrick had been taken to the emergency room."

The doctor leaned forward, smoothed his white coat, and put his hands on his knees.

"Mr. Bontempo, I'm terribly sorry. Your son passed away earlier this afternoon."

The room whirled, its furniture growing larger with each revolution, the faces of the three men sitting with me, smaller.

"We did everything we could, everyone did."

I stood up and felt the ground sinking away from me.

"Patrick!"

Mick stood next to me.

"Gabe," he said quietly. "You'll see Patrick. First, let's let the doctor talk."

Mick did not turn his gaze. On his face I saw my pain.

"Okay, Mick," I said in a choked voice, and sat down.

The doctor sat up straight and crossed his legs.

"We don't think your son was alive when the rescue team arrived. He wasn't breathing, his heart had stopped beating, and the body wasn't warm."

I banged my hand on the little table, and the priest caught the lamp before it fell over.

"*The body!*" I shouted. "Jesus fucking Christ, doctor!"

Mick took hold of my shoulders and addressed the doctor and the priest with more authority than I'd ever heard in his voice.

"Are Patrick's friends outside?"

The priest nodded.

"Either bring them in or take Mr. Bontempo to his son."

The priest sprang to his feet.

"Excellent idea, Senator. I'll get the young lady and her brother."

I closed my eyes against the fluorescent light overhead and saw Patrick holding the red pulp he had scooped out of the old-growth cedar tree. When Isabel came in, sobbing in fits and starts, she stood in front of me and hesitated, her eyes unable to blink back the tears. I stood up and gave her a long hug. Behind her stood Jeremy, his eyes red and dry.

"I'm sorry, Mr. Bontempo," Jeremy said. "I feel terrible."

"We know that," Mick took charge. "We want to know what happened, from the beginning."

Jeremy looked at his sister.

"I'm not okay, but I can do it," she told him.

The priest brought in two additional chairs and Isabel sat down, blew her nose, and began to tell her story.

"After you left, Mr. Bontempo, we walked and walked. We took a water break in a clearing around noon. Everyone was hungry, but Patrick said if we walk till we're starving, lunch would taste better. We did—but, you know, around every nice bend, somebody says, 'let's stop here,' and somebody else thinks there'll be a better spot . . . " She trailed off, twisted her handkerchief around her fingers, and Jeremy came to her rescue.

"About two, we came to a gorgeous little meadow above the mudflat where Lake Sacagawea was."

"Everything was fine," Isabel interrupted her brother, sniffling into the handkerchief. "Patrick and I were done eating first. Jeremy said everyone could take a nature break or sit and rest or read or talk—whatever—till quarter of two. Then if we took the shortcut down from the top, we'd come to the trailhead before five and make it to Vanport by six," she paused, dabbed her eyes. "And Patrick and I would be on time for dinner with you and Senator Whelan."

Saying those words, Isabel broke down. Only when I held her hand and patted it was she able to keep going.

"Patrick and I went off—not out of sight. Just hanging out."

Now she was deep into her story and I with her—as long as Patrick was in her story, he was alive.

"We were at the edge of the meadow. There were butterflies everywhere, then this huge yellow-and-black guy flew in a circle round and round my head, then Patrick's, and didn't go away. My scarf's yellow and black," she touched the wrinkled cloth around her neck. "Patrick said the butterfly thought the scarf was the Almighty Butterfly."

She laughed at the thought, and her grief began to melt into the story.

"'Wow,' I said, 'that's neat, Patrick.' That butterfly kept flying off and coming back, so I took off my scarf and ran, twirling it over my head. Patrick caught up, and we sat down together, you know, messing around. Pretty soon the sun went behind some big pinkish clouds—you know, like cotton candy. I got cold and looked for the scarf. Patrick said the wind must have taken it. He stood up right away to find it—that's the kind of guy he was."

She stopped to blow her nose, and I winced. When Mick touched my hand, I didn't feel a thing.

"My scarf was sort of floating, that same black-and-yellow butterfly flying next to it.

"'Look, Isabel,' Patrick said, 'the butterfly is stealing your scarf.'

"I stood up and gave him a push—'Patrick to the rescue,' I said."

Overhead, there was a squawk from the intercom box—a tuning fork for the voice that followed.

"Father Mooney, please come to cardiac. Father Mooney, this is an emergency," the soprano of disaster repeated her aria.

"Ah, what isn't an emergency?" Father Mooney sighed.

The interruption broke the spell and brought me back to reality with a rush. Suddenly, I didn't give a damn about the story; I wanted to know what happened to Patrick. But part of me identified with Father Mooney, who rose slowly from his chair and excused himself with a thin smile.

As the door closed, Mick and the doctor scraped their chairs on the tile floor and began to speak at the same time.

"Isabel," Whelan began, then deferred to the sound of the doctor's voice.

"Tell us what happened next," the doctor said.

A minute before, Isabel had been a storyteller; now, she was a shattered fourteen-year-old girl fearful she'd done or not done something that made her responsible for Patrick's death.

"The sun came back out," she told us. "I started walking toward Patrick. A gust of wind caught the scarf and took it out over the mudflats where the lake used to be. Patrick was running past some reeds. I could see him and the butterfly following the scarf. I don't know—all I know is, I was behind Patrick and he was running."

Isabel looked down and picked up the handkerchief that had been resting on her bare knees.

"I was at the edge of the meadow, and Patrick was running out over the mudflats. Then he started to go in slow motion, and fell down. I hollered, 'Are you okay?' He shouted yes and went to get up, but when I looked, he was in mud up to his knees. 'Forget the scarf,' I told him. 'Come back.' I could see he was having trouble. He slipped down a little at a time, and I heard him cry for help.

"I started running. I got to the mudflats and his hips were sinking. His arms had nothing to hold on to, so I went back and broke off a long reed. When I turned back, he was in up to his waist and so scared he kept yelling, 'Help, Isabel! Get help! Get Jeremy!'

"Senator, I was scared. By now, I couldn't see Jeremy. We had wandered pretty far. I started toward Patrick—if I couldn't pull him out, I could hold on and stop him from going under.

"'Isabel, go back!' he yelled. 'Get help!'

"I looked down and there were cracks in the dry mud where I'd been walking and squishy noises coming from under my feet. I screamed. I tried to be calm.

"'Patrick,' I said, 'hold on, I'll get Jeremy.'

"I told him to keep his legs moving because I'd read that sinkholes aren't very wide, and maybe his leg would kick into some solid mud and stop sinking. Then I ran. But I couldn't run—I had to tiptoe around the cracks. At the meadow, I turned around and all I saw was Patrick's head and the top of his shoulders.

"'Jeremy!' I cried, 'Jeremy, help!'

"I ran and ran. No one heard me until I was almost at the trail. Jeremy wanted me to tell him what was the matter, but I couldn't.

"'Follow me!' I kept screaming.

"Halfway down the bank to the meadow, I told Jeremy we should break off a branch from one of the trees, but he kept going.

"Oh, God," she sobbed.

As she described the others running toward Patrick, she fastened her eyes on Mick.

"It was awful, Senator. Running across the lake all we could see were Patrick's arms; there was this little crease on one of his elbows. Oh, God, why didn't I run back when he first told me to?"

Mick took hold of her knees with his hands. She had scrubbed the mud off, but her yellow hiking shorts were stained brown and red from crawling around the sinkhole that had swallowed Patrick.

"Isabel, you did everything you could," Mick said. "You were brave."

Her sobs slackened to sniffles.

"Anyways, Jeremy was ahead of me. I tried to warn him about the mud cracks. He kept on—like a guy," she looked at her brother sitting off to one side beyond Mick. "You didn't listen."

Jeremy twisted his body in the chair.

"It's all right, Jeremy," Mick said.

"Patrick's arms were slipping into the mud, and the mud was cracking at Jeremy's feet."

Isabel looked directly at Mick.

"Now I could just see Patrick's wrists. Jeremy crawled over and grabbed them, but his hands were slippery and his grasp slipped down to Patrick's fingers. Poor Patrick was in the mud—all Jeremy had was his fingers. Oh, God."

Isabel slumped to the floor.

"She's in shock." The doctor hesitated, looking from Jeremy to Mick to me.

"Jeremy, can you take over while the doctor sees to your sister?" Mick asked.

The boy's hands shook.

"I'm sorry, Mr. Bontempo."

I thought of Patrick and reached for Jeremy's hand.

Jeremy's was a hurried epilogue to his sister's story. His struggle to

318

save Patrick's life turned into a struggle to pull my son's body out of a murderous sinkhole concealed by the surface of a moribund lake. Like his exertions, his words were halting. It had taken precious minutes for him and another young man to lie flat with a firm grip on each of Patrick's hands and for Isabel and the remaining two hikers to seize their legs. With excruciating slowness, Patrick emerged far enough for Isabel to crawl forward and give him on-again, off-again artificial respiration. Jeremy remembered Patrick's skin having a bluish tinge once the mud was rubbed off. Eventually, they carried him to the meadow, put him down, and Jeremy gave him CPR. He sent one of the hikers to summon help, but the best he could do was have an emergency medical vehicle waiting when he, Isabel, and their friends got to the bottom of the mountain with Patrick.

I was suddenly exhausted. I wanted to see Patrick, and the doctor's details about the paramedics' state-of-the-art attempts to bring my son back with great gouts of oxygen and hypodermics of adrenalin shot into his heart made me conscious of the one thing that mattered: I had not been with Patrick. I had trotted off to a godforsaken hearing of Mick Whelan's Senate subcommittee on refugees.

"My son's the refugee," I sobbed.

The only thing that kept me there listening was my dread at calling Kate and the certainty that she would want every fact there was to know and some that weren't. During the doctor's commentary, Mick kept his eyes on me. At length, with the courtesy and authority of one professional to another, he interrupted.

"Doctor, maybe you can finish while you take Mr. Bontempo to see his son."

The doctor rounded off his sentence and stood up.

"Certainly," he said.

"I'd like Senator Whelan to come with me."

We walked along the corridor, Mick next to me, one arm out in case I needed steadying.

"Oh, God," I said when the doctor pulled down the sheet and I saw my boy's face. "My poor Patrick bear."

Mick held my shoulders, but I didn't fall. Looking at my dead son, I heard that bright voice of his and the clay features before me changed into the quick, fluid face I had kidded with that morning. *"Love you, Dad,"* I heard the last words he had spoken to me.

"Let's go," I told Mick. "Please, let's go."

On the walk back, I thought of Kate in New York, having dinner, unaware that Patrick was anything but safe and sound and happy.

"Doctor," Mick said, guessing my thoughts, "is there a phone where Mr. Bontempo can make a long-distance call?"

There was, and I did. But it was nine o'clock in New York, and she was probably out. I imagined her finishing a second glass of wine while telling her companions she better not be tipsy when her son called to tell her about his hike around Mount Loowit.

Outside in the hall, Mick was waiting.

"Just as well," he said when I told him I couldn't reach Kate.

"I better go back to The Blue Hour," I told him.

As we turned into the lobby, he put out his arm to stop me.

"Gabe, I know this is a lot." He hesitated. "Are you up to five minutes with the kids?"

I looked blank.

"Isabel and Jeremy."

Mick turned me around, and I saw them sitting in a faraway corner of the lobby. Seeing us, they clung to each other until I stepped up and put one arm around each of them.

"Listen," I said, "I want to thank you, for myself and Patrick's mother. You were there for him. He knew that."

Jeremy disengaged from my arm and stood ramrod straight.

"You shouldn't feel bad, Mr. Bontempo. If you'd stayed, Patrick and Isabel would have gone off the same way, and you would have stayed talking with the rest of us."

"He's right," Isabel said.

"You're generous, brave kids," I told them.

After a ferry ride during which images of Patrick, bright and alert and alive, pierced my catatonia in flashes, Mick Whelan and I sat in my suite at The Blue Hour waiting for Kate's call. When the phone finally rang, he stayed in the living room discreetly in my line of sight while I lay propped up by three pillows on the king-size bed.

Kate, naturally, thought I had called to tell her about the glorious hike. When I said hello, she called me Patrick. She had been thinking of him, she said, and she was sure he would answer the phone.

On my end, I put everything I had into speaking slowly, carefully, gently, sparing the harshest details, conjuring a picture of Patrick on his last morning, which someday might be a comfort. There was no consolation, and I told her so.

After she thought to say how awful it was for me and sobbed that I shouldn't blame myself, that I had done all I could to save Patrick, my silence blocked her words. To this day, I cannot remember the exact phrase she used to pin down my whereabouts. What I will always remember is the cry of pain that came through the telephone when she realized I'd been in Vanport while Patrick was suffocating in the mud.

"You weren't there?! You what?! You were where?! . . . Patrick died without you?"

I sat up and absorbed the blows, not listening so much as taking what I had coming. Through the doorway, Mick knew what was going on from my expression and the silence. I held the receiver tight against my ear so that he wouldn't be able to hear Kate's words or the even more-painful silences between her strangled cries.

After a while he came in and dropped a note on the bed. Would it help if he talked to her? I pushed the note away. He nodded and went back into the sitting room, closing the door except for a tiny crack through which I could see a last shaft of sunlight.

"Kate, I'm sorry," I said. "You don't know how much."

She took a long time breaking the silence.

"It's done, Gabe. He's gone," she said. "Don't make any arrangements until I get there."

"Kate?"

There was a long pause.

"I'll let you know my plans," she said, and the line went dead.

By the time I threw cold water on my face and went out to the sitting room, Mick was on the phone with Sarah. When he put me on, she told me that she would offer to fly out to Portland with Kate.

In the bar sometime later, Mick pretended to sip and I periodically gulped double martinis.

"Poor Kate," Mick said. "Sounds like she wants nothing to do with Oregon."

I nodded. My nose touched the lemon peel as I took a long swallow of martini.

"With me either."

"Wait a minute, Gabe," he said. "Patrick is your son. Won't it be harder if you two just take him back to Washington?"

The gin was beginning to numb me.

"Kate can decide. Patrick's gone. I had his last days."

The waiter came. I raised two fingers, signifying another round. Mick shook his head, then turned to me.

"Listen, Gabe," he said. "You ought to put something in your stomach to keep the booze company."

Mick ordered two bowls of French onion soup and a large order of French bread. When the waiter left, he took me by both hands.

"Gabe, listen. It's going to be crazy tomorrow. Maybe you should figure out what you want to happen."

I looked out the bay window at the river. Lights were blazing on the Columbia stern-wheeler on the return leg of the dinner cruise.

"What do I want?" I shouted. "To go with Patrick and find Isabel's scarf."

Mick ran his hands over the worry lines suddenly running up and down his forehead.

"Remember what Jeremy said. If you'd stayed, you wouldn't have been close enough to help."

In the candlelight, I noticed that an unruly swirl of curly hair at each of Mick's temples was turning gray. In ten or fifteen years, white curls would make him distinguished as he gave away his girls to two lucky young grooms.

"Goddamn it, Mick. Don't be the politician making things right. You can't, so don't try. It hurts more when you do."

Mick took my abuse, then poked at his bread and soup and nursed his martini in silence until I spoke.

"Jesus, I'm too much of a coward to take responsibility so I dump my trash on you."

To the right of the bar, a young black man I recognized from Ship of Zion came back to the piano and started to play Ellington tunes the names of which wouldn't come off the tip of my tongue until, as if sympathizing with my memory lapse, he doubled back to "Mood Indigo," the one I'd known all along. Mick went back to making the case that I should take half the initiative about arrangements for Patrick.

"Kate will want to see where it happened. Patrick loved those old-growth cedars. Why not have something for him near the meadow where he had that last good time with the girl?"

Aided by the piano player, who segued into a medley of Cole Porter tunes, including "Night and Day" in a swinging tempo that made my ears ache with pain, I tuned in and out of Mick's proposal.

"I've got to wait," I said.

I was having trouble keeping my head up. I toyed with my soup until the once-crunchy Gruyère turned sodden and begin to slide down the sides of the bowl.

"What say, Gabe?" Mick nudged me. "Time to quit."

I downed the remains of my warm martini and stood up, feeling dizzy like I had a few days before rounding a steep, narrow curve of trail high above Crater Lake. Suddenly, it hit me that stillness is an illusion, lulling us to forget about nature's violent insides. All is vertigo, I thought, and the sinkhole that swallowed Patrick only hints at the bubbles of fire seething uncontrollably deep in the cauldron of the world.

Upstairs, I tried to say good night at the door to my suite, but Mick would not let me go through the hours alone, so he slept in Patrick's room. As he hugged me, I reminded him of his call on the day of Patrick's birth, March 17, 1974.

Alone in bed, my tears became a rush of sobs until I fell asleep and dreamed that I was walking on an endless mudflat holding a butterfly net and looking for Patrick, before sinking back into the black silt of my unconscious. . . . The next thing I knew, sunlight streaming through the wispy inner curtain prodded me awake. I had almost finished showering when it hit me that my son was dead. By the time I knotted my tie, slipped on my jacket, and appeared in the living room, Mick had placed two mugs of steaming café au lait on the coffee table. He informed me that the desk had called to say that Kate's plane was due at eleven forty-four.

The coffee burned the remains of sleep and last night's martinis off the roof of my mouth. My tongue felt normal size again, and I wanted to talk.

"Christ, when I got up, I couldn't find my toothpaste, and I started to call to Patrick to borrow his . . . It's funny, Mick, it's supposed to be gray and rainy the day after someone you love dies. I wish it was—the blue sky makes it harder."

I went on like that for a while, the sound providing odd reassurance

324

that Patrick remained within range of a human voice. During my on-again, off-again monologue, the phone rang several times, each time for Mick. Finally, his driver called from downstairs, telling him it was time to leave for the airport.

"Do you want me to go along?" he asked.

"I think so."

At the airport, Mick waited in the town car with its government plates and windshield stickers while I hustled to the gate. Kate arrived alone. When I went up to her, she slipped out of my hug into a half embrace. She carried her purse over her arm.

"Is Sarah on a later plane?" I asked.

"I told her to stay with her girls—one dead child is enough," she said, walking toward the terminal. "Was having her come Mick's brainchild? Or yours?" she asked, eyeing me suspiciously.

"Hers—the second thing she said to me."

"You could have alerted me."

"Kate, you and Sarah are old friends."

"Whatever you say."

I veered toward baggage claim, but she stayed put.

"Shall I get your bag?"

"I don't have one," she said.

I took a step toward her.

"That's okay. We'll get what you need here."

I took her arm, glad I could offer to do something for her.

"Gabriel," she said as if talking to a child, "I didn't bring any luggage. I'm leaving as soon as I arrange for Patrick to be flown home—tonight at the latest."

She hesitated, waiting for me to show the way.

"Kate, that's too soon."

She cut me off.

"Where's Patrick's body?"

"O'Sullivan's. An undertaker Mick knows in Vanport."

"I see."

I took her arm, which she then let fall back to her side.

"Mick suggested . . . ," I began. "I mean, I thought we might have a little gathering for Patrick out here before we bring him back to Washington. Something simple."

Kate had liberally applied a light-pancake-colored makeup to cover the red blotches on her cheeks. Now in the bright fluorescent light of the terminal, there began to be cracks in the façade of her face.

"Mick thought that would be nice, did he? Maybe he could give one of his eulogies," she said, her hazel eyes blazing. "Good God, Gabriel, your son is dead."

"Kate, stop," I said. "Patrick loved Mick."

"And where would you and Mick like to have this little sideshow? I'll bet it's that black church. Ship of Canaan."

"Zion," I corrected automatically, steering her to a waiting area with a vinyl couch and chairs. "We need to talk, Kate. Mick's in the Senate car outside." I bent down to sit in one of the chairs while she remained standing.

"Which is it, Gabe? Talk or not keep Mick Whelan waiting?"

"Okay, Kate, I'm not going to fight about arrangements. If you want Patrick brought to Washington right away, fine, let's do it. Blame me all you want, but Mick had nothing to do with it."

She stood, hands on hips, while an attendant wheeled a frail elderly traveler past.

"Mick asked you to break your word to me about Patrick," she hissed. "How can I forget that?"

"No, he didn't. He asked a perfectly innocent favor. I'm the one who decided to go back after I saw what the trail was like."

"A lot you saw."

Through the revolving door, I saw the exhaust from Mick's limousine turning red under the taillights.

"For God's sake, Kate, you make it sound like I knew there were sink-holes in that damn lake."

A crowd of people heading down to the baggage carousels flowed toward the escalator on our left, paying no attention.

"You *didn't* care, Gabriel. Patrick didn't come first. For years it's been Whelan, Whelan, Whelan!" she shouted.

I shifted my front foot back and my back foot front.

"I'm sorry, Kate," I said. "I wish you knew how sorry."

The cresting wave of her anger had broken. Her face told me that beneath her accusations lay a terrible, overwhelming, tragic grief.

"All right," she said with a sigh and a contorted smile. "Let's not keep the senator waiting."

With Mick, Kate observed the protocols. She acknowledged his kind-ness, informed him she had told Sarah that she would need her when she was back in Washington, and thanked him for arranging for Patrick's body to be taken to O'Sullivan's. I became her silent partner, and, along with Mick, we persuaded Dermot O'Sullivan to prepare the body for shipment to Washington on that night's red-eye. As a favor to Mick, Kate agreed to see Isabel and Jeremy late that afternoon. She couldn't bear to go near The Blue Hour, so she met them in Mick's office while he and I cleared out Patrick's belongings from the hotel suite. As we did, he responded to my melancholy brooding.

"At least Kate takes your mind off the worst of it," he said.

"I'd rather face the real grief."

He handed me the last of Patrick's clothes, which I folded and placed in my son's carry-on bag. I turned out the light and followed Mick out of the suite. With a pang, I realized that, leaving this room only a day before, Patrick had been certain he would return.

"Mick," I told him in the hallway, "I hope you go before your daughters."

"Old Gabe," he hugged me. "Dear old Gabe."

When we arrived at the office, Kate was pacing back and forth, a lit cigarette in her mouth, several dead ones in the ashtray.

"The two kids waited for you. I thought they'd never leave."

"I'm glad Patrick knew them, especially Isabel," I said.

Kate inhaled, blew a line of smoke between us, and stabbed her cigarette straight down into the ashtray.

But Mick stuck it out. He dismissed his driver, chauffeured us to the airport, and saw to it that Patrick's casket was properly stowed in the baggage compartment. So we wouldn't have to endure a deathwatch at the gate, he took us to the VIP lounge for a cognac.

"Look after each other," he said, holding up his snifter until Kate and I touched his glass with ours.

On the walk to the gate, Kate said she hoped he, Sarah, and the girls would be able to come to the service in Washington. She promised to call Sarah, then went to the ladies room.

"They bumped you and Kate to first class." Mick took my arm and held tight. "I'll be back in Washington for the funeral," he said, giving me his signature tap on the chin. "Look to Kate, Gabe. She's the only wife you've got."

Kate approached us as she walked down the concourse, shifting her purse from her right to her left shoulder. When she reached us, she put out both hands to Mick.

"I mean it, Mick, thanks for everything."

"Kate, look to Gabe."

"Yes," she said with a tight smile, "and you to Sarah."

We were ushered down the ramp to the plane by the chief stewardess who, assuring us that our son's casket was safe and secure, escorted us into the first-class cabin. Settled in our seats, Kate and I rested, heads angled away from each other during the flight to Dulles Airport. First light yielded to a foggy sunrise that obscured the ground during the slow, shifting descent of the plane.

"Did you sleep?" Kate asked while I raised the lid of the overhead bin to hoist down my bag and Patrick's backpack.

"Off and on," I said. "You?"

"Not a wink."

Walking through the dim tube leading to the airport gates, I was relieved to see Sarah Whelan first in line at the rope. Grasping the situation immediately, she gave Kate a long, lingering hug of maternal solidarity, and then embraced me with a quick hang-in-there pat on the shoulder. The flow of human traffic hurrying to dozens of gates pushed the three of us into one another until Kate took Sarah's arm. Bringing up the rear, I felt like a eunuch guarding the two most prized wives in the sultan's harem.

But before long, I was grateful to Sarah for acting as a buffer. Sure enough, Kate took her cue from Sarah and busied herself over the endlessly multiplying details of Patrick's funeral service and burial. At Kate's insistence, the only eulogies would be remarks made by the headmaster at Patrick's school, the history teacher who doubled as his soccer coach, and a fellow student, teammate, and friend of Patrick's.

Mick and Sarah were there. So were L. A. and Yvonne Jackson and Ted and Victoria March. Later, after prayers at Rock Creek Cemetery, Kiem Phuong, dressed in deep purple suggestive of Vietnamese mourning immemorial, her teenage son and daughter in tow, bowed to Kate. When Kate looked past her and took the outstretched hands of the next woman in line, Kiem bowed again, then presented me the light-blue tile on which she had painted a likeness of Patrick's travel bear. Mick, observing Kate's slight, told me to forget his campaign and stay in Washington.

"Look to Kate," he said again as he left Patrick's grave.

Later that week, I met Kate in a Georgetown wine bar. After we ordered, I brought up the future.

"Kate," I began, "we're strangers in the same house. I can't bring Patrick back, but I'd like to be with you."

She lit one of those long, slender cigarettes pitched to professional women, held the match until the flame guttered, then snapped her wrist and watched the dead match drop into the ashtray.

"I still can't accept you leaving Patrick for Mick Whelan's hearing."

"Kate—" I tried to resume.

"These things aren't two-minute drills, Gabe. Besides, you've got the Whelan Senate campaign to run."

Our glasses of wine arrived, and the waiter mistakenly put the Gris in front of me, the Grigio next to Kate. When I mentioned it, Kate sniffed the wine, pronounced it satisfactory, and took a goodly drink.

"To you," I said, raising my glass. "I'll stay back here as long as it takes to work things out."

She turned her wineglass around in a circle.

"Or until Mick Whelan asks you to take charge of some crisis." She snuffed out her half-smoked cigarette and excused herself to go to the ladies' room.

While she was gone, I looked outside at the rain. Though it was late August, the temperature had dropped and gray clouds hung low over the city as if Oregon weather had followed us east. Rain fell on the windowpane in round, lazy drops interrupted every once in a while by a thin slash.

"Look at the rain," I said to Kate when she returned. "I've never noticed those slashes before."

"Sure," she said. "On the diagonal."

"No, I mean the straight slashes," I told her. "I understand how they fall through the air like that, but how in the world do they end up in an absolutely straight line on the windowpane?"

Her curiosity piqued, she joined in the speculation, fascinated and stymied at the same time. Suddenly, she was crying.

"Good God, Gabe, it's the sort of thing Patrick would know, or if he didn't, he would find out and surprise us."

I reached for her hand. She hesitated, then pulled back and shook a second cigarette loose from the pack next to her glass.

"It's too soon, Gabe. I need time. You go out to Oregon and run Mick's campaign like you were going to do."

"Kate, I want to be with you. To watch the rain and maybe figure out what Patrick would say about why the odd drops fall straight down on the window."

· Her eyes misted over. The waiter appeared at her side with a lighter, but she waved him off and put the unlit cigarette on the table next to her glass.

"You just don't get it, Gabe. I can't right now," she picked up her cigarette. "You go back to Oregon—that's the best."

I didn't argue. I couldn't blame her, yet I wanted to do anything rather than seem to obey her. But after my anger died down, I realized that if the alternative was tagging along, waiting for her to grant me audience after audience, hoping she might agree to a new chapter in our marriage, then, in my hurt, I would choose Oregon.

"Whatever I decide," I said stiffly, "I respect that you need time to yourself."

I hadn't meant to be distant or grudging, but her look told me she was not unhappy to have pushed me that far. Two days later, I packed my bags and returned to Oregon to manage Mick Whelan's reelection campaign.

CHAPTER 19

During the night flight to Oregon, I sat in a window seat looking into the blackness as another airliner swam into view and began to glide past in the other direction, heading east. Staring at my reflection in the window, I dozed off fitfully until the face that came back was Patrick's. I pressed my face against the window and waved. He waved back. And as his plane came exactly opposite, he smiled. I felt a glow, then felt myself disintegrate as the plane he was in exploded in a ball of fire that turned yellow and black, then was gone. With a start, I woke up and saw only the dark beyond my little window.

In Oregon, I was a troubleshooter in Mick's campaign to keep his Senate seat, and Mick a troubleshooter in my campaign to reclaim my life. Knowing the therapeutic value of long drives, he put me on the road, sometimes solitary, sometimes with him riding shotgun. At the end of September, coming back to Vanport from central Oregon, he told me that Isabel and Jeremy wanted to hold a small private service in honor of Patrick and plant a cedar seedling just off the trail to Mount Loowit. As we approached the distant white triangle of Mount Hood on Route 26, the flurries of the high desert became flakes flying so thick and fast that the road turned white.

"I'm ready, Mick, but what about you?" I said, recalling how painful the spot was for him.

Full of that extraordinary human warmth, he leaned over and rubbed the back of my head. My eyes filled because it was the same gesture he'd made to Patrick the first time he saw him and rubbed his head and hunched over to make himself the little guy's equal on the floor of our town house.

To give Kate as much notice as possible, I picked the third Saturday in October. She responded with a polite note to Isabel and Jeremy. She had commitments in Washington, she wrote, adding that "emotionally, it's too early for me, but you young people should go ahead."

The day of the ceremony dawned in impenetrable fog that burned off to reveal a sky of heavenly blue above air as dry and crisp as the crimson and ocher leaves. When we reached the meadow, Mick and Jeremy hunted for a spot where the seedling would get plenty of sun and I took Isabel's arm as she made her way into the clearing. As we walked, the musical charm bracelet on her left arm chimed in tune with her voice.

While she tuned her instrument, I wandered down the meadow to the mudflats. There were still indentations where Jeremy, Isabel, and their friends had dragged Patrick over the mud, and a slight depression marked the place of his fatal descent into the muck. I was turning around to head back when a ray of sun refracted off something half buried in mud. Remembering Isabel's harrowing story, I walked on my toes. But no cracks appeared as I reached the silvery bit. When I picked it up and wiped it off with my handkerchief, I recognized a miniature violin an inch long with a tiny loop at the neck. I turned it over and found the inscription: "To Isabel from Patrick." I began to cry. Momentarily dizzy, I turned around toward Mount Loowit. Soon I heard footfalls break out of the pack and then a voice.

"Gabe!" Mick cried out strongly then again, softly, "Gabe?"

"I wanted to see where . . . ," I said, approaching him.

Along the former lakeshore were the snags and stands of dead trees, some standing as straight as they'd been when the cloud of ash and fire stripped away their branches so many years ago, others drooped over, still mourning their stunted, amputated limbs. Beneath these trees were green signs of life, while on the near side of where the mudflow had occurred, dead trees mingled with sturdy new ones that were already taller than Patrick. The vine maples were back, too, blazing with autumn fire. Just before we reached the little circle of people, Mick turned to scan mountain and lake, his hand cupped over his forehead. He put his arm around me.

"Strange, Gabe. Rebecca's out there somewhere under all that muck."

In the sunlight I saw new creases in a face teetering between youth and middle age. Mick was forty-six. Without the creases, he looked less than forty; with them in stark relief, a man of fifty.

As we waited, the wind whistled in the tops of the trees at just the right transitional pitch. Before Isabel played, I fingered the silver violin in my pocket and watched the natural flush in her cheeks turn sunrise pink as she placed a handwoven cloth on her shoulder and adjusted her violin, her face shining as if she already heard the music.

"Samuel Barber's 'Adagio for Strings,'" she said.

As the melody ascended, my eyes stung. Kate and I had heard the piece played by a string orchestra at the Kennedy Center on the tenth anniversary of John Kennedy's death—dozens of strings sighing and straining as if Barber needed every violin in the world to express the slow, painful harmonies of human loss. Now, against the grain of music composed for the multiple violins of a string quartet or symphony orchestra, everything depended on one slight girl and her violin as the composer's struggle to give form to his grief became her struggle to become the voice of our grief for Patrick.

High in the trees a wind began to gust, then dipped lower and lower until the music ascending from Isabel's violin fused with the notes of the air. A bird trilled in a nearby cedar, the scales of the adagio became Isabel's lullaby, and I heard Patrick's coos and gurgles in his cradle and, later on, his squeals as he delighted in drawing breath after waking up from his nap. My tears flowed as I realized all over again that he was gone. Looking at young Isabel—her loveliness taut while she wooed the notes from her violin—I cried out silently against my son's fate never to have her love or the warmth of any woman. Isabel strained to release Patrick, but he was already elsewhere among unheard harmonies beyond the reach of her solitary violin. As I overflowed with grief during a long, sweet crescendo and climax, the composer came to the rescue with a bar of silence, and Isabel played the theme again. In the lower registers, the roll of grief sounded slowly, more unbearably, as Isabel's heartstring strained beyond the fiddle strings of her single inadequate violin. Her eyes briefly caught mine as she tautened her fingers and flexed her elbow for the final bars. For a few more moments, all eyes were on her. While she held the final notes of rest and resolution, the wind died down, and her silence was also the world's. As one, we resisted the impulse to clap when she took the cloth from her neck and held her bow and violin so still they seemed part of her.

In the bright silence, every eye quickened. Before anyone spoke, Jonas and Martin Fitch stepped forward. Jonas brushed the branch of a birch tree out of his face, and in his bass voice sang "Swing Low, Sweet Chariot." Then he yielded to Martin's tenor for the verse "coming for to carry me home" before father and son joined in a repeat so full of breath that the birch leaves trembled. Jonas looked at Isabel, and when she looked down at her violin, he nodded, and she played an accompaniment, tentative at first, then steady and true to their voices.

> *If you get there before I do,*
> *Coming for to carry me home,*
> *Tell all my friends I'm coming, too,*
> *Coming for to carry me home.*

The Fitches paused. Jonas hummed the refrain, then raised his hand to the rest of us, and we sang. When we were finished, we reached for the hand of the person on either side, surrounding the tiny cedar in a circle too imperfect to be traced by any compass. After an interval of silence, Mick broke the spell by tapping a marker into the rust-red earth. On the cedar chunk he'd carved Patrick's name and the dates of his birth and death. When Mick was done, we joined hands and sang together a last time.

Swing low, sweet chariot,
Coming for to carry me home.

I was sharing Isabel's hand with her bow. As our hands parted, the charms on her bracelet rang on the air with the high, faint tinkle of tiny invisible bells. While she and I took our places in the double-file line of departure, I opened my hand and put the tiny silver violin into hers.

"I found this near the spot where you found Patrick."

Her eyes brightened with tears as she read my son's inscription. She leaned toward me, then stopped. Her eyes offered a hug, which, if given, would have broken the intimacy.

"Oh, God," her voice broke. "Just before Patrick ran off, he said he had a surprise," she sobbed out the words. "I'll wear it for him when I play."

My eyes full, I nodded, and hearing the footfalls of Jonas and Martin behind us, we made our way down the trail.

In the meantime, as the Whelan reelection campaign purred along, I gravitated to the young people. In the past I had shunned them because they were kids—self-absorbed, sometimes know-it-alls, often earnest to a fault. Now, I took them under my wing and taught them the tricks of a campaign: how to cull likely voters from the unlikely; how to set up a canvass and keep your canvassers honest; how to disarm the press by seeming to know less than you did; how to attract free media; how to orchestrate political appearances by Senator Whelan as nonpartisan events. I pitched in on the tedious, messy jobs, such as washing storefront windows and scrubbing the floors, tables, and chairs for older volunteers, especially the women, who do most of the work in campaigns; organizing counter space for coffee, juice, and cookies; and hanging the vertical white-on-green Whelan for Senate banner from the front of headquarters to contrast with the horizontal signs of other candidates. The students couldn't get enough of my war stories about the sixties, and the more I sensed their conviction that the nineties could be a decade of idealism and activism, the more I craved their respect.

The leader of Students for Whelan was Jeremy Riggs the Mazama. Retro Gabe, he called me one night in a campus beer joint after noticing that I had gone without a haircut for more than a month.

"I've been meaning to ask you something," he said after licking the foam off a microbrew flavored with oatmeal. He looked around, as if expecting to see a Republican waitress listening around a pillar. "Is it frustrating to speak for the senator on every issue under the moon but never appear with him?"

It was after eleven. A two-hour drive from Eugene to Vanport loomed, and I began kicking myself for getting so chummy.

"We talk all the time."

"But not in public."

Finally grasping his point, I broke discipline.

"You want me to debate Senator Whelan?"

"Not exactly. Be on a platform together maybe . . . "

He took a swallow of beer and looked at me sheepishly.

"It's a stupid idea," he said. "It's not the way things work."

I left a ten for the beers and got up to go.

"I don't know about stupid, but you're right, it's not how things work."

A few days later, trolling for a laugh, I mentioned the exchange to Mick.

"Jeremy's right," he said. "Besides, if I keep quiet and healthy, the election's a walk. Let's do it."

Once he overcame his euphoria, Jeremy acted as if I had put him in charge of an old-growth forest. He scheduled the Whelan-Bontempo Show at the end of a statewide student-government convention on Halloween, about a week before the election. Going over the details, I put on my advance-man's hat.

"No press?"

"None."

"Publicity?"

"Announcements, no flyers."

"If press shows up?"

"It's private."

"By student preference?"

"Yes."

Halloween afternoon, Mick wouldn't stop ribbing me as we drove over to the Portland State University Student Center. "I need a skull session," he teased. "I need a speech coach and a makeup man."

At the ballroom, we walked up the ramp behind Jeremy so everyone could see us approach the stage. My practiced eye calculated the house at two-thirds full. Half the kids were in Halloween costumes, some dressed as figures from the sixties. Riveted by the mix of real and surreal faces, I sat down at a table on which three cardboard signs read, from left to right: Senator Michael Whelan; Jeremy Riggs, Moderator; Mr. Gabriel Bontempo, Administrative Assistant.

Before I knew it, Jeremy's introduction ended, and I was up first. As the applause died down, I told the students that at first I had turned down Mick's offer to work for him because I hadn't wanted to put our friendship in harm's way on the chameleon field of politics. Finishing up, I felt I had talked too much about resisting signing on with Mick, too little about how we worked together on the particulars of legislation and congressional maneuvering. But Mick covered me, and then some.

"In politics, you never want to speak first. But Gabriel Bontempo is not a politician. A politician warms up by listening to the other guy. But instead of listening, he's really rehearsing his own lines—lines he might not remember if he had to break the ice and be first."

Mick had most of the students leaning forward, laughing.

"But because Gabe told you why he didn't want to work for me, I'll tell you why I wanted him so badly."

He looked at me, his smile almost a grin, and took a long swallow from his glass of water.

"We met in 1963 during the March on Washington. He worked for the Justice Department; I was a student volunteer."

First fall to Mick, I thought, and the image I saw was not the settled figure of Senator Whelan, gray streaking the brown curls over his temples, but the fiery, wiry renegade who dared me to shame my superiors in LBJ's Justice Department into giving the seats belonging to Mississippi at the 1964 Democratic National Convention to Fannie Lou Hamer and the others who were risking their lives to defy segregation and the Klan. Not Senator Whelan in his chocolate-brown pinstripe suit, but young Mick Whelan in jeans on the steps of the Alabama state capitol in Montgomery in 1965 answering Martin Luther King's call of "How long?" with shouts of "Not long!" while I, still working at Justice, felt the words form silently on my lips.

Applause from the students interrupted my reverie. Senator Whelan was saying he had needed me at his side to tap the spirit of the sixties, and telling the students to "keep the faith" and pick up in the nineties where we left off in 1968. My head spinning, I thought how different the embers of '68 were for me, because I could never be free of the what-ifs for me or the country if Bobby K had lived.

Suddenly, the doors to the ballroom swung open and Miles Stein burst up the aisle. Black French cap on his head, video camera in hand, Nikon looped around his neck, he knelt and filmed Mick finishing his statement. While students with questions lined up at the microphones, Miles moved here and there, shooting. The questions failed to compete with him until a guy dressed as Mick Jagger asked Mick Whelan if there had been times when I had intended to resign or when he had been inclined to ask for my resignation. Without hesitation, Mick deadpanned a one-liner.

"Resignation, never. I've wanted to fire him a few times."

Soon Jeremy announced there was time for one more question. Immediately, a shaggy-haired guy in a jeans suit bent over one of the mikes.

"You broke your word, Riggs." He pointed a bony finger at Jeremy. "I went along with no press coverage because you said Senator Whelan and his man wanted a private discussion."

Obviously experienced at campus rabble-rousing, the young man turned the mike sideways and threw a scathing look at Miles, who was on his haunches, pointing his state-of-the-art Nikon.

"No one can move without this creep filming or snapping our pictures. Who is he, Riggs? FBI, CIA, or a Portland undercover cop?"

There was a ripple of assent as others in the audience followed the questioner's finger. Hearing the young agitator's *j'accuse*, Miles intensified his behavior. Without rising from a squatting position, he advanced, clicking rapidly until he had a close-up.

"No need to embarrass anyone," Jeremy answered. "The man shooting film sometimes works for Senator Whelan, but today he's here on his time."

A few scattered boos were heard. Mick lifted the microphone and brought it down with a thump on the table.

"Mr. Stein is here on his own, but a deal's a deal. I agree he shouldn't shoot anyone who doesn't want to be filmed."

At this, there were cheers from a few kids wearing Whelan buttons. Sensing his moment ebb, the shaggy young man fired an insinuating question calculated to restore his grip on the crowd.

"Who gets the film, Senator?"

Mick spotted Miles and beckoned him to the stage.

"Ladies and gentlemen," Mick said. "Miles Stein rushes in where angels fear to tread. He's a holy fool, and to introduce him, I'll call the roll of places he's been with his camera: Birmingham and Dallas, 1963; Meridian, Mississippi, and Atlantic City, 1964; Selma and Montgomery, Alabama, 1965; Memphis and Chicago, 1968; Kent State, 1970. He's lived in the line of fire, so don't let our friend here . . . " He pointed to where the shaggy guy stood, arms akimbo, legs straddling the microphone.

"Don't put words in my mouth, Senator!" he yelled.

But the interruption was red meat for Mick Whelan.

"Mr. Stein won't defend himself," Mick continued. "But like the black folks he filmed in the South, he goes ahead and does his work. His photographs and film clips stirred the conscience of the country."

By now, Miles had huffed and puffed up the stairs to the table, camera straps flapping at his sides like extra arms.

"Trick or treat?" he said.

"Who controls the film, wise guy?" the shaggy guy shouted.

Mick moved his chair so that Miles could bend over the microphone and speak while standing up, while Miles curled his forefinger through the thinning tuft of gray hair where his cap stopped.

"Film's mine unless you sign."

"Double-talk." Mister Shaggy shifted from insurgent to heckler.

Again, Mick took charge.

"How about giving him his say?"

Most in the audience stirred uneasily.

"Sit down, Gordo!"

"Yeah, shaggy, let the man talk."

Now the rhythmic clapping and stomping of feet irritated the antagonist into silence.

"Okay, sports fans," Miles told the crowd. "Negatives, mine, but I don't use prints without your permission. Pulitzer Prize, I don't care—no film goes out without your permission."

There was applause. Some kids stood as Miles walked off stage pantomiming snapping shots of shaggy head as he took the long way up the aisle. Before Jeremy could reach for the mike to close the meeting, I moved it in front of me.

"This wasn't planned," I said.

Again, there was laughter and impatient applause. The kids were restless and ready to party at the Halloween shindig.

"But it's a good example of how Mick Whelan works. He doesn't say he'll have an answer after he meets with his advisors. He's comfortable letting people around him speak their piece even when he might be better off telling us how it's going to be. But then he acts," I said, trying to paddle out beyond the shallows. "Mick Whelan's a senator, and people who work for him get paid. But without his friendship and respect, I'd get a real job."

I stopped long enough to think of a parting line.

"Miles," I said, "take a shot of me—use it any way you like."

That line got me more applause than anything else I'd said, and a pat on the back from Mick as I sat down. After an instant of indecision, Jeremy asked for a round of applause for the two surprise performers who had almost stopped the show.

"Jeremy might find himself in D.C. someday," I told Mick after he'd engaged shaggy Gordo for two minutes of back-and-forth on the First Amendment.

"I missed the violin," Mick winked at me, "as accompaniment to your riff at the end."

Election Day, the question wasn't whether Mick would win, but by how much. As usual, I took nothing for granted, monitoring the get-out-the-vote drive from a ten-line phone console at state headquarters in Vanport. At about three o'clock, a maternal volunteer brought me a Reuben sandwich, along with a letter that had come overnight from Washington, D.C. When I was alone, I noticed my home address in Kate's handwriting in the top left-hand corner, and ripped open the envelope without heeding the instructions to tear the flap across the dotted line. Dreading the red lights that were likely to flash at any moment, I buzzed the outer office and told them to hold all calls until I was through with my sandwich. Although the letter was handwritten, its consistent margins and careful spacing told me that Kate had roughed it out, revised it, then copied it over.

My dear Gabriel,

Forgive me if I have been hard to reach or less than responsive when you called. As I told you when you left after Patrick's funeral, I needed time to sort things out, and there was plenty to sort out after the shock of the accident and the awful way it happened. Not a day goes by I don't blame myself for leaving Patrick in Oregon. Something told me not to, but against my better instincts, I gave in, as I have done too many times in our marriage. They say your whole life passes in front of you at the moment of your death. I have felt something like that the past two months. Feeling responsible for Patrick's death hasn't left me, and never will. I am reconciled to that now. Knowing I will live with it every day of my life makes it easier for me to carry on. Not with the old life—the work I've been doing has shown me that I am able to take responsibility only by beginning a new life. That is why I am writing to you now—even though my lawyer advised me not to contact you.

With my thumb and forefinger, I detached two sheets of paper from the bulk of the letter; the top sheet was letterhead from a D.C. legal firm, the second a parchment document embossed with the District of Columbia seal.

I am not taking his advice. We have had a marriage, whatever its faults, and a wonderful son. These last years I fell into the trap of going on day to day as if the good outweighed the bad. Now that Patrick's gone, I can't kid myself that your love is anything else than politics with Mick Whelan.

I'm not blaming you—that's for you to sort out—but it's not an accident that what pulled you away from Patrick after you had promised to stay with him was a last-minute request from Mick Whelan. It's what you wanted to do; I realize that now. I'm not blaming you. You did the best you could. I've come to believe that. I didn't at first; I was bitter and angry. But now that Patrick's gone, you have to live your life, and I have to be free to live mine.

I hoped your being in Oregon for Mick's campaign might change things. Above all, Gabe, I was hoping for clarity. I have that now, and so I am filing for divorce. I came to this decision some time ago but wanted to live with it for a while. So please believe me when I say that it is the right thing for me. I also wanted to wait until the election season was over, for your sake. On that score, everything I hear is that Mick is a shoo-in, so I decided to get this to you when you might have the peace and quiet that you've always told me comes on Election Day.

I hope what has been between us—not just Patrick, but the other good things you and I have shared—will help us be as amicable as possible.

Then she signed her name—not *love* or *sincerely*, but simply *Kate*. Below her name was a hastily written postscript.

Unless you contest my right to do so, I plan to stay in the house. I've arranged to be away from November . . .

For a while, I sat in silence so deep, I heard the hum of the wall clock and a small sharp click each time the second hand passed twelve. Around me, everything vanished except the phone console. The conscientious volunteer had set a timer, and now lights flashed and several lines rang at once. By now, I was so far behind, I never did catch up. Each caller had a manufactured emergency, and I fought off numbness by responding as if Mick's reelection depended on me solving each and every problem, no matter how miniscule.

Telephone traffic slackened off ten minutes before the polls closed. Cheers from the big storefront room signaled the Whelans' arrival. Soon Mick poked his head into the inner sanctum.

"What's up, Gabe?"

"Looks like a low turnout—bad weather in the mountains and on the coast, but it will hurt him," I said, speeding like the auctioneer in the old Lucky Strike radio commercials.

"I meant with you."

I tossed him the envelope and watched the second hand swing twice, three times, around the face of the clock before he looked up.

"I'm sorry, Gabe. I'm really sorry."

He held out his hand to mine, his grip at once firm and gentle. Then we sat without talking.

After a while, Mick broke the silence.

"Sarah wondered . . . ," his voice trailed off. "Hell, Gabe, it's my fault for calling back about that damn hearing after you told me you'd promised to be with Patrick. I feel awful."

There was a knock on the door, and Sarah popped her head in.

"Mick, the natives are restless."

Looking from him to me, she sensed she'd interrupted something, but tact steered her back to the business she'd come on. "Your press man wants to know if you'll make a statement to reporters."

"Not until there's a result. He knows that."

He took her arm.

"Come right back."

When we were alone, he came and sat on the edge of the desk. Beyond him the room was beginning to blur. When Sarah returned, I told her the news.

"Let's cut things short," Mick said, looking from Sarah to me, "and slip over to York Island for a quiet drink and a bite."

"I'd like that."

Mercifully, by eight thirty every network projected Whelan a comfortable winner. After thanking his supporters, he met briefly with reporters and told them he'd be making a statement at the Portland Hilton.

Outside, he opened the door for Sarah and me. At the reserved parking space, he started the motor, then eased the dark car into the street.

"I'll make this quick," he said, pointing to the lights of Portland in the distance, "then The Blue Hour."

The Oregon Democrats' party at the Hilton had more the feel of a Greek wedding than an Irish wake, the faithful whooping it up as if carrying Oregon compensated for the ticket's landslide national defeat. Mick saw to it that he was the first speaker called to the podium.

"Not only is the Democratic presidential ticket leading in Oregon," the state chairman shouted in the voice of the union organizer he used to be, "but our great senator Mick Whelan has won a sweeping victory. Senator, come up here."

After congratulations to the victorious, condolences to the defeated, and second helpings of hope to those whose races were too close to call, Mick broke my distracted reverie with stirring words.

"I'm proud to be a liberal. Contrary to what we've heard from the Republicans and the press in this campaign, the *L* word is a good word—a word that pledges liberty and justice for all, a word for American ideas and ideals going back to the Declaration of Independence. So take heart, fellow Democrats, and remember that the people of Oregon have kept the faith despite the national defeat in this presidential campaign. Next time, we'll take this country back from those who say liberalism is finished."

Cheers erupted. There were shouts of "Whelan! Whelan!" from people I recognized from Mick's first election-night celebration in 1974, older now and graying, but still responding to Mick Whelan with piss and vinegar.

As Mick and Sarah made their way through the crowd, I heard a single foghorn voice holler, "Whelan in '92!" Several voices picked up the chant, and someone scrawled Whelan in '92 on the back of a placard for the defeated 1988 ticket. Momentarily, I felt an adrenalin surge, but when Mick saw that our path was directly in line with the guy holding the improvised Whelan for President sign, he changed direction. In a series of calculated, casual gestures, he dove in and out of the swells of Democrats in his path. Watching his practiced act cheered me: a handshake here, his hand on an elbow to steer him to the right, the other hand on the shoulder of the next person, then a swivel-hipped move and he was in the clear, smiling and talking all the while, face turning right, then left, not missing anyone as he passed, all the while keeping Sarah in close range. Starting for the revolving door, he stopped to shake hands with the doorman.

Outside, Sarah's teeth chattered as she put her arm in Mick's. "Brrr."

Three abreast, we walked down the block, then got in the car for the drive back to Vanport and the ferry to York Island.

"Are you sure you're up for this?" I inquired from the backseat.

"Absolutely," they answered together.

During the five-minute ferry ride, we stood against the starboard bow and watched the wind stir the tips of the dark waves into froth. Mick sheltered Sarah against the drizzle mingling with spray from the Columbia.

At The Blue Hour, we slipped into an inconspicuous booth. As soon as Horace, the bartender who sang tenor in the Ship of Zion choir, spotted us, he came over.

"Senator, from what I hear, it looks like there won't be peace and quiet for you. Yes, sir," he leaned over in a confidential way, "you didn't pay those 1992 signs no mind. 'That's the Mick Whelan I know,' I thought, 'got to let that Greek fella get over the hurt,' But people watching on television at the bar, they allowed as how you might be as good a candidate as the Democrats can find next time—for number two, if not the top spot."

"Good God," Sarah said. "We're barely through one election."

"That's true, Missus. But folks talking about the handsome couple you and the senator make—fine as a new dime."

Horace paused, then proceeded to take our order as smoothly as he changed keys on Sunday mornings.

"Mick," Sarah said, "those nuts holding up the sign about 1992—the eager beavers on your staff didn't put them up to it?"

"If they did, they'll be looking for jobs in the morning," Mick answered.

For a while we ate in silence. Every time I looked at Mick and Sarah as they exchanged glances or passed the salt and pepper, my head turned and sought a line of sight on the river beyond the French doors. But, apart from flotsom bobbing up and down, there was no point of reference—no stern-wheeler churning downriver, cruising toward Vancouver, its necklace of lights framing the nightly ritual of couples dining and dancing.

Suddenly, I was a teenager again on Shelter Island *imagining the goings-on aboard what I took for a pleasure boat off Big Ram Island. Lights bobbed up and down along the deck, and ashore, the girl I was parked with thought she heard a calliope playing. But the next day, the island was in an uproar at the news that the owner of a garish mansion on Big Ram was dredging his cove under cover of darkness and destroying the refuge of nesting herons along the shore.*

"Gabe," Sarah said, picking at the tangled remains of croutons, grains of Parmesan cheese, and scraps of lettuce on her plate, "is there anything we can do?"

She saw me wince.

"I knew things were rocky," her voice drifted and her eyes veered off course from mine, in Mick's direction.

I swallowed, my mouth too dry to speak even if I had had words. Again, I looked out at the river. The shimmering flotsam had run south with the current, and it took my eyes a few seconds to track its dim, shifting course.

"I let things go for too long," I said, readjusting to the light in the cocktail lounge as I turned back to Mick and Sarah and let the words tumble out. "I was hurt when Kate turned cold after Patrick's accident—after he died. I didn't blame her for blaming me. But she made a cause out of it."

I took a sip of cognac. "Her not wanting anything in Oregon, I could handle. And her not coming out, I could handle. But when I called to tell her how the ceremony had gone, I couldn't get five words out of her."

I took another sip from the enormous snifter in front of me and rolled the cognac around in my mouth.

"She rattled on about the Freer and Mick's campaign. God, when I said I was hurt, she acted like I was from another planet."

Sarah leaned to her right and put a hand on my arm.

"Shows *she's* hurting."

Across the table, Mick looked from our faces into the bottom of his brandy and up again.

"Go home, Gabe. You never know."

As he talked, the palms of his hands stayed anchored to his brandy snifter while his fingers moved out in space as if describing the journey. "Be matter of fact if you write."

Sarah's eyes flashed. "Mick," she said sharply, "he's not writing a press release."

His fingers closed over his glass. "I don't know, Sarah," he said nonchalantly, "people are always talking about love and politics."

"Don't you two start a small war over this," I said, trying to break the tension.

At that same moment, they reached for each other's hand, and I no longer felt like Joe Btfsplk, the vowel-less man in "Li'l Abner" with the gray cloud over his head wherever he went. At the piano, the torch singer launched into "A Tisket, A Tasket." Kittenish at first, she became ever more urgent, sultry, and vulnerable as she reached for the lower registers that Ella Fitzgerald had made famous. She was backed by a piano player with short salt-and-pepper hair that looked like a cap woven around his head. Wherever she went, he followed her on the keys like a lover. As the song wound down, I felt close to Mick and Sarah. For the first time since reading Kate's letter, I felt she and I might be able to put Humpty Dumpty back together again. In my moment of inattention, Mick grabbed the check, and he and Sarah got to their feet.

"I'll see you to the ferry," I told them.

"No need," said Mick.

"Too cold," agreed Sarah.

While Mick lingered, accepting congratulations from a couple at the bar, Horace sidled up to Sarah.

"Missus," he said, "don't take this wrong, but I won't be surprised you and the senator have me singing 'Amazing Grace' come Inauguration Day in 1993."

"Good night, Horace," we said serially, each off key.

Outside, Mick and Sarah walked with their arms around each other along the path to the ferry, and the three of us embraced before they stepped across the metal grate to the boat.

"You're true friends," I said.

As their ferry chugged away from the dock, I stretched out my arms. "I almost forgot!" I shouted. "Congratulations, Senator!"

In my room at The Blue Hour, I left the balcony door open a crack before climbing into the king-size bed and arranging the pillows into a tunnel for my head. In the morning, there was steam at the edges of the sliding-glass door and frost outside on the balcony railing. Sitting up, I was shocked into alertness by the air and by the lingering impression that during the night Patrick had tiptoed into my room. I remembered straining to speak to him as he rubbed his hand back and forth across the top of my head, but I'd been unable to move. Now, jarred out of bed by an image of him that was more apparition than dream, I grabbed my clothes and dressed by the balcony door. In the eastern sky, the massed blue-black shapes of dawn retreated before streaks of red and yellow—a snappy vanguard marching west to clear out any pockets of resistance to the sun's advance over the dark peaks of Loowit. Seized with anxiety,

I checked out, and made sure that Kate's letter was tucked away in my brown leather pouch in front of the papers I needed for Mick Whelan's postelection press conference.

Chapter 20

Stuck in a holding pattern outside Washington, my plane wheeled over the Shenandoah at Harper's Ferry. Looking down, I tracked the Potomac's dark, narrowing path to Washington. On his final approach, the pilot banked left, then right, so passengers could catch a glimpse of the Capitol Dome dimming from rose to lavender, the ghostly green glow of the Washington Monument, and, finally, the brightly lit columns of the Lincoln Memorial, where he dipped in salute. Exhilarated by the markings of the nation's past, I forgot to grip the top of the seat in front of me, and when the wheels bumped on the runway, I jounced forward, smacking my forehead against the plastic traytop of the seatback in front of me.

On the ground, my mind went blank. The more imposing the monuments in the distance, the more lonely it felt without Kate and Patrick, and the more the marble of Washington mocked my unchiseled face of grief. For almost twenty years, I had shared the glories and shame of the nation's capital with my wife, and then my son. Recalling that Kate and I put our money on Washington when most of our friends were moving to the suburbs of Maryland or Virginia, it occurred to me that having a family and going to work for Mick Whelan had been my attempt at e pluribus unum. But when my cab turned out of Rock Creek Park, it took me two tries to come up with my street address. The driver, wearing an old beat-up Washington Senators baseball cap halfway up his bald head, chuckled at my lapse.

"Been gone so long, you done forgot home."

"Something like that," I said, opening the rear door of the cab as I tipped him.

Inside, I switched on the lights, dropped my bags on the landing, hung up my coat in the little vestibule, and headed to the kitchen. Wandering the downstairs, a glass of Irish in my hand, I noticed subtle changes. I liked a book and one or two magazines on the coffee table, but Kate preferred it bare; now, before me, was only a stack of brass coasters stamped with the logo of the Freer Gallery. Upstairs, later, I unpacked my bags. Finding only Kate's special hard-as-a-rock pillow on the queen-size bed, I went across the hall to Patrick's room. His things were arranged like an exhibit, his single bed stripped, so I went back downstairs, poured more Irish, and looked out the French doors at the headlights exploding silently though the trees in Rock Creek Park. Under the arch between the living room and the kitchen, I traced the forms of the two peacocks on the Whistler lithograph I'd had framed for Kate the Christmas before.

"Fuck it," I said, and left my drink on top of the coasters, went upstairs, got into bed, and read briefing papers from the Latin American Affairs Subcommittee before falling asleep.

Several days later, I was working late when the buzzer buzzed on my private line.

"Gabe?" I recognized Kate's voice.

"Kate, hi."

"Gabe, tomorrow's the day I wrote you I'm coming back."

"Everything's fine with the house."

There was a half click and a sigh.

"Hello?" I said.

"I'm here," she said as if only the therapeutic patience of Job kept her on the line. She breathed in at the other end, then exhaled with a sniff through her nose, a mannerism that kicked in whenever she tried to keep irritation in check. "I don't want you in the house as a boarder."

"I want to see you."

"Certainly."

"In our living room."

"Gabe, for God's sake."

"Look, I'm going along with you on the house. Can't you go along on where we meet?"

"Tit for tat," she said. "Tit for tat."

I was too upset to say anything else. Beyond the office window across the street from the Russell building I recognized John Lewis, the old SNCC hero, now a congressman from Georgia, walking toward the Capitol arm in arm with his wife. As they passed the guardhouse, they started to kick up leaves piled high on the walkway as if they were leading a chorus line.

"You win," Kate said into the silence.

The appointed afternoon was one of those November days after the time change when the sun signs off prematurely, leaving a cold red glow in the sky. Kate had the furnace setting a couple of degrees lower than I was used to, and I offered to make a fire. She nodded assent, and I laid the fire, struck a match, and, as the paper and kindling caught, looked around for the aluminum tube I used to blow the embers into full flame. Expecting to become a New Age Edison or Ford, a ne'er-do-well cousin of mine had manufactured fireplace blowers by hand for a while in the seventies. On Patrick's first Christmas, he gave us a designer model fitted with a leather mouthpiece. The object was a natural conversation piece that transformed me into a mean guy with a match. But for years the gadget had kept falling down from where I leaned it against the fireplace, and I never followed through on promises to rig a clasp that would keep it upright.

"Have you seen the blower, Kate?"

She was sitting on the couch, leafing through a folder whose contents were attached to the file with a peacock-shaped paper clip.

"Hmm?"

"The aluminum tube my cousin made after Patrick was born."

Looking up, I saw Kate's face in the oval mirror on the opposite wall. Behind her image a purplish red blotch of sky was fading to blue-black in the glass.

"I gave it to Goodwill."

I stared at her in disbelief.

"Gabe, the thing kept making spots on the rug."

I squatted down in front of the fireplace, poked the sparse sticks of wood to let more air in between the paper below the grate and the logs above, then leaned over and blew into the fire until sparks flew in my face and out over the little courtesy rug protecting the hardwood floor. I stamped my foot on the runaway cinders and took the Lord's name in vain.

"Don't 'Jesus' me," Kate said.

"I wasn't."

By now, the fire was sputtering. Without my cousin's tube it was sure to go out, so I pulled the little wire mesh curtains closed and sat back down on the couch.

"Gabe," she said, "I want a clean break."

I exhaled as if I was still tending the fire.

"If that's what you want," I said, wishing I had some say but realizing for the first time that the connection I'd flown across the continent to remake was severed—for me as well as for Kate.

I declined her offer to call a taxi. At the door, she handed me a large manila envelope of keepsakes and extended her hand straight and true as an arrow.

On the way over to Massachusetts Avenue, I remembered first seeing Kate on the Mall this time of year at a 1969 moratorium protesting Nixon's continuation of the Vietnam War. She arrived dragging a sky-blue banner on which she'd drawn a white dove in the shape of Vietnam with blood-red markings on its breast, but as she unfurled it on the grass, the banner was wider than the wingspan of her arms.

"Damn," she said, loud enough to be heard by several admiring young men.

I was the first to move in. "You hold one side, I'll hold the other."

She looked over the competition, her gray hazel-flecked eyes flashing above a full-lipped mouth that changed from a pout into a smile that made my insides jump.

"I'll take you up on that," she said. The sea of potential admirers parted, and, holding the banner aloft, we stepped off to scattered clapping and several envious stares.

The day after Kate made her clean break, I rented the three-room ground floor of a narrow townhouse a ten-minute walk from Capitol Hill. There was living space for one and, as I got my bearings, once in a while, two. In my solitary routine, the kitchen, living room, and bedroom became separate sites for acts of cooking and eating, reading or watching television (though often I hustled back and forth from the couch and a magazine to the stove where my dinner was cooking), and sleeping. But far from picking up the slack of my life, for the first time working for Whelan became only that—work.

As the eighties passed into the nineties, gotcha politics were in vogue. Confirmations were voted down because of allegations of boozing or womanizing; congressmen and senators were videotaped accepting cash; leaders resigned over shady book deals. All the while, the urge for higher ratings and profits drove television networks and newspapers of record to cover scandal more conscientiously than policy. Through the looking glass of the Cold War's ending, while the citizens of East Germany poured through gashes in the Berlin Wall singing, "We shall overcome," government in Washington became government by veto. When I told Mick I'd had an offer from the lobbying firm I'd turned down more than a decade before, he flipped a stack of nominations for law-school deanships across his desk. In the past, he'd made jokes about being dean for a day, but now he traveled to several institutions delivering his Abraham Lincoln "Politics and the Constitution" talk. Still, nothing came of the grousing, and the Senate remained a holding operation until the spring of 1991.

Ticker tape was still blowing in the streets from parades in celebration of the end of the Gulf War when word leaked that the White House was preparing a resolution authorizing the president to use military force anywhere in Latin America to stave off threats to America's well-being. The president's advisors were confident that Democratic senators who had opposed the Gulf War wouldn't dare vote against a resolution offered by a triumphant president to protect American interests close to home. In Mick Whelan's case, they didn't know their man. He took seriously his new assignment as chairman of the Senate subcommittee on Latin American Affairs. I didn't know how seriously until I returned from lunch one day to find that Marva had put out an all-points bulletin.

"The senator's been looking for you," she said when I strolled in. "He's with Congressman Hart."

Entering the inner sanctum with my folder on the military-force resolution in hand, I was surprised at the frail, forlorn old man who welcomed me.

"Well, well, Gabriel."

With an effort, Henry Hart stood up, favoring his back.

"Henry," I said, shaking hands warmly, "I'm surprised to see you on the Senate side of the dome."

Hart sat down slowly and crossed his long legs, his arms dangling over his knees until both hands met.

"It's this damned resolution, Gabriel," Hart said.

Whelan stood up behind his desk and began pacing while Hart got comfortable on the couch and leafed through a page or two of notes.

"Michael, I've been working the phones on the House side so I would have something concrete to tell you." He tossed his legal pad on the table. "The boys and girls are playing defense for 1992."

Hart acknowledged Mick's frown with a wave of his hand. "Michael, you say this resolution could turn the countries of Latin America into provinces of the United States—I agree. But you asked for a reading of Democrats in the House." He sighed. "Many House Democrats who stuck their necks out on the Gulf War see the president as vulnerable on the economy. But the Gulf War was such a popular success—so few Americans killed—they want the party strong on defense and national security. They remember that fella in the damn tank."

Hart shook his head with the resignation of an old man who no longer believed in his power to dominate reality. Without unthreading his fingers, he removed his hands from around his knees and rested his arms on the back of his head.

Sneaking a look at the top sheet of the congressman's pad, I saw numbers circled in red. In the meantime, Hart eased over to the middle cushion of the couch so he wouldn't have to shade his eyes from the sunlight pouring in through the sparse branches of a swamp oak on the Capitol lawn.

"Gabriel, your eyes are younger than mine. Read off the numbers in red on my pad."

"One forty, fifty, seventy-five."

"That's a rough breakdown of House Democrats. The fifty no's you can count on, Michael; some of the yes's are soft; the seventy-five undecideds are sniffing the wind. But the White House spin machine is making sure representatives know the approval rating of the Gulf War in their districts. No one in the House is prepared to get out front, especially not with our old friend César Rivera chairing the Military Preparedness Subcommittee and calling the tune on base closings."

"So the Senate's the ballgame," Mick said, turning to me. "How do you call it, Gabe?"

"Knee-jerk supporters of the president, fifty-five. Doves, fifteen. Head in the sand or don't know, thirty."

"That's bad," Henry said.

Mick looked beyond Hart to the greenish light rippling through the trees.

"Not necessarily. Hell, Henry, we started farther behind on national service and high-speed trains and pulled it out."

"That was in the House," I butted in, "with a friendly chairman."

Congressman Hart looked at Mick and dismissed my compliment with a curt wave. I would not have wanted to have been a lawyer defending a shaky case in his Texas hill-country courtroom.

"But Henry," Mick said, "you taught me how to change the count."

Hart laughed and leaned forward, tense for action.

"Michael, you're just the senator to fight this resolution. And there is one other thing in your favor. Some in the Senate haven't forgotten their constitutional role in foreign policy."

Mick slipped his hand into his jacket pocket, his fingers probing the silk lining.

"Henry, there's something else I need your counsel on."

For a moment, the old twinkle lit Hart's eyes and propelled his hands forward in their former strong, sure gesture. "The republic's come to a fine pass when a second-term senator turns to a dried-up old pecan like me."

"That's where we are, Henry." Mick gave the old man's knee a quick pat, then took a tin of little cigars from his pocket. "I've got to figure out a way to open the debate."

"Well, now, Michael, what's a subcommittee for if not to take up matters its chairman deems of national importance?"

Hart stood up and walked to the window. He began to pace slowly and unsteadily back and forth, like a show horse at his last competition.

"Tell them the president's resolution is a chance to look at American interests and policy in Latin America. If you're lucky and call the right witnesses, CNN might televise a session."

Lighting his cigar, Mick considered and got to his feet.

I stood up, too, and as soon as they noticed me, they sat down again.

"Michael, you're doing the Senate a favor. No matter which side they're on, if you play it fair—patriot that you are—true senators will thank you for letting them be senators."

Whelan made a fist and punched it into his other hand, and, for a while longer, Henry Hart remained the Have a Heart of old. As Mick stood up to show him out, Hart beat him to the door without a hobble.

"I can't deliver the House, Michael," he said, "but I'll be your eyes and ears with former members now in the Senate."

I was present in Mick's office the afternoon he went over details of the hearings with the subcommittee's vice chairman, the senior senator from Wyoming, or, as both Democrats and Republicans on the staff called him behind his back, the senator from Grizzly.

"Senator Whelan, you are most kind," the vice chairman said while, obeying the command of Mick's outstretched palm, he settled into the leather chair with the best view of the Capitol and the Mall.

"My pleasure. I love that view," Mick said, moving the ashtray to the end table next to the senator.

"Yes," the senator responded, "that, too," running a hand through his iron-gray wavy hair. "But I meant having a private chat on these hearings of yours. You may hang your hat on the other side of the aisle, but you bend over backward to be fair. If, as I expect, Republicans gain control of the Senate next year, I will reciprocate."

Mick shifted his eyes to the window, passing mine but never lingering. "We've got two and a half days for the hearings. I've looked over time slots. You're welcome to all seven witnesses you asked for at an hour each—or you can cut one or two so each one will have more time."

The senator looked down his tortoiseshell bifocals at the list in his hands and stroked his chin until an I-may-be-a-nice-guy-but-I-know-how-to-drive-a-hard-bargain expression captured the landmass of his face.

"Senator Whelan, I'd like to cut my witness list to six, give two an hour and the other four an hour and a half."

"Eight hours," Mick said, and turned to me. "Gabe, how would that work?"

"It would play havoc with the majority witnesses and also shorten the time for senators' final remarks."

Whelan stroked his chin in silence. "The hell with it. I'd like to oblige the senator." Then he addressed his colleague softly. "Would you agree to have senators on both sides limit their closing remarks to five minutes, with ten minutes for you as vice chair, ten for me, then call it quits?"

The senator from Wyoming beamed. "It was wise of me to come alone," he said, then coughed into the folds of his immaculate white handkerchief. "Senator Whelan, sometimes I think the Senate would be a more civil body if we limited our staffs to a driver, a valet, a personal secretary, and a stenographer for each committee."

Then he looked over at me as if one of us had come in without knocking.

"You seem old school, too," he said out of the side of his mouth as if I was a Cheyenne brave and he an agent from the Bureau of Indian Affairs puffing a peace pipe. "My man is the new breed—discourages me from looking a man of different views in the eye, shaking hands, and calling a deal a deal."

He slapped his knee with one hand, mine with the other. "Sometimes I get the impression he doesn't think I'm too bright."

The senator replaced the white handkerchief in the upper pocket of his jacket, and, while he was at it, removed two ten-inch cigars. He masked a sense of unworthiness behind one of the most ponderous self-presentations in the Senate, but his cigars puffed him up to where he felt equal to his betters.

"Senator Whelan, will you have one of these to seal our agreement—they're Havanas."

"I'd like that, Senator," Mick said, looking past my head before reaching for the cigar.

The Republican vice chairman of the Latin American Affairs Subcommittee slid the band off his long panatela and watched Mick grip the band on his cigar as if to peel it off.

"If I may, Senator Whelan," he reached for Mick's cigar. "A man ought to let another man do what he pleases with his cigar, but I'd like to keep your band in one piece for my grandson."

The senator unbuttoned his jacket and reached inside for the monogrammed cigar cutter that dangled from a gold chain like a Phi Beta Kappa key. He passed it to Whelan, who had reclaimed his cigar, moistened it, and was preparing to bite off the end. Again looking at the wall, Mick snipped off the end of his cigar with the gold cutter. Business done, cigars lit, Whelan became inquisitive about his colleague's grandson. Fortunately, at my suggestion, he had instructed Marva to interrupt any meeting he was having with another senator after the first half hour and every fifteen minutes thereafter. Sometimes he waved off the buzzer; at others he brusquely told Marva whoever it was would have to wait. But picking up the phone now, he became excessively interested in her phantom message, listening with a graver and graver expression.

"Tell him I'm sorry," he said, then, after repeating "I understand," hung up, holding his cigar aloft as if supplicating the gods to save him and all good senators from obtuse secretaries.

"This is an amazing cigar," he told his colleague.

"Well, now, Senator Whelan, here's hoping the taste and aroma stay with you. Jack Kennedy liked a good cigar. I always thought he would carry the country with him in a war with Cuba if he'd made Castro choose between cigars or the missiles."

Mick laughed, a little more than was polite. In a minute, the Republican vice chairman flicked the ash from his cigar and slapped his free hand on his knee.

"I better be moseying." He stood up. "Senator Whelan, you're a good man to do business with."

Mick walked him to the door.

"Thank you, Senator. You drive a hard bargain but offer the best cigar."

The senator beamed again, this time wide enough so that a gold tooth appeared, its shine the exact shade of his cigar cutter.

"Gabe will review the order of the witnesses with your man."

The senior senator from Wyoming nodded.

"By the book, Senator," I said. "Strictly by the book."

He put his hand playfully on my shoulder.

"Don't worry, young man, I'll tell Joseph everything is settled."

As he left, he winked at Marva, his cigar almost out of sight until he was in the corridor where a cloud of smoke reassured him and he waved to us, a big smile on his face.

"Son of a bitch filibusters against relaxing the trade embargo with Cuba and brags about his supply of Havanas," I groused as Mick closed the door of his inner office and we sat down.

"He's all right," Whelan mused.

I sprawled on the couch while Mick sat in one of the leather chairs, his hands folded against the back of his head, the cigar tendered by the senator from Wyoming glowing faintly in the ashtray.

"What now?" I asked.

"Ask the Democratic members to get back to me if they have any suggestions, but make sure they react to my witnesses first."

Then he lowered his voice so I'd know the next point was important. "And give me a fallback name for every slot by breakfast."

I stayed in the office until after midnight, tracking sources at State, Defense, and the CIA. At seven, Mick and I met over café au lait and apple crisp at Au Bon Café, a hole-in-the-wall café adjacent to the Library of Congress. Mick cleared a space in the middle of a tiny marble table for my list of witnesses.

As he talked there was a lull in the line of federal employees coming in for their early-bird coffee and croissants. Hearing a sweet, sassy Jamaican voice, I waved at the manager.

"Hey, Mistuh Gabriel, what you mean not telling Eulalee you bringing Senator Whelan this mornin'?" She shook her finger. "De archangel Michael higher up de Lawd's food chain than de angel Gabriel."

Eulalee rubbed her hand on her light-blue starched apron and stuck out her hand, which Mick took in both of his.

"So you're the woman who puts café au lait and apple crisp into this man's belly so he can do a decent morning's work."

She lingered until she could no longer ignore the half a dozen impatient customers lined up along the granite counter.

At our cramped corner table, Whelan peered at my list, made several switches between my first- and second-string witnesses, asked me to alert the press for a two o'clock open-mike session with the senator from Wyoming, and told me to come by after lunch. As we were leaving, Eulalee swayed over again.

"Senator," she said loud enough for everyone, including several Republican types who were waiting for their eight o'clock lattes, to hear, "my mahn Jomo, he drive a cab in dis town. He say dat mahn Whelan, he from O-ray-gone—dat's true—but we need him for dis whole countree."

"Tell Jomo I hope he passes by the Capitol next time I need a ride," Mick replied in farewell.

Outside, he and I headed toward Independence Avenue.

"That Eulalee's some number," he said.

I stopped at the Library of Congress to bone up on oil reserves in Latin America. Later, when I got back to the office after a meeting at the Interior Department on old-growth forests and a long leisurely lunch afterward, Mick was pacing back and forth in his inner office muttering uncharacteristically incoherent phrases.

"Today of all days to take a three-martini lunch."

"Chianti and pasta," I said. "At Boccaccio's, like we did when you were trying to hire me."

He laughed, but his eyes burned. "Can we talk?"

It was my habit to remain on my feet at tense times with Mick until the old waves of the Sound Connection began to surge over us.

"A couple of Democrats want me to throw off the Republicans' four-star general or find one opposed to the president's resolution authorizing military force in Latin America."

"Everything else okay?"

"Check," he said, coming back to Earth. "Before I forget, you must have given away the store this morning. I had calls from the Interior undersecretary and the executive director of the Sierra Club, both telling me what a great job you did."

I snapped my fingers.

"By the way, Mick, Jack Phillips stopped in from the woods. He wants to pay a courtesy call on you."

"I don't have anything else to do. Why don't you bring in everybody else I've done a favor for in the last ten years?"

I waited.

"Sorry, Gabe," he stopped carrying on. "How did Jack do?"

"Every so often that scary, faraway Vietnam look comes into his eye, but when he stays on point, he's a good witness."

Suddenly, Whelan doubled up both hands into fists and slammed them on the desk.

"Damn it, Gabe, that's it! Young Jack is the perfect foil to the Republicans' four-star general—an ordinary soldier with combat medals whose father was one of the congressmen the military most respected."

Before Mick got carried away, it was my job to anticipate even the most unlikely mortar shell that might be lobbed his way.

"Suppose Jack's not up to the strain," I said. "Suppose the press accuses you of using him because of his father. Suppose someone in the White House with access to Army records feeds a reporter the story of the Mexican G.I. who threw himself on the grenade instead of Jack . . . Is it worth the risk?"

Whelan considered.

"Find him."

"Let him find you," I said. "Last thing he said was that he'd look you up."

Mick swung forward in his chair and pressed the buzzer.

"Marva, when Jack Phillips Jr. calls me, put him through. If he stops in, show him in—no matter who I'm with or what I'm doing."

Young Jack showed up after Marva left for the day, and he was intense enough for the twentysomething manning the phones to buzz Mick. She told me she'd never seen Senator Whelan move so quickly; he came out, gave the visitor a handshake and a hug, and ushered him into his office. Fifteen minutes later, I was summoned to buy young Jack a beer and brief him. The whole time, I watched for the wandering eye, the high, harsh laugh, the tight mouth, but none came. By now, Jack had something of his father's gravity as well as an occasional otherworldly look that marked him off from the rest of us.

Jack had also wanted to see Mick about the president's resolution. Settled into his Forest Service job, he had become active in the national organization of Vietnam veterans and was serving a term on the board of directors. According to Jack, plenty of vets were worried that if the president's resolution passed, men would die before the American people knew what was happening. In short, he was a well-informed, eager potential witness. Concerned that people would accuse him of trading on his father's name, Jack insisted he not be identified with his father or the Vietnam veterans' organization.

"Winter soldier. Take me or leave me," he told Mick.

Then Mick got another break. The day before the hearings, a story broke in the *Post* that the petroleum lobby had orchestrated the gist and timing of the president's resolution. Big oil companies were dismayed when Saddam Hussein remained in power with his hand on the spigot. One of their lawyers wrote a top-secret memo urging that the resolution give this and future presidents authority to commit peace-keeping troops indefinitely upon the threat of insurgency or unrest in Venezuela—whose proven oil reserves were next in line behind Iraq—or anywhere else in Latin America *without* further action by Congress. Finally, the story alleged that the memo had been funneled to the White House, intended for the eyes of the president's nephew, a less-than-successful former Texas oilman.

By the time Mick gaveled the first session of the subcommittee to order, senators on both sides of the aisle were grumbling about White House insensitivity to the Constitution's checks and balances and separation of powers. And because the hearings were the only game in town, cameras and notepads were out in full force.

"The Latin American Affairs Subcommittee will come to order," Senator Whelan began, blinking into the glare of the stationary CNN camera that was pointed straight at him. "This hearing is not a direct response to the resolution about to be sent to both Houses of Congress by the president, but testimony offered here may provide a context for the debate on the floor of the Senate next week," he added, then introduced the senior senator from Wyoming.

Once he had run his fingers back and forth like the teeth of a small rake to delineate the ridges in his hair, the senator seconded Mick's every word, and then some.

"For the bipartisanship of this hearing," he said, "each of us owes a debt to the senator from Oregon. He has structured these hearings as an exercise in representative democracy. Senator Whelan, I yield the floor back to you."

Predictably, several senators pursued lines of questioning that argued for or against the upcoming military-force resolution, but the chairman and vice chairman took turns keeping the subcommittee from breaking up into competing factions. In the meantime, more and more doubts surfaced about the resolution, whose language an overconfident White House insisted was nonnegotiable, causing a few more senators to slip off the presidential bandwagon. There were also reports in the press that roving bands of paramilitaries funded by the CIA were preparing to disrupt the elections in Venezuela, even to the point of Civil War, should the candidate in favor of nationalizing the oil companies pull farther ahead in the polls. Through it all, Mick held his fire, and no one objected to young Jack Phillips as the last witness. During the recess just before his testimony, I tipped off media people I knew that the dramatic moment was at hand.

"It better be, Bontempo," grumbled Nick Smart, a CBS reporter who had showed up because I warned him he'd be scooped if he didn't. "My editor's already accusing me of chasing skirt down here."

When Jack came on, in place of green-camouflage fatigues, the uniform of choice for most Vietnam vets appearing before congressional committees, he wore gray slacks and a blue blazer with silver buttons. In his right lapel was a tiny American flag, in the left, his Marine Corps insignia with the letters *VV* sewn in scarlet underneath. But the statement he read was prosaic, in places pedantic and tedious. Likewise, in his answers to senatorial questions he sounded like a pious son striving to say what his father might have said rather than a man testifying from the marrow of his own experience and conviction. Nick Smart glared at me, but his cameraman left his red light on. As I brooded on the damage control I would have ahead of me, the lean and hungry voice of the last senator to question the witness broke through my daydream. He was a nondescript Missouri Republican. Elected by a fluke, he knew any chance for reelection depended on great gouts of cash from the Republican National Committee, an arm of the White House if there ever was one.

"Now, Mr. Phillips—you do go by Mr. Phillips? Or do you still hold your lieutenant's commission in the Marine Corps?"

"*Mr.* is correct, Senator."

"You are currently employed by the Forest Service?"

"That is correct."

"In which jurisdiction?"

"Mount Hood National Forest."

"In Oregon?"

"That is correct."

"Did Senator Whelan provide one of your references?"

"He did, Senator."

"Now, Mr. Phillips, would you tell the subcommittee . . . "

The flush drained from Phillips's face, giving him the reddish brown look of volcanic cinders in central Oregon.

"Excuse me, S-senator, Senator Whelan wrote the reference ten years ago when he was a congressman. Since that time, I have worked my way up to the rank of s-senior ranger."

There were titters of laughter followed by a short drumbeat of applause from the uniformed Vietnam veterans in the last two rows. Except for the laser glint in his eyes, Mick's expression was as impervious as the chief croupier's in the swankiest casino on the Vegas strip might have been watching a high roller lose the biggest pot of the night. Before the senator could resume questioning Jack Phillips, Whelan banged his gavel.

"Order in the hearing room, so the senator from Missouri may complete his questioning in a dignified manner."

Grins flashed on several faces, and the senator did not acknowledge his chairman's comment by word or look.

"Mr. Phillips, I did not know your father, the late congressman from

Oregon, but I respected him. I particularly admired his ability to anticipate threats to our national security, as does, umm, the president's military-force resolution. Now, Mr. Phillips, I honor your dedicated service in Vietnam."

The senator minced a look in Whelan's direction.

"I am also pleased to note your progress up the ranks of the Forest Service bureaucracy. I have no further questions unless, umm, Mr. Phillips, you have anything you wish to add to the expert testimony already heard by this subcommittee."

Mick skillfully interposed his person and gavel between the senator and the witness.

"Mr. Chairman," Jack said, "there is something I would like to say as a private citizen who has served his country as a soldier."

"I object, Mr. Chairman," came the lean and hungry voice.

Mick was silent, and the senator plunged ahead.

"My question limited further testimony by the witness to matters of expertise, not opinion."

"The chair takes the senator's point," Mick said in a low, deliberate voice. "But the senator yielded, and the rules leave recognition to the chair's discretion."

He banged the gavel.

"Mr. Phillips, you have three minutes for your statement."

Young Phillips took a gulp of water and wiped his lips with the back of his hand.

"As senior ranger, it's my responsibility to know the forest. Starting backfires can work when a fire has gotten out of control, but you don't begin there. You come to know the forest on its terms. As an American citizen, I'd say the same thing is true of Latin America. It was true of Vietnam. None of us knew the country or the people, not soldiers like me in the field, not the career men and politicians who made the policy—the experts, Senator."

Jack took another drink, his handkerchief coming to the rescue before water spilled down his chin. "Vietnam was a m-mirage, Senator. The purposes of the soldiers who fought that war were confused. So were the purposes of those who planned it from Washington—the experts." He cupped his hand around his water glass. "Yes, Senator, my f-father voted for the Gulf of Tonkin Resolution, but he came to believe that he and almost everyone else in the government played fast and loose with American and Vietnamese lives—and with the honor of America."

Mick lifted a finger in Phillips's direction as the yellow warning light flashed on.

"Senator Whelan and senators of the Latin American Affairs Subcommittee, I leave you and the American people with a simple question—the question of an American citizen-soldier whose congressman f-father regretted the haste with which experts set in motion so much killing and devastation in Vietnam: *How can you ask a man to be the first to die in a war that isn't a war?*"

The red eyes of the two television cameras glowed steady, one camera panning the room, another holding its close-up. The silence, followed by a collective intake of breath after Jack finished, was broken by applause. In the aisle, Nick Smart directed his CBS cameraman to pan from Mick Whelan to Jack Phillips.

"The chair recognizes the vice chair," Mick said, and the senator from Wyoming nodded to Jack Phillips, then once more noted Mick's impartiality as chairman during the hearings.

"As a member of this subcommittee who supports the president's resolution, I would like to commend the senator from Oregon on hearings that have brought so many useful views to bear on American policy toward Latin America at a time and in a setting when another chairman," he glanced at the two Democrats who had tried to turn testimony into a brief against the pending military-force resolution, then, with a withering flick of his eye, at his lean and hungry Republican colleague, "might well have twisted things said here in good conscience to partisan, political advantage."

The senator's other remarks were embarrassing bromides about the special responsibility of the United States toward the people of Latin America. He all but invoked the white man's burden for his little brown brothers and, remembering it was 1991, sisters. Then the floor belonged to Mick.

"I thank the members of the subcommittee and the witnesses for their testimony," he began, every inch the statesman described by his Republican colleague. "Some in the press have written, and one or two witnesses on both sides have implied, that this hearing has been a distraction from issues raised by the military-force resolution about to be sent to Congress by the president. But it's the other way around. The president's resolution is a distraction from unresolved questions about the relationship between the countries of Latin America and the United States. Whether the resolution is approved, whether military force and American troops, not to mention special forces, some under the supervision of civilian contractors, are sent to Venezuela and elsewhere in Latin America, the people of this country and their government have choices to make that will affect the republic well into the twenty-first century."

Mick looked up and down the row at his fellow senators.

"In that spirit, I hope these hearings inform the debate on the military-force resolution in the Senate next week and the discussion about what kind of great power the United States will be south of our borders and elsewhere in the world. Will we encourage the poor in Latin America to risk democracy, or will our actions persuade them that democracy is only a word, an idea to be abandoned when it suits powerful interests in this nation? It was one thing to stretch history and invoke the Monroe Doctrine during the Cold War when the Soviet Union was active in the hemisphere. But the Soviet Union is disintegrating. There remains the United States and the countries of Latin America—each a sovereign nation, none an empire."

From my seat behind Mick, a CBS monitor caught the keen blue of his eyes as well as the touch of gray in his brown curls.

"When Thomas Jefferson drafted the Declaration of Independence to justify the creation of this nation, he wrote that those who spoke and acted for the revolutionary government did so out of a decent respect to the opinions of mankind. I remind you that no delegate changed one of those words on or off the floor of the Continental Congress in 1776."

Mick glanced at his watch and began to speak faster.

"Nor should *we* omit Jefferson's words and their spirit from our debate. The temptation to act as an empire when there is not a single nation or group of nations with the might to challenge us is great. But living out the true meaning of our democratic principles on occasions when we might do otherwise gives other nations powerful reason to follow our example. Let the day not come—as it has with every empire in the history of the world—when an imperial United States of America will be vulnerable to challenge and harm."

Mick picked up the gavel and pointed it toward the witness.

"However high-sounding, resolutions like the one soon to be debated have consequences, so let us keep in mind the eloquent question posed this afternoon by John Phillips Jr.—in another time a soldier, in our time a vigilant citizen: 'How can we ask a man to be the first to die in a war that isn't a war?' I declare these hearings adjourned."

As Mick brought the gavel down on the mahogany block, the glare from the television lights intensified and boom mikes swung out over the audience to record the applause, which was gathering force. Like a bull moose whose antlers shone in the headlights of the cameras, the senator from Wyoming rose and came over to shake Whelan's hand. Deftly, Mick put an arm on his shoulder and led him toward the private door so that whatever questions the stampeding reporters shouted could be answered in passing, and collegiality would be the prevailing mood when the president's resolution came to the floor of the Senate.

"The senator from Oregon and I will take counsel on where the sub-committee goes from here," boomed the senator from Wyoming.

When the host of a national talk-radio show bumped the vice chairman's jaw with his mike and demanded the senator's opinion of Jack Phillips, Mick stepped between the two men and pushed the offending mike near the intruder's chest.

"Give the senator room," he said.

Moving away, the Wyoming Republican turned and faced the reporter who, thanks to Mick, now stood several feet away.

"Mr. Phillips's view of the president's resolution differs from mine. I knew his father, Congressman Phillips, well enough to say without fear of contradiction that he would have been proud of his son. I support the president's resolution—but I respect Lieutenant Phillips's sincerity and patriotism."

Then the two senators slipped down a side corridor into the commotion of other senators and staff.

"Senator," I said, catching up. "Senator Whelan."

As soon as I was sure he heard me, I retreated outside the ring of senators until they said their good-byes and walked off in the direction of the elevator to the private underground subway that runs from the Capitol to the Russell building. But Mick veered off toward a side exit that led outside to a garden, walking so fast I had to break into a trot to keep up.

"I don't know about you," he said over his shoulder as he reached the door, "but I'm not up to riding the circus car. Let's stroll and smell the flowers."

CHAPTER 21

Eager to see what the morning papers had to say, I showed up at Au Bon Café on the dot of seven.

"Mistuh Gabriel," Eulalee cried from behind the counter, her apron half fastened. "I was tinking you be here dis mornin'."

She handed me the *Post*, pointing to the headline above the fold, "Oregon Senator Lauded." The article quoted several senators, Democrats and Republicans, to the effect that in his hearings on Latin America, Senator Whelan struck a constructive, if skeptical, tone for the forthcoming debate on the president's military-force resolution. Below the fold was the arresting subhead "Son of Former Congressman Testifies; Vietnam Vet Warns Against 'A War That Isn't a War.'" In the accompanying photo, Jack Phillips's eyes burned so fiercely that my elbow came down on the marble-top table and spread a coffee stain over both photos.

"Eulalee worry about dat face, too. Den I read what he say, and I know why your bossman have dat mahn talk," she said, returning with a steaming café au lait in a yellow cup the size of a soup bowl. "You tell Senator Michael he better bring his sword to dat big meetin' next week."

At the office, Mick's door was ajar, but he was nowhere to be seen. Once inside, I smiled, remembering the rule of a grizzled, long-since-retired AA whose bite was worse than his bark: "Never trust a staffer who arrives before you do or stays after you go home." I laid the morning paper full-length across Mick's desk just before he came in, preoccupied and short of breath.

"Seen the *Post*?"

"No," he said, "I walked over to the Vietnam Memorial."

He stood behind his desk, hands on top with his thumbs hooked under for balance as he read from one story to the other.

"Maybe we've got a chance," he said, swinging around to sit in the chair next to me.

"Gabe, who's your contact at the Library of Congress?"

I told him, started to give him her number, and stopped. "If you need something checked, I'll do it."

"I'll take care of it," he said quickly.

Mick moved to the window, raised it, and craned his neck out in the direction of the Mall. "God, in the early light the names on that wall are something."

That's all he said before he went off to huddle with colleagues on the Foreign Relations Committee anticipating imminent approval of the president's resolution by the House of Representatives. I had a couple of hours free, so I walked in his tracks down the Mall beyond the obelisk of the Washington Monument, where rectangles of green grass yielded to the shining oblong of the reflecting pool. There, a mirage from almost thirty years before appeared in the broken clouds shimmering on the water. For a few seconds, I was back watching Mick do a broken field run through the ranks of dignified, well-dressed black Americans stepping toward the Lincoln Memorial. For old time's sake, I climbed the steps to that president's austere marble chair. Held by his sheltering gaze, I scanned the words of the second inaugural chiseled on the wall. The last time I had done this, little Patrick tugged at my sleeve until I followed his finger and noticed the pigeon resting on Lincoln's head. Concealing my impatience, I heard my son giggle and looked up at a thin white stream trickling down the great emancipator's ear. Despite disapproving looks thrown my way, I had patted Patrick's head, sure that old Abe, father of Willie and Tad, would have wanted me to look to my little boy at that moment instead of his words.

Halfway down the marble stairs, I looked left to where the black granite of the Vietnam Wall glinted through the trees. Before I could get my bearings, a live round from an old nightmare burst in my mind, and for an instant *I stood in a jungle clearing in my best blue suit in terror of the ambush that was coming.* Carved on the westernmost panel of the wall was the solitary name of the first American soldier to die in Vietnam. As the panels rose higher, perished comrades joined him by ones and twos, then by tens, and, finally, hundreds, as the slabs, once no higher than the lip of a foxhole, rose ten-feet tall, the names bunched close together until I imagined their remains stacked in body bags on the landing strips in raw, bulldozed clearings. Eerily, Vietnam veterans fell in on both sides of me until the wall of names felt like a bunker shielding us from hostile and friendly fire alike.

On my way back, the Capitol Dome seemed to pull the light into its self-aggrandizing bulk. On the fourth floor of the Russell building, an eager beaver announced my presence as soon as I opened the doors to Senator Whelan's suite.

"Senator's looking for you," Marva said.

On important days, even an experienced hand like Marva slipped into the imperous singsong phrases I remembered from teachers' pets back in parochial school.

"Where's himself?" I asked, feigning terror as I backed away from Mick's door one foot at a time.

"All he said after he hung up with Congressman Hart was to tell you the snapper blues are biting in Long Island Sound."

I shrugged and made a nonchalant exit, but once in the corridor, I took the stairs two at a time. Outside, I raced across Constitution Avenue to the Capitol. In the rotunda, I found Mick in the middle of the spit-and-polish marble floor holding court before a knot of reporters. I stood in the back between a Greek column and the torso of a television camera, the busts of long-forgotten vice presidents on either side of me like mementi mori. Mick's catch consisted of two television-network cameras, several radio microphones, the ubiquitous C-SPAN tripod, and more than a half dozen newspaper reporters.

"Senator Whelan, are you charging the White House with pressuring the House of Representatives to bring the military-force resolution to a quick vote? Are you accusing the leadership of your own party of caving in to the president?" asked ABC's congressional correspondent.

"Shepard, the answer is no, and no."

Looking in the direction of several shouts of "Senator," Mick saw me, then smiled at the ash blonde reporter from NBC.

"If you'll let me explain my answer . . . "

Like a school of fish satisfied that enough bread would be cast on the waters to feed the lot of them, the reporters stopped darting and their arms fell slack at their sides like fins.

"The House is an independent body free to act as it sees fit," Mick said, flashing a twinkle of light in my direction.

"But, Senator," interrupted the correspondent, "doesn't the two-to-one vote in the House make it a foregone conclusion that the Senate will approve the resolution?"

"The Senate is charged with providing advice and consent to the president," Mick answered. "Voting first, the House has underscored our constitutional responsibility."

A black reporter, his salt-and-pepper hair bristling in a military cut corresponding to his prickly questions, sidestepped to the front of the queue. "Senator Whelan, when word of the president's resolution leaked, you were one of the first senators to object. You used your position as chairman of the Senate Latin American Affairs Subcommittee to hold hearings, which many observers considered a backdoor way of building opposition to the resolution."

Other reporters edged closer to the questioner. Mick waited for quiet, then looked keenly at the CNN interrogator, whom he liked despite his pushy questions.

"Reuben, I think even Ronald Reagan would have had trouble finding a pony in all those words. Is there a question?"

The man's nut-brown face turned ruddy, and he carried on more portentously and humorlessly than before.

"Surely, sir, you don't believe today's vote in the House helps your chances of defeating the president's resolution in the Senate?"

Mick put one hand in his suit-jacket pocket as if fishing casually for an answer. "There's usually a wild card or two in the Senate, Reuben. A lot depends on whether senators come to see the vote by the House as an act of courtesy or desperation."

He caught my eye again. His twinkle brightened into the quick, bright flash that rides from wave to wave at break of day.

"I don't follow, Senator," the reporter from the *Post* said.

"Nor do I," echoed a writer from *The New York Times* who spoke with the same acid tone rumored to have caused her to be passed over twice as the paper's White House correspondent.

"I think," Mick showed his incisors in a merciless smile that delighted me and made the reporters uneasy, "even senators disposed to give the president the benefit of the doubt want a full and fair debate. Allegations that the Pentagon and the CIA are hiring independent civilian contractors to supervise interrogation and undertake limited combat missions in Venezuela go against the grain of American tradition as well as congressional authority. They need to be addressed."

"Senator, are you saying—"

Mick broke in.

"I'm saying no one is immune from the Constitution."

For a minute, the scraping of pencils on steno pads and the faint hum of the cameras were all that disrupted the silence.

"There are reports," Mick went on, "that one or two of the big oil companies advised the administration on this resolution."

A freelance reporter whose thick black eyebrows traveled up and down when he talked moved into Whelan's line of sight.

"Senator, sources tell me the administration used the Gulf of Tonkin Resolution as a model? Is that of concern to you?"

Whelan moved his head to the left until he was looking between the eyes of the two television cameras.

"My concern is the constitutional role of the Senate in 1991. Rather than the Congress encouraging military force as a first resort in Latin America, I am in favor of a national security policy for this country that respects and pursues our mutual well-being."

The woman with *The New York Times* logo on the lapel of her dark-blue tailored pantsuit had taken over postposition from the CNN correspondent. Now, diminishing the critical distance between her and Senator Whelan, she threw her shoulders forward, tossed her head back, and began.

"Senator, getting back to the nub of the matter, how do you expect to win anything more than a moral victory in the Senate?"

A flick of Mick's eye signaled that he would like to finish on this question.

"Andrea, from my conversations with senators in both parties, I'm convinced there are enough open minds for the vote to go either way."

While Mick was talking, he moved away from Hubert Humphrey's vice presidential bust and closer to Harry Truman's. "The president's resolution asks Congress to endorse a doctrine of unilateral preemptive action in Latin America anywhere and anytime he or a future president sees fit."

In counterpoint to his voice came the rapping sound of several canes striking the floor as a group of senior citizens passed by in summer pastels.

"I ask the press to report this resolution for what it is—a challenge to the constitutional relationship between the Congress and the president. Opposing the resolution, I also oppose a policy that allows the president to impose a Pax Americana on the countries of Latin America."

As Mick started to walk off, the CNN correspondent, now directly in his line of vision, lobbed a rhetorical live grenade at his feet.

"Senator, Congressman Rivera, one of the floor managers of the president's resolution in the House, has accused you of divisiveness for inviting the son of the late Congressman Phillips to testify before your subcommittee. After the vote this morning, he appeared before the press with the nephew of the private who fell on a grenade and saved Lieutenant Phillips's life twenty-five years ago. The nephew said that bringing Vietnam into this debate on Latin America was an act of disrespect to his uncle."

For a moment, those listening held their breath; even the tap tap of senior citizens' canes seemed suddenly muted as Senator Whelan replied slowly, almost in tones of mourning.

"Reuben, I assure you and my former colleague César Rivera that I regard both Private DeJesus and Lieutenant Phillips as American heroes. Private DeJesus died saving the lieutenant's life; his act of valor enabled Lieutenant Phillips to evacuate the rest of his company, including the wounded, during a desperate firefight in Vietnam."

In the hubbub, I reached Mick's side. Moving and speaking deliberately, he put one hand on my shoulder blade and propelled me forward while addressing fragments to the reporters.

"Yes. I think so . . . No, but I will be speaking with him . . . "

Spotting a private Senate elevator open, its doors just beyond the press of reporters and television crews, Mick stepped inside. I followed, unscathed except for a scuffed shoe. As the elevator ascended, another senator asked what the fuss was about.

"The press," Mick said. "This resolution has them stirred up."

"That bunch looked like a posse of hound dogs hot on your scent," the nattily dressed junior senator from Tennessee said before leaning close to Mick.

"'Course, as I see it, Senator Whelan, in those hearings of yours, you were the lead dog trying to get the rest of us to pick up the administration's trail."

The elevator opened and the senator stepped out and waited, thumbs stuck in his plaid vest. "You did the Senate and the country a service."

In the next few days, straws multiplying in the wind swirled wildly around the president. In a remote village of Venezuela, two American nuns were abducted and murdered. Evidence pointed to a local atrocity, but a CIA spokesman pinned the crime on leftist terrorists. Meanwhile, a band of paramilitaries broke up a rally in Caracas and beat up supporters of the Social Democratic candidate for president. There were also intimations by a military attaché that Muslim fighters from the Middle East, enraged by the continuing American military presence in Saudi Arabia, were converging with other militants, local and foreign, in Latin America. According to intelligence reports cited by administration sources, insurgents would soon move, country by country, to tie down the United States in its own hemisphere, stir up world opinion, and revive the old cries of "Yankee, go home!" against American multinational corporations.

The day before the Senate took up his resolution, the president addressed the James Monroe Society. For the first time, he made the case explicit for expansion of the Monroe Doctrine. In what Mick and other senators found a case of Orwellian doublespeak, he used Venezuela as the "test case of a country where American peacekeepers are needed to help democratic forces maintain order and stability." The president did not take questions, so, naturally, reporters went to the chairman of the Senate subcommittee on Latin American Affairs, and Senator Whelan responded that the true "democratic forces" in Venezuela were citizens of all persuasions participating in the ultimate test of democracy: free and fair elections. He also chided the president for not instructing the

CIA and the military attachés to the American embassy in Caracas to cease communication with individuals and groups seeking to sabotage the presidential election.

Although many senators fumed over Congressman Rivera's bitter, daily criticism of Senator Whelan, in a closed-door meeting the Senate Democratic caucus took no position on the president's resolution. Nor did any senior Democrat step forward to lead the opposition. Instead, Mick's colleagues passed him the hot potato because of his chairmanship of the subcommittee on Latin America, his reputation as a savvy, fair-minded senator, his growing public identification with the issue, and, I heard it whispered, his expendability as a second-term senator from a small western state. Before agreeing, Whelan exacted a promise that he be allowed to manage the speakers and time slots as he saw fit. But Democrats will be Democrats, and when Mick agreed to the other side's suggestion that debate be limited to eight hours in favor and eight hours against, there was grumbling in the cloakroom. In the meantime, supporters of the resolution, in collusion with the White House, lined up sixteen senators, half to make the case, the other half to rebut objections.

"But the Earth is moving," Mick told me at a skull session before the opening of debate as he checked off names on his tally sheet. "A couple of senators who were in favor are undecided, and two of the undecideds are now leaning against. One Republican who's bending over backwards to vote yes despite his reservations told me that the president's nephew accused him of being soft on national security."

"Poor inchworms inching along," I said.

"Trouble is, they want to speak," Mick said, looking up from the sheet of letterhead on which his doodles were beginning to resemble the arcs of Senate desks. "But if I lose a vote to extend debate, the resolution's a sure thing."

He pushed the sheet of paper to one side of his desk. "Maybe the best thing is to leave the loose ends loose and reconnoiter later this afternoon."

He checked his watch and frowned. "Gabe, remind me to call Jack Phillips and tell him I've got a gallery pass for the last day of the debate."

Mick stood up and gave my shoulder a soft punch. Following habit, he and I walked over to the Capitol. On the elevator up to the Senate chamber, he ran into three senators; two asked him if there were speaking slots open. The door slid open, and the senators walked toward the Democratic cloakroom a few feet ahead of me.

"We'll work it out," I heard Mick say before he melted into a large knot of senators and their aides at the cloakroom door.

I stayed behind. Some senators made a show of being clubby with their top assistant while around other senators; Mick acted with a reserve that suited me. I preferred to seem to know less than I did. On this occasion, I knew he would figure out a way to let wavering senators speak. But he needed intelligence, so I staked out the cloakroom, listening and waiting until senators relaxing on the several couches or using the telephones on the far wall strolled into the chamber. A few minutes before the call to order, I pushed through the swinging doors and walked around the four tiers of desks, counting senators. As the gavel banged, I eased into one of the straight-backed chairs along the side of the chamber. There were sixty-eight members present; more than I expected, fewer than Mick had hoped. As arranged with the majority leader, the presiding officer was the junior senator from Iowa, an undecided Democrat and a man so allergic to conflict that Mick could count on a free hand. Waiting, I thought of Patrick's nap-time refrain, "I'm sleepy, but I'm not tired"; in the Senate chamber, I knew my challenge was to look sleepy but keep my yellow pad at the ready.

The first speaker for the resolution outlined the administration's case, and left succeeding speakers to fill in the particulars. He alluded to bombings of American embassies in Venezuela and Ecuador; the need to safeguard oil reserves and production in Latin America; the fury of radical Muslims at the American military presence in the Middle East and their links to international terrorist groups with other grievances against the United States; the president's bold reinterpretation of the Monroe Doctrine; CIA reports that Castro's Cuba was once more a clearinghouse for subversion throughout the Southern Hemisphere; and the need for preemptive action to prevent attacks on vital American interests in Latin America, especially Venezuela. The veteran Republican ended by invoking the success of the Gulf War and warning against complacency at a time when the United States enjoyed military and moral superiority all over the world.

"It is wisdom and common sense," he said, "for Congress to authorize the president to take appropriate action, military and otherwise, before, not after, this nation faces the out-and-out crisis of an attack."

The senator sat down to cheers from a claque in the gallery, nods of assent from many in the chamber, and respectful looks from some senators who were undecided or opposed to the resolution. But Mick Whelan had chosen his first opposition speaker well. He was a bantam rooster of a Republican from Vermont, a protégé of the late Senator Aiken, whose advice to Lyndon Johnson on Vietnam ("Declare victory and get out") still resonated among senators wary of military adventures and imperial presidential power. Instead of rebuttal, he treated his colleagues to a historical exposition of the Monroe Doctrine. It was not, nor had it been at first, he explained, a self-evident policy. In effect, it was the name of an elastic practice that first targeted Britain, France, and Spain; only later had Teddy Roosevelt proclaimed the right of the United States to intervene in response to *internal* misconduct or disturbance in order to forestall action by any European power. The current resolution, the speaker reminded the Senate, revived a policy toward Latin America that the State Department had repudiated in 1928. Worse, it flew in the face of commitments made by FDR to the Organization of American States in the forties and JFK's Alliance for Progress in the sixties.

In short, the opening speech staked out the case in the form of a history lesson. As Mick had intended, it drew blood from supporters in the form of impassioned justifications of a sacred American principle, and, for the rest of the afternoon, the speakers in favor remained off balance. By the time the last speaker walked from her burnt-sienna desk to the well, I detected a sea change. Senators I read as undecided had begun to shift restlessly in their chairs and, between speeches, wander about in the aisles. Now, as the senator addressed her colleagues on the resentment that unilateral action by the United States stirred up in Latin America, several senators burned to speak. Perhaps more comfortable asking a woman to yield than a man, four male senators were on their feet at once, seeking recognition.

Mick hesitated. Then, as the senator from California looked from one imposing presence to another, he came smoothly to her rescue.

"If it please the distinguished senator from California, may I ask the gentlemen for what purpose they seek recognition?"

"You may, Senator Whelan," she told him.

Mick stepped to the lectern and rapped lightly on the wood. "I acknowledge the senators from Kentucky, Delaware, Colorado, and New Mexico. Will the senator from Kentucky state the purpose for which he seeks recognition?"

The senator from Kentucky was in the tradition of former senator John Sherman Cooper, who, like Senator Aiken during the Vietnam era, had been best of breed in that now-endangered species of moderate-to-liberal Republicans.

"I rise for the purpose of adding an aside to the fine remarks of the senator from California," said the senator, a large man whose florid face and chestnut ties suggested the bourbons and thoroughbreds for which his state was famous. "The hour grows late, but nevertheless I rise to ask if my colleague from California will be so gracious as to yield."

The senator from California fiddled with the single string of pearls over her powder-blue cashmere sweater and stayed silent. After glancing in my direction, Mick turned to face the senator from Iowa who was presiding at the dais behind him.

"Mr. President," Mick began, "I would ask the senator from California to yield to our several colleagues and assure her that the time they use will not be subtracted from her minutes but from time remaining to the opposition after her remarks."

Whelan then turned sideways so he could face the assembled senators without turning his back on the presiding officer. "Mr. President and members of the Senate, in view of the issues raised this afternoon, a number of senators may wish to address their colleagues before the time set aside for debate has expired. To keep faith with the procedures agreed on and to allow senators to be heard, as the leader of the opposition, I will accommodate senators who wish to raise a question or deliver short remarks on the resolution."

As I wondered what effect Mick's offer would have on the ebb and flow of senatorial speeches prepared as careful expositions of the flaws in the president's position, an imperious voice boomed out from the middle of the chamber.

"Point of information, Mr. President."

The presiding officer gaveled the buzzing chamber into sudden silence, and the senator from Connecticut, a large, gangly man who confused his Lincolnesque physique with the latter's wit and political acumen, rose ponderously to his feet.

"Mr. President, I respectfully inquire of the chair if it would be in order to extend the hours for debate?"

The presiding senator leaned close to the microphone.

"Is there objection?"

Shouts of "No!" and "Out of order!" echoed off the walls and rose toward the dome above the chamber.

"Mr. President." From his front-row desk, the senator from Connecticut moved into the aisle and backed up until he looked down on his colleagues. "If it please the chair, I move to extend the time of debate beyond the sixteen hours previously agreed to by the two sides and the Senate."

In response, shouts of "Hear, hear!" and "Out of order!" sounded like competing drumrolls. From where I sat, it was impossible to tell the respective strength of those in favor and those opposed. Just then, Mick Whelan took a backward step toward the dais.

"Mr. President?"

"The chair recognizes the senator from Oregon."

"Mr. President, I respect the senator's wish to extend the hours of debate. But I would like time to confer with my colleagues on the other side of the question. I therefore ask my distinguished friend to hold any procedural motion until tomorrow morning, at which time the Senate may vote up or down on a motion to extend debate."

The mouth of the senator from Connecticut was working furiously in pantomime. During the silence that followed, the presiding officer brought down the gavel.

"Without objection," he bellowed, "so ordered."

Then he addressed Mick directly.

"If it please the senator from Oregon, the chair recognizes the senator from California for the nineteen minutes remaining of her time as the final speaker of the day."

Whelan sat down in the leather chair adjacent to the lectern.

"Thank you for not letting the clock run out," the senator from California resumed. "But time is running out for the United States in Latin America. Mr. President, I submit that democracy and our national interest are one and the same. Nowhere is this more important than south of the border, where our diplomats and even presidents are not greeted with 'sweets and flowers' but by mobs shouting 'Yankee, go home!' and 'Death to the Gringos!'"

Here and there, senators—by now upward of eighty were present—whispered to each other, and their body language suggested most were poised to head for the cloakroom. Once the senator from California finished and the gavel sounded adjournment, I slipped to the rear next to the swinging doors and took up a position that enabled me to hear snatches of conversation from senators lingering and others bustling to be about their business. Back in the office, I wanted to compare notes when Whelan returned. But from experience, I knew to be discreet, and, sure enough, with my door cracked open, I heard Mick's voice from the outer office along with those of three senators: the senator from Virginia, the leading supporter of the president's resolution; the senator from Connecticut; and the senator from Wyoming. All three greeted Marva with an excess of courtesy—a sign they were important senators gathering for an important meeting with an important colleague. I had just finished putting a Y, N, or U by each senator's name on my tally sheet but had not added up the numbers when the buzzer on my phone rasped once, twice, three times.

"Gabe," Mick's voice said when I picked up, "will you come in a minute?"

I tucked away my tally sheet, straightened my tie—loosened ties suggested the wearer had worked up a sweat—and went down the hall to Mick's office, where Whelan's senatorial guests sat warily in leather chairs.

"Gabe, we've got wildly different estimates of how many additional senators want to speak." He pointed to the senior senator from Virginia.

I tried to figure out Mick's game. He knew I had no idea who wanted to speak. I thought fast and decided he must want me to tell the truth; that meant speculation. It also meant that how I spoke was more important than what I said. Knowing that words I hadn't yet formed in my mind had value in the hand Whelan was playing did not put me at ease. But while I was shuffling the cards, the senator from Wyoming came to my rescue.

"None of us expects you to know any more than we do, though you very well might," he said, after clearing his throat of a huge frog. "No, indeed, I asked Senator Whelan to bring you in because I saw you sitting through the debate with a yellow pad on your knee."

"I knew I should have loosened my tie, Senator," I said, sitting on the couch across from the senator from Wyoming.

He laughed, and reassured me. "Speaking for myself, I'd like your sense of the Senate's mood as the debate progressed."

Relieved and wishing I could do public penance for every reference I'd made to him as the senator from Grizzly, I plunged ahead.

"That's a tough one, Senator, but from my seat, it looked like a lot of players on the bench wanted to be on the field."

The senator from Wyoming beamed and slapped my knee.

"Hell's bells," said the president's man, the senior senator from Virginia, who favored the bright satin waistcoats he supposed evoked the eighteenth-century Cavaliers. "No offense," he addressed his colleague from Wyoming before turning his gaze on me, "but it wouldn't surprise me if Mr. Bontempo wouldn't play back our opinions to each of us if asked the right question."

Beyond the window the sky was a racing jersey of bright red and yellow whose uppermost stripe abruptly took on the scarlet, black, and blue discoloration of a cyclist's angry bruise.

"Now, Senator," huffed the senator from Connecticut, "I may be a Connecticut Yankee, but Senator Whelan's office is not King Arthur's court."

"Friends, senators, countrymen . . . ," Mick said, mingling Shakespearean echoes of history and tragedy with the provenance of comedy.

Nervous laughter broke out as each senator looked around to make sure the other two didn't know where Mick was headed.

"Thanks, Gabe," he said, more to his guests than to me. "Unless one of the senators has something else, you can go."

I was on my feet and pointed toward the door before he finished. I thought I saw the lips of the senators from Connecticut and Virginia about to part, but before any words sounded, I was gone. I went through the outer office, pausing long enough to tell Marva that I was going out. Forty-five minutes later, I was back in Mick's office with my tally pad and a couple of sharpened pencils.

"You were drop-dead good on Wyoming's caper," Mick said when we'd settled down.

I put the tally sheet on my lap. "How the hell did you know what I'd say?"

"I didn't," he told me. "I figured nothing you could say would be worse than having you say nothing."

"What happened after you kicked me out?"

Outside, shafts of declining light were fast turning the Washington Monument from a pillar of fire to a pillar of cloud.

"Your line about senators as players on the bench got them going. The Connecticut Yankee wanted unlimited debate; the Virginia Cavalier said a deal's a deal. Finally, after I led him a little, Grizzly proposed a compromise—extend debate for an hour on each side."

By now, it was dark enough that George Washington's obelisk simply marked the halfway point on the Mall rather than bridging the gap between earth and sky.

"Anything else, Mick?" I asked.

"No," he said, flipping off his desk light.

Except for an intern at the Xerox machine, no one remained in the office.

"For God's sake, Dusty, turn on the overhead light. What will I tell your father if you lose your sight?"

Mick tousled the boy's hair and we headed out. Walking down Constitution Avenue, I noticed the shadows were bare of the solitary women who usually waited in the dark between streetlights. Saying good night, Mick spoke for the first time since we left the Senate Office building.

"That woman at the Library of Congress? Is she reliable?"

"The best," I said. "Need some help?"

"Just butterflies before the big game."

I went off to the Irish Times, a pub not far from Union Station. By the time I copped the last stool and pivoted around, a ceili band from West Cork was setting up on the makeshift stage. Out in front, the crowd looked like an advance guard of the twentysomethings who had swooped down on Washington like killer bees. In three-piece suits reduced to half price because their pinstripes were too unfashionably wide or narrow, the young men were on the make, eager to leave jobs on the Hill for entry-level positions in one or another of the lobbying firms up and down K Street. Their young women looked like daughters of the sixties' princesses who had left small towns for careers as actresses or models. The daughters had gone to college, majored in politics, and followed the flow to D.C. Lured by reports of inexorable upward mobility in the civil service, they accepted jobs in the lowest classifications, and stayed put. Like the young men they dated, they quickly learned that networking was everything and that much business was begun, if not finished, in the archipelago of bars and bistros that dot downtown Washington.

I ordered corned beef and cabbage, and my concentration on the Senate debate drifted away under the influence of two pints of Guinness. I listened to the wild reels from the West of Ireland and watched the action unfold at ground zero. The winding path of the music had the feel of walks in County Kerry with a girl I'd courted there and lost long ago. Through the mist of memory, I saw her in the face and slender-solid build of a young woman sitting near the band. Off and on, she seemed to be looking my way, so, going to the john, I veered in her direction for a closer look. The resemblance stuck, and to my surprise, she smiled and spoke to me.

"Don't you work for that Oregon senator who's opposing the president's Latin American resolution?"

The others at the table also knew who I was and invited me to sit down. Before long, the woman who looked like my old flame engaged me in an excited two-way conversation against a background of louder, coarser voices. After a second round of drinks, she confided her secret wish to work in a Senate office. I looked at her, a question forming in my mind, and heard a pint glass crash to the floor. Someone's arm had knocked over my Guinness. Feeling the dark stout spread over my trousers, I pushed back my chair, but not quickly enough to avoid the embarrassment of a thoroughly wet crotch. As a waiter rushed up with a damp towel, I excused myself amid apologetic grins from my tablemates. To break the tension, I assured everyone all I needed was for someone to order me another pint of Guinness.

In the men's room, I waited while a couple of pinstripe suits splashed cold water on their faces, combed and patted down their hair, and went back to battle. With the help of paper towels, warm water, and my handkerchief, I made the stain respectable, buttoned my jacket, and headed back to the lounge, looking better, I thought, than when I had entered the pub. As I emerged into the lighted room, the two fiddlers were finishing a slow, haunting air. In the haze, I couldn't find my table; only when the band moved without transition to a fierce, defiant reel did I spot it. But except for a single glass of stout sitting in the middle, it was empty. Stunned, I looked toward the bar and saw no one. I picked up the half-pint glass and noticed the coaster underneath. Below the presidential seal was scrawled *Sinn Fein*—We Support the President.

I put down the glass, slopping stout over the table, and sought the bartender.

"Your friends paid, me boyo," he told me.

I put a five on the bar.

"Sure, they were a merry bunch," he said, and with a magician's sleight of hand spirited the bill from the slippery bar top into a pint glass stuffed with silver and singles. "Have yourself a good night," the curly-haired black Irishman told me, an insincere twinkle flashing in his eyes.

Outside, I declined a cab, put my head down against the fine drizzle, and soon was walking down First Street between the Capitol and the

Supreme Court. By the time I arrived at my ground-level flat, I felt sober enough to review my tally for the next day's vote. Before falling asleep, I revised my estimate to fifty votes for, thirty-eight against, and twelve undecided or indeterminate. During the night, snatches of dreams broke over my mind like waves. In one, I was in Vanport witnessing Congressman A. S. Corbett being declared the winner over Michael J. Whelan. In the last, the young woman from the Irish pub was in my bed stretching without a stitch on when she excused herself with a lovely kiss. I waited, arching toward the peak of desire, before it dawned on me that she was not coming back, and I woke up.

Chapter 22

When the hottest hot water didn't banish the shadow of the enticing, disappearing girl, I gritted my teeth and turned the shower knob over to cold. Afterward, chattering, I prepared to enter the world of the Senate. This day, nothing but my best suit would do—navy, without pinstripes—tie splashed with rich reds and purples given to me by Kate the last Christmas Patrick was alive, and a light-blue dress shirt as brilliant as the summer sky over Shelter Island. For shoes, I chose my oxblood loafers, which a spit shine restored to the prime of life. At the front door before leaving, I looked in the mirror and felt revived—like my shoes. By God, I thought, if something should prevent Mick Whelan from being present today, I could step into his place and make him proud.

At Au Bon Café, I was Eulalee's first customer.

"Ah," she shouted over the whirr of the latte machine, "you know why I believe you come dis mornin'?"

"Because on this day of days, I need your café au lait."

"Shame on you, Mistuh Gabriel. Eulalee believe you come because I have some good luck for your senator mahn."

I sat at the far end of the counter on a wire stool whose filigreed legs and back made me feel like the truncated torso of a postmodern sculpture. I blew waves across the steaming surface of my coffee mug and watched Eulalee fill orders while she kept up her peppery chatter. Pretty soon, there was a hiatus in traffic, and Eulalee stood on the other side of the counter, drinking her coffee. She closed her eyes for a minute to catch her breath, then took something wrapped in tissue paper from her purse.

"My gran, she carve dis in Jamaica." Eulalee unwrapped a small figurine. "She start wid a hunk of white coral and keep on wid her seashell knife till de angel appear."

Gazing at the figure on the marble counter, I saw wings on either side of the torso, one stretched in flight, the other shining like a sword, while from every nook and cranny of the tiny sculpture bits of bright coral made the inanimate animate.

"My gran, she worship spirits from de old country along wid de Good Book. She tink gods from Africa fly away and become angels in America," Eulalee said, turning the angel over in my hand. "Long time past, my gran tell me de archangel Michael, he cast down de devil mahn."

Hypnotized by the exquisite little figure, it occurred to me that Mick Whelan also needed to soar and make his tongue a flaming sword to bring a touch of heaven to the kingdoms of the Earth. I took two gallery passes out of my pocket and handed them to Eulalee.

"For you and Jomo to hear Senator Michael."

She leaned over the counter and hugged me. "Eulalee wave to you from high up in dat balcony like I used to do in dat old-time movie house on de Island."

When I got to the office, three or four people were already at their desks, determined to convey the impression that whatever they were doing was sure to tip the vote Mick's way. Undisturbed in my office, I scoured the morning papers for hints of indecision among the senators and went over my tally sheet one more time, but I could find no reason to change my estimates of the night before. The president's forces were poised to sneak over the top. Once that happened, I feared enough undecideds would fall off the wrong side of the log to give the resolution between fifty-five and sixty votes. I was trying to think of a gentle way to break the news to Mick when he and Marva burst into my office.

"Problem, Gabe," he said, halfway between the door and my desk, "the intern handling gallery tickets delivered Jack's single to Sarah and her three to Jack. Can I have yours for the girls?"

"Jesus, Mick. I gave them away."

"Shit," he said. "This is the last thing I need."

"I'll take care of it," I said. "Go work on your speech."

Whelan retreated to finish sketching out what he was going to say, and I told Marva to call my counterparts in four or five senators' offices. Fortunately, three were in, and two of them came up with a ticket. Marva left to pick up the tickets, and I went back to Mick's office. Tossed to one side were notes scribbled on several sheets of paper torn from his yellow lined legal pad. Laid out neatly on the desk in front of him were four or five Senate envelopes with the main points of his speech neatly printed in block letters.

"Mission accomplished," I told him.

He waved a hand in a single gesture of thanks, dismissal, and concentration on other matters.

"Your girl is all right."

I felt my head jerk. Had he slipped over to the Irish Times and observed me? He saw me start and laughed.

"I meant the gal at the Library of Congress."

He rolled his chair back and to one side so he could look at both the window and me. The midmorning sun knifed through the open French windows at an angle that cut the room into equal parts light and shadow.

"Speech ready?" I asked.

"This kind is never ready. It depends on what's said before I come on. But *I'm* ready, if that's what you mean."

I moved my face out of the sun and into the shadows, got out my pen, and held it in position above the blank top sheet of my yellow pad. "What's your guess on the damn resolution, Michael Joseph?"

"We need three or four more votes."

I looked heavenward, and suddenly remembered the charm in my pocket.

"Eulalee gave me this for you from down on the Island."

He took the figurine, turned it over from hand to hand, and looked at it a long time. "I hope the thrones and dominions of the Senate listen." He rewrapped the angel, put it into his suit coat pocket, and untucked the flap.

As I passed through the outer office, Marva told me there was a message from Sarah Whelan to meet her and the girls on the Capitol steps, and a call from Mr. Phillips on the private line in my office.

"What's up, Jack?" I said, closing the door.

"Gabe, I gave away the two extra tickets, but the senator can have mine if he needs it," Jack said in a low voice.

"And have you miss what you and he started? Hell, no! Some reporter's liable to say Rivera's crowd scared you away."

"I'm a f-fighter," Jack shot back, his voice rising. "No matter what Rivera says, Whelan's no slick Mick."

"Atta boy, Jack. And no matter what happens, hang around afterward. Sarah's throwing a little shindig for Mick."

Because security was tighter than usual, I was waiting for Sarah and the girls at the Capitol a good half hour before the gavel was scheduled to hit the mahogany. A long line of people, some with passes for the Senate gallery, others who were merely eager to wander through Statuary Hall, were in a line that snaked halfway to the Supreme Court. I escorted the three Whelans through the VIP checkpoint. On the way to the elevators, Molly Whelan looked around, distracted.

"Uncle Gabe," she said shyly, "a girl in U.S. history said there was a saloon where senators snoozed and spit tobacco into spittoons."

"She means the cloakroom," I laughed. "Let's have a peek."

"You sure you want to barge in there?" Sarah asked.

She was right. Outsiders, even family members, were not permitted in the cloakroom except in the presence of a senator, but not wanting to lose face in front of the girls, I decided to risk it.

"A quick surveillance mission," I told her.

As we approached the door, a voice boomed out from behind us in the corridor. "Mrs. Whelan, how do you do?"

It was the senator from Wyoming, with his AA, Joseph, in tow.

"Senator, I'd like you to meet Maud and Molly Whelan," Sarah said proudly.

Molly looked at the three cigars jutting out of the upper pocket of the senator's suit jacket, so I told him what she'd heard.

"Well, well, young lady," he said, his voice rumbling like summer thunder over the Continental Divide. "You'll just have to see."

To the ill-concealed impatience of his aide, the senator, charming and grandfatherly, showed the girls and Sarah the row of telephone booths, the couches, and leather chairs. In a coup de grâce, he urged the two girls to try the swinging doors that opened into the Senate chamber.

"See, no spittoons, Molly," he said, "though I won't say there were none here when I was first elected. And I won't say they were never used," he chuckled.

"Senator, you're due on the floor." By now, Joseph was literally pulling his boss's coat.

"Well, now," the senator said, his face clouding over. "Senator Whelan is half an hour away from leading the opposition in an historic Senate debate, and his man is escorting his family to the visitors' gallery."

He looked at his exasperated aide. "Joseph, I wish you would learn from Bontempo here that a senator can take care of himself."

The aide backed away from the senator, who shook hands in a courtly way with Sarah and chucked Maud and Molly under the chin. "Who knows, you girls may wind up the first sisters to serve in the Senate together."

With that, the senator from Wyoming bowed and pushed his way through the swinging doors while behind him, his aide caught the backswing of the door on the forehead, reeled backward, then staggered ahead into the chamber.

Upstairs, the press seats were occupied and the visitors' gallery was filling up fast, but I found three seats in a front row reserved for senators' families.

"Make sure Mick's free afterward, Gabriel," Sarah instructed.

Standing at the edge of the gallery I sensed the same vicarious excitement I'd felt in college at the first game of the World Series. In the expectant hour before the first pitch, the grass looked greener, the sky bluer, the uniforms whiter, the flags snappier; even the dingy, sweating façade of Yankee Stadium had sparkled in the sun like the Parthenon. Strangely, I'd never had an aerial view of the Senate chamber just before a session. Below were the four curved rows of red mahogany desks, a matching leather chair behind each desk. Waiting for the call to order, senators lounged in the aisles and at the well in front of the dais. Most of those scheduled to speak sat at their desks going over their addresses, several young pages hovering close by in case a senator should require a last-minute check of a fact or a quotation. Today there were enough senators present for the hum ascending from the chamber to hold the descending buzz from the galleries to a draw.

As I stood at the railing, Mick emerged from a side door into the chamber. Quickly spotting his family, he waved and curved his hand up in my direction. I took my time, for I wanted the panorama of the Senate to recede until only the dais and the front desks, where the leaders for and against the motion would stand, were visible. From the top step, I stopped and winked at the bust of Vice President Adams across the way, high above the spot where the current vice president would soon preside over the Senate—without, I hoped, breaking a tie in favor of the resolution.

Downstairs, television monitors glowed on both sides of the cloakroom doors, and flashbulbs popped as I entered behind a small crowd of senators and their aides. In the world of the Senate, the how-do-you-dos to aides were often reliable expressions of a senator's opinion of the senator you worked for. Today the greetings told me more about the prospects of the resolution than anything I'd read in *The Washington Post* or *The New York Times*. Senators who sided with Mick were friendlier than usual—not a big surprise, but two Midwestern senators on the fence detained me to ask how Mick's morale was holding up. Judging by the teeth-clenching excuse for a smile flashed by the resolution's chief sponsor, the self-styled Virginia Cavalier, whose narrow eyes were the color of slate, Senator Whelan was making progress.

Inside the chamber, Mick was shooting the breeze with a page, his foot resting on one of the chairs along the far wall, the spot I had occupied the previous day of debate. Although he stood there like he had nothing else to do, I knew he was saving the place for me.

"All set?" I asked when the page was out of sight.

Mick nodded and strolled off to take his seat alone at the near table beneath the dais while the Republican and Democratic cosponsors of the president's resolution settled on the far side. The Democratic majority leader remained at his desk. In recent days he had privately assured Mick that he would vote against the resolution, but he had not called Senate Democrats together to reassess the vote-your-conscience position adopted at an earlier caucus. For one thing, he did not want to tip off the lobbyists for the big oil companies and defense contractors. For another, he favored Mick keeping the pose of the lonely voice joined one by one by other senators during the debate, the same advice tendered by Henry Hart. "Sneak up on them, and when they falter, show no mercy," old Have a Heart had said, and when I looked up, there he was, sitting in the gallery, long legs out in the aisle.

Presently, the vice president arrived. After more than two years in office, he still looked like he did the day he broke his first tie in the Senate—a schoolboy answering the bell rather than the headmaster ringing it. The lines that wrinkled his face showed the wear and tear of ridicule; only the apparent triumph of the Gulf War had quieted calls for the president to appoint him secretary of the Navy to clear the way for a worthy successor. On this day, he looked chastened by the president's displeasure at an impolitic remark, overheard by a reporter for *The Washington Times*, that he wished the vote would be even so that he could break the tie. In his first year as vice president, the sergeant at arms had tried to help by announcing his entrance, but the smirk that crossed his face offended so many senators that they took to leaving their desks and joining conversations on the floor as soon as they spotted him. To his chagrin, the din of conversation increased as senators became aware of his presence. But this afternoon, senators came to order on their own—a sign that no one was merely going through the motions on the words to be spoken or the votes to be cast.

Finally, acknowledging the silence, the vice president tapped the great gavel lightly on the block of wood before him. "I recognize the majority leader."

"Mr. President, I move that the remaining time for debate on the resolution be extended from eight to ten hours, each side having five."

For a minute no one spoke. Then the senator from Connecticut rose.

"Mr. President, may I address the senator from Oregon?"

"So ordered."

"Senator Whelan, will you confirm your intention and the intention of speakers on your side of the question to yield to senators wishing to raise questions or briefly speak in opposition?"

There were murmurs at the open-ended quality of the understanding sought by the senator from Connecticut.

"The chair recognizes the senator from Oregon."

I scrutinized Mick's face for signs of irritation, yet he looked blandly, even benevolently, at his colleague, as if they were old friends.

"I thank my colleague from Connecticut," he began, "who, except for a trick of fate, might well be my senator today."

Whelan's reference to his Connecticut background drew good-natured laughter from a dozen senators whose patron saint was the angel of wit.

"The senator from Connecticut is correct, and I thank him for reminding the body that senators who yield are entitled to reserve the balance of their time."

Whelan's nonchalant tone belied his intention to keep the parliamentary reins in his own hands.

"I yield back to you, Mr. President," he said.

"Is there objection to the motion?" the vice president asked.

In the hush, the senator from Connecticut half rose, then wisely sat down. To object to a unanimous consent request was a nonstarter. Every one of his colleagues would see there was no principle at stake. The shrewdest among them would sense a jockeying for position with his presumed ally, Senator Whelan. And the senator from Connecticut would be the loser—today in the Senate and in the press tomorrow. So he sat down.

"Hearing none, the chair yields to the senator from Virginia."

Stepping to the microphone, the senator tapped it with his forefinger. "Mr. President, there has been distortion in the press regarding the intent of the present resolution and the political and diplomatic situation in Latin America. Extending debate gives the Senate an opportunity to correct this misinformation, and before recognizing my esteemed colleague from Michigan, I would like to thank Senator Whelan for supporting the extension."

From the earnest expression on Mick's face, you would never have known that he had initiated the proposal for extra hours of debate or that the senator from Virginia had agreed only when his aides told him that if he opposed a motion to extend, he would lose.

Under the guise of refreshing senators' memories—a task never to be taken lightly in that national cathedral of vanities—the senator from Michigan recapitulated the points of contention. His words drifted past less vivid than the atmospherics. More than ninety senators were on hand, the galleries full, and—a sure sign that the margin was narrowing— senators on both sides were on good behavior. As the dinner break approached, the energy in the chamber ebbed, but once the Senate reconvened, the tension rose and fell and rose again when the senator from Virginia, natty in his tattersall vest, came forward and bowed to his colleagues. As he grasped the lectern, the hands on the golden face of the clock, which stood high on the façade dividing the chamber from the galleries, stood together at quarter of nine. By now, not only were all the seats full, but many other spectators, some in suits, some in shorts, some, including Eulalee Marley and her husband, Jomo, in work uniforms, sat on the gallery steps. At this hour, security guards, too, were standing there as much to listen as to enforce the fire marshal's regulations.

In his speech, the Virginia Republican unwittingly did Mick a favor. Because he laid out the points of the case at methodical length, he set up a challenge to the premises behind the facts. Also, looking to conclude in a way that brought in the recent triumph of arms in Kuwait and Iraq, he gave Mick an opening. In the end, he spoke too long for a senator long on high policy, short on narrative drive. As I contained my restlessness to the jiggling of my feet, I saw similar efforts under way among senators and many in the gallery. By the time the senator finished to a thin patter of applause, the hands on the clock were touching at ten to ten.

Only then did the senator from Virginia play his hole card. After the applause died, the vice president banged his gavel to make sure all eyes were on him, and spoke in a well-rehearsed fashion. His role in the plot was to remind us all that supporters of the resolution were not completely out of time.

"Does the senator from Virginia yield the balance of his time?"

"Mr. President, I do not," came the hominy voice.

Against a murmuring backdrop of surprise and dismay, several senators jumped to their feet.

"Will the senator yield?" came half a dozen shouts, identical in language, different in accent.

On cue, the cosponsors of the resolution stood—four or five on the Republican side, one or two among the Democrats. The senator from Virginia recognized his colleagues one by one, and each spoke his appointed line.

"Mr. President, I rise in support of the resolution on the grounds that our national security demands action in advance of attack," the senator from Colorado proclaimed . . .

"Mr. President, I rise in support of the president's resolve to send a message to the last remaining Marxist dictator, that infamous, washed-up baseball player, Fidel Castro, that the United States will preempt subversion and leftist expansion anywhere in Latin America," declaimed the senator from Florida.

"Mr. President, I, too, rise in support of congressional approval for the president's plan to implement a bold new mobile, flexible military force to keep the peace and protect American interests in Latin America," declared the senator from Arizona.

So it went until the senator from Virginia turned his head to the left of the chamber and recognized the senator from Maine.

"Mr. President, I rise as a Democrat and a proud American, not simply to support the resolution, but to urge my colleagues to follow the great tradition of bipartisan foreign policy—a policy that won World War II, won the Cold War, and, most recently, although with far too many defections on my side of the aisle, liberated the Republic of Kuwait."

The vice president's gavel came down as an exclamation point to the senator's concluding sentence: *"Let Republicans and Democrats stand together as Americans in support of this forward-looking resolution."*

The senator from Maine sat down, and Mick Whelan walked past his Connecticut colleague's desk, paused fractionally, and nodded before continuing to the lectern.

"The chair recognizes the senator from Oregon."

In all four arcs of desks, I now counted only two empty chairs. Before Mick began to speak, my eyes roved the gallery and spotted two conspirators from former days in the House, Ted March and L. A. Jackson. Dressed in dark three-piece suits, they were sitting next to each other on the top step of the aisle in the middle of the gallery, enjoying as distant and direct a line of sight to Mick as bleacher bums beyond dead center field have of the hitter at home plate. In the meantime, Mick pawed his feet at the lectern as if digging into the batter's box. Finally, he smoothed his notes and raised his left hand in a fraternal gesture to his Senate colleagues.

"Mr. President, I share the national security concerns of those who have risen in support of this resolution. But I do not share their unilateral, preemptive framework. When the founders were creating this nation, before there was a president or a Senate, the Declaration of Independence tied the American cause to 'a decent respect to the opinions of mankind.' Where is that 'decent respect' in the resolution before us?" he asked, his voice soaring out over the senators arrayed before him and up to the gallery.

"Why should the United States of America, a nation founded on ideas, fear the opinions of mankind, especially in Latin America? This administration warns that the Gulf War has stirred up nests of militant Arab terrorists who are preparing to make common cause with anti-American groups in Venezuela, Ecuador, and Colombia. Oil fields will be nationalized, supporters of this resolution tell us, looking to Latin American oil and natural gas as a hedge against terrorism and militant Islamic states in the Middle East. But the way to checkmate terrorists, Islamic or otherwise, in Latin America is to work with the Organization of American States. If we've learned anything since Teddy Roosevelt's dispatch of American troops without congressional approval early in this century, it is that Latin America is not a province of the United States."

Mick paused to look up at the great seal of the republic on which the American eagle, symbol of war and peace, grasped an olive branch in one talon, a sheaf of arrows in the other.

"Mr. President, I did not vote to authorize the president to take us to war in Iraq. But he did what he said he would do: throw Saddam Hussein's army out of Kuwait. He did not invade Baghdad. He did not garrison the Middle East. So why should he now seek to garrison Latin America? Some say the resolution to authorize mobile military force in Latin America is an effort to make up for not finishing the job in Iraq. Others say this hemisphere is American ground. Mr. President, Latin America is ground for a true Alliance for Progress, not a Pax Americana. Mr. President, there are reports that the Defense Department has military advisors in Venezuela, Colombia, and Ecuador, and that the CIA is hiring private security companies to complement its own special forces."

Whelan took a drink of water and moved his notes to a corner of the lectern.

"Mr. President, this resolution is an imperial decree, appropriate to the Roman Empire, not the American republic. This nation is a great power, yet the resolution suggests we lack the will and integrity to sustain a republic. From the earliest days, some have dreamed of an American empire. On occasion, we've leaned over the precipice, but the better angels of our nature have called us back to the firm republican ground of the founders."

Like the senators whose occasionally drumming hands or tapping feet betrayed a slight restlessness, I did not yet know where Mick was headed.

"A few mornings ago, uncertain what I would say, I walked the Mall—behind me, the Capitol, which Lincoln insisted go up during the Civil War as proof that the Union would not perish; ahead, the Washington Monument, ramrod straight and upstanding—like the man who was his country's surveyor as well as its father; and in the distance, Lincoln's Memorial, that true resting place of the American spirit. For the first time, I was struck by how the spaces in between—the grass, the paths, the reflecting pool—stand for the open space in the American mind."

Behind the lectern, Mick uncrossed his feet and looked out at the senators in front of him and the slice of the American people listening in the gallery, high above the chamber.

"Walking, I realized that the Mall keeps faith with the founders and leaves room for future generations to contemplate our history and destiny without imperial monuments."

Mick looked down at the notes written on white envelopes against the burnished red of the lectern. Before he resumed, he raised his left hand and held it high, perhaps in brief salute to Jackson and March, whom I was sure he had spotted on the highest stair of the gallery.

"I stayed in the open, keeping Abe Lincoln in my line of sight. The sun slanted in front of me, and, as I looked through the trees, the light flattened out against the Vietnam Wall."

As Mick uttered the word *Vietnam*, I noticed a sprinkling of Vietnam vets in the gallery who were wearing the camouflage fatigues, green hats with company insignia, and various peace buttons I had seen at the wall.

"Like the war it remembers, the wall is off to the side, maybe a reminder of the American people keeping Vietnam in a corner of the national conscience."

In rapid succession, Mick made eye contact with one or two of his Senate colleagues on each side of the aisle.

"Down I went along the wall. Name by name, the dead passed, and there I stood, knowing my name would be called today on the floor of the Senate. But many of the men these names stand for had no say in their fate. Black soldiers from the South could not vote when they died in Vietnam in 1965, and many of their white and brown comrades were too young to vote. Yet all went to Vietnam and died pledging allegiance to the United States and the republic for which it stands."

As Mick paused, a senator who had been missing entered the rear of the chamber. In the silence, the swinging doors squeaked. Like a savvy conductor, Mick held his hand up until the noise subsided beneath the faint hum of the air-conditioning.

"Behind the clouds reflected in black granite, the names stood at attention: Gonzales, Lowell, Lee, Morgan, Kowalski, Harper, Brownstein, McCarthy, Cuong. Anyone who doubts this country's debt to the peoples of the world should come to the Vietnam Wall."

Whelan stopped, and someone cleared his throat in the gallery near the VIP row where Congressman Rivera was sitting.

"For a minute, I thought that if I spoke the names one by one, the lost soldiers would appear." Mick reached into his pocket for a thin square of white paper and put it on the lectern. "When I stopped and looked straight ahead, one name shook loose from the others and swam into focus behind a passing cloud: Michael Joseph Whelan. Letter after letter tiny bamboo spears in my heart, I tried to imagine Michael J. Whelan. *How had he died? Had he been scared? Was there a buddy with him? What were his last words? Did he sigh? Did he cry or did he curse the sky or curse the senators who sent him to die in Vietnam? I'll never know.*"

Mick gripped the square of paper, then put it down again, a smudge of charcoal visible.

"But I do know that the Michael J. Whelan who died in Vietnam grew up in a small town in Ohio. His grandfather, like mine, came from Ireland. Like me, he served Mass on snowy mornings. Like me, he was a high-school athlete. Like me, he had curly hair, but his was black like many in County Cork where centuries ago his people rescued sailors from the Spanish Armada. As far as I know, we were not related, but I consider Michael J. Whelan my younger brother, and the sons and daughters he never had, nieces and nephews. He died in Vietnam in 1969, and that's another grief, because if politics in 1968 had worked out the way a majority of the American people wanted, Michael J. Whelan would have come home to Ohio alive, and would be living his life today."

Again, Mick picked up the square of paper and held it out to the listening senators.

"The other morning, I borrowed pencil and paper from a young man who was searching for his father's name and took this rubbing."

Mick looked up toward the great seal of the republic. "I've paced back and forth in front of the wall many times and missed this name. Standing in the well of the Senate, I know why I saw my shadow in the form of a name I had never seen before: this name—his name, my name—is a sign of the faith I'll keep tonight."

Mick put down the rubbing and his eyes lingered on one of the envelopes on which his notes were written.

"Mr. President, this resolution authorizing military action anywhere in Latin America any time the president chooses is a mistake, perhaps with even graver consequences than Vietnam. Last week a question was put to a subcommittee of the Senate by a Vietnam veteran: *'How can you ask a man to be the first to die in a war that is not a war?'* Without this resolution, Mr. President, there will be no war and no first or last dead American in Latin America."

The hum of the air-conditioning system died away as Mick Whelan uttered the last words of his speech.

"Mr. President, tonight the Senate can see to it that the poet's prophecy of 'small war upon the heels of small war' does not become America's legacy. For the sake of the republic and the Constitution, for the sake of our fellow citizens whose well-being we are sworn to protect and preserve, I urge defeat of the motion."

As Mick turned his head, his profile was in sharp relief to both the vice president and the members of the Senate.

"Mr. President," his voice rang, "I ask for the ayes and nays."

With a jerk, the senator from Virginia came to his feet.

"Has the senator from Oregon's time expired?"

"It has, Senator."

Stymied, the senator from Virginia carried on.

"Mr. President, is it not the Senate's custom to call for a brief recess before a vote?"

Walking the Oregon coast as the denouement unreeled in my mind, I stumbled, remembering how I started up in my chair at the Virginia senator's snarling question. My God, I thought all over again, there won't be a vote after all. Then, hearing a passing beachcomber say that the recount in Florida had resumed under court order, I tuned back into the Senate drama of almost ten years before.

The vice president bent over and listened to the parliamentarian whisper in his ear, then answered.

"It is the last speaker's right to call for the ayes and nays."

"Point of order," the senator from Virginia persisted.

"The senator from Virginia will state his point of order."

"I move for a fifteen-minute recess."

The vice president looked uncomfortable but had no reason to consult the parliamentarian.

"The senator's motion is out of order. The senator from Oregon has acted within the rules unanimously agreed to by the Senate when it adopted procedures for this debate."

Half a dozen senators were now on their feet.

"Point of information, Mr. President."

"The senator from Connecticut is recognized."

"Mr. President, I rise to remind my good friend from Virginia that should he move to suspend the rules, the will of the Senate shall be determined by a nondebatable motion requiring a two-thirds majority."

The parliamentarian leaned over to the vice president.

"The senator from Connecticut is correct," the vice president replied. "Does the senator from Virginia so move?"

The silence on the floor of the Senate drowned out the excited murmurs in the galleries.

"Hearing no call to suspend the rules, the ayes and nays are ordered," the vice president said, his eyes doleful at being unable to prevent what the president, who knew little about the Senate, would expect him to prevent.

So the Senate waited, the gallery waited, and I waited for the clerk to call the roll. Mick had cut the heart out of any maneuvering by supporters of the resolution with his immediate call for the ayes and nays. Losing a vote on procedure would telegraph to fence-sitting senators that the ayes might lack the votes to pass the resolution. As for Mick's speech, I hoped he had swayed a vote or two, but when I watched the cosponsors converging at the dais to make sure the vice president stayed put, I thought they had it figured at worst case a tie, at best, victory by one or two votes.

Calculating votes in the Senate during the fluctuations of a roll call is a little like keeping track of the red and the black at the roulette wheel. No matter how even the vote, there are always consecutive runs of ayes and nays, and the alphabet is the only constant. The first three senators voting on the president's resolution responded aye. Through G, the resolution was ahead by six, where it stayed until the Ms and Ns brought a surge of nays. It stayed in front by one or two through the Ts, and I began to think that Mick Whelan might cast the tying or tie-breaking vote. I was too nervous to trust my count. Only two senators remained to be called after Mick, and as the clerk called out, "Mr. Whelan," the page boy kneeling in front of me whispered that it was tied. Sure enough, when Mick answered nay in a clear voice, applause broke out in the gallery, and in the chamber a stifled shout of "Right on!" came from the page.

"Quiet," I shushed, fearful any breach of decorum might alienate the last two senators, a Democrat and a Republican from the Midwest known to be undecided, who sat directly across the aisle from each other.

I was wrong.

When their names were called, each senator voted nay, the first in a whisper, the second in an unparliamentary *No!*, which unleashed a roar from the gallery and from Mick a sigh that I heard across the chamber. While the clerk went over the official tally sheet with the vice president, I looked up and saw the hands of the gilded clock lock at five to eleven. In

412

the meantime, the president's men fanned out on the floor, desperate to round up a switch or two that would pass the motion outright or allow the vice president to break a tie. Finally, the senior senator from Montana rose unsteadily to his feet.

"Mr. President, I seek recognition to switch my vote."

"The gentleman is recognized."

With both hands on the front of his desk, the senator spoke in a cracking voice.

"Mr. President, I cast my vote in error. I vote aye."

"The clerk will change the senator's vote to aye," said the vice president.

Christ, I wondered, how many senators did the bastards hot-wire to switch if they were a vote or two short?

Mick looked my way with a frown followed by a wink, telling me, yes, the fix might be in, but it wouldn't work.

"Thank you, Mr. President," the senator from Montana said.

He then dropped some papers on the floor so that it took him a minute or two to sit down. But seeing no other senators on their feet and hearing no further calls for recognition, the vice president pushed back his chair, accepted the tally sheet from the clerk, examined it, scanned the Senate desks from left to right, cleared his throat, looked up once more at the senator from Virginia and out over the Republican desks, gulped, and read the vote.

"The vote," he began, speaking slowly enough to allow for a tardy switch, "the vote on the resolution authorizing the president of the United States to use appropriate force in Latin America, at times and in places, as he shall see fit, to safeguard national security and protect American interests, is as follows."

The coughing and clearing of throats that accompanied the vice president's stalling tactics subsided all at once.

"Yeas: forty-nine; nays: fifty. The motion fails."

As bedlam broke out in the galleries, the Senate chamber remained quiet. Looking this way and that, the vice president banged his gavel and called for order. Knowing that the battle was over for now and that they could only come back and fight another day, the sponsors of the resolution joined the rest of the Senate and voted to adjourn. As several of them huddled with the senator from Virginia in a far corner of the chamber and the galleries began to empty out, most senators stood in the aisles and chatted until the way was clear to the well, where Mick stood accepting congratulations and thanking two or three senators who told him his speech had swayed their vote. As Mick's top aide, I stood off to the side and basked in the congratulations sent my way by men and women on the staffs of senators who had voted both ways on the resolution. Soon a page rushed up with a note scrawled on ABC stationery asking if Senator Whelan would speak with its correspondent.

"He's waiting outside the cloakroom," the boy told me.

He offered a pencil, but, seeing that Mick would be occupied for a while, I hurried out to the corridor.

"Hell of a speech the senator made," the correspondent, in a dark-blue ABC blazer, told me.

I muttered a guttural thanks the way I was supposed to but could not stifle a grin.

"I've got a live feed to Ted Koppel," the ABC guy said. "He'd like to interview Senator Whelan on *Nightline*."

A few feet away, the cameraman and his assistant were setting up a little stage against the backdrop of the newly installed bust of former vice president George Herbert Walker Bush. I went back into the Senate through the cloakroom. Of course Mick would do Koppel. The trick was not to announce it, but to disengage Mick and wait until we were alone to tell him what was up. Nonchalance was the game, so I strolled up to the well, where he stood listening to half a dozen senators reconstruct the debate. He was especially attentive to two Republican senators who, though they had voted for the resolution, were telling him how much his remarks had moved them. Nodding and shaking my head by turns, I gave Mick the sign. His eyes glinted on mine as he concentrated intently on his colleagues. After granting each one audience for a moment or two, Mick shook hands, slapping his left hand on their right before letting go. Then he walked up the center aisle of the chamber to a chorus of approval. From the gallery came one or two yells and several thumbs-up signs, mostly from Vietnam vets.

"What's up?" Mick asked me at the swinging doors.

"Koppel," I said. "There's a live feed."

In the cloakroom, Mick gave brief audience to a knot of senators waiting to congratulate him. Again, one or two who had voted for the resolution were at pains to tell him they had almost been swayed to vote no. A low cheer went up in the corridor when he appeared. Not far from where the ABC camera was set up, L. A. Jackson and Ted March held court with Sarah and the two Whelan girls. As he approached, Mick held out his arms and caught his wife and daughters in a single embrace. Off to one side, young Jack Phillips hung back, this time wearing his combat camouflage fatigues from Vietnam. I waved him over, but not before L. A.'s booming voice closed the little circle.

"Man, you did some mighty preaching. Talking about your name on that wall. And those senators hustling for the Pentagon saw a ghost or two. I'm telling you, bro, that was a sight to see."

The ABC monitor flashed from the set for *Nightline* in the New York studio to a commercial where the silver blur of a sleek American car named for a jungle cat darted around a mountain curve into the sunlight and vanished down a long straightaway.

"Koppel-time, Senator," I said, thinking of Miles Stein.

"Aren't we important?" March said with a grin that told Mick how well he'd done and how glad March was that he'd been there.

Before March or L. A. Jackson had a chance to kibitz anymore, Sarah shushed them and turned to me. "Go ahead, Gabe, help the man of the hour."

Sarah was not the least bit like Senate wives who turned their husbands' senior staff into colonial servants the minute a television camera appeared on the scene. And I obeyed her, making sure the microphone bit into Mick's lapel as he checked his image in the monitor and straightened the tilt of his head in the nick of time.

"Good evening, Senator Whelan," Koppel said as his groomed image filled the screen. "May I congratulate you on your stunning victory?"

"Thank you, Ted," Mick said, his face on the left of the split screen.

"Senator, the House is more solidly Democratic than the Senate, yet its members voted two-to-one for the president's resolution. What happened in the Senate to change so many minds?"

At the edge of the knot of onlookers, Jack Phillips was staring at Mick, his fixed expression a mixture of awe and some other emotion I could not place.

"The Senate took its time, the evidence came out," Mick answered. "The Pentagon and the CIA have personnel in Venezuela working with paramilitary groups and dissident army officers to undermine the presidential election. There were also reports that American civilians have been hired by our government to train paramilitaries—actions that are turning the people in Latin America against the United States. So one senator after another came to feel that the administration was deliberately turning something not a war into a war."

On the monitor a tight close-up of Koppel replaced the medium shot of Mick.

"Senator, well-placed sources in the administration tell us there is talk of a reconsideration motion. Are you concerned?"

As Mick began to answer, the cameraman went to a shot that enlarged Mick's head enough to catch an eagle-eyed glint.

"Reconsideration is a matter for the Senate to decide, not the White

House, Ted. Twice the senator from Virginia and the vice president invited senators to switch their votes. Only one did. The president is free to send up another resolution, but I think a clear majority of senators on both sides of the aisle accepts the verdict rendered tonight."

A wide-angle shot of the ABC studio zoomed in on a color-coded map of Latin America behind Koppel. But before Koppel could launch into his pundit's close, Mick seized the floor.

"Ted, the Senate met its responsibility to the Constitution and rejected putting young Americans needlessly in harm's way and inflaming the nation's relations with Latin America and the world."

Now Koppel truly was out of time, so after a swift pro forma sign-off, the monitor in front of us went dead. While Mick said see-you-later farewells to Sarah and the girls and the crowd thinned out, I headed over to Jack Phillips. Before I reached him, he was at my side, his intensity concentrated on me for a change.

"Tell the senator that was a fine speech," he said, with tears in his eyes and a fierce set to his mouth.

I took his arm. "It would mean more from you, Jack."

He had turned to leave, but now he hesitated, and waited until Mick disengaged from the ABC crew.

"Those bastards better lay off M-Mick," he told me.

"You mean those few angry vets?" I asked.

"No, the ones b-behind them—Rivera and his lobbyist friends. They better stop lying—better stop calling my f-friend Slick M-Mick."

When Mick saw Jack's lower lip quiver and heard his halting words of friendship and praise, he put his arm around the other man's shoulder and walked him away from the microphone and camera. "The speech was for you, Jack—you know that."

Jack's eyes glistened. Mick made a fist, tapped Jack lightly on the shoulder, and turned to me. The three of us walked toward the checkpoint at the rear of the Capitol.

"Gabe, I was telling Jack his senator's a plagiarist."

An unsettling faraway look of admiration came into Jack's eyes again.

"You're my h-hero," Jack said.

"What say we bring Jack to the Irish wake Sarah's putting on?" Mick said, an open, welcoming look on his face.

"You're not supposed to know about that."

"Gabe, if you're a senator's wife and you want to keep something from him, don't tell his private secretary."

Then he turned to Jack. "I'd like to have you there."

"Senator, are you sure?" Jack looked directly at Mick. "I mean, s-sure, I'll come."

On our way out, the guard asked Senator Whelan to autograph a gallery pass for his grandson. Outside, a restless wind amplified the noises of the early summer night. I raised my arm for a cab, and as I opened the door for Jack and Mick, the horn blared from an old green TR 4, a relic of the sixties, in which a handsome young couple—the woman Georgia brown, the man Rocky Mountain ruddy—were riding with the top down. They gave Mick the peace sign and waved.

"Good going, Senator Whelan!" the young man hollered, his voice cresting on the night air.

"*You* ought to run," his companion added before the taillights of their sports car, one flickering like a dying star, the other a deep, pulsing red, vanished up Constitution Avenue.

CHAPTER 23

The next ten days, I pretended that the telegrams, letters, and phone calls pouring into Mick Whelan's Senate office were a pain in the ass. But how could I fool even the most callow intern when I hounded everyone within earshot to send a veteran Washington pundit's column to every soul on the mailing list?

In the aftermath of Senator Michael Whelan's triumph on the floor of the Senate, a growing number of Democratic professionals are saying the party could do worse than nominate the eloquent forty-nine-year-old senator from Oregon as its presidential candidate in 1992. Because of the Gulf War, conventional wisdom has it that next year will not be a Democratic year. But the pasty needs a fresh face. And as he showed leading the opposition and defeating the president's military-force resolution, Whelan, a veteran of four terms in the House of Representatives, and respected by Senate colleagues on both sides of the aisle, possesses formidable political skills and a remarkable sense of timing . . .

Whelan's stance on the lessons of Vietnam could lead the way to healing the Democratic Party and the country more than fifteen years after America's sorry departure from Saigon. Word around Washington is that the Oregon senator already has enough pledges to fund an exploratory campaign . . .

Predictions are never legal tender in politics, but after hearing the cheers cascade down from the Senate gallery last week, this reporter would not be surprised if Senator Michael "Mick" Whelan became the dark-horse candidate of choice in the 1992 presidential sweepstakes.

Late one afternoon, Mick called me into his office. He was sitting at his desk, tilted precariously, arms folded behind his head. After I sat down, he shook loose a couple of little cigars, extended the tin box, then snapped his lighter and held the flame until our cigars glowed into life.

"You've got one more chance to talk me out of this," he said, exhaling a thin stream of smoke that traced a low flight pattern above my head.

"That's one more than you gave me in 1974."

Mick's extended palms gave me leave to continue, so I told him that César Rivera and the same bunch he and L. A. Jackson had stirred up with their bills on compulsory national service and high-speed trains back in the House in the late seventies were out to bring him down after his defeat of the president's resolution. "Bad enough Senator Whelan, but President Whelan?"

He tapped the tips of his fingers together and waited for the rest of what I had to say.

"I know you don't scare. How about Sarah?"

As he spoke, his face grew sober.

"She's gung ho—maybe more than I am."

Mick wasn't kidding. Since his speech, Sarah Whelan had taken to calling me almost daily. At first, she'd been skeptical about her husband running. But she quickly warmed to the idea, and within a week floated the names of several campaign managers, passed on the resumes of a half dozen hungry young advance men, inquired about delegate selection for the 1992 convention, and suggested a sequence of appearances for Mick on television interview programs. "Sarah for press secretary," I told her, and she demurred—sort of. *A man never knows about his own house,* I thought, but when I remembered Sarah's kindness after Patrick's death, I stifled an impulse to caution Mick about his wife's take-charge attitude. Listening to him that afternoon, I realized I was the only living soul he had told about Rebecca Phillips. I also sensed his fear that he might look like a fool if he ran for president, so I told him that was one of the few things in his power to control. Reassured, he stabbed out the glowing embers of his cigar and shifted to talk of the press conference announcing the Whelan-for-president exploratory committee.

"I was thinking of the caucus room, but Henry Hart's leery of the Senate." Mick shuffled the remaining cigars in the tin box.

"He's wrong," I spoke up sharply. "The Senate's your house."

Mick nodded, and a week later Congressman Hart stood at a podium between the marble pillars of the vaulted Senate caucus room blinking into the small explosions of flashbulbs. Despite his bad back, Hart stood ramrod straight.

"It's been said that the United States Senate is a body of a hundred men and women who, hearing the words 'the president of the United States,' all turn around at once. But now Democrats across the country are turning to Senator Whelan because they believe he can chart the direction the party should take in the nineties."

Hart turned his head toward Mick.

"I watched Michael Whelan grow into a courageous, effective leader on domestic policy during his four terms in the House of Representatives. And last month, many senators who had doubts about the president's military-force resolution followed Senator Whelan's lead on the most vital foreign-policy issue of our time. He was the one senator with the courage and judgment to know when and how to act. There is something to be said for a presidential candidate who can anticipate the country's best desires and who is willing to risk his future to move out ahead in that direction. Ladies and gentlemen: Senator Michael Whelan of Oregon."

Mick looked at Sarah and his daughters, and, after going to Hart's side to shake hands, waited until the old man toiled back to his chair. At the lectern, he took a single folded sheet of paper from his pocket and smoothed it on the wood. At Mick's insistence, the press conference lacked the trappings of a rally. The friends and supporters who showed up sat scattered behind the row of reporters and bank of television cameras. He had come a long way from the great room at the Oregon state capitol, where, as a lark, he had filed for Congress on Saint Patrick's Day in 1974. Now, as he stood at the podium in the same room where Jack and Bobby Kennedy and his friend Eugene McCarthy had declared for the presidency, words that had sounded logical and even inevitable in the privacy of Mick Whelan's mind must have seemed more than a little presumptuous.

"I take this step toward becoming a candidate for the Democratic presidential nomination because there is a yearning among Americans for a politics consistent with our first principles, and for policies able to meet the challenges at home and in the world as we approach the twenty-first century. "

Mick took a half step back from microphones clustered oddly like the Indian paintbrushes I'd passed hiking the Loowit trail with Patrick. Because Senator Whelan had not given the press corps an ounce of red meat, they sharpened their pencils to an edge fine enough to take a man's head off. They were led by the correspondent from the *Chicago Sun-Times*. His albino baby face belied the fact that he'd gotten close enough to the bone of scandal in Chicago politics that, on publisher's orders, his editor assigned him to Washington, a venue less tied to the paper's advertising revenues.

"Senator, some Democrats, in particular Congressman Rivera of California, are complaining about divisiveness and opportunism on your part, even suggesting your candidacy could lose the House of Representatives for the Democrats. How do you answer that?"

Mick glanced my way, perhaps wondering why I hadn't prepared him for this question.

"On the contrary, Peter, Democrats around the country want last month's Senate debate extended to the country at large."

"Senator," began an oily-tongued columnist notorious for deflating

Democratic candidates before they posed a serious threat to Republicans, "you come from a state in the Northwest that most Americans have barely heard of. You have no personal fortune, no experience in a national campaign."

Mick stood motionless while the reporter looked over at the nearest television camera and back to Whelan.

"Isn't this committee a front to give you enough national exposure that the eventual Democratic nominee will consider you for the vice presidential nomination?"

There were rumblings of displeasure in the audience, and the hiss of "Kiss my . . . " from where L. A. Jackson was sitting between Ted March and a restless-eyed Jack Phillips under a black-and-white photo of FDR.

"It's the other way around," Mick replied. "The national exposure generated by the Senate's rejection of the president's military-force resolution is why Democrats are asking me to run for president."

While I was kicking myself for not planting one or two favorable questions, the correspondent from *The New York Times* jumped to her feet, eager as always to show she was more in command than the person holding the press conference.

"Senator, you alluded to a progressive agenda without mentioning specifics. Can you tell us what you have in mind?"

Crouching a little, as if the pitch he'd been waiting for was on its way to the plate, Whelan seemed to tense his hands and extend his arms, ready to hit the ball on the sweet spot of the bat.

"Andrea, after defeating the president's preemptive initiative, and with the Cold War over, we need to talk about a true America: about creating jobs, providing health care, cleaning up the air and water, preserving the natural resources we've been blessed with, and moving toward a society where the good life is a reality for everyone in the United States of America."

Mick stopped and pointed to a short man who stood up with a CNN mike in his hand.

"Senator, that sounds like rhetoric Democrats trot out every four years. Anything new?"

On the left, Miles Stein was panning his handheld camera from Mick to his wife and daughters to L. A. Jackson and Jack Phillips.

"Charles, in 1944 Franklin Roosevelt promised full employment, health care, housing, and education as priorities after the war. In 1948, Harry Truman added civil rights. But in the sixties, when we were about to make good on the old promises, the president and Congress put a foolish and tragic war in Vietnam ahead of building a great and good society at home. Then the great chance we had in 1968 was lost. Now, more than two decades later, after Vietnam and Watergate, after the so-called malaise of the late seventies and the me-first spirit of the eighties, the time has come to tap the spirit of public happiness."

Mick looked toward the glowing red lights of the television cameras. "Now is the time to tell the American people the truth—the Earth's oil supply is running out, but we have the ingenuity to develop technology and sources of energy friendly to the environment and to our relations with the rest of the world."

Mick had taken a step away from the podium when an earnest young woman I recognized as a freelancer spoke up along the far wall.

"Senator Whelan, two weeks ago no one would have taken this press conference seriously. What's moved you to take the leap?"

Mick came back to the microphone, a faraway look in his eye.

"Simple, Marilyn," he said, beckoning her to a seat at the end of the front row. "People who had sworn off politics see the 1992 election as a chance to take back this country. A nation can't be an empire to the world and a republic to its people. My purpose, like Benjamin Franklin's after the Constitutional Convention, is to challenge the American people to keep the republic."

Walking off, Mick held his head at half-mast, downbeat as if unaware that the tougher the questions, the better he'd done. But he needn't have worried. Both print and electronic media pulled the fragments together to support the theme that Whelan might be the politician able to ignite the smoldering conscience of the Democratic Party. Meanwhile, pledges of support flowed in from many men and women who had cut their political eyeteeth with Gene McCarthy or Bobby or, later on, Ted Kennedy, and now looked to one of their own to redeem the promise interrupted in 1968 by hubris, nemesis, and the lesser foibles of politicus Americanus.

At the end of June, Mick hit the road for a collage of speeches, media interviews, meet-and-greet events with the party faithful, and one-on-one sessions with leaders in New York, Pennsylvania, and Illinois. Everywhere he went, Mick's riff about the imperial danger to the republic turned people on. And when the Commonwealth Club booked Whelan for a July speech in California, Ted March set in motion a fund-raiser at five grand a head in Silicon Valley the day after the long-scheduled Fourth of July dedication of the John D. Phillips Research and Observation Center on Mount Loowit, where Mick was the featured speaker.

The night before the ceremony, I camped out in the bar of The Blue Hour with members of the national press corps for whom Loowit's eruption, a half dozen years before Mount Saint Helens, exerted a nostalgic pull. Usually wary of briefings by a candidate's aide, the reporters were eager for details of Mick's wild ride down the mountain. I obliged, embellishing the story but declining a nightcap until they left and Harry Hacker sidled into the booth.

"You've brought your boy a long way in seventeen years," Harry said, rolling a swallow of Courvoisier to and fro in his snifter.

"Mud in your eye, Harry." I lifted my glass.

"Better not be any in yours," he said, "or Jack junior will end the Whelan campaign before it gets started."

I looked at Harry through the enormous snifter and I saw the unquiet eyes of someone bursting to pass on bad news.

"What have you got?" I bit off my words.

"A headwaiter in Washington saw young Jack throw a punch at that Mexican congressman last week."

"César Rivera?" I said.

"Yup," he nodded, knowing he had my attention. "Rivera told Jack to watch out for Slick Mick—called him a ruthless son of a bitch out to use Jack like he'd used his old man. Good thing Rivera ducked or he'd have been one cold-cocked congressman," Harry said, exhaling like the cognac was firewater. "Better keep junior hugging trees."

Before Harry could order another, I had the waiter bring the check, and Harry matched my ten spot.

"No fear, no favor, old sport," he said with a mean wink.

In the morning, Mick and I followed Miles Stein, who was in the lead car scouting locations for shots of the blast zone below the blown-out remains of Mount Loowit's north face. Once out of Vanport, I followed the Columbia gorge, one hand on the wheel, the other on a clunky early-model car phone.

"How many interviews, Bontempo?" Mick asked after I clanged the phone back into its cradle.

That was like Mick, to call me by my last name after almost thirty years. But sensing he might have hurt my feelings, he added we as if it took both of us for him to be Senator Whelan.

"You taped 60 Minutes. There's the Times, the Chronicle, the Post, and the Trib. Don't worry, I'll stiff the locals," I told him while he shaded his eyes from the sun and looked straight ahead to the east before putting one of his stocking feet on the dashboard.

"Stall the Times but not the locals," he said abruptly.

Here I was driving my boss of a dozen years, friend for thirty, up the mountain to commemorate the eruption, and he was telling me how to handle the press. That was why he was the senator from Oregon and a likely candidate for president, and, on the record, I was a defeated candidate for Congress. I veered southeast from the old Gorge Highway to Route 200, a two-lane road that wound through the lush, dark-green countryside into the blast zone for twenty miles until it came to an abrupt end at the Phillips Observation Center. Every few miles, I noticed a stand of trees that had been planted each year by the timber companies since 1975—Douglas, noble, and other indigenous species of fir decimated by the avalanche of ash and boulders that had swept down the mountain over the tree line. High above the gorge, the color of the sky changed from the pigment of Giotto's frescoes—a pale-blue hint that, little by little, the world was wearing out—to the eternal deep blue of the mountains. As we climbed to three thousand feet, I felt part of the sky and was glad I'd accepted the Avis manager's upgrade to a convertible. Suddenly, there was a sickly rasp from the car phone. Mick waved it off, and I ignored it till the noise ceased. Then I flipped the *off* switch, and we slipped into companionable silence. After a few miles more, the lead car stopped beside a stunning overlook. By the time I parked, Miles had positioned his camera to the right of a sightseeing telescope.

Below, I saw a vast field of mud halted in midflow.

"See the silvery line," Mick said, tapping me on the shoulder. "That's the Clark River. Kayaks used to ride the rapids down there."

Chattering in time to the whirr of his camera, Miles shot Mick surveying the landscape. As we waited for him and his sidekick to pack up and shove off, Mick adjusted the telescope and told me to look.

There were no trees in sight, only elk grazing, the color of mud except for the white patch on their behinds, while the silver thread of the river unspooled westward in fits and starts.

"A whole herd," Mick said. "Jack Phillips told me they'd come. By the way, remind me to catch Jack after the dedication. Rivera and some of the oil and defense boys in D.C. are whispering in his ear."

Ever impatient, Miles pulled out of the overlook and honked for us to follow.

As our convertible climbed up the mountainside, a sign marked the elevation at four thousand feet, and endless dots of trees receded into the distance on every side. Around the next bend, the remains of Mount Loowit rushed into view, chalked with a thin film of snow. To catch a last glimpse of the river, I looked sideways past Mick, and saw a tear winding down one of his cheeks. I turned my head, but he saw me and touched my arm. We rode in silence for a while before his voice reached me, not forlorn or faraway, but matter-of-fact and immediate from the next seat.

"Rebecca, the love of my life," he said, dabbing his face with his handkerchief. "And Sarah, my wife."

Ahead, spreading out below the crater, logs that had been huge Douglas fir were splayed out over hills of mud like fistfuls of pick-up sticks hurled once upon a time by a petulant child. I looked at Mick, but a rush of memories and old feelings stripped my gears of speech.

"With one thing and another, things don't get told," he mused. "I was about to before Sarah's miscarriage with our little boy . . . ," his voice faded out, then came back strong. "But now, with this presidential thing, I've got to tell her about Rebecca."

He sighed. Silent, he stretched his neck and hands straight up in the air until the wind tunneled through his hair and seemed to deepen the creases in his face.

"Here we are," he said a few minutes later, taking a comb out of his pocket as I pulled into the parking lot below the Phillips Observation Center. Seventeen years ago, the force of the blast had pulverized the soft rocks below the north face and blown tons of debris over a campground that doubled as a listening post. Now there was a visitors' center of stone and glass next to an L-shaped research laboratory and residence built of cedar. Outside the entrance, a banner flapped and went limp as nomadic gusts of wind blew down the mountain. In the midst of the hoopla, an advance guard of press and media angled Mick toward the shoulder of the steep path. Like a blocking back, I slowed up the first two reporters before Whelan zigzagged in the other direction, bantering the whole time.

Inside, a young woman wearing a blue badge rushed up. "This way, Senator," she said, unclasping the rope that kept us on the business side of the ticket line. "You're a special guest."

"All the more reason to pay my way," he laughed, then edged closer to the kiosk.

On the other side of the rope, Miles was shooting visitors who milled around enormous before-and-after photographs of the mountain. The young woman with the badge was still gushing over Mick when he returned with two thin, green wraparound paper bracelets signifying that we were paid customers. Two guides led us outside to a wooden platform, sideways to the mountain, where the governor, Mrs. John Phillips, and other dignitaries stood along a cedar railing facing the shattered features of Mount Loowit. Whelan hung back until the governor and the congress-woman from Vanport spied him and approached. Because of the hubbub about the presidency and the large contingent of press and media, Mick was no longer simply an Oregon politician, but you wouldn't have known it from his demeanor.

Presently, a string quartet led by Isabel Riggs finished playing Vivaldi's "Summer," the choir from Ship of Zion sang Ray Charles's jazzy version of "America," and the auxiliary bishop of Vanport gave the invocation. Mick sat in the front row between the governor and Mrs. Phillips, who turned a little toward the seat reserved for her son. The sun burned my neck as the governor paid tribute to the late congressman and introduced Senator Whelan as the man responsible for making Mount Loowit a household word in America and sponsoring legislation to fund the magnificent John D. Phillips Center. During applause that rose, fell, and rose again, Mick made his way to the podium. He shook hands with the governor and scanned the mountainside and, beyond the gaping crater, a sliver of lake whose shoreline receded before broken cliffs of caked mud. Then he acknowledged Mrs. Phillips, praised her late husband as the driving force behind the center, and fleetingly mentioned the daughter whose loss had moved the congressman and his wife to do what they could to prevent another catastrophe from catching people unawares. The preliminaries over, the Fourth of July duly noted, Mick looked through shimmering heat at the diminished majesty of Mount Loowit.

"This spot is the beginning and the end and the beginning of my world. I see so many people here whose lives have touched mine because of this mountain: Jonas and Martin Fitch who saved my life and gave me purpose in the chaos of the eruption; Gabriel Bontempo, who has kept me on course, beginning with my first campaign for Congress; Elizabeth Phillips; and Isabel Riggs, whose violin I have heard before on this mountainside."

The sound of his voice and the expression on his face told me that Mick was already in a world far from the press, his fledgling presidential campaign, and the conventions of the dedication.

"Today I'm conscious of the Bible's words 'Remember, man, that thou art dust and unto dust shalt thou return.' Those words are true of Mount Loowit, too, and the whole round Earth revolving through the limitless sky."

Mick turned his head in a half circle, taking in the gaping peaks of Loowit, the glint of the Clark River across west-running fields of mud, and the human microcosm before him; then he searched from one face to another.

"Seventeen years ago, the mountain in front of us unleashed its fire against the valley below. But that devastation was not the end of the world. Look around—beginnings are everywhere. Look at the mountain flowers in their bursts of red and orange, yellow and lavender. A few miles back, a herd of elk grazed near the mud field. Elk didn't come up that far before the volcano—they do now. On the path a little while ago, two marmots darting between flowers in the sand showed me how to zigzag past a pack of reporters."

During the interval of laughter, Mick wiped his forehead, then took off his jacket and slung it over the podium.

"Look at the giant butterflies flying around in pairs. They alight on flowers and on tree trunks splintered by the blast. Just when I think they're tame and reach out to see if they'll alight on my arm, they dart out of sight."

As he spoke, a yellow and black butterfly, larger than the others, flying solo, flew around his head, swerved, and alit on the pocket of his jacket. "This one's alone. Maybe his mate's gone."

Its wings taut, the butterfly rose and buzzed Mick's head before it disappeared beyond the railing and flew off toward the mountain. Mick ducked, then laughed at his instinctive flinch.

"Everywhere, a world is beginning. But I can't look at what's left of that lake—the dead trees floating down there—without thinking of those who were buried in their cabins."

Mick swung his eyes to where Mrs. Phillips sat, her jacket folded neatly on the chair next to her while stones clattered down the mountainside from a large boulder above the observatory.

"Today I look north and see a lake that wasn't there."

He stopped to absorb the natural scene before focusing on the people in the back rows who strained forward to hear him. "Let us pay our respects to the beginning of a world, the natural world and the historical human world shared by visitors like us and by the scientists who live and work here. To have the beginning of a world that's happening now, there had to be the end of the old mountain and the fragile life on the mountainside."

The sun slanted through Mick's hair, lighting up the patches of gray above and behind his temples.

"My friends and fellow citizens, it falls to us to live in the world with life and death. It falls to us to know that respect for nature and one another is necessary to change history and create a society where all people can have a share of the good life. For this reason the Fourth of July not only celebrates our independence, but also our interdependence on one another and on nature."

He stopped, picked up his jacket, and folded it over his arm. As the applause grew and echoed into the world beyond the human outpost of the center, Mick descended the makeshift platform. Off to one side at a table covered by starched white cloth, waiters stood with champagne flutes and bottles of recent Oregon vintage. The associate director of the center, a tall, athletic woman in a peasant blouse and flowing matching skirt, took Mrs. Phillips's arm and motioned dignitaries toward the refreshments. I stood nearby, keeping the impatient press on a leash so Mick could spend a decent interval with the other speakers and officials. After the governor offered a toast, Mrs. Phillips disengaged from the noise and flow of people and stood along the red cedar railing a few feet away. As soon as I caught her eye, I went over. We chatted for a few minutes, and, as Mick approached, I heard Miles calling from behind and excused myself. By the time I settled him down and returned, Mick and Mrs. Phillips had moved out of range. Moving closer to her, Mick bent over and nodded. When I was about ten feet away, she put out her hand, as if to touch his arm, then drew back and said something in a low voice. I stopped. The hum of voices was too loud for me to be sure, but I thought I heard her say, "Forget." Then a surly voice broke my concentration.

"The senator's talking to Mrs. Phillips," I told the burly reporter from NBC. "What do you need?"

"The sun is at a perfect angle for a shot of Senator Whelan looking toward the mountain."

At that moment, Mrs. Phillips looked up, startled, from her conversation with Mick. From the left came rude shouts, and from the right the center's hostess was bearing down. Before she arrived, Mick patted Mrs.

Phillips's arm and walked toward me, looking away. I couldn't be sure because the sun was in my eyes, but I thought he blinked away a tear.

"What's happening?" he asked.

Before I could answer, the NBC guy barged in again about the sun. Mick looked back over his shoulder toward the spot where he had been standing. By now, the woman in the peasant blouse and skirt had spirited Mrs. Phillips off to the refreshment table. Mick shrugged and turned back to the reporter.

"Let's do it."

The reporter walked him to where the railing jutted farthest out from the patio while I joined Miles in a triangle of shade. As Mick moved into position so that the cameraman stood at an angle beyond the line of sight, Miles ridiculed the NBC rigamarole and chattered on about the perfect shot he had in mind.

"Puts that little lake in—Papoosie. With the mountain in the middle."

Miles's staccato was welcome counterpoint as my mind veered back and forth between arranging an efficient schedule for the growing number of reporters and television people who wanted to interview Mick and imagining what had been going on with Mrs. Phillips.

"See?" Miles tugged at my arm. "The angle's all wrong."

He was so agitated, I thought he might hustle over and halt the shoot. I laughed as the cameraman backed away from Mick, who was looking beyond the railing, a touch of sadness deepening the serenity in his eyes, his weathered profile in peaks and valleys like the mountain.

My mind emptied. There was only sun and sky, mountain and lake in the quiet drama Mick had called the end and the beginning of a world when, from the uphill side of the railing, I heard sharp staccato sounds, and the *bap-bap, bap-bap-brup* of an automatic rifle broke the sound barrier of silence on the mountainside.

In the aftermath of the screams, I froze before I saw the figure charging down the hill, sunglasses down, weapon pointed at Mick. Before I could process the frames flashing in front of my eyes, Mick was hit three, four, five times, and crumpled to the ground, sighing a long sigh.

Involuntarily, my legs moved forward in a safe, straight line before I steered them along the quickest diagonal to Mick. I knelt down and saw a shaking, sickening chaos of flesh and blood where his torso had been. His face was whole when I reached him, but all I could do was cradle his head. The intense blue of the sky in his eyes slowly dimmed to a mottled violet. Unbearably aware that below his head his body was quivering, I took in his face. His mouth moved silently, his lips struggling for a word as he took a breath and quickly another, then whispered, "Why? Why now?"

His face went still, the lines invisible in shadow, all hint of speech gone from his mouth, all tremors from his body except the brown-gray curls lifted into the sunlight by a gust of wind.

On the patio some people were screaming, some were quiet, some pushing and shoving, some face down on the ground, some running, some helping those too feeble or scared to do anything but remain exposed. In the accelerating commotion, three or four men vaulted the railing in pursuit of the figure in military fatigues who by now was galloping up the hill uttering strange insensate sounds. At a sail-shaped boulder, where he must have been hiding, he stopped, pulled a grenade from his belt, and waved it at his pursuers.

"Jesus, no!" he yelled, biting off the pin. "No, Jesus no . . . , I got your back."

Now the screams on the patio were wordless and terrible. But the soldier on the hill clutched the grenade to his chest, then turned his back and dove to the ground behind the rock. After seconds that lasted hours, an explosion boomed off the rock and echoed toward the mountain like a distant avalanche followed by silence so terrific and desolate that I wished for more gunfire.

By now, a medevac team had reached Mick, followed by photographers, whom Miles, a lion among hyenas, roared away from their prey. I helped the medics wrap two sheets around Mick and place him gently on the stretcher. At the ambulance, Jonas Fitch stepped forward with his son.

"Want us to ride down with you?"

"Yes, Jonas," my lip quivered. "Mick would want you and Martin keeping him company."

Between sobs on the way to Vanport Mercy, I relived the murder and blamed myself for not saving Mick.

"No," Jonas patted my knee. "You were the first to move. Wouldn't a mattered if you done a high jump."

A mile or two down the mountain, the driver turned off the sirens, and Jonas shook his head and broke the silence.

"Now why would that Phillips fella want to kill Mick Whelan?"

"What?" I said, jolted out of numbness.

"Sure enough, I saw his face sure as I'm seeing yours. Jack Phillips come running down that hill like he was back in Vietnam."

Maybe because I had been there, I had considered the murder somehow an act of God. But now, spinning toward delirium, I hallucinated that Mount Loowit had blown again, and I was driving. *Grabbing one of Mick's ankles, I felt a pulse, saw Patrick giving him artificial respiration in the seat beside me, imagined Kate waiting in the emergency room, and knew that this time everything would be all right.* At Vanport Mercy, Jonas saw to it that a doctor gave me a shot. Then he took me back to The Blue Hour and talked to me like a Dutch uncle.

"Look here, Gabriel, you the only one can do certain things need doing, hear me?"

Overlaying Mick's account of how Jonas compelled him to act like a grown-up after the 1974 eruption, the words towed me back to the painful, living present. Jonas was right. Things needed doing, so I did them. Mercifully, Sarah Whelan had not seen Mick's murder on television. Telling her, I broke down, and Jonas Fitch again came to the rescue. He told her I had been with Mick, cradling his head at the end. In a husky, halting voice, he also told her that if it would be a comfort, he and the brothers and sisters at Ship of Zion would be honored to hold a service before the official rites in Washington. But he had been too far away from where Mick was standing to give her the details survivors crave as bits and pieces of the person they've lost. As I heard Sarah's voice break at the other end, Jonas held out the phone without cupping his hand over the receiver.

"Gabe," he said, after wiping his nose, "will you talk to Mrs. Whelan again?"

"Sarah," I began, then stopped, my words aborted by the shots echoing in my mind and the sight of Mick torn up yet somehow whole in the last moments of his life.

"Gabe, at the end, was it, were there . . . ?" she paused, her sobs trailing off as she gave me time to loosen my tongue.

Briefly, I thought of telling her that Mick's last words were her name and the names of his daughters, but a glance at Jonas made me ashamed of my cowardice.

"He was just there, Sarah. In shock more than pain. His eyes were open like he was waiting . . . "

I couldn't go on, and her quiet, intermittent sobs told me she had crossed over into her own private country of grief.

"I'm glad you were with him," she told me in a voice once again in the here and now.

With Jonas's presence for moral support, I told Sarah as tactfully as I could that I would enlist someone to handle the phone and keep the curious away from her door, especially ambitious reporters eager to make their careers by solving the mystery of why John Phillips Jr. would kill his friend Senator Michael "Mick" Whelan. More painful was counseling her not to talk to agents from the FBI or the CIA without a lawyer present, because I was sure the circumstances of Mick's murder would ignite conspiracy fever inside and outside official Washington.

At first, it looked like vindication of that old saying "Anybody ain't paranoid got to be crazy." Within a day, the FBI found e-mail on Jack Phillips's computer sent two days before the murder. In a clever impersonation of familiarity, the message urged Jack not to be hoodwinked by the likes of Mick Whelan, a slick, self-promoting opportunist who had not fought in Vietnam and was manipulating Vietnam veterans for suspect, treasonable political purposes. The language was inflammatory, almost violent, and the press ran with it for a day or two until FBI agents in the field discovered that the same message had gone out to hundreds of other veterans. Following Sarah's lead, I put conspiracies out of my head and focused on the arrangements. Half kidding, Mick had once told her that if anything happened to him, he wanted a service at Ship of Zion. He hadn't left anything in writing, but she decided to honor his words. Somehow she also found it in her heart to be sorry for Mrs. Phillips. In response to a heartrending letter sent overnight, with a pang Sarah put herself in the other woman's shoes. Elizabeth Phillips had lost her husband, and before him her daughter; now, after he had killed Mick Whelan in her presence, her son was dead by his own hand. Hearing Mrs. Phillips's voice break on the phone, Sarah invited her to the service at Ship of Zion, and went so far as to say that young Jack would be remembered with compassion as a friend of Mick's. At first, Mrs. Phillips declined, but at Sarah's request I called to tell her that I, too, wanted her with us.

Almost ten years later, the memorial service at Ship of Zion remains as blurred as Mick's last moments are stark and vivid. I remember battling Sarah over her wish that I speak. I told her I knew she felt she had to ask, but that deep down, she expected me to refuse. Accepting would be self-serving, I said, and besides, I was a rotten speaker. When none of this changed her mind, I blurted out that having been with Mick at the end, I wouldn't be able to go through with it.

"You were Mick's friend for thirty years, Gabriel. I've got the service at the National Cathedral to worry about—L. A. Jackson and Ted March are speaking—maybe Ship of Zion is hard, but your name is on the program. You have to speak even if all you say is that you can't say anything."

Before I left The Blue Hour for the service, L. A. Jackson came to the rescue long-distance, over the phone. "I say, look, man, I'm there with you—you know that." Then he broke my resisting silence. "No need for you to be Mick's keeper. Just be his friend. The brothers and sisters will do the rest, hear?"

I heard, but listening to Brother Horace sing "Amazing Grace," my mind went blank until I was left with my own diminished self. In desperation, I thought to repeat what Mick had said about old Jack Phillips, that he was a man you could love. Finally, grasping the podium that Mick had liked to call the prow on the Ship of Zion, I bit my lip and said what was in my heart . . .

The world is full of men you could love. But Mick Whelan was a different breed—he was a man who could love, who did love, and so he was not just a man you could love. He was a man you did love, a man I loved and continue to love.

The other thing I remember from Ship of Zion is Mrs. Phillips afterward at the little reception in the basement. (Little reception, hell! The sisters heaped their finest china with fried chicken and ham, potato salad, mustard greens, corn on the cob, black-eyed peas, and pecan pie, all carried piping hot from the kitchen on gleaming silver trays.)

"Gabriel, please eat something," she said, handing me a plate with an expression as close to a smile as she could muster.

My numbness was wearing off, and the mother of the fucked-up, crazy bastard who killed my best friend was not someone I wanted to see. Sensing this, she was brief, saying only what she had come over to say.

"I want to thank you for your kindness, Gabriel."

"It's a hard time."

"For all of us," she said. Picking her words carefully, she added, "I hope you'll come see me on the Metolius."

"It's a lovely spot," I said, my voice breaking.

She put her hand on mine. "I mean it," she said, then took her leave without saying good-bye.

On my way out, I saw Miles Stein manically snapping a cheap insta-matic. Squatting down, he shot me, then rushed forward until his head came to rest on my shoulder. He cried and cried, and I patted his head where gray tufts of hair swirled behind his ears.

"Couldn't shoot the service," he sobbed.

I looked at him uncomprehendingly.

"Forgot to load my camera."

"Miles," I said, hugging him again. "Miles."

"Couldn't shoot you speaking. Let everybody down. Let you down. Let Mick down," he went on, sobs muffling his staccato as if he'd hit a slow-motion switch on his voice box.

"Miles," I said, holding his head in my hands. "Sweet Miles."

His eyes locked on mine, the light came back to them, and he snapped the little borrowed camera in front of my face. "Gotta shoot Mrs. Fitch holding the tray of pies. Mick would like that."

"Yes," I started to say, "he would," but Miles raced off, and I was alone, talking to myself.

CHAPTER 24

The month after Mick Whelan's murder, Washington was a den of conspiracy theories aided and abetted by the tabloids and cable networks. Each succeeding hypothesis flared into a headline more lurid than the last before dying for lack of oxygen. One week, Jack Phillips had acted to avenge the names of the American dead in Vietnam taken in vain by Senator Whelan; the next, he'd been an undercover agent programmed by the CIA to assassinate Whelan then kill himself to conceal the conspiracy; finally, in a grotesque parody of the Sinn Fein gibe I'd endured at the *Irish Times*, an IRA splinter group issued a proclamation—"Remember Bael Na Mblath"—insinuating that Mick Whelan, like Mick Collins before him, had met his maker because he'd betrayed the struggle for a united Ireland. But when the autopsy found a trace of amphetemines in Jack's bloodstream, these inventions yielded to the view that the tragedy was the aberrant act of a troubled, suddenly berserk Vietnam veteran with a well-concealed drug habit.

Gradually, I became less and less at the mercy of FBI men flashing their badges on Capitol Hill as I went through the motions of putting Mick's Senate affairs in order. Throughout the ordeal, I could not get the encounter with Mrs. Phillips at Ship of Zion out of my head. I didn't mention it to anyone, but when I flew to Oregon in mid-August to clean out Mick's Portland office, I called her from a pay phone, half hoping the conversation would be my last hurrah with the now-defunct Phillips clan.

"I'm putting you to too much trouble," she said. "Perhaps we can meet some other time."

"I may not be back," I said. "Maybe I can drive over day after tomorrow."

"Wonderful, I'll expect you at two."

Not a single cloud obscured Three-Fingered Jack on the last leg of my drive. Seeing the amputated peaks brought back young Jack's tragic act. Not until I was in the driveway of the Phillips compound did I recall the vigorous old congressman rescuing me from a snowdrift on my first visit a decade before. But this time, Mrs. Phillips welcomed me from the doorway, smoothing her hands on her apron.

"Have you had lunch?"

"Yes," I lied.

Looking around, I noticed wool place mats on a round log table in the middle of wild grasses growing up to the cabin. Here and there, wooden birdhouses painted in bright pastels and decorated with silvery glitter were attached to the ponderosa pines.

"I have iced tea and lemonade," she told me at the doorway, "and I bake the best scones east of the Cascades."

I sat down on a chair made of logs and watched three craggy fingers claw at the sky from the mountain in the distance. Presently, Mrs. Phillips reappeared, took her seat across from me, and placed a silver box on the log table.

"Gabriel, I didn't invite you all the way out here to taste my scones."

She lifted the latch on the strongbox between her thumb and forefinger but did not open the lid. "Secrets are best kept, but sometimes you have to tell someone and still keep the secret."

High in the sky, west of where the sun was beating down overhead, a wolf-gray cloud prowled past Three-Fingered Jack.

"I have no family left and no friend I can trust with this. Perhaps you have a right to know. Something tells me you'll keep what I tell you between us."

I decided not to fake it. "Mrs. Phillips, if I can keep your secret, I will, but I won't know until you've told me."

She smiled the biggest smile I'd seen on her face since she'd handed Sarah and Kate the batch of homemade cookies the afternoon of old Jack's funeral. Then she put her hand in mine and swung our hands straight up and down in the strangest handshake I've ever had from a woman before or since.

"Gabriel, if you hadn't given that answer, I would have put this"—she patted the strongbox—"back inside and said good-bye."

I moved my chair free of the table and crossed my legs.

"When I tell you the story, you will know why telling anyone else would only do harm."

"All right," I said in the most neutral tone I could muster.

"I know you feel terrible you couldn't save Senator Whelan's life on that patio. Well, I feel worse because I believe I could have saved his life and Jack's."

She brushed a few long strands of white hair out of her eyes, smoothed them back over her temple, and eyed me without a trace of emotion.

"Jack came down here on the third of July. We were to have dinner together and drive over to Loowit in the governor's limousine early on the Fourth. Jack was so proud Senator Whelan had used his testimony in his speech opposing that foolish resolution."

She stopped long enough for me to get something off my chest.

"Mrs. Phillips, I worried Jack was upset that Mick didn't give him more credit."

She shook her head, and a wisp of hair fell over her ear.

"Oh, no. He thought he was given too much—so much more than his father ever gave him. Your Mick Whelan was the older brother Jack never had."

Her eyes caught movement in the grass. She held a finger to her lips and pointed in the direction of the ponderosa where two chipmunks were having a tug-of-war over a pinecone. Lost in thought, Mrs. Phillips and I watched the wind sweep over the wild grasses in the meadow, and then she resumed speaking.

"Jack was so excited Mick Whelan was going to run for president—he talked about taking a leave from the Forest Service. He was beside himself with that congressman for saying that Whelan used people he knew to get what he wanted."

Warily, the chipmunks took turns pulling the pinecone.

"The afternoon Jack arrived, I had an engagement in Sisters. When I returned, it was almost six, and he was gone. He left a note. That's why I didn't think too much about it. 'Dear Mother, something came up—sorry to miss dinner. See you at the John D. Phillips Firefight—Jack.'"

"God," I cringed.

"I can see why you'd react like that," she said, putting aside her pain. "But Jack was a ranger—he also liked to kid me, so I thought he was telling me his leaving had something to do with a forest fire. Vietnam didn't enter my mind. And even if it had . . . ," her voice trailed off.

"I still don't get it," I said.

"I didn't either until I came back here after the . . . after he did what he did. I was looking through some family things in the attic"—she pointed to the eaves under the cedar shake roof. "The box where I keep Rebecca's things had been opened. Rebecca did a little drawing of herself for me one Mother's Day and I taped it to the lid. I never would have put it back upside down."

I tried to keep my face from betraying my hunch that her tale was leading to a destination as defunct as the incendiary e-mail on Jack's computer. Finally, I spoke.

"But surely he wouldn't . . . "

"No, Gabriel, Jack would not have killed Mick Whelan because his sister and Mick were lovers."

I blanched, and she placed a vivid green pine needle on top of the box.

"I'm an old woman, Mr. Bontempo, but I'm not a fool. I have known that Mick Whelan confided in you about my daughter the way a mother knows. Hasn't it ever occurred to you that Rebecca might have confided in me while she was alive?"

She looked away, her nose and cheekbones as craggy as the peaks on Three-Fingered Jack.

"I'm sure you noticed my coolness toward Mick Whelan over the years. Before you came into our lives it was easy. But I liked you and his wife and girls—I liked him, too, in spite of—"

She broke off and reached into her apron for a handkerchief to blow her nose.

"I did wonder," I began, then stopped.

During the silence, the peaks of Three-Fingered Jack stabbed a long cloud and it broke into three ragged gray fragments.

Unperturbed by the mountain or me, Mrs. Phillips continued.

"Ever since Jack and Rebecca were little, I kept their treasures—letters from their father, birthday cards, things they wrote. When she was older, Rebecca kept her keepsakes locked in a little silver strongbox at the lake—I had her name, birthday, and zodiac sign engraved on the outside for her twenty-first birthday. Last summer, someone found it where the old shoreline used to be. He was trespassing, but he remembered reading about Rebecca being in the cabin when the volcano buried the lake. So he dropped off the box and left without telling me his name. I had to have a locksmith open the box. I intended to put another lock on and have a key made that I could tuck away, but I never did."

Beyond the unfenced boundary of the Phillips compound, a doe that had been feeding, oblivious to everything else, sniffed our scent and faded away through the wild grass. Mrs. Phillips turned her head toward the doe, then returned her gaze to me. She took out her hand-stitched handkerchief again and dropped it in her lap.

"While Jack was rummaging around, I believe he came across

Rebecca's silver box and found her diary."

A posse of white clouds was overtaking the sun. Suddenly chilly, I was eager for Elizabeth Phillips to come to the point.

"I'm not telling the story in a straight line," she read my mind. "Why don't I let you see for yourself?"

Opening the box, she handed me the diary. I turned to the place marked by a dry pine needle. Beginning at the top of an immaculate page of parchment, Rebecca's last entry was written in a hand marked by bold vertical strokes and gently flowing, sensuous loops:

Friday, May 17

> *I could have driven down to Vanport, but Mick wants to be together. He'd rather have time at the lake. I could tell when I called him . . .*
>
> *So sweet . . .*
>
> *I couldn't sleep. I've known for three weeks. I can't wait any longer. Before I see a doctor I want Mick to know . . . I love him . . . too much?*
>
> *And the baby?*
>
> *I could go away . . .*
>
> *I can see his little boy—what if he looks like me? What if it's a girl with Mick's curly hair and black like mine?*
>
> *I want to tell him here, where the baby started. I know the afternoon. Maybe he does, too . . .*
>
> *He loves me—does he love enough to tell her—the woman he's been with on and off? Love me enough? As soon as I see him, I'll know.*
>
> *When I heard his voice—quick and strong, gentle,*

*too—I wanted to be with him . . . I'll go out on the deck
and feel the sun while I wait for that funny car of his.*

*Is that Mick on the other side of the lake? Too
loud—sounds like the sky.*

I'll go see . . .

God, that's close—all dark in the east.

I better get my things and be ready . . .

I read the entry again, then left the diary open to the breeze.

"I wish he'd known," I said, feeling my tears rise.

"When, Mr. Bontempo?" Mrs. Phillips asked me in her coldest voice.

Angry she was writing Mick off, I let my grief tumble out.

"Before, after, right now!" I stopped. "He loved her, Mrs. Phillips."

She raised herself up on her elbows, even with me.

"You'd never know it," she said in the cross, timeless voice of a mother. "Michael Whelan loving Rebecca never crossed my mind."

The *rat-tat-tat* of a woodpecker on the ponderosa pine above us punctuated Mrs. Phillips's statement with exclamation points.

"Well, he did," I told her. "He never stopped loving your daughter. He was beside himself after the eruption. He told me again when he saw what used to be Lake Sacagawea on the day he died."

Suddenly, my mind flashed back to my last glimpse of Mick and Mrs. Phillips, and I stood up. "Wait a minute. At the dedication, you and Mick went off to one side after his speech. What were you telling him?"

She smoothed her hand over Rebecca's last page of writing and the blank page across from it and placed the diary in the middle of the table. "I told Mick Whelan I forgave him."

I looked at her without comprehension and sat down again.

"But he didn't know."

Her eyes filled with a pain deeper than words. She spoke so softly of her daughter and the lost child that I needed the wind of the high country to carry her voice to my ears.

"My dear Gabriel, I meant to include a dear one he knew and one he didn't."

A spray of needles from the ponderosa directly over our heads dropped and landed on the blank page of the open diary.

"He wiped away a tear while he was leaving you."

She reached over the table and covered my hands with hers.

"Thank you for telling me how Mick felt about my daughter."

"Poor Mick," I said, shaking my head. "Poor Rebecca." I paused. "And Jack. Poor damn Jack."

She took her hands back and folded them on the table.

"Jack's troubles go way back—his father, what happened in Vietnam . . . I couldn't expect him to tell me what he found in his sister's diary. But I can't forgive myself—I thought to cancel tea with my friends—Jack and I were to have dinner . . . I didn't know he was back to using drugs."

She shivered as a sudden shaft of light lit up the snow on the highest crag of Three-Fingered Jack. There was one more thing to say, and although she was very tired, Mrs. Phillips fastened her eyes on mine.

"Gabriel, there's no one living who would be served by knowing about Mick Whelan and Rebecca and their baby. And there's no one else served by knowing what you've told me about how much Mick loved my daughter."

"Mrs. Phillips," I got to my feet. "I think you know what I'll do."

She saw me to my car and said good-bye. I rolled down the window before heading out on the loose red earth to the road. As I waved, she called to me.

"One more thing, Gabriel."

I leaned my head out the window.

"You're the only other living soul who will ever see Rebecca's diary."

I put the car into first gear.

"I know," I said.

451

Elizabeth Phillips died a couple of months later when the last leaves were turning and early snow dusted the crabbed knuckles of Three-Fingered Jack. I kept her secret. But as I brooded on the story, my own losses erupted all over again like molten lava from the volcano. Alone in Washington, I cried out at the loss of my son and his mother, my wife, whose features at last I superimposed on the glimpse I'd had of Patrick's face nine years before as I turned away to head down the mountain to the hearings in Vanport.

And Mick Whelan? Few days pass in my Neah-Kah-Nie hiding place that I don't miss him as my best friend, and the politician whose passing—I know all the more after the lost chances of the nineties—diminished the possibilities of the country. Even now, despite, or maybe because of, my blood count and the doctored and undoctored vote count in Florida, I am heartened by his words the day of his death about endings and beginnings. Last week, climbing Neah-Kah-Nie Mountain, I looked east above the December fog and heard his voice from an evening in the sixties at the One Step Down. As the tenor sax player held the last notes of his solo in the smoky air, Mick grabbed my arm and shouted, "Live, man, live!" slamming his beer glass on the slab table.

Those words sounded again when my doctor at the Health Sciences University reported that my blood cells were both stable and erratic. "Like radio frequencies," he said, returning to his diagnosis of a month before. "I was wrong to call your red and white cells undecided voters. They're votes all right; the question is whether they'll be counted." The doctor stopped, folded his hands over the red, white, and blue tabs sticking out of the medical folder on his desk, and gave me a wicked look. "That's more than I can say about the count in Florida." And when I responded with the silent resistance doctors endure from their patients, he carried on more bluntly. "Whether you live a full life is up to you. Your weak spot—your susceptibility—is not going away. So, really, Gabriel, from now on, your

452

life is a matter of what's inside you. No reason you can't make a commitment to that lady friend you told me about and start over on Shelter Island. What's your heart like, that's going to be your question."

On the drive back to the coast, my heart beat faster and my mind saw double in a fashion reminiscent of Miles's split-screen commercials for Mick Whelan's campaigns. On one side stretched a diagonal from Shelter Island past the northwest tip of Long Island to the blue blur of Connecticut across the Sound; on the other, the sad, lovely, alluvial-brown face of Kiem Phuong as she waved good-bye at the Portland Airport two weeks before. Back at the A-frame, I leapt before I looked. I called Shelter Island, rented a house through the millennial New Year, then phoned Kiem and invited her and her two childen to join me.

"I waited, Gabriel," she said, a cautious beckoning in her voice.

Later, I turned on Oregon Public Radio for the latest news from Florida, and heard the Republican congressman from Blackjack Phillips's old district say he was positive that if Phillips were alive, he would urge Al Gore to concede for the good of the country. My juices sizzling, I phoned in, offering to give chapter and verse on the air about Judge Phillips's dedication to the Constitution—"a document you could die for," he once called it. But the twentysomething taking calls told me that the Republican congressman's comments were merely an opinion. If I cared to send mine, it might be read on the air during the station's mailbag segment.

I slammed down the phone. The circuits were jammed when I tried to reach Miles and L. A. in Florida, so I prowled the beach staring at yellow butterfly clouds on Neah-Kah-Nie Mountain for clues to the Supreme Court's leaning in *Bush v. Gore*. The next morning, I had coffee at first light, and before day dawned an immaculate dark blue, I grabbed my ski gear and headed for Mount Bachelor. I sped toward Salem, drove east over the Santiam Pass, and wound down through Sisters and Bend to the mountain beyond. It was early in the season, so I had little company on the slopes. My legs came back slowly, and after flying high for an hour, I sensed fatigue.

To the west, a column of white clouds was beginning to march toward the Three Sisters, so I decided to ski the highest, longest run.

From the summit of Bachelor, literally the mountaintop, the Cascade Range was visible from Shasta in California to the great snow hill of Rainier south of Seattle. In between were the Oregon Cascades, and I quickly fastened on Three-Fingered Jack to the north and that old nemesis, Loowit, slightly northwest of Hood. I rested on my skis until a touch of vertigo passed, and I surveyed the world before using my poles like crutches to shove off down the mountain. By fits and starts, I bumped down the slope, thighs burning, knees aching so much that a couple of times I traversed the slope sideways, laughing when I heard Mick Whelan's old command ring in my ears. "Point them downhill," he used to say, knowing I was more of a zigzag man. Before long, I relaxed and was going well enough that I skied the last half of the run without stopping. At the bottom of the hill, I had a burger and a pint of microbrew in the bar. The television was on, and the anchors on one cable network after another were in a frenzy about the imminent Supreme Court decision. "As we speak," said the most insistent of the millennial furies, "the Supremes are almost certainly putting the final touches on a decision that may name the next president of the United States."

Outside the plate-glass window, snow clouds from the west were rolling in fast and furious. The sky had the look of a whiteout, so I took my last run down the beginners' slope and called it quits. By the time I reached Sisters, it was four o'clock. I got gas, and, passing mounds of burning brush in between stands of ponderosas on Route 20, I decided to stop at the Phillips compound. I needed to be quick because the radio said a bad storm was brewing west of the Cascades headed straight for Santiam Pass. Around a familiar bend on the road to Camp Sherman, shafts of brilliant light lit the trees, but several turns farther on, the sky was almost dark. Here and there, a few lights twinkled in the scattered cabins. At the Phillips compound, the birdhouses with their glitter had been taken down; in their place plaster casts painted a garish green and black to resemble the faces of garden creatures were now attached to the trees. The wild grasses, too, had yielded to a lawn bumpy with molehills. Missing the sense of home I remembered, I turned away.

I stopped by the country store to buy a drink and a sandwich for the long ride back to the coast. The radio was on, and the man behind the counter struck up a conversation by grumbling about what was and was not worthy of airtime.

"Florida, hell," he said. "I got morning deliveries scheduled. I want to know whether the snow's likely to close the pass."

I mumbled unconvincing assent, cocking an ear to the radio, while he slathered mustard on my turkey on rye and shifted to a more personal tone.

"Ever since old Jack Phillips died, and his son killed that Whelan fella, I haven't paid attention to politics."

I told him I had known all three men.

"That so? Well, you ought to take a look at how Mrs. Phillips fixed up the boneyard just before she died."

He wrapped my sandwich, made change, and I decided to double back and stop at the little family graveyard in the stand of ponderosas that had gone into conservancy at Mrs. Phillips's death nine years before. I could hear the river rushing by, and overhead the solitary honk of a wild goose that must have missed the takeoff for the migration south. Below were four headstones covered in pine needles. I squatted down to pay my respects, and as I stumbled, favoring my sore knees, off beyond the graves I noticed a small cedar rectangle fixed to the stump of a once-splendid ponderosa: *Michael J. "Mick" Whelan*, it read, *Senator from Oregon and Friend to the Phillips Family*. Dizzy, I held on to the nearest tree, and my sobs joined the rush of wind and water as I saw Mrs. Phillips toiling over the red earth, hammer in hand, attaching her memento to the rugged pine stump.

The wind was roaring high in the trees when I got back to the car. My headlights showed dark water from the river flashing white where it broke over hidden rocks and burst toward the sky like shooting stars going home. As I nosed the car back to the road, noise blared from the radio—static and the announcer's voice harmonizing in the eerie whinny of a centaur. I switched off the dial and made tracks for Route 20. There was no denying it: bad weather was on the way. But with luck, maybe I could make it over the pass before the storm broke and I heard the decision handed down by the Supremes.

Acknowledgments

I wish to express my gratitude to the Caldera Foundation for awarding me a residency in the spring of 2003; to David and Nancy Stern for several generous, extended residencies during 2004 and 2005 at their compound in Camp Sherman; and to my dear friends Michael Mills and Laureen Bidell for offering me the inspiration of Shelter Island, summer after summer, before, during, and after the writing of *A Man You Could Love*.